THE GAILL

THE GAILL SERIES BOOK ONE

LO MEYER

Book Cover by Books & Moods
Formatting by Books & Moods
Editing by Victory Editing
Proofreading by Victory Editing
ISBN 979-8-9891731-0-5 (print edition)

To my fellow dreamer.

Don't give up. Your dream is worth it. And so are you.

Stay Deviant ☆

TRIGGER WARNING

The Gaill is an action-packed speculative romance that contains subject matter that may be difficult for some readers, including graphic violence, torture, combat, attempted sexual assault, blood, kidnapping, and all-around deviant behavior.

NEW
MERICA
White Point
NOR
GAILL
Gaill
Stronghold
The Cape Inn
& Tavern
Atlantic
Ocean
Catham
KINGDOM OF
CALDERONE

CHAPTER 1

THE HEIR

I wasn't avoiding the inevitable. Not exactly. I'd just spent the past hour awake in bed, retracing the patterns in my canopy and willing my mind to get lost in the maze of stitching. It was a temporary sort of solitude. No kingdom, no Gaill, no nightmares, no betrothal. Nothing except the scratching of the old oak at my window and the heavy thud of my heart. Today everything would change, and I wasn't sure if it was dread or excitement consuming me at present. The tightening in my chest told me it was dread.

A sudden swoosh of skirts outside the curtains drew me from my daydreams and reminded me that from now on, my only moments alone would be like this—stolen and elusive.

Miranda, one of my principal ladies-in-waiting, ripped back the heavy beige canopy surrounding my bed, blinding me with the rays of a fully risen sun, and began pulling my duvet off. She didn't bother to make sure I was up; she already knew I was.

Moaning, I tried to grab the covers back as she dragged my limp body halfway across the sheets and incidentally smeared some of last night's makeup on the white silk.

"Unhand the duvet, Mir, and I'll give you all the lands in Gaill Country." I smiled up at her, barely able to keep my eyes open against the light.

"Like I'd want those." Miranda snorted as her dark braid flew over her shoulder, a few springy curls fighting their way loose in the struggle. She tucked the stray hairs behind an ear and lowered her voice. "Did you sleep after I left?"

Shrugging and flopping back, I gave up the fight and rolled into the nearest pillow, relishing the feel of the soft silk against my skin. I could only evade reality for so long though. Today was my eighteenth birthday. In exactly a year, I, Jacqueline Louise Livingston, would be crowned queen of Calderone. I would call the shots.

One more year.

My chest constricted again at the thought.

"It's already noon, and Queen K is on the verge." Rachel, my second lady-in-waiting, hurriedly wheeled in my hair-and-makeup cart, her brown eyes focused and determined. She was followed by Maxwell, my cousin and third principal lady-in-waiting—regardless of his gender.

"And *you* look awful, J." Maxwell cocked a dark brow as he assessed my current state. Not waiting for an answer, he grabbed my arm, hauled me into the large bathroom attached to my chambers, sitting me down at the vanity before going to help Miranda and Rachel draw a bath.

Stifling a yawn and rubbing my eyes, willing the black spots still clouding my vision to fade, I blinked against the bright lights that surrounded the mirror. Once the spots cleared, I barked out a laugh.

My long black-brown waves were wild around my head like I'd just stuck my finger in the nearest socket. My eye mask was halfway off my head. And last night's eyelashes clung to my cheek below my sleepy, bloodshot, usually bright blue eyes.

I was dragging. Clearly.

Too tired to even contemplate brushing through the mess of waves or dealing with the makeup still caked on my face, I swallowed another yawn and peeled off the outfit from last night's festivities that I'd managed to fall asleep in.

"Aren't you excited, J? Today you turn eight-teen." Maxwell met my eyes as I plodded over to the now-steaming bath and settled in. He enunciated the word like I didn't already know the implications of the day. "You're officially an adult. You get to drink with the big kids, read in public"—his hand flew to his chest as Miranda and Rachel let out gasps of mock horror—"and vote… sometimes. Yes, only one more year until this is *our* court. And only one more day until *you* start your worldwide takeover."

"Right." I snorted, rolling my eyes and dipping below the surface before anyone could respond. Max was doing what he did best—using sarcasm in an effort to distract me. But neither sarcasm nor the momentary silence of the water could drown out my thoughts.

I *was* excited about my birthday. I was. Really. Not only was it my birthday and the start of my ascent to the throne, but it was also the last day my identity would be kept hidden from the world. So I *was* excited.

Just equal parts excited and scared out of my mind.

"You okay, J?" Miranda asked when I resurfaced, the same concern from the night before crossing her gaze.

I nodded, though she likely didn't buy it.

She'd woken with me last night as she'd done every night this month. As she'd done since we were kids. Miranda knew all too well of my troubles—the anxieties that plagued me by day, the nameless nightmares that haunted my dreams at night. My *weakness* as Father called it.

Taking a deep breath, I locked away the anxious feelings, willing the heaviness in my lungs to lighten. I'd be fine. I was *born* for this. And I *was* excited, wasn't I?

I'd be *fine.*

I just needed to make it through the next twenty-four hours of pure mayhem first.

"This isn't one of your plays or little novels, Jacqueline. This is *Calderone.*" My mother chuckled heartily at her own joke as her closest ladies smiled behind their white silk gloves.

I didn't attempt to hide my eye roll or sigh. Could they come up with anything new—*ever?* As if reading the classics of Shakespeare and the Brontës somehow made me a dumber person.

"Jacqueline." Fixing me with a disapproving eye, my mother sighed as she reached over and plucked a nonexistent speck of lint from the shoulder of my white gown. Her eyes lingered on the dainty black pearl necklace that permanently sat around my neck—the one that clashed horribly with the beige image she always insisted on. And the one that had belonged to the grandmother she had never let me meet.

"I don't know how you do it, Queen Katherine. My daughter can read now"—Lady Lewis shot me a glare like giving Miranda access to my tutor was akin to treason—"but she is much too busy with her duties to waste time on such a venture."

"As she should be." Mother continued as if I weren't standing in their circle, as if this wasn't *my* private birthday celebration before my public debut tomorrow. "Poor Jacqueline is at such a disadvantage and stretched *so* thin, expected to tackle her homemaking duties as well as the education necessary for her role as heir."

She took a drink, fidgeting as she fanned herself and patted her dark waves back in place though they hadn't moved from their tightly bound chignon at the nape of her neck.

"Mother." Taking advantage of her momentary pause, I placed my hand on the silk glove that covered a majority of her arm. "If you'll excuse me, I believe I see Captain Adams and must go say hi."

"Oh yes, dear. Please let him know to stop over as well."

Nodding, I gave her and her ladies a forced smile as I backed away.

I had no intention of seeking out Phin Adams, but the mention of his name had granted me the quick escape I so desperately needed.

After a quick look around, I beelined it for my group of ladies assembled in the corner next to one of the many floor-to-ceiling windows that lined that particular stateroom. It wasn't hard to pick them out; they were the only ones wearing amethyst in a sea of white. My idea—about the darkest I could go without dressing them in black.

I had about ten or so in total, though Miranda, Rachel, and Max were the ones most often at my side. All had noble parents who were top-ranking members of my father's government. To serve a future monarch was a position of great honor as they became intimately acquainted with the future king or, in my case, queen.

Most were a few cocktails in, lounging on the considerably uncomfortable modern furniture my mother had insisted on when she redecorated the palace for "the debut." Not that she asked my opinion on anything; she just needed an excuse to redecorate. Again.

"Let me guess," Maxwell drawled as I approached, swirling around the minimal amount of champagne left in his flute as he leaned against the back of the chaise Miranda and Rachel were sitting on. "It was the reading again."

I rolled my eyes. "Is it ever anything else with her?"

Women generally weren't allowed to learn to read and write in Calderone. It had been decided that our skill set was geared toward the more particular *arts* of homemaking—sewing, child-rearing, and gossiping.

However, when I was reluctantly declared heir, it was determined that I needed to know *something*, so at the age of ten, I was given about five tutors and seven years to cram into my brain what boys would have twice the time to learn.

You would think since I had caught up to where every other heir had been at this point and was *literally* reading Shakespeare in my free time, my mother would be impressed. But in truth, I think it terrified her. Or just irreparably damaged her ego given she herself wasn't able to read.

"Incoming, six o'clock." Rachel's eyes grew wide as she watched someone approach over my shoulder, and all of a sudden, my ladies did their best to look very *busy.*

"Happy birthday, J. You look beautiful."

I didn't have to guess who was behind me. If the deep voice hadn't given him away, the reaction of all the other girls and Max in front of me would have.

"Thanks, Phin." I turned, a smile spreading on my face despite my efforts to stop it as Captain Adams grinned down at me.

Phin Adams. The boy I'd grown up fishing in the mud with who had become a Calderonian warrior overnight. *The* Calderonian warrior. The one half of the court wanted and the other half wanted to be.

"Save me a dance later?"

I grimaced, instantly regretting the smile. "Sure."

His face fell, making me curse, yet again, that the mask of apathy that came so easily to the rest of the royals had always been a challenge for me.

I mean, Phin was a good-looking guy. Probably the best at court. By all accounts, he was the perfect betrothed. He was tall with a toned body he'd grown into now that he was almost twenty, and his blond hair was usually styled off his face in a sort of wave that reminded me of old Hollywood photos from the early twenty-first century, which with his dark blue eyes, angular jawline, and red military uniform made him the classic type of handsome most girls wanted.

And he was exceptionally nice. Ridiculously so. *Infuriatingly* so.

I actually wasn't sure he was capable of saying the wrong thing in any situation, whereas I never seemed to say the right thing.

Mother and Father loved him.

I took his hand and gave it a squeeze. "*Of course* we can dance later." I mustered up another smile I hoped was convincing. "I'm sorry. It's just that you know how these events set me on edge, and with tomorrow being what it is—"

"I get it, J. You never have to explain yourself to me." Phin's signature smile returned, but it only served to tighten the anxious knot in my chest.

Phin and I had been friends since I could remember. And I might not have feelings like that for him, but we'd always been close, which made my change of heart that much more difficult to digest.

Because Phin had been my first... *everything.*

My first friend, his father being the military commander and chief advisor for mine; the first one who snuck out of the palace with me to go mudding; the first one to stand up for me against the boys who made fun of me for being a girl; the first one to try to understand my panic attacks; my first kiss; and the first and only guy I'd ever been with like *that*.

It'd happened almost six months ago. I thought I loved him.

We were always meant to be married. We'd known that since we were six. But two years ago, things changed. Phin changed. He entered the army, started thinking like everyone else, treating me as everyone else did—like I was this object always in danger of shattering. As if my brain was wired for only *feminine* pursuits and even mentioning government matters would send me spiraling. As if, even as heir, I couldn't possibly handle what every other male heir had before me.

I thought if we got together before our forced engagement, it would make him see me as he used to. Instead, it had confirmed what I already knew in my heart—the love we had could never be what it should be. Not anymore. Not when he saw me as a child perpetually in need of coddling and protection.

But it didn't matter what I wanted. We'd be married regardless—the union being "advantageous to the monarchy" in the words of my father a few days later when I asked him to break it off.

"You know"—I quirked a brow and looked around to ensure we weren't being overheard—"the girls, Max, and I are going out to Crash after the first dances if you wanna join. It's been over a year since you were out with us last, and this will be the only time we can do it before the big reveal." I widened my eyes sarcastically as I said the last part.

His features instantly went taut. "Jacqueline. You shouldn't be leaving the palace, especially to go to a place like Crash."

He really had gotten exceedingly lame since becoming an army captain.

"That club is notoriously dangerous, especially since it's so near the Wall."

"the Wall? We haven't had a breach in over a hundred years, Phin."

"There have been reports of unrest in the suburbs. Things we're looking into." He licked his lips.

"What reports?" I did little to hide the irritation in my voice. Not only was I being told what to do, it was also clear I'd been left out of current events happening in our country. Again.

"It's nothing, J; we're handling it."

"If everyone could move to the dining room, we will start the dinner," one of the underbutlers announced, his voice echoing through the room.

Phin threw me an apologetic smile before making a quick escape through the archway to find his seat.

"And so with that came the change to the Oath of the Heir Proviso."

Father had been droning on for a solid twenty minutes, and I was alternating between giving my best princess smile to the intimate group of one hundred courtiers assembled in front of us, all dressed in varying shades of white, and taking small sips of my champagne, forcing the glass to last what was likely to be another thirty minutes of his speech.

"For those of you who are not familiar with the Proviso..."

We were *all* familiar. But we were also all ready for another lecture.

The Oath of the Heir Proviso was one of the cornerstones of monarchical law—every heir had to swear to obey it in order to claim his title. The Proviso not only set term limits on the monarchs but also established that a king's successor must be his direct descendant.

It further stipulated that, to protect his life and the monarchies against the dangers of a disruption to the political order and the

Gaill, the heir must keep his identity secret until his eighteenth birthday when he'd be presented to all society at a grand ceremony where representatives from the world's five monarchies would be in attendance. Throughout the next year, the heir would tour the country and the world to meet with his subjects and diplomats and handle legislation before ascending the throne upon his nineteenth birthday, at which time his father would peacefully retire.

When I was ten, it became clear my mother wasn't having another child, let alone a male heir, and the Salic Law that forbade a woman from holding the throne was quietly dissolved. Never before had a queen held one of the five thrones—not since their inception in 2075, three hundred years prior. Most thought it was luck or a blessing to the kingdoms; I knew it had to be planned somehow. My father and the other kings were far too controlling to let something like legacy and power be left to chance… or a woman. My birth had screwed up the plan.

But in 2365, without another option and given the sanctity of the Proviso, my father and his advisors quietly ended Salic Law by slipping its dissolution into pressing, must-pass legislation, reasoning that drawing attention to it would most certainly make it known that the heir was a girl. To protect my safety then, it was quietly done away with, the pronouns in the Proviso changed to the ambiguous "their."

And although the Proviso stated that only the *heir's* identity be kept a secret, *my* identity had always been kept secret even before I was declared the official successor. Whether for extra security, as my mother insisted, or just to keep me a secret in general, it was really hard to say.

A genuine toss-up.

Watching my father now, I wondered if he felt the impending shame of it all. Having to announce that not only was your only living heir a girl but that you'd had to change the law to make her claim legitimate.

"It is with great pleasure that we come together tonight to celebrate my very beautiful daughter, Princess Jacqueline Louise Livingston, future queen of Calderone."

The entire room broke out in applause then, and I stood on instinct, hand to my heart as I flashed the assembled group another smile, mouthing silent thank-yous, and blowing air kisses as required.

This was the easy part. A rehearsal, really.

At midnight, I would officially become the heir in the eyes of the monarchies, and tomorrow the true chaos would begin. In twelve hours' time, at 0800, my name and image would be released by the palace and subsequently broadcast on all TVs and newspapers across the world. Even our currency would change.

Tomorrow night would be the grand ceremony. The one where I'd be presented to the world.

But tonight? This crowd? They were considered my father's closest confidants, all of whom lived in the palace and were sworn to secrecy because of that.

Outside this palace? I didn't exist.

Yet.

"Wonderful job tonight, Princess." My father's twinkling eyes turned to me as the applause slowly faded, and people started to get up. Placing a perfectly manicured hand on my shoulder, the dark red velvet of his military tux shining under the glow of the chandeliers, he gave it a reassuring squeeze.

"Thank you, Father." I forced myself to hold his gaze.

We'd never been good at the father-daughter thing without that awkward tension. I suppose he still saw me as nothing but that ten-year-old tomboy with ratty hair and wild blue eyes. The one who would never be the prince he so badly wanted.

"Your Majesty." Albert, our butler, approached him from behind, bowing deeply. "The cigars and brandy are ready in the drawing room. Should I gather the council?"

"Yes, Albert. That would be fine."

Albert wasn't gone a second before I took my opportunity.

"May I join you, Father? Captain Adams mentioned potential issues in the suburbs. Perhaps I can be of assistance? Offer a new perspective?"

"Ah." My father squeezed my shoulder again and smiled at me as one might smile at an ignorant child. "Don't worry yourself over it, Princess. All will be handled. Governing and politics can fatigue a woman, given your disposition. And I would hate for you to miss the dancing. I know how you love it so."

With that he turned, dismissing me like it was nothing, and walked to the drawing room located behind the two great golden doors at the end of the hall.

We were flying down the causeway that led to the city a short while later, the relative darkness of the palace fading behind as the lights in the valley spread before us below.

"You smell that, ladies?" Max asked from behind the wheel, elbow on the rim of the open window as he gripped the top of the door and leaned his head out to take a huge sniff of the humid, citrus-scented night air. "Smells like freedom."

"You're ridiculous." I laughed, shaking my head but really loving every second of it because we were free.

For a few hours at least.

The past couple of years, we'd been sneaking out of the palace at least one or two nights a month.

Choosing to scale my trellis, take a set of keys from the valet lock box that we'd learned to pick, and force Max or Miranda, whose only experience was driving small carts around the estate, to drive us to the city always seemed like a great use of what little power I had.

Typically, we stuck to nightclubs, bars, or concert venues close to the palace in case we had to get home quickly. But tonight we were going all out. Tomorrow my face would be plastered across every billboard and note in the country, and soon these nights would be a distant memory.

Crash was the club on the outskirts of our province, Chatham, and was nearest to the Wall. This made it the most dangerous club in Calderone—for us anyway—both because of its proximity to Gaill Country and because it was about the farthest from the palace we could go and still get back before dawn.

My father would kill me himself if he found out we were this close to the Wall without a security detail. The thought of him breaking his composure made me smile a bit.

"Phin didn't make it sound too bad, did he? Suburb Five is right next to Crash." Worry seeped through Rachel's tone as she attempted to pull her jeans on while crouched in the back of the service van we'd hijacked for tonight's escapades.

It was rather large, but the completely tinted and open back gave us an easy place to change out of our formal attire. And it was a certainly less conspicuous than our only other option—a stretch limo.

"He mentioned unrest, but neither he nor Father seemed bothered by it. He seemed more worried we were going to be near the Wall." I shrugged as I shimmied into the black V-neck top I'd packed, brushing my front layers out of my face as they whipped around from the open window, then reaching for my black jeans and boots. Black was not only my favorite color, but dressing as plain as possible ensured we blended in with the rest of the Calderonians at the club. The last thing I needed was for someone connected to the palace to spot me and report back to Father. His spies were everywhere.

"Well, if Daxinius or the other Deviants want to climb the Wall and take me home tonight, I won't complain," Max replied in a half-joking, half-serious tone as he weaved in and out of traffic, hitting the highway to head north.

"Please." Miranda scoffed behind me, meeting his eyes in the rearview mirror. "You're aware those probably aren't even real people, right? Just stories made up to scare us as kids? Roll your window up, by the way; you're ruining my masterpiece." She moved to fix the layers slipping from the side braid she'd woven into my hair for the evening.

"Or so they say..." Max waggled his eyebrows.

"Max, pictures of the Nor Gaill king and prince have been the same for centuries. Literally. They're either made up, which is probably the case, or from another planet. Humans don't live that long."

He looked over his shoulder, his eyes shining with laughter as they met mine. "I mean, obviously they're not humans, J. Have you *seen* how good-looking they are? Which"—he did a quick double take—"have you seen *you* lately, Miss Heir-Bearing Hips?"

Laughing, I just shook my head and stuck my tongue out at him. My curves had filled out in the past year, much to the happiness of my mother. Max and the girls never let me live it down.

"They *are* gorgeous." Rachel giggled, referring of course to the Gaill royal family.

And as much as I hated to admit it, King Aidoneus Da Luca and his son, Prince Daxinius, *were* inhumanly gorgeous if you believed the photos. But more importantly, they were our number one enemy, the storied leaders of the Nor Gaill—the warring faction of barbarians that lived several hundred miles to our north. Or so we thought.

It was hard to know exactly where or what the Gaill were. Whether that was from our relative lack of information or from the lack of information relayed to me, I wasn't sure. I wasn't even sure where their name came from.

But we all knew one thing. The Gaill were traitors to Calderone and the common good. They sought to undermine the monarchies in their infancy immediately after the Nuclear War. King Richard, my distant relative and second monarch, had valiantly banished them in 2100 even after it ended up his dear friend and confidant, Giovacchin Da Luca, was their leader.

And because they were banished outside the Wall to what we now call Gaill Country, most of them succumbed to the radiation left over from the War. A group that survived, however, had formed the rudimentary monarchy that now called themselves the Nor Gaill. There were rumors some of the Gaill had deviated—had come to possess superhuman abilities from the radiation, like certain powers and immortality, but Father said that was simply Gaill propaganda made up to scare us as kids.

I'd say it worked.

Every child in Calderone knew not to repeat the name Daxinius out loud when you were alone in a darkened room or he would be sure to appear, slaughter you mercilessly as he had done to the villagers around our borders, and then take your remains back to the Deviants as a sacrifice.

Or so the rumor went.

I tried it once, and he never appeared. Though I did look under my bed every night for a year afterward.

Grabbing our bags, we jumped from the back of the van to the darkened street behind the club. Straightening hems and applying a last touch of gloss under a nearby streetlamp, we made our way toward the source of the music bumping through the streets.

We got through the line immediately, Maxwell not so subtly bribing the bouncer, and were led to a secluded spot on the second floor where the lights were low and the music not quite as deafening. We were near enough to the less crowded balcony bar but also near to the women's bathroom. Perfect.

Flagging down the nearest waiter, we acquired a round of perfectly toxic cocktails and then another. By 0100, we were all downstairs on the crowded dance floor, avoiding the creeps and getting lost in the music with one another.

"Refill?" Miranda shouted over the music, pointing at her empty glass, then to the empty one in my hand. The lights from the DJ flashed across her face in varying shades of neon, but I could tell from here she wasn't drunk. Just slightly buzzed.

"Yes!" I gave her the thumbs-up and went back to twisting my hips and shimmying into a very tipsy Maxwell as she and Rach went for refills.

"Bathroom," he said suddenly, grabbing my hand and pulling me through the crowd.

Throwing apologies out as I ran into people, we made our way across the sticky floor to the side of the club where the main bathrooms were. Leaving him, I entered the ladies' lounge, which was really just a room with a beat-down love seat, one stall, and a small vanity already crowded with a few girls.

My heart suddenly felt heavy as a wave of future nostalgia hit. I'd miss being able to be an anonymous nobody in places like this. Somehow I don't think Mother would approve of this venue as a stop on my countrywide tour starting next month.

Not having to go to the bathroom myself, I moved to the mirror to reapply my lip gloss, smiling at the girl next to me as I squeezed in. "Excuse me."

She smiled back, making room for me on the counter so I could set my small bag down. Taking out my compact and gloss, I tucked in a few stray hairs as I stepped back to inspect my makeup in the dim lights that hung above the mirror.

And of course, in that moment, the power went out.

Sighing, I was feeling for my bag on the counter when a bloodcurdling scream pierced the air, followed by an explosion so massive the ceiling began to fall in.

Ducking instinctively, I threw my hands over my head, bag completely forgotten as more screams erupted around me, followed by a deafening ringing in my ears.

My hands shook, and I was barely able to stow the lip gloss in my bra and whip open my compact mirror. Its light illuminated the floor enough to see around me, and I swallowed against the pounding in my chest as I realized the people on the couch had been knocked unconscious by sizable falling chunks of ceiling.

Breathing through the fear seizing my lungs, I stepped over the people lying unconscious on the floor and pulled the bathroom door open. A mass of smoke billowed in my face. I coughed into my elbow and fell back, temporarily blinded. I let the door close and waited until my eyes stopped watering, then made my way into the hall, pulling my sleeve over my hand and burying my face to keep the smoke out.

Crouching close to the ground, I used my compact and the lights near the floor to see, flattening myself against the wall as people ran past. It was too smoky to see who anyone was or where they were going, but I managed to make my way along the wall and down the steps to the dance floor, which was covered in stone, glass and splintered wood.

The sprinklers were going off haphazardly, leaving certain areas aflame and others in heavy smoke as debris continued to fall from the ceiling.

The smoke was getting thicker. It scorched my throat, filling my lungs with what felt like ash, making it increasingly harder to breathe.

I had to find the others and get out. *Now.*

Just then I felt a hand on my arm and turned in time to see Miranda, a mix of pure terror and determination etched across her face.

"Run!"

She pulled me with her, and we ran blind through the smoke, jumping fallen bodies and stools and weaving our way through people fighting.

Fighting? Wait—*is that a sword?*

"Duck!"

I looked forward just in time to avoid a dagger as it whipped over my head.

I crouched, frozen in fear, the ringing in my ears reaching a deafening level as reality hit me. Much more than a fire was happening at Crash.

"J, we have to go *now.*" I felt Miranda nearby, but her command sounded like it came from a million miles away.

"Jacqueline!"

And then we were running again. I didn't dare look around, didn't look back, just ran, following Mir, the one assigned to our exit route, as she found our way to the back entrance where Rachel and Max were already waiting.

We burst into the alley behind the club and sprinted to the van parked at the end, our feet pounding the pavement and our shapes momentarily illuminated every time we passed under the glow of the street lamps.

My combat boots echoed off the buildings, but all I was aware of was the thundering of my heart and my ragged breathing as my lungs struggled to function.

I couldn't seem to run fast enough. I had to run faster.

My steps faltered as I struggled to keep up.

"J, we have to keep moving." Miranda's muffled voice met my ears as she looked back, tugging on my hand. Her eyes, rounded in terror, met mine.

"Go!" I summoned every last bit of strength I had as I ripped my hand from hers. "That's an order, Miranda."

Her eyes pleaded with me, but she couldn't disobey an order. Not from me. And I'd rather die than let my inability to control my anxiety jeopardize her life.

"J—"

I shook my head.

A second passed before her mouth flattened in determination. "Keep moving, and I'll drive the van to meet you." With that she bolted down the alley.

I pressed forward, but it was as if my legs had turned to granite—each step was like wading through quicksand.

My stomach started rising, threatening to choke me. And I began to wheeze, struggling to find air. My lungs felt like they were still filled with smoke, like they themselves were on fire, and I was only moments from passing out as spots filled my vision.

That's when I heard it. Heard *them*.

Fast as light. Deadly as a nightmare.

I focused in front of me, ignoring my nauseating levels of fear, but then a primal terror erupted deep within my gut when I saw Mir ahead in the distance under the glow of a street lamp. Somehow I'd fallen too far behind. Rachel and Maxwell were already at the van, and Miranda threw herself into the driver's seat.

I willed my body to move quicker, but my lungs refused to fill, and I could feel myself gasping for air as panic took hold.

There wasn't enough time.

Max threw open the van door, and Rachel jumped in. He turned around for me, but I was still half a block back when his face contorted in shock, and I felt a sting in my neck.

Then something hit my head.

And everything went black.

CHAPTER 2

ARRAIGNMENT

My mind was thick, like it was plodding through mud as I tried to keep up with everything happening while doing my best not to panic, not to fall apart. Small flickers of light made it through the roughly woven material of the sack that covered my head, and I was vaguely aware of time passing as the fabric scratched my skin.

The road was bumpy, and there was a faint scent of exhaust. That, together with whatever they'd used to knock me out and what felt like life-threatening dehydration, had me drifting in and out of consciousness despite my efforts to stay awake.

As to who had taken me, when they'd taken me, and where I was going, that was a mystery. Their accents, from the little they'd spoken, were unrecognizable.

I shifted as much as I dared between two hopefully alive people I was positioned between. Settling back, I willed myself to stay awake. Being alert was my best chance for survival no matter where I was headed.

Just as I felt myself drifting back into another state of nothingness, the truck jerked to a sudden halt, sending me flying into the person next to me.

"Sorry," I croaked, attempting to right myself when the doors screeched open.

Rough hands grabbed me and hauled me out of the truck, causing me to bump against the others before I stumbled into the open air. A cool breeze hit my skin through the thin top I wore, carrying with it the overwhelming scent of cold ocean and old pines.

My stomach instantly twisted to a sickening level, and sweat broke out on my forehead, but I willed my knees to hold.

We were nowhere near Calderone, which was currently in the midst of a very humid summer.

We're somewhere much *farther north.*

Before I could lapse into a full breakdown, another pair of hands grabbed my upper arm, positioning me in place before ordering us to walk.

We entered a building that was silent except for the echoes of our steps along the hard stone floor. There was a dripping sound in the distance, and the damp atmosphere seeped into my skin even though I couldn't actually see anything.

We halted abruptly a few minutes in—someone grabbing my arm as the other footsteps receded. There was a jangle of keys and a great sound of metal on metal; then the hood over my head was ripped off, and I was shoved forward into a small, darkened cell.

I whipped around, but the door was already locked and bolted, my captor gone before I could see their face.

Turning back, I swallowed against the tightening in my chest, my mental fog evaporating in a wave of adrenaline as I dutifully counted my breaths.

Think, Jacqueline.

I had to get out, but how?

I ran over what little I'd determined in my bouts of lucidity on the long drive but came up with nothing.

There had to be a way to escape. A way out. As far as I knew, I'd been captured by a group who didn't know my identity. If they did, surely they'd have asked for a ransom, right? That's how these things work in books.

Then again, no one even knew for certain the king had an heir. That was the whole point of the Proviso.

A clanking sounded, and I looked up to see a man dressed in all back with a sword strapped to his back sliding a tray with a glass bottle on it through a hatch in the door.

Walking forward cautiously, I realized an apple, a bowl of what looked like porridge, and a bottle of water sat on the tray. Oddly balanced for a prisoner.

As he latched the little trap door back up, I noticed a glint of gold on the breast of his black uniform. I moved forward to get a closer look, only to pause immediately once I realized what it was.

A golden crescent.

Looking up, the guard made eye contact, a dark smirk appearing on his lips as he took in my expression, took *me* in, before he turned and walked away.

Warning bells went off in my mind, and I stumbled back onto one of the few filthy mattresses lying around the small room, leaving the tray on the floor. The knots in my chest tightened, threatening to cut off oxygen to my lungs as tears flooded my eyes before I could stop them. Letting them fall freely, a choked sob escaped, reigniting the fire in my throat.

I crawled to the tray. Inspecting the bottle quickly and finding the seal unbroken, I opened it and drank heavily. Coming up, gasping for air, I hiccuped as the reality of my situation hit me again and a new wave of tears fell.

I was a Gaill prisoner. And not just any Gaill prisoner. *Their* prisoner.

A prisoner of the Nor Gaill. Of the Da Lucas.

My breaths came in short bursts, panic took over, and my control slipped. I was sure my heart would stop beating at any moment—the pain was unbearable.

Slaves, torture, human sacrifices…

No one captured by the Nor Gaill had ever made it back to Calderone alive. *Ever.* Usually there wasn't even a trace of their bodies, as if they were swallowed whole.

And the two members of the royal family who had been unlucky enough to be captured while outside the Wall a few decades ago? Father had said they'd been returned—in pieces, a letter accompanying their remains and signed in their blood by the fabled Prince Daxinius. No one could doubt the Nor Gaill were responsible.

My tears fell freely as I sat on the freezing floor of the cell. My mind reeled, stumbling through every possibility but always ending at the same conclusion: my title was my death knell. It wouldn't buy me time or the hope of negotiating a ransom—if that was a thing. No, it would only buy me certain death where the Nor Gaill were concerned.

And besides, in admitting who I was, I'd break my oath under the Heir Proviso.

I felt days pass by, but it was likely only twenty minutes before the gurgling in my stomach brought me back to reality. And my overwhelming hunger.

It probably actually had been days since I'd eaten.

Drying my tears on the back of my sleeve, I set the bottle on the tray and grabbed the apple before crawling back to the mattress in the corner.

I probably shouldn't eat it, but not having anything in my stomach made me nauseated. I figured maybe, if I was lucky, the apple would take me kindly and painlessly like in the fairy tale.

I ate it to the core before tossing the remains in a bucket in the center of the room that I had the sinking feeling was my new bathroom.

Willing my tears not to come, I folded my arm beneath me, avoiding the still-tender spot where I'd been knocked out, curled on the mattress, and faced the wall. I was counting my breaths when my fingers brushed the strand of pearls. My grandmother's necklace was still in place, unbroken.

The tears fell then, and I was powerless to stop them.

Falling. Falling. Falling.

Bright blues and purples rush past.

I sat up, panting, my hand clutched my heart. Beads of sweat ran down my forehead, my head instantly pounding from both the movement and the nightmare.

Gray morning light streamed in through the small barred window in the corner that I'd missed the night before.

And there were people in the cell with me now, talking. Arguing.

"Yeah, looks like she works for one of 'em, dunnit?" the woman with the black snarl of a ponytail said to the one on her right.

"Uh-huh," replied her friend. Both had on worn-out blue jeans that looked like they were from the 2350s with dirty, oversized tees covered in holes.

I instinctively shrank back into my corner. They weren't paying attention to me, and I planned to keep it that way.

"How much you bet we can get for this getup at one of the camps?" Said the first woman. They moved apart a bit, and I saw who they were talking to—or about, rather.

A petite girl near my age with a head of wild blond curls sat on the mattress at their feet. Her brown eyes were so wide with fear I felt my heart breaking on sight.

She was wearing a typical Calderonian housemaid uniform that was in considerably better shape than anything the other two women were wearing.

"I'd bet a gold note or two." The woman with the ponytail leaned down, shoving the blond in the shoulder, making her fall back into the wall.

"Yeah, girl. Why don't you take that off? We'll trade. And when we make it back, maybe we'll let you get back to your fancy job at the rich folks' house."

They moved toward her then. I wasn't sure what their next move was, but I wasn't about to let them make it.

"Stop right there." I drew myself up, my voice sounding much stronger than I felt thanks to the fact that I was still so dehydrated it came out two octaves lower than normal.

"Oh, who's this? Didn't see you there in the corner." The woman's friend turned to me, her eyes black with a desperate type of hate, and a cruel smile spread across her lips as she took in my clothing.

"Those are nice boots… would certainly come in handy if we have to go back to the camps."

The look in her eyes should've terrified me, but I felt a surprising sense of rage quell my fear as I stared her down.

I didn't know who those women were, how I was going to get out of this mess, or if I'd even make it to tomorrow, but I wasn't going to allow this place to strip me of my dignity. Or my boots.

I opened my mouth to speak when I noticed the dark-haired woman advancing on the blond, a look of intent on her face like she'd rip the clothes from her back if necessary.

And then I was speaking before I knew it.

"If I give you my boots, is that enough? Will you leave the two of us alone?"

The two women exchanged a conspiratorial glance. The one nearest me opened her mouth to respond when there was a clanking at the cell door.

All four of us looked, the women backing away from the door, as two Gaill guards entered.

"Which two of you were in the camps?" the slightly taller one asked. I didn't recognize either as the guard who had given me my food yesterday although both had the same golden crescent on their uniforms.

Having no idea what the camps were that both the women and now the guard referred to, I remained silent. The two women, however, exchanged a glance between themselves, apparently all the confirmation the guards needed.

Walking straight for them, the guards grabbed the two and with no further explanation, walked out.

"What about us?" I recklessly shouted as they were closing the door. The guards didn't bother acknowledging my question before leading the now-silent women away from the cell and out of sight.

"Thank you" came a small voice from behind me a minute later.

Sighing at the guards, I turned to find the girl with the wild curls looking at me, a grim but relieved look on her face.

Nodding to her, I crossed the room to where she stood. "You okay? Those women were rough."

She nodded. "Normally I can handle their type. Guess this whole thing has me pretty shaken up." She laughed. I had the feeling it was an attempt to cover her fear.

"Yeah, me too." I laughed too, hoping it covered mine as well.

There were really no words that could describe the maelstrom of anxiety and emotions storming through me at the moment. Fear didn't seem an adequate enough word.

"I'm Lana." She stuck her hand out by way of introduction.

"Jacqueline." I shook her hand in a gesture that seemed oddly normal in this totally abnormal situation.

She sat back on one of the mattresses then, motioning for me to sit next to her, which I did. I didn't know Lana, but I wasn't about to pass up kindness when it was offered.

We spent the next few hours distracting ourselves by getting to know one another, talking about home and generally avoiding the topic of our current situation except to cement the fact that neither of us knew where we were in relation to Calderone, how we could escape, or how much time had passed since we'd been taken.

I did learn that Lana was one of seven children in her family. After her father left, she helped support them by working as a housemaid for Lord Duvay, a lord I knew to be rather harsh and unforgiving. She'd been meeting with someone when she was captured outside Crash and brought here.

Managing to avoid topics surrounding my background, we focused mostly on her, but I was finally forced to admit how I'd ended up sitting beside her on that dirty mattress in the middle of Gaill Country.

Father always said if you're forced to tell a lie, you should stick as closely to the truth as possible so that it was easier to remember your story when you needed to. Having no other plan of action at the present, that's what I did, weaving a background for myself as believable as I could. And one I could easily remember.

Namely, that I too was a housemaid, though I avoided saying who for, and had snuck out to Crash with a few of the other maids when I alone had been captured. Lana gave me a quiet, assessing look as I told her this before moving on, seeming to buy my story and not saying anything otherwise.

As the daylight in the cell waned, we moved on to more pressing topics like why they were serving us actual food—I was almost positive our prisoners at home got no more than a slice of bread and a cup of barely potable water—and if we were going to live to see another day.

"Do you think they'll kill us?" Lana picked at the banana they'd given us with lunch.

I didn't want to lie, but I also didn't want to acknowledge the truth because that somehow made it more real.

"A girl I knew back home said they raided a village along the Wall near to hers a few years ago," she continued before I could speak. "Killed everyone within minutes except a couple of women they tortured and raped. They dismembered them, leaving the pieces scattered around like a scavenger hunt for the authorities to find."

I shivered. My eyes met hers, and I'm sure the look of fear in hers mirrored the look in my own. I didn't want to tell her the story was probably true, but Phin's warning of unrest echoed in my mind.

"I don't know." I reached for her hand and squeezed it. "But either way, we have each other now, and that's better than being alone."

"Wake up."

A command sliced through my dreamless sleep in the early hours the following morning.

Blinking slowly, I opened my eyes to find a Gaill guard standing over the mattress where Lana and I had curled up next to one other in search of warmth. I hadn't realized we'd both fallen asleep.

Without waiting, the guard yanked my arm with such force I was standing in a second.

And in the next, both Lana and I were pushed into the dimly lit corridor outside the cell where there was already a line of other captives waiting, shuffling their feet to keep warm in the damp chill of the prison.

No one spoke as we moved along the corridor except for a few grunts from the guards. It was slightly warmer than it had been in the cell thanks to the torches that lined the wall, but I still hugged my arms to keep my body heat from escaping, silently cursing myself for choosing the more fashionable top over an outfit requiring a jacket.

As we moved through the corridors, I attempted to keep track of where we were. There had to be a way out of here, and I was determined to find it when we returned.

Hopefully, we return. Alive.

I shuddered. Thankfully, I hadn't eaten much in the past few days, or else I wouldn't have been able to control the nausea now roiling through my gut.

Swallowing, I worked to keep my emotions off my face as I took a deep breath, feeling fresh air fill my lungs as we exited the prison.

The air was cool, the sun having barely risen, and mist hovered above the dewy grass as we were led through a small courtyard to a compound that resembled a royal palace more than a military fortress. I reminded myself it technically *was* a palace considering who supposedly lived there.

And I was in no way prepared for them.

The Da Lucas.

I was trained in the arts of literature and good manners. I highly doubt these royals renowned for their brutality would be impressed by my knowing which fork to use first.

But I had one advantage—no one knew who I was.

If they did, this would be much, much worse.

Guards were everywhere as we were led through a giant Gothic stone archway and into the palace itself. We passed guard after guard as we walked through the corridors before eventually rounding a corner only to encounter a chamber full of people.

Not unlike Father's court, men and women, obviously noble from the quality of their attire and general air of self-importance, milled about, turning to watch our sorry parade as we marched through. I thought I caught a few snickers and glances in my direction while we walked. A few of the women turned to whisper in one another's ears. I couldn't really blame them though. I probably would have done the same thing if a girl wearing a low-cut top with combat boots had walked through my court when it was obvious that modesty reigned supreme here. All the women wore similar day dresses in somber hues, complete with mock necks and hair back in braids. Back home I looked chic. Here I probably looked like the new court harlot.

Not to mention I hadn't seen a mirror in days or bathed for that matter. I could feel my makeup crusted around my eyes, and I had no doubt I resembled a raccoon at this point. My dark curls were still in their side braid but barely. It lay tousled over my shoulder as my waves ran wild, and I resisted the urge to fix it as we passed the last group of ladies, my pride nearly getting the best of me.

Approaching what I assumed was a receiving hall of sorts, guards opened two sets of giant oak doors with a Gaill crescent above to let us through. This hall was even more imposing than the corridor we'd just left.

It had the same Gothic architecture as the rest of the palace, which had the disorienting effect of making me feel like I was in one of the great ruined cathedrals in Old Europe that I'd seen in photos. It was as if the castle already stood from eons past, and the Gaill simply outfitted it for their use. Though I knew that couldn't be the case; we were still on New American soil.

My eyes caught the light as it streamed through the stained glass windows lining the top half of the hall. Stealing a quick glance, I recognized the first window as depicting the Fight for Freedom—when the dictators were finally defeated, signaling the end to the War.

There were tapestries and candles covering the giant stone walls as well, but though we moved forward slowly, it was hard to make out what any of the tapestries depicted through the crowd in front of them. It was then that I actually took note of the people we were passing through. They were all silent, kneeling and facing the front of the room. Most had their heads bowed, others just stared blankly, eyes fixed forward.

Resisting an urge to shudder, I attempted to see what they were waiting for but couldn't see a thing from my five-foot three height. I craned my neck as far as I dared, barely peeking over Lana's shoulder in front of me, when I felt it.

Power. All-consuming, electric, magnetic—*terrifying*.

It creeped into every bone and fiber of my being, infiltrating my very blood and making my hair stand on end as we drew nearer. A fear deeper and more sinister than any I'd ever known, far worse than that which had paralyzed me in the ally, pressed on my chest, making it impossible to breathe. I could swear there was smoke surrounding me again, the air felt so thick. Every instinct told me to run, but my limbs propelled me forward in an automatic way toward what was most certainly my doom.

The pressure only intensified the nearer we got to the front, and I concentrated on my breathing again, taking deep breaths in an attempt to calm myself. The room remained deathly silent while we slowly shuffled in behind the row of captives in front of us.

Determined not to look my death in the face, I kept my eyes on the ground a few feet ahead of me as the guards led the captives in front out. I'm not sure I could've looked forward had I tried. The power was the strongest it had been so far, and I felt like I was moving through quicksand as my body tried to navigate the foreign energy permeating the room. A glance in my periphery told me that no one was looking forward. Not even the guards.

"What're these?" A deep voice with what I now recognized as a Gaill accent boomed out across the hall, causing us all to flinch. Annoyance, arrogance… and lethal power followed in its wake.

"The most recent captures, Your Highness. Gathered from directly inside the city three nights ago and immediately transported here."

It had been three days. Three days.

I already knew I was in the palace of the Nor Gaill. And from what I knew—how long it'd taken us to get here and how cold it was outside—we were far from home. I had arrived sometime yesterday, likely very early in the morning based on the light outside the window of my cell and how long I'd been with Lana, which meant it had taken us just about a day to travel. I concentrated on that new kernel of knowledge as the voice again spoke out.

"General Romano, approach."

A blond-haired man wearing a military uniform stepped from the row to my right and approached the front out of my view.

Counting my breaths to remain calm, I tried to sort a way out of this. I *had* to.

I could try to beg for mercy though I knew I'd find none—I wasn't a fool.

Should I give up my identity? Violate the oath I'd sworn to honor? Would they ask for a ransom?

No, they'll probably just kill me.

Ending the royal line was their ultimate goal anyway. And by the looks of the palace, they likely didn't need our money.

So any option leads to my death; it's just a matter of when.

I closed my eyes, swallowing as an involuntary shiver snaked down my spine. No matter what happened, I was determined to go down fighting. Taking a few more deep breaths, I honed in on the general, Romano, talking.

"The raid near Suburb Five didn't yield much new information. These are the resulting captives we were able to grab from the few hundred who fled the area. It's not known who they are or if they know anything of value, but they were at the scene."

None of what the general was saying made any sense, and the power radiating through the room was making my mind more of a jumbled mess than it already was after days of dehydration and no sleep.

Nervously licking my lips, I chanced a quick glance to the front of the room before I thought better of it.

Once I looked though, I couldn't tear my eyes away.

Lounging on a throne carved entirely from stone, black military boots kicked out in front of him, one hand splayed on his outstretched knee, the other holding up his jaw in a picture of boredom, was the most terrifyingly beautiful man I'd ever seen.

He didn't look much older than me, likely early twenties, with an angular, hard-set jaw darkened by stubble that I'd never seen on any man back home. His shoulder-length, dark brown hair hung in loose curls with two braided pieces at the front framing his face. The braids somehow only added to his brutality.

His broad shoulders shifted, muscles taut as they rippled under his slightly open tunic while he addressed the general, revealing a maze of tattoos against brown skin. They were *everywhere*, extending from his neck down to his exposed forearms, hands, and fingers. He moved with deadly energy, and the more he moved, the more it became apparent this wasn't just a soldier—this was a warrior. Born and bred.

Daxinius Da Luca.

He existed.

The air got knocked from my lungs by the realization that my worst fears, my worst nightmares, could all be real.

He was more stunning than any photo. Striking, really. But no legend or photo could have prepared me for the innate terror his palpable power triggered within me. No warning would have adequately sufficed.

I didn't know where King Aidoneus was. Perhaps dealing with Calderonian captives was beneath him. Though it didn't matter in the present moment. If you believed the rumors—which were becoming alarmingly accurate—both Aidoneus and Daxinius were cruel, but Daxinius was the brute force behind the Gaill throne. The punishing force. Crossing him was the same as signing your own death sentence.

As if someone dared test that theory, a voice rang out from my left. "Long live King Manasseh of Calderone!"

The silence blanketing room reached a suffocating level as everyone's eyes moved to the man who dared speak out against the Gaill prince. His hair was cropped in a high and tight, his back rigid, and jaw set. Though he wore civilian clothes, only members of the Calderonian military had that hairstyle.

A sense of pride in his service and defiance washed over me, then was quickly drowned by the fear instilled by the prince's gaze. His eyes were now a glowing white-green.

Before I could blink, he was right in front of the Calderonian soldier. His size was impressive from the throne, but it was even more intimidating only ten feet away.

"What did you say?"

An involuntary shiver ran down my spine as I desperately worked to keep my knees from knocking together.

"Long live King Manasseh. The one true king." The Calderonian soldier remained defiant as his head tilted to meet the prince's gaze.

There was another moment of silence before the prince threw his head back and laughed. A sound so cruel it seemed wrong to associate it with something usually reserved for happiness.

Daxinius addressed the general he'd spoken to earlier while keeping his eyes trained on the Calderonian soldier. "A member of their military, Romano? Are you and your team so incompetent you mistake a soldier for a civilian?"

"Your High—" Romano began, instantly falling silent as the prince raised a hand in his direction.

"You choose to defend a tyrant?" Daxinius's tone was nothing but lethal as he directed the question at the soldier.

"L-long live King Manasseh." His resolve was wavering.

"I'll take that as a yes." Daxinius turned, holding his hand out, and a sword that had been resting near the throne literally flew into it. It was mammoth and had a Celtic cross at the hilt that was visible even from where I stood. Before I could process what the prince had done, he turned and drove the sword directly into the heart of the Calderonian soldier.

Blood exploded on Daxinius as he drove the sword deeper until it went clear through the man's heart and protruded out his back.

My heartbeat went into overdrive as my hand flew to my mouth in an attempt to stifle a sudden rush of nausea at the sight of the blood dripping off his sword and gushing from the soldier's mouth.

Daxinius twisted his sword into the soldier's chest, a manic look on his face before he withdrew the sword in one swift motion and let the man crash to the floor. A horrible gurgling sound came from the soldier as he proceeded to choke on his own blood, red covering his convulsing body and the surrounding stone. It began pooling beneath the feet of the captives standing next to him, but not one moved. They were likely frozen by the same fear I was.

Ringing sounded in my ears as my heart continued to pound. The weight on my chest grew impossibly heavy, threatening to cut off any bit of oxygen I had left.

"I have no use for a heart that remains loyal to the man who calls himself king of Calderone."

And with that Daxinius walked back to the throne. His sword remained in his right hand, blood dripping from it as he moved, leaving a trail of death behind him. Placing the still-bloodied sword on its stand next to the throne, he once again took his seat. His mask of boredom slipped back in place as he watched a group of Gaill servants drag the soldier's limp body from the chamber.

My mind stuttered as I attempted to process what just happened—both the man's death and how Daxinius could be seemingly so unaffected by taking the life of another.

I heard a small squeak next to me and, pulling my attention from the Gaill prince, glanced over to see Lana's eyes fill with tears. The fear was evident on her face.

"It'll be okay, Lana," I whispered quickly before I could think.

The moment the words left my mouth, I felt a pin-prickling

sensation as dread washed over me. I was being watched, and I knew by whom.

Sliding my eyes back to the front of the room, it felt like the world stuttered to a halt as the prince's light green gaze locked onto mine, pinning me to the spot. My breath hitched under his examination, his eyes so intense I could do nothing, say nothing but be stripped raw by them. Another shiver raced down my spine, and I had to remind myself to breathe against the building pressure in my lungs. I had the creeping feeling he could read every thought in my head.

I felt the unwavering need to look away then, but it was like my eyes were glued to his through no will of their own. And suddenly he was looking at me like a puzzle he couldn't solve but had to. Like his whole world's existence depended on it. Then I blinked, and the look was gone, replaced again by the same mask of annoyed indifference he wore earlier.

Glancing down, I attempted to slow my breathing as a cold sweat broke out at the base of my neck.

Why do I feel like I just let the enemy in?

Taking in a harsh breath, I forced my eyes closed and held it, hoping to keep the panic at bay. I couldn't forget who I was.

I was the future queen. A sudden rush of hate, so palpable I could practically taste it, flooded my system. He could go to hell if he thought I would cower before him, his throne, and the court of murderers he had the audacity to represent and defend. If I'd let them break me, give away who I was, or share any information about my monarchy. I had one mission, and it was to get out of there alive and back home as quickly as possible.

I glanced up and found his gaze still on me. I glared back—boldly—and forced myself not to flinch at the power he emanated in return.

What is *this guy?*

Phin had that quiet dominance to him, a demeanor honed over years of training. But the prince? That power wasn't normal.

How long had he been alive anyway? *Could radioactivity actually give you powers like this?*

No. No, it was all in my head. All a product of insane levels of fear and relatively no sleep.

As I returned his gaze, I could've sworn his mouth twitched ever so slightly, and it gave me the creeping feeling that he might actually be able to read every thought in my head.

Suddenly losing interest in us entirely, Daxinius turned his attention to the general. And if his arrogant smile wasn't enough to make my blood boil, what he said next definitely was.

"Well, hopefully the rest of the captives are more compliant, Romano. Although we all know how useless Calderonian women are for our mission."

A familiar sense of anger fell over me. I was once again being written off as nothing all because I was a girl. The irony this time being that it might save my life; I had a feeling whatever they planned for the men to make them compliant would break me.

Unless being useless meant my existence here was also useless.

Panic surged in my chest at the thought.

Closing my eyes again, I concentrated on my breathing. If I left this room alive, my identity would surely be my death sentence. I needed the right plan in place. So as far as everyone was concerned, I was a lady's maid. I would use Miranda's family name if I could; then maybe, if the monarchy caught wind of our capture, they'd connect the dots since Miranda hadn't gone missing.

She hadn't, right? I watched her getting in the car… saw all their faces as I felt those feet running up behind me.

Stop.

I couldn't allow myself to think of them. I needed to stay strong.

Gathering my nerves, I opened my eyes only to find myself once again the subject of *his* gaze.

"The women, as maids, shall help in the palace. They're not likely to know anything of importance anyway. The men will be questioned about their knowledge of Calderone... and its suburbs."

At that, he got up, his towering presence again filling the room and dwarfing General Romano next to him. Without another word, he grabbed the sword resting near the throne, not bothering to wipe off the blood still coating its blade. Sheathing it across his back in one swift movement, he turned on his heel and moving with inhuman speed and fluidity was gone, leaving us to the mercy of General Romano, who couldn't be bothered to hide the look of annoyance on his face as he turned to us.

I let out a breath I hadn't realized I'd been holding when it hit me that the prince had just sentenced Lana and me to living and serving there in the palace, under *his* rule. The relief knowing we'd keep our lives was instantly soured by suspicion. Having prisoners work in a palace? I'd never heard of such a thing. Father certainly would never consider having Gaill work in our palace back home, whether they'd formerly been maids or not.

And who told him we were maids, anyway?

I looked to Lana, who appeared just as confused as I was.

"You heard His Highness. Be thankful he showed you mercy today." The general was addressing us as he strode toward our disheveled group. He had the same power radiating from him that the prince did. It wasn't quite as intense, but I still felt it. "Especially you two." He directed his stony blue gaze at Lana and me. "Calderonians have never served in the palace before. Don't mess up." His eyes shifted to the men in our group. "You lot are to be prepped for questioning. Depending on what information you provide, the prince may let you keep your lives." Romano motioned to the men in our group to follow a bald, built Gaill soldier with a mean grin standing beside him.

I exchanged a relieved glance with Lana that neither of us would be going anywhere with the man.

"You both follow me."

Turning back to General Romano, I wasn't sure if we were much better off. He was looking at us like we were leeches, dirt—practically nothing. It was clearly beneath him to be dealing with us directly.

Screw him, I thought. Some of the fire in my chest returned as the air in the room continued to lighten after the prince's departure.

Without another word, he brushed past us, striding for the great oak doors at the back of the hall. The Gaill guard walked alongside him, the two talking quietly before the rest of the group broke off shortly after we exited the room. I watched them leave wondering if any of us would see each other again. Alive.

The general led us down a back staircase wide enough to fit several people but clearly worn and so plain it likely never saw foot traffic from guests. We were going down to the servants' quarters.

We landed in a large chamber, making our way along a hallway that was open to a courtyard on one side. The morning was warming up now that the sun had risen, but it was still notably cooler than Calderone. All the servants we passed hurried to stay out of the chill of the exposed hallway as they rushed about their morning duties.

Birds I'd never seen before flitted between the well-kept hydrangeas growing in the courtyard, while others took turns sunning themselves in the rays shining on a nearby bird bath. If I hadn't been so terrified for my future, it would've seemed rather beautiful.

Keeping up with General Romano, we passed several rooms on

the right.

"This hallway houses a chapel, a private office, and a storage hallway. There is a locked service door in one of the storage rooms that leads beyond the outer ward. It's strictly off-limits unless Madam Scarletti assigns you to unload shipments arriving for the kitchens." The general looked over his shoulder long enough to level us with a glare that sent a storm of emotions rolling through me.

I wasn't sure who Madam Scarletti was, but I did know an access point to the outside, even if forbidden, meant one thing—a chance to escape. I cataloged this new information as the three of us rounded a corner and were immediately confronted with the din of the kitchen. The clanking of silverware and the shouts of instructions from the cooks reached us though we were still far from the entrance.

Swallowing audibly, I realized I had no idea how to find my way around the lower levels of a palace let alone serve people. Romano's warning to not mess up settled like a weight in my gut as I rifled through all the things Miranda and Rachel had told me, but I could only remember the gossip and cursed myself for all the times I'd tuned them out as they went on about the more mundane aspects of their day.

The sounds of the kitchen grew louder as we moved down the hall, and people began pouring out of an open archway to another room on our right. Peering in as we passed, I noticed what looked like a giant hall with its own kitchens in the back and even more servants. Broken sunlight filtered through the bars that lined the windows and danced across the floor. I swallowed again over the growing lump in my throat.

Did I trade one prison cell for another?

I picked up my pace as the general turned left, away from the hall, into the bustling kitchen and strained to hear him over the noise. He continued muttering instructions on basic rules and the areas of the palace we weren't allowed to enter. I caught that we'd just come from the throne room and that the south wing, where the military was housed, was off-limits, then the rest of what he said was swallowed by the hum of the servants.

Steering us toward the ovens in the far corner, the general stopped in front of an austere, rather stout older woman who was reprimanding a young cook.

"Madam Scarletti." He raised his voice, interrupting her. "These two belong to you now." He motioned to us over his shoulder with his thumb, not bothering to dignify us with anything more.

The young cook made his way around our small group, embarrassed as evidenced by the redness in his cheeks but probably thankful for an easy out.

"Very well." Madam Scarletti gave us a long look, her gaze assessing, questioning, and not at all friendly. Her eyes landed on my neck for a beat, and it took me a moment to realize she was staring at my necklace. I resisted the urge to rip it off; the pearls were a dead giveaway that I likely wasn't a maid.

"Follow me." Her only command before turning and making her way through the kitchens.

Lana and I exchanged glances. We were not welcome, that was obvious.

We followed Madam Scarletti through the large kitchen, and when I looked back, Romano was nowhere to be found. Breathing a sigh of relief, I felt my heart rate slowly returning to a bearable place. With his presence gone, the atmosphere was somewhat less charged.

I glanced around the hot kitchens as we passed through; there had to be at least three separate rooms, each with large wood-burning ovens and people rushing about. Two women tended to a large pot of oatmeal on an even larger stove, and in the next kitchen, two men were preparing what looked like a couple dozen omelets.

Then there were the boys—they couldn't be much older than twelve or thirteen—kneading the day's bread for the slightly older boys to toss in the ovens as the girls next to them were sorting the day's fruit. As I watched, one of the younger boys threw a piece of dough at a girl, hitting her in the arm and causing the whole group to burst into giggles. I smiled in spite of myself before that knot of worry returned.

We got a few looks as we continued through, but I was more concerned with what the servants were doing.

Everyone moved so well together, like they belonged there and had been there forever. Each group had their own duties. And each group appeared happy to be there, and if not happy, at least content.

Rolling up my sleeves, I felt a flush that wasn't entirely due to the heat from the ovens as we started up a narrow winding staircase at the back of the kitchen. Climbing past the second floor, I noticed a long stone hallway lit by torches with wooden doors on either side.

"You two will have quarters on the third floor, girls' wing," Madam Scarletti advised us as we ascended to the third floor landing and made our way down the hall, which was identical to the floor below.

Stopping a few doors in, she turned to us. "Names?"

I stuttered, thrown off by both the question and her bluntness.

"Lana Jones, ma'am," Lana responded before looking at me, waiting for me to follow suit.

"J-Jacqueline, ma'am. Jacqueline Lewis."

Madam Scarletti only raised an eyebrow in response.

I had no idea what I was doing.

"Right. Well, same rules apply to the both of you. You will be palace maids—changing the linens, the firewood, fetching meals on occasion as I'm sure you know." Madam Scarletti again fixed me with her stare as if she could tell that I definitely did *not* know.

"You will begin at 0630 daily to help prepare breakfast," she continued, "and so that you may start your daily duties. Curfew is at eleven every evening. Meals are served in the dining hall across from the kitchens at 0830, 1230, and 1930. There's a front staircase you can take at the opposite end of the corridor that will take you nearer to the entrance of the dining hall." She motioned to the opposite end from where we stood. It dawned on me that the room I noticed across from the kitchen, the one with the barred windows, must've been their dining hall—as if even during free periods the servants needed a reminder of their lack of freedom.

Taking another deep breath, I reminded myself that being outside a prison cell was better than being in it, even if it meant a few weeks of dodgy work and servant meals. Surely being here, with a chance of access to an outside entrance, would make it easier to escape regardless of the bars on the windows.

Unlocking the first door, Madam Scarletti turned to Lana. "You"—she pointed a long, crooked finger—"will be here."

Lana walked in, grabbing an extra key from Madam Scarletti as she passed. Peering in, all I could see was a narrow, modest room with white walls, a small window, barred of course, a bed, desk, and a wardrobe. Although plain, it would do for a few weeks.

"And you, here," she said to me. Unlocking another door nearby, she pushed it open and moved aside to let me pass.

I got the feeling she didn't remember our names.

"Wash up and then head straight down to the kitchens. Inquire with Master Pepridge, the butler, as to your duties today." Without another word, she handed me a key and closed the door, her heels clicking as her steps receded down the hallway.

Washing up didn't make any sense until I saw the small sink in the corner along with a bathroom that couldn't have been more than a few feet across. Even considering the size, the Gaill court had to be bringing in some serious money to afford these bathrooms. Our court, considered the most affluent in the world, had centralized bathrooms and showers for servants.

Before I could move, there was a knock at the door. I opened it to find a plain-faced, dark-skinned girl staring back at me with bright green eyes.

"Here." She awkwardly handed me a folded pile of clothing. "Scarletti told me you needed these."

"Thanks," I replied, mustering up a smile. The girl couldn't have been more than ten and looked so timid. It took me a second to recognize her from the group giggling in the kitchen.

She smiled back before turning down the long hall toward the stairs.

I closed the door, putting the clothes on the bed before starting to take out the numerous pins still in my hair.

Had it been just three nights ago that Mir and Rach had pinned it up? That I'd blown my mother off? Been annoyed with Father and Phin? Now my biggest worry was how I was going to survive the day.

The Gaill's not knowing my identity was both a blessing and a curse. It meant I might be able to escape by flying under the radar, but it also meant they could kill me off and no one would know. My gut twisted at what that would do to my friends and family. And my country.

I never wanted to be queen. But I loved my country and my people. And the thought of leaving the throne without an heir...

No, that wasn't an option. All I could do was escape.

Retrieving the last of the embedded pins, I loosed my hair from its braid. Finding a comb in the basket under the sink, I began the arduous process of untangling my wiry mess of curls, assessing the rest of my damaged state in the process. I couldn't see any visible cuts or markings, but my makeup was now smeared across my face, even down to my neck. My earlier assumptions were correct—I more closely resembled a wild animal than a future queen.

At least no one will suspect you for royalty, I thought sardonically.

Sighing, I washed my make up off and brushed my teeth with some products in the same basket as the comb. I had to admit though they were modest, the Gaill were accommodating. I wondered how many other servants they had in the palace to afford such luxuries. And why? Surely the servants could afford their own personal toiletries.

I was surprised to find I'd dramatically improved upon the disheveled mess I'd been just minutes earlier. My lashes were back to their regular black fullness, and my eyes were clearer.

Blue, like Mother. Most other Calderonians had brown eyes. My gut twisted at the thought that I might never see hers again.

My parents had never been particularly loving. Having a child always seemed more of a duty than a desire for them. But they were my parents. My only family. And all our squabbles suddenly seemed so petty in comparison to my current reality.

Blinking away thoughts of home, I inspected the rest of my appearance. My cheeks had regained some of the natural rosy glow that helped tone down the severity of my cheekbones, the defining feature of my slightly heart-shaped face, my nose a small ski jump and my lips of average fullness otherwise. And not a trace of makeup. I hadn't even seen a speck of it on any of the servants or courtiers. The all-natural look would take some getting used to.

Wandering to the bed, I picked up the first dress on the pile and saw the ones below it were almost identical. They were simple, all black with long sleeves, a mock neck on some, modest V-neck on others, with skirts that hung to the ground. The material was soft wool, breathable yet warm given the cooler temperatures. And it was cooler here—wherever *here* was.

I peeled off the outfit I'd worn to the club, desperately wanting to shower, but that would have to wait. The last thing I wanted was to arouse more suspicion by taking too long.

Putting on the new dress along with a new set of undergarments I found in the wardrobe, I went for the small black boots the girl brought next. The ankle was on the shorter side, yet they had a slight heel and a rubberized bottom. They were the type of boots that looked nice but were actually practical—the type I rarely wore. I found they fit, just as everything else Madam Scarletti had sent, and were surprisingly comfortable.

I combed my hair into a low bun—slightly unkempt, but it would have to do—and tucked my pearl necklace under the dress's high neckline. Should anyone question it, I could say it was a gift. Surely that would be believable. I'd given my ladies jewelry on more than one occasion.

I dug my peach lip gloss out from my pile of old clothes and hid it in my wardrobe. My necklace was easy to hide, but I wasn't about to draw attention to myself by wearing lip gloss, which apparently didn't even exist this side of the Wall.

After a once-over, I left the room, tying one of the aprons Scarletti sent around my waist, and made my way down the deserted hallway to where we'd left Lana.

"Lana? It's Jacqueline." I knocked softly.

When she didn't answer right away, I grew worried. If she left before me, I was screwed. That much was certain. I didn't know where to go to find the butler. But just as I was about to knock again, she opened the door. And, she was smiling.

"Uh, did you see these dresses and the rooms? You couldn't force me to go home." She stepped back and finished zipping the top of her dress.

Are the dresses that much better too?

"Yeah." I played along. "What kind of money do they have to give us all our own bathroom?"

"A lot. Way more than the monarchy, that's for sure." Lana shook her head like she couldn't believe this was all real as she combed her hair into a similar low, albeit much smoother, bun.

Did they really have more money than us? The servants' quarters certainly suggested it. But we treated our servants well. At least in the palace we did.

"I know one thing," Lana said, bringing me out of my thoughts. "I miss the makeup." She eyed herself in the mirror above the sink before meeting my gaze and laughing.

"Me too." I smiled back at her. "It's definitely going to be an adjustment. That and the lack of good skincare."

Her expression suddenly became more serious as she turned to face me. "Hey… Thanks. For earlier. When we were in front of the prince," she said with a shrug.

Walking up to her, I pulled her in for a hug. "Of course, Lan. Anytime."

And I meant it. We'd only known each other a few days, but after those twenty-four hours in the prison cell and surviving our first encounter with Daxinius Da Luca together, Lana felt like a sister to me.

Plus she was kind.

So maybe this wouldn't be so bad—being here for a few weeks.

The servants didn't seem to totally hate it here, and I'd have Lana, who clearly wasn't my enemy, by my side along with a decent place to sleep and food while I figured out my escape. I could make this work if I just played my part as a maid convincingly enough.

"Come on, gorgeous." Lana squeezed me back before looping her arm through mine. "Let's go find this Master Peptide or whatever and see if we actually have work to do or if we're just being prepared to be their next human sacrifice."

CHAPTER 3

DEVIANT

“But did you see Master Pepridge’s face when you fell? He looked just like that portrait of Antonio above the fireplace.” Lana screwed up her face, making me smile despite the dread that had lodged itself in my chest ever since I tripped over a bucket of dirty water and spilled it all over the floor of the newly cleaned receiving room.

Master Pepridge, every bit as austere as Madam Scarletti and then some, had Lana and me work together, along with a few other experienced servants. I had managed to clean most of the room without issue. It was only when we were rushing to pack up our supplies before the room was needed by the prince that I tripped over the bucket, dirtying the clean floor thirty minutes before he was set to arrive.

The looks Pepridge and a few servants gave me were enough to flay me live, even if I did manage to escape any physical punishment. Well, except being forced to clean up the mess with the added pressure of doing it before the prince’s imminent arrival. Lana had volunteered to help me, and though we managed to finish up and leave minutes before he arrived, I wasn’t sure my heart would ever recover. It was still pounding as we made our way back down the dimly lit corridor to our rooms.

"Antonio... you mean the old guy who looked like he was suffering from a massive case of indigestion?" I asked matter-of-factly, meeting her gaze.

She snorted, which caused my smile to widen, and a surge of gratitude hit me. She'd not only stayed behind to help me clean when no one else did, but was actively trying to lighten my mood now.

Sighing, I stopped outside Lana's room as she unlocked the door. "How do you suppose we ready ourselves for dinner?" I asked, hoping it was a normal question.

Luckily, it didn't seem to raise any alarms.

"Since we only got a few dresses, I assume we just wash up and leave our aprons here." Lana shrugged.

"Easy enough. Be back in five minutes."

Making the short walk to my room, I made quick work of ditching my apron and resetting my bun, which still more closely resembled a rat's nest than anything else. I made a mental note to slyly ask Lana for some hair tips as I went to meet her in the hall.

A few people milled about, but I kept my head low, not wanting to draw attention to myself. Lana was talking to a guy practically twice her size, and they turned to me as I approached, the man cracking a smile that took over his entire face.

If I had to guess, he was close to our age and was most definitely born on this side of the Wall. His features and entire demeanor screamed Gaill—everything from his slanted, icy blue eyes to the tattoos covering his muscular forearms up to his angular jawline. I would not be surprised if something different, something inhuman, ran through his veins. A familiar power seemed to thrum from him—although nowhere near as suffocating as the one earlier in the throne room.

"Hey, I'm Axel." He extended one tan, tattooed hand to introduce himself while the other, equally tattooed one, combed back his messy blond hair. "Lana was just telling me how you two landed here. Quite a surprise..."

He trailed off as he looked me up and down as if trying to figure out exactly why we were here. His smile never wavered. It was unnerving.

Clearing my throat, I reached for his hand. "His Highness showed us great mercy by letting us stay here and serve in the palace." I had lived among royals long enough to know that the best type of answer was always the one that flattered the monarch. It hurt to give the prince even a fake compliment almost as much as it hurt to meet Axel's practically glowing eyes, but I forced myself to do so while we shook hands. His were as cold as ice.

"Ah yes, the prince can be quite… merciful." Axel's smile remained, but there was a certain edge to it. He lightly squeezed my hand before dropping it. I resisted the urge to blow warm air on it.

"Well, Lana and I were just going to dinner." I looked to Lana before starting down the corridor again. The power coming from Axel wasn't as strong as the prince's, but something about it and that unwavering smile tightened the knot of dread in my chest.

Apparently, Lana felt the same. She immediately fell into step beside me, and we practically jogged down the hall.

"What a coincidence! So was I." Axel caught up to us almost instantly. "You two can sit where I usually do. It'll be nice to have some new blood in the group."

"O-oh, that's so…," Lana stuttered.

Axel cut her off with another wide smile. "Please." He placed a tattooed hand over his heart. "I insist."

As we neared the giant dining hall I'd seen earlier, I could barely make out what Axel was saying over the chatter and clanking of silverware coming through the open doors. There were so many people in there.

"Because accommodations are good and pay is pretty steady, families often work here for generations. You two are in single rooms like me, but they have family apartments that house up to ten on other floors," Axel was saying as we made our way into the line.

Food was served like I had seen in old American photos: we waited in lines while workers served us across a counter. I didn't know places like this still existed.

Following Axel's lead, we got drinks and food—some sort of chicken and veggie dish that didn't look too bad—and made our way to a table in the far corner with a few empty chairs. It was hard to read Axel. We might be making a huge mistake sitting with him, but we didn't have much of a choice. He'd probably just follow us to wherever we sat down, and considering everyone in the hall was eyeing us with outright suspicion, I doubted we'd receive a warm welcome anywhere else.

Axel greeted the few people already sitting at the table—a girl and two guys, all about our age.

"Pick up some strays, Ax?" The guy with the wavy black hair threw a smirk our way and leaned forward, folding his tattooed arms on the table.

"Ha, yeah, more like Dax's chosen ones." Pride laced Axel's voice as if we were a trophy he'd won.

"Wait, seriously?" The guy sat up straighter.

"Yeah, in the flesh." Axel nodded to us as we set our trays down.

"Never thought I'd see the day."

The group appraised us with questioning eyes, a certain power radiating from them.

Axel clapped his hands together, his smile giddy as he looked from us to the group. "Lana and Jacqueline, meet everyone. Everyone, meet Lana and Jacqueline."

The guys at the table just laughed and shook their heads, but the girl got up, throwing her long, straight strawberry blond hair over her shoulder as she made her way for us with ethereal grace. Tiny tattoos and freckles peaked out from the sleeves of a dress identical to ours.

"You never were any good with new people, Ax." She sighed, pushing past Axel and immediately drawing me into a hug.

Caught off guard, it took me a few seconds to realize she was sincere, and then I hugged her back on instinct.

"Kacey." She leaned back, showing me a pair of slanted bright hazel-orange eyes and a smiling face full of freckles before she then moved over to Lana and gave her a hug as well. "Finally some girls here. The testosterone in this group is absolutely nauseating."

I cracked a smile at that, and Lana laugh-coughed, smiling back at Kacey, whose orange eyes twinkled.

"I've barely survived these past few minutes." The words were out of my mouth before I could stop them.

"I like her." Kacey laughed, flashing a smile at me before going back to her seat.

"Well, I know I'm just a testosterone-filled caveman," the one with the wavy black hair said, playfully nudging Kacey and rising from his seat, "but I do have manners. Name's Killian." He extended a tattooed hand to shake mine, then Lana's, then gestured with a thumb to the redhead sitting at the table. "And the shy one's Maverick. Seriously though, welcome."

"Thank you." I flexed my hand at my side as I sat down. Whereas Axel's hands were icy cold, Killian's held the strength of a giant.

Like Axel, Killian was extraordinarily tall, well over six feet. But Axel was lean and muscular while Killian's wide shoulders and imposing girth made the surrounding table and chairs look like doll furniture. Killian's nails were painted a chipped black too, and his tattoos covered every inch of his dark skin—except his face, which was covered with piercings in his brow, nose, and lip. His eyes were a rich hazel brown and, like every other Gaill sitting at the table, seemed to have an electrical current running through them, like flames of different colors.

His black hair sat in loose waves, lazily pushed off his forehead, as opposed to the man named Maverick, whose bright red hair was slightly longer on top with designs shaved into the shorter sides. He hadn't spoken a word since we'd sat down except to whisper something in Kacey's ear, who was now facing him, talking animatedly while eating an apple. A few tattoos dotted his skin as well, but more striking was his resounding paleness in juxtaposition to the fiery redness of his hair and the amber color of his eyes together with the black work shirt, pants, and boots he and the other two wore.

I did my best not to feel intimidated.

These… *These* were the type of Gaill that had frequented my nightmares as a child.

I concentrated on eating. It wasn't hard, though the food wasn't the best I'd had. I couldn't remember the last time I'd had a full meal, and I practically inhaled the tray.

I took a large gulp of water to wash it all down when a blur of movement flashed in my periphery, and I felt the water go down the wrong tube. Tears pooled in my eyes as I coughed, but it was only moments before Axel reached over and pounded my back.

"You good, Jac?" He grinned.

I nodded as I coughed again, swallowing around the tightness in my throat. A minute passed before my heart rate returned to normal. "What was that?" I asked once I caught my breath.

"You choked. On your water."

"No, I mean that movement. It startled me."

The group of Gaill exchanged looks.

"You mean the person who shifted?" Killian's brows drew together as he met my gaze from across the table.

"Shifted?" Lana interjected.

"Yeah, when a person moves so fast their image blurs?" Killian arched a brow as he looked between us.

Lana's confused eyes met mine. I didn't know what caused someone to move like that, but it definitely didn't happen our side of the Wall.

"Wait." Axel laid both palms on the table. "You two don't know what shifting is? Don't they tell you anything in Calderone?"

"Calderone?" I tried not to sound suspicious as I sipped the water. We hadn't told them where we'd been taken from. So what gave us away?

"Yeah…" He screwed up his face in confusion. "Your accent? Clear Calderonian."

"That's for sure. What were you, girl, raised in the heart of the country?" Kacey's eyes danced as she met mine.

"Um, yeah, something like that." I dropped my gaze to my plate, avoiding eye contact.

Luckily, Lana interjected before I had to field any more questions. "What are your accents? 'Cause I've never heard anything like them before."

"Strictly Nor Gaill—we're the result of a melting pot." Axel waved his fork in the air as he spoke. "Our accents are a result of those from Old Europe who came over and mixed with the people already here."

"They're a hell of a lot easier to understand than the Eur, that's for sure." Killian mumbled between bites of his rice.

Since the Eur Gaill—the Nor Gaill's counterpart in Eurasia—didn't exist on our continent, I knew even less about them than about the Nor Gaill. But I did know that some of those who were part of the mass exodus from Old Europe after the War had settled with the Nor Gaill just as some had continued farther south and now lived in Calderone.

"So can the Eur Gaill—the Eur—shift too?" I ventured, pushing for any information potentially useful to Calderone whenever I managed to escape.

"Of course. The perks of all that lovely radiation we've been exposed to this side of the Wall." Axel's cheeky grin reappeared.

I blanched. Everyone in Calderone knew the stories of how the radiation changed the Gaill were made up. Tales to scare us into remaining fearful of the Gaill.

But what else could cause that power I felt from them? The shifting colors of their eyes?

"So the radiation causes you to move like that?"

"You're full of questions, aren't you?" Killian raised another brow at me.

I opened my mouth but closed it again. If these Gaill were like in the stories, then not only were they much more powerful than me, but they were also much less merciful.

The image of the dead Calderonian soldier in the throne room swam before me, warning me not to test the extent of their mercy.

"Of course she has questions." Maverick spoke for the first time. "They don't teach Calderonians anything. Especially Calderonian women." He met my gaze, and I could swear pity swam in the amber depths of his eyes. A pang of annoyance hit my gut, but a look of pity was better than those of outright distrust we'd received from some of the other Gaill that day.

"Don't worry, girl." Kacey gave me a friendly smile. "We know how Calderone works." She threw a glare at Killian, and he rolled his eyes. "Knowledge isn't kept for the few this side of the Wall." She smiled again. "And, yes, radiation causes changes like shifting."

With that, the Gaill moved on to discuss their work assignments for the next day as if they hadn't just completely altered my reality and everything I knew.

It was entirely possible they were lying. Women weren't educated in Calderone, but the men were. So if what the Gaill said about the radiation was true, someone—*surely Father*—would know about it. And the Gaill hated the monarchies. They might pity us and our lack of knowledge as women, but that didn't change the fact that our countries were enemies. And hadn't Father always said the Gaill were the ones spreading the propaganda about their supposed powers?

Still, I couldn't deny what I felt from some of them. Confusion and a fresh wave of anxiety rippled through me. I had to get out. Because either the Gaill were lying—and therefore proved themselves our enemies—or they were telling the truth, which meant the stories were at least partially true, and our lives were in even greater danger.

The instinct to flee hit me at light speed. I stood, sending my chair screeching behind me and startling everyone at the table. "I-it looks like they've served dessert." I pointed aimlessly toward the front where people were walking away with various cakes and puddings.

Before anyone could answer, I booked it for the dessert line.

My heart hammered in my ears as the Gaill around me went about their everyday lives, talking animatedly with one another, oblivious to the fact that my entire reality was crashing down around me. I took a deep breath and held it, then repeated the process until I felt myself gaining more control over my emotions.

I had to escape. Not only to uphold my duty as heir but to warn Father and others in Calderone about what was happening with the Gaill. I might not know whether they were telling the truth about the radiation, but I knew the power I felt from them was real. And that they weren't just a group of traitors living some rudimentary life outside the Wall. They were flourishing. Which meant they were an even greater threat to Calderone.

The service door in the storage room was the only access to the outside world I knew of right then. I just needed to plan how I'd get there without anyone noticing.

By the time I got to the counter, the desserts were pretty picked over. But it didn't matter; my appetite had fled once fear had settled back in.

I grabbed a slice of chocolate cake and turned to leave, locking eyes with a tall blond man not ten feet away.

He stood, leaning against a table with his arms crossed over his broad chest and looking down his nose at me with light gray eyes alive with that same flame-like quality. There was a hollowness to them, and another set of warning bells rang in my mind.

"So, it's true. The prince let a Calderonian serve in his palace." He shifted so he was right in front of me, disdain replacing the hollowness in his eyes.

"His Highness showed us great mercy by letting us stay here and serve in the palace." I concentrated on my breathing as I repeated what I'd said to Axel earlier.

The man scoffed before shifting again, this time knocking the plate from my hand so that it shattered on the floor. I barely controlled my gasp as everyone in the vicinity turned to stare. Time seemed to slow as my eyes moved to the broken pieces and the frosting smudged on the stone. He lowered his lips to my ear, causing my cheeks to heat.

"Watch yourself, Jacqueline Lewis." His voice was a cold whisper, and I worked to keep myself from cowering. I didn't dare ask how he had learned my name. "Your kind isn't welcome this side of the Wall. Wouldn't want any more *accidents* happening." He looked down, kicking some of the glass shards across the floor before shifting around me.

I stood frozen for a few moments before chancing a glance behind me. The man was gone, and everyone nearby was staring.

Crouching down, I moved to clean up the glass when someone squatted beside me. A deep brown tattoo-covered hand wrapped itself around my wrist.

"I got it." Killian's low voice rumbled. The brown of his eyes had lightened a few shades. "Go."

I opened my mouth to insist on helping. Fear might have taken up a permanent residence in my bones, but I wasn't about to let others see me as weak. It would only put a larger target on my back.

But something in his gaze had me nodding instead.

Standing, I turned to find Lana already waiting by the entrance. She was shuffling from one foot to the other, her eyes darting among all the people watching me.

I made my way for her, doing my best to appear unaffected though my emotions were likely splayed across my face. We didn't say one word to each other as we made our way back to our rooms except to say good night and set a time to meet in the morning.

Once back in my room, I locked the door and fell on the mattress. Closing my eyes, I loosed the breath I'd been holding since leaving the hall.

As the last of the daylight receded and darkness moved in, the adrenaline coursing through my veins wore off and the magnitude of what was happening to me and what I had to do hit me in full.

I'd survived day one somehow.

And I had done so well keeping it together, but there in the dark, alone, I let the tears fall. Silent but unrelenting, they burned my eyes and trailed down my cheeks, pooling on the sheets around me. A knot formed in my chest making it hard to breathe. Images of the alley, the prison cell, Daxinius on his throne, and the Calderonian soldier bleeding out were replaced by the angry face of Pepridge, the looks of suspicion from the Gaill, and the man in the hall. And eventually, images from Crash took their place.

The blinding smoke. The looks on their faces before it all went black.

I gasped a shuddering breath as I felt my lungs seize. Rolling to the side, I curled into a ball, willing my breathing to steady as I counted to ten in my head.

I was strong. I could handle this. I knew I could. Wouldn't I be expected to handle more as queen? Wouldn't it take extraordinary strength to lead the greatest country in the world? Especially as its first female monarch? I had to survive this. I didn't deserve to be anyone's queen if I failed.

The tears fell a while longer until I rolled over with a sigh and sat up. Reaching behind me, I unzipped my dress and stood, letting it fall to my feet as I stepped out. Bruises had formed on my upper arms and ribs from where the Gaill had grabbed me. I reached back to confirm I still had a bump the size of an egg on the back of my head, which I assumed was from when they knocked me out.

It seemed slightly better tonight, but maybe the past seventy-two hours had just made me delirious. Pulling my hair out of its bun and finger-combing through it, I searched the wardrobe for suitable pajamas. Finding a button-up shirt and shorts, I changed and crawled back into bed.

I didn't even know what time it was or how long I continued to lie there, silently crying, but my eyes grew heavy, and I gradually lost focus as broken rays of moonlight slowly made their way across the ceiling. In my haze, I vainly tried to remember my friends' faces, times we'd had together, and promises we'd made before my world was turned upside down. And as sleep took me, I only hoped I'd make it out to see them and home again.

I was up by 0550 the next morning thanks to the alarm clock preset in my room. I hadn't been able to find the clock before but had no problem now as I walked over to where it was nestled on a shelf and turned it off.

Instead of going back to sleep, I turned back and forth, running over how today could go in my mind. Closing my eyes and steadying my breath, I reminded myself who I was.

Showering and putting on a dress and apron, I went to meet Lana and find Pepridge. Because we didn't eat breakfast until 0830, just as the court was eating theirs, we had a few hours of work ahead of us.

We were assigned to make the loaves of bread for the day. Having never made anything a day in my life, I was hoping Lana knew a thing or two about baking. If she did, maybe I could fake it enough so she wouldn't notice that I, once again, had no idea what I was doing.

"Wanna grab the yeast?" Lana began pulling a jar forward that read FLOUR and another labeled SALT.

"Oh yes, of course." Yeast… yeast. Right, easy enough.

Before panic really set in, Lana grabbed my hand and pointed to a canister sitting on the counter. As I was pulling away, she tightened her grip, causing me to look back.

"Jac, I know who you are," she rushed in a whisper.

For ten seconds, the world stood still.

I opened my mouth to say something, *do* something, though I had no idea what, when she continued. "You're a lady. Of the monarchy."

Clearing my throat, I loosed a breath and let myself relax a bit. She didn't know who I *actually* was.

"How did you know?"

"The first sign? Your hands."

Confusion must've shown in my eyes, because she turned my hands over to show me my palms.

"See, no calluses. And your nails are way too clean, long, and healthy." She turned them back.

Nervous and not wanting to be overheard, I just gave her a subtle nod.

Looking at me, she held my hands and whispered, "I won't tell a soul, my lady. You are one of the kind ones, and how you ended up here I do not know. But I'll do everything I can to help you."

"Thank you, Lana. Your kindness will not be forgotten or go unnoticed. I promise you."

Giving Lana's hands a squeeze, I let go to reach for the yeast and handed it to her. For the next hour, she subtly taught me the art of baking bread.

It was only when we were placing the loaves in the oven that I realized the blond man from the dining hall had been watching us.

Once breakfast rolled around, we found spots at the same table.

The group eyed me warily, but no one addressed what happened the night before. Whether to save me the embarrassment of reliving it or because what had happened was expected given the Gaill's hatred for Calderone, I wasn't sure.

The guys apparently chopped wood most mornings. And they certainly looked like they'd been out working for hours. Axel and Killian's long hair was drawn back into messy buns, and Maverick kept his off his face with a rolled black bandanna. All three had their black work shirts unbuttoned at the top and rolled up at the sleeves, and they busily chugged their coffees like it was their number one task from Pepridge.

Kacey had been assigned to dusting the libraries and looked remarkably chic with her long, sleek ponytail hanging down her back. She and Lana were talking quietly. I preoccupied my time with drowning my pancakes in syrup to avoid any questions I couldn't and didn't want to answer.

I managed to get through the rest of the day with only minor hiccups. Lana and I were assigned to clean a section of guest rooms after breakfast, a task pretty self-explanatory, but I managed to use the dusting solution on the windows in half the rooms, causing a streaky mess that took us twice as long to clean up. We finished right before we had to head back to help prepare more loaves of bread for dinner.

By the time we were walking out of the dining hall later that night, I couldn't help yawning. Even with little going wrong, it felt like I had been awake for ten years and could sleep for another ten.

If this was what every day was going to be like as a palace servant, I'd never stay awake long enough to plan my escape.

"No yawning, ladies." Axel threw his arms around our shoulders. "We're heading to Mav's room tonight."

Lana and I exchanged a wary glance, causing Killian to scoff and clutch his chest, feigning offense. "Don't tell me you're too cool to hang with us?"

Lana laughed, and I felt myself smiling at his theatrics despite my uncertainties.

Though they were our enemies, the group had been strangely kind to us. Distrusting and a little demanding at first? Yes. But at least they didn't treat us with open hostility. I wasn't sure what their true intentions were, but spending more time with them was the only way to find out. And being friendly was my surest way of surviving while gaining more information for Calderone until I figured out a way out of there.

Sighing, I took a risk and matched Killian's sarcasm. "Of *course* we're too cool. But we'll do you this favor and go to Maverick's."

Killian's smile was practically blinding as he started backing toward the staircase that led to the servants' quarters. "Knew you'd fit in, Calderone."

A weird, calming feeling settled in my gut before it was replaced by both guilt and apprehension. Shaking it off, I looked to Maverick. "What's your room number?

"412. They gave me a single-family room on accident, so it's slightly larger than the standard rooms." Maverick shrugged, a blush coloring his cheeks.

Four floors. Just for servants and workers. Calderone had a lot to learn.

Killian narrowed his eyes at Axel and Maverick. "Last loser there has to get supplies for next time." And with that he took off at a blindingly fast run toward the stairs, Axel and Maverick hot on his heels.

Lana and I laughed as we watched the three dodging and tripping one another as each tried to get to the stairs first.

"Idiots." Kacey laughed, shaking her head. "Like Kil said, cavemen."

"You got that right." I laughed with her as we trailed after the guys to Maverick's room.

It was definitely bigger than a normal room, if only by a few feet, with a slightly larger bathroom attached. Still, it felt more spacious.

Kacey dragged out two large, overstuffed pillows from under the bed and sat on one, pulling her reddish-blond hair from its ponytail and running her hands through it. She motioned for us to share the other—they were easily large enough to fit two people.

Killian, making it apparent he was the troublemaker of the group, plopped down on the bed with Axel and withdrew a slim bottle from under his jacket, grinning.

"It's been so long since she's had the good stuff." Axel half moaned as he eyed the bottle and went to the wardrobe, pulling out a stack of cups and a pitcher of water.

Killian started portioning out a knuckle's worth of brown liquor into the glasses and handing them out as Axel poured waters.

Swirling the drink in the glass, the heavy aroma of whiskey—*good* whiskey—hit me. I felt slightly drunk from the smell alone. How did a servant afford liquor like this?

"To the One," Killian stated emphatically as he raised his cup.

"The One," chorused the other three.

Silently toasting to whatever the One was, I took a sip from the glass. The slightly honeyed flavor of the whiskey did nothing to still its fiery warmth as it rolled down my throat. My eyes watered on instinct as the taste momentarily blinded my senses. I never could handle my whiskey.

"Here, Calderone." Killian laughed and handed me a cup of water from where he sat on the bed.

"Thanks." I gave him a small smile as I sipped the water, feeling the effects of the whiskey as it swam through my blood.

"So are we just not gonna address how Tynan harassed Jac in the hall yester— Ow!" Axel rubbed his arm where Killian had punched it.

Kacey rolled her eyes. "These girls are probably having a hard enough time being away from home and adjusting here; no need to make them relive something like that, Ax."

Ax met my eyes and shrugged.

"No, it's okay." Everyone's eyes whipped to mine. "I-I mean, yeah, it's been hard, but he—Tynan—said something that's been bugging me." Taking a breath, I decided to let the whiskey do its work and give me the courage to ask a question that had bothered me since last night. "He seemed to have a really big problem with our being from Calderone and serving in the palace, so… Why are we here if some people hate us enough to wield threats before they even get to know us?"

"What did he say exactly?" Maverick looked over from where he was sitting next to Kacey.

"Just that an accident could befall me and that my *kind* isn't wanted here."

"Well, he's not wrong—What?" Killian returned Kacey's glare. "He's not wrong. There's a reason Calderonians don't normally serve in the palace. Most people here don't have a very good history when it comes to Calderone's cruelty. Many families have suffered because of it."

"Calderone's… cruelty?" I could see why they thought their initial banishment was cruel, but it was due to their own traitorous actions. Anything Calderone had done since then was simply in self-defense. We weren't the ones raiding borders and taking citizens captive. "Calderone is largely an accepting place. Sure, they don't treat women as well as they could, but the citizens are well cared for..."

I trailed off, managing to stop myself before I could say anything else and give away that I knew more about Calderone than most given my education and position. Lana had accepted that I was nobility, but admitting that in a room full of Gaill, no matter how kind they seemed, was pure idiocy.

A knowing look passed between the Gaill, and even Lana didn't meet my eyes. Axel opened his mouth before Kacey shook her head, silencing him. Instead, she turned toward us. "If Dax let you live and work here, other people shouldn't question that." Kacey looked back to the Gaill in the room. "We know firsthand that not everyone is defined by where they came from. There's good and bad in every kingdom."

Awkward silence filled the room. A feeling took hold of me I couldn't quite place because I knew more about Calderone than any of them, right? And what was so bad about it? For all I knew, they were just trying to turn us against the country we called home simply because Calderone banished them three hundred years ago and never let them back in.

I took another sip from the cup of whiskey, but it did little to ease the mounting tension in the room.

"Is Tynan... like you guys? I mean I saw him shift around Jac when he left," Lana asked, reminding me of the other question I had had since last night—the radiation and what exactly it did.

"A Deviant like us? Yeah." Killian said as simply as if he was stating the weather.

Lana's breath hitched next to me, and I stopped breathing altogether as we waited for him to explain what exactly that meant. Because the Deviants we'd been told about should have already been torturing us or sacrificing us to whatever moon god they worshipped.

Certainly not working as servants in the Nor Gaill Court.

"But probably not the Deviants the monarchy warned you about," Maverick raised his brows at us.

"Yeah, I've never been one for killing and eating young babes." Axel laughed, standing to grab the flask before giving himself another knuckle's worth of whiskey. "Or virgins for that matter."

"Nah, too easy a target. I prefer to kidnap them for my homemade radiation experiments." Killian's voice dripped with sarcasm.

"So what you're saying is the Deviants we've been warned are synonymous with the Devil really aren't Deviant at all."

"On the contrary, my dear." Killian leaned forward again, a playful look in his eyes as he answered my question. "We *are* Deviant, just not in a devilish sorta way."

Kacey huffed, her face one of pure annoyance as she pulled herself up to swipe Axel's whiskey from his hand. "What they're saying is we're not psychos. We're like any other Gaill except our ancestors were the first generation outside the Wall and had more exposure to the radiation, so we *deviated*—we adapted to the radiation. We eat, sleep, and drink like you do. We're just stronger, faster, live longer, and are, in the most basic sense, better than our more human Gaill counterparts," she finished with a smile and a wink at us humans.

I closed my eyes against the spinning that was suddenly taking over the room.

They *had* adapted to the radiation. As much as I wanted to believe they were spreading Gaill propaganda, the power I felt from them told me otherwise. Their eyes, the way they moved, the way

Daxinius—*Dax*—made me feel… even from fifty feet away, in that massive throne room, I had felt his power, had felt *him*…

It had to be true. And that meant the Gaill were far stronger than we realized.

"So there are two types of Gaill then—the humans and you guys. Deviants. And if you live longer, how old *are* you?" Lana asked, pulling me from my thoughts.

"I think I'm technically a hundred and something, but I honestly stopped counting years ago."

The stark honesty in Kacey's answer made it apparent how normal this was for them. And how ignorant we were.

"So that's why you have so many loyal servants. The multiple generations," I reasoned.

"Partly. A longer life is certainly a common trait among families outside the Wall. And our powers allow us to heal more quickly so our rates of mortality are low. But the palace also provides security," Maverick replied, his expression darkening slightly. "Beyond the palace's outer ward, your safety and your next meal are never a guarantee."

A shudder ran through me, reminding me that, though these Deviants seemed different, I was still stranded in the middle of Gaill Country.

"We'd always been told the whole radiation-Deviant thing was made up."

I looked at Lana and nodded in agreement. "But radiation *does* actually do something?"

"Well, sort of," Kacey replied before setting Axel's whiskey on the desk and grabbing a fresh glass of water. "Even though there's still radiation out here, it's been three hundred years. It's not like when we were first in exile. There's not enough of it now to seriously cause damage or make you deviate unless you were born outside the Wall and carry the genes of the first generation."

"Kacey's dad was a Gaill nuclear physicist. Well, the *head* nuclear physicist for the Nor Gaill actually, so she knows basically… everything. Right, Kace?" Axel raised his brows at me, but I could see the amusement behind his eyes.

"Exactly. Don't question me," she joked, narrowing her eyes at him to which he gave her a big smile in return. Sighing, she looked between Lana and me. "Don't worry, ladies. You're safe out here."

Safe wasn't exactly the word I'd use to describe my time outside the Wall. But it was good to know that at least the radiation couldn't kill us.

Lifting myself off the pillow to stand against the one free wall next to the door, I undid my bun, running my hands through my waves as I pulled in my bottom lip. "So if you all are… extra powerful or whatever," I added with a wave of my hand, the other one coming to rest on my hip, "why are you all servants and not commanding an army?"

Killian sipped his whiskey and smiled. "Don't worry about it, Calderone."

At that, Kacey yawned and started piling up the empty cups. "All right, where are you two tomorrow?" she asked, changing the subject.

I wanted to pry more—figure out what Killian meant by Calderone's cruelty, the extent of their powers, and why they would be working as servants. And the real reason they took us captive. But the monarch in me also knew not to push my luck. Not when they were being so open and providing new information that could be useful to Calderone. The last thing I needed was for them to become suspicious and start questioning *me*.

"No idea," Lana stood and started stacking the rest of the cups. "I assume Pepridge will tell us tomorrow morning."

"Well, hopefully you two don't get dusting. That shit gets *so* boring."

"If any of you ladies wanna come help us in the woods tomorrow at five, be my guest," Axel interjected, earning himself some side-eye from Kacey.

"We're good, thanks." I laughed, appreciating his sarcasm.

"Well, I hate to kick you all out, but bed is calling." Kacey wiggled her brows suggestively.

Snorting, I walked over to help Lana finish putting the cups away. I couldn't help but smile because, remaining questions aside, I had had a seminormal evening. Even if it was with a group of Deviants.

The feeling faded quickly though as guilt settled like a weight on my shoulders. These Deviants might be friendlier than most, but their history and very existence still told me I should be wary of trusting them. Especially when my friends and family back home were probably beside themselves with worry.

"Come on kids, gotta let mom and dad have their alone time." Slinging his arm around our shoulders, Axel corralled Lana and me out the door.

Killian chuckled behind us, and I'm pretty sure I heard Kacey shout some obscenities as he closed the door.

Laughing as we made our way to the staircase, I turned to Killian. "Are you on the same floor as us?"

"As you two and Ax?" He pointed between us and Axel. "Yeah, boys are in a separate wing. Lest we get any wrong ideas." He winked.

"Do Kacey and Maverick room together?" Lana asked from the other side of Killian.

"No, they wish." Axel chuckled to my left, quickly moving behind to allow us girls to head down the staircase first. "Kacey technically rooms just a few doors down from you two. That's whose room I was coming from when I ran into you last night. I thought everyone was in there, but they'd actually ditched me to head to dinner early."

"If you didn't take two hundred hours to fix your hair before dinner, you wouldn't have missed us," Killian joked, to which Axel promptly punched him in the shoulder.

"Well, thank you for, you know, inviting us tonight. You didn't have to..." I felt awkward as we paused at the entrance to the third floor corridor, suddenly self-conscious as the whiskey and general lack of sleep slowed my mind.

"Don't sweat it, Calderone." Killian put his hand on my shoulder. "Anyone who's saved by Dax is one of us. And being self-proclaimed head of the servants, we kinda had to claim you two as our own."

Setting loose a laugh, I smiled up at him. "So this is really just a power thing for you all?"

"Basically." He laughed and straightened up, folding his tatted arms across his chest. "All right, you two think you can make it back from here?"

"Yes, silly," Lana replied, giggling and letting a small hiccup slip as she playfully slapped his arm, which only elicited a smile from Killian in return. "Come on, Jac."

"Night, boys," I said with a small smile before turning to follow Lana toward our rooms because we were most definitely out past curfew. I had a feeling the rules didn't apply for this group. But given neither Lana nor I were Deviants, and I wasn't willing to risk getting caught by Scarletti or worse, Pepridge.

Wishing Lana a quiet good night, I unlocked my door and let myself in. Falling on the bed, I let sleep take me without even changing out of my dress.

CHAPTER 4

THE MEETING

"I'm to serve whom tonight?" I asked Madam Scarletti at approximately 0700 about a week later, earning myself an immediate eyebrow raise in return. Blame it on the lack of coffee or my eighteen years of royal upbringing, but I still wasn't used to waking up and taking orders before breakfast.

"Is it an issue to serve His Highness, Miss Lewis? Many would consider it the greatest honor."

"Of course not, ma'am." I bowed my head in a show of servitude. "I'm only a bit shocked is all, having been here just over a week." I hoped that would convince her to reassign me. The last thing I needed was to be around Daxinius Da Luca. His level of power made my mind such a jumbled mess that one false move could reveal the truth behind who I was and mean instant death.

"He requested your service. I'm assuming because of your previous work as a lady's maid." She gave me that same assessing look she had the first day, like she could see through my lie. "He is to host our allies the Eur Gaill tonight and would like things to go smoothly."

Biting my bottom lip, I only nodded as she turned away, effectively dismissing me as she promptly laid into a servant who had folded a stack of towels incorrectly.

I grabbed a few dusting cloths and a spray bottle to go meet Lana and Kacey in the galleries where we were set to work while I mulled over the absolute mess I'd gotten myself into. I really couldn't see how I could get out of working for the meeting tonight. Dax knew where I was from and where they'd captured me, so why ask me to attend a meeting where there was no doubt going to be confidential information exchanged between the two Gaill factions? It made no sense. But I had a sinking feeling whatever his reasoning, it wasn't good.

"So that's all she said. Nothing more?" Kacey paused in her dusting of an old placard below an ancient map. I had found them in the World War room, and we were currently making our way through the maps from every battle in the Vietnam War.

"No, nothing." I fiddled with my spray bottle's nozzle. "Except to instruct me that I'd be handing out drinks, biscuits, and cigars upon request."

Kacey set down her bottle and rag. Looking around to ensure no one but the three of us was nearby, she motioned for Lana and me to follow her to a corner of the room.

"Listen, he's done this before, albeit with servants born and raised here, but regardless, nothing comes from it. But there's one thing you should both know." Her hazel-orange eyes lightened a shade as they moved between Lana and me. "We told you last week that radiation causes us to develop certain abilities. But there are differing levels to what we can do depending on how long we've been exposed. There are those who, after centuries of exposure—some of it purposeful—are a *lot* stronger than any others."

"Those like Daxinius?" Lana asked.

Kacey nodded. "Yes. He's one as is the king and most of the leaders he's meeting with tonight."

My breathing labored a bit as that familiar weight settled on my chest again.

"How did he get… overexposed? Is it because he's been alive for centuries?" Part of me asked because I knew that information would be vital to helping Calderone fight powers like Dax had. But another part of me was still desperate to prove to myself that the stories I'd grown up on were simply that—stories.

"That's a story for a different time. But yes, he's older than any of us, which is part of the reason."

The levels of exposure explained the differences in power then. Why some of them seemed to give off a little and why Daxinius's—Dax's—felt so much more palpable. So terrifying.

"So Dax is actually the lethal Gaill prince we grew up hearing stories of? The warrior who mercilessly razes his enemies to the ground, can destroy an entire army in the blink of an eye, the one true threat to Calderone? All that?" I asked.

"He's not as merciless as he once was. But he's been known to slaughter an army or two in the past."

"Holy hell." Lana voiced exactly what we were both thinking.

Swallowing and nodding, I tried to process what I was hearing. Not only were the stories—all of them—apparently true, but tonight I was going to be in possibly the most dangerous situation of my life.

"Any tips? What do I do? What if I mess up?" The whispered questions rushed from me.

Kacey took my hand in hers and gave it a gentle squeeze. Her hand was inhumanly warm, and its warmth was instantly calming. "It'll be okay, Jac. Once the meeting starts, serve everyone a drink, a biscuit, and offer up cigars. They typically only serve brandy at meetings. Scarletti will give you a tray with everything to bring up, and there will be another decanter in the back should you need it. And whatever you do"—the intensity of her gaze nearly paralyzed me—"do not show emotion. Whatever they discuss, whatever plans they make, reveal nothing of how you feel. Because the last thing you want is to be interrogated."

A trickle of sweat made its way down the nape of my neck as I nodded back, understanding her completely. "I just don't get why Dax is playing games like this. Assigning us as the only Calderonians to serve and now having me do this?"

"I'm not sure of his intentions. But what I do know is that Dax doesn't play games. If he wanted something from you, he would just take it. Including your life."

I nodded again, the only thing I was capable of as my heartbeat rushed in my ears.

"Sucks that you won't be there tonight, but I know you'll do okay." Giving me a reassuring smile, Lana took my other hand and squeezed it.

Tonight the Deviants from the lower levels—lower guards and servants—would be getting together to celebrate the full moon. No one could tell us exactly when this tradition started, but everyone could tell us the reason behind it. Their powers were the strongest at the full moon, and they celebrated by getting together, drinking, and usually causing chaos.

The Full Moon Festivals had been more tame in recent years though after Ax and Killian downed a full bottle of scotch and then bet each other on how many walls they could break through using just their bodies. They'd all had a good laugh at my and Lana's reactions after telling the story over dinner one night last week.

King Aidoneus let the festivities go on, saying it was good for morale. Killian said it was likely because they'd do it anyway and the king wanted to look like he was in control.

Either way, both sides had agreed that the celebrations would always take place on a Saturday even if the full moon was during the week since most servants had off on Sundays, and inevitably most of those who attended struggled to perform their duties the next day.

I was sad to miss it not only because it meant a night off any duties but also because it was going to be my chance to scope out the door in the storage room while most of the servants were distracted.

"Yeah, maybe Killian will make the first move tonight." Kacey playfully nudged Lana in the ribs.

"Yeah, right. We're just friends. He doesn't think of me like that. And I barely know him anyway," she gushed, smiling down at her hands, a blush creeping up her cheeks.

Kacey and I exchanged a knowing look. There was definitely something between the two of them if their glances and banter at meals was any indication.

I squeezed Lana's hand back. "Well, I for one am sorry I'm missing it. While I'm passing out brandy and choking on cigar smoke, you all will be partying."

"And potentially breaking through walls." Kacey crossed her arms and raised a brow.

"And that." I smiled, some of my worries temporarily fading at the thought of the group and the insanity that was about to take place tonight. My conclusion from last week had been right—rules didn't seem to stop the lot of them from doing what they wanted.

"Well, hopefully, I'm not back too late. Save a dessert and drink for me?"

"Always!" Kacey patted my arm with a small smile before picking up her cleaner and rag and heading to the opposite side of the room. Lana smiled in agreement before turning back to her work a few frames away.

I began to dust the golden frame for the map of South Vietnam, concentrating on Dong Ap Bia, Saigon, and anything else that could distract from the growing pit of dread in my stomach as I again lamented why I, of all people, had been asked to serve the leaders tonight.

At approximately half past seven that evening, carrying a tray laden with biscuits, drinks, and cigars, I backed through the door that led from the hidden servant's staircase to the main gallery of the prince's apartments. I set the tray down on an empty table and adjusted my dress and apron while surreptitiously looking around.

I breathed a sigh of relief. Scarletti had told me I was to serve the leaders in the drawing room located off the main gallery, but I was nervous a few stragglers would be left behind. Only a few guards kept me company now, and all four looked straight ahead, completely disinterested in what I was doing.

My hair was in a loose side braid, which I had sort of perfected over the past week. Still no makeup to be found, but I was starting to like going without it. I pushed away a few front pieces that'd fallen forward and squared my shoulders. I was determined not to show any fear.

I picked up the tray and headed for the open door at the opposite end of the gallery. I assumed it led to the drawing room, given that the double doors located in the center likely led out of the prince's apartments if this palace was anything like home.

Home.

No. I could *not* think of Calderone right then.

Burying my longing for home deep down, I steeled myself as the guards let me pass. I entered the drawing room to find a group of maybe ten people—men and women—all talking among themselves.

Before I could freak out about what to do next, the room stilled, and I felt that power from the throne room creeping into my mind. I couldn't even see him yet, but I felt him—a vibrating filled my body the nearer he came.

Rooted to the spot, I barely felt him as he breezed past me, grabbing a glass off my tray on his way to the large chair stationed at the front of the room. I thought I smelled a woodsy trace of pine and cold ocean air as he passed, but in a second it was gone, only his power left in its place.

"Sit," he commanded, taking his seat.

Instantly, they all obeyed.

With everyone seated, I began passing out drinks and silently offering cigars and biscuits while Dax addressed the group.

"You all know why you're here." His voice boomed across the room as he got right to the point, not wasting time with small talk. "Michail, are you prepared to provide the agreed-upon forces in exchange for the position of prime minister upon our victory?"

I chanced a glance to see the man I assumed was Michail give a curt nod.

Prime minister? What even was that? And victory over whom?

"Good. Now, Romano, the papers."

I moved to refill another glass as I saw the same general who brought us down to the kitchens move toward the prince with a few rolls of paper. He caught me looking, disgust and annoyance crossing his face before he turned to his prince and commander.

I felt my cheeks heat as I turned and hurried to the back of the room where a fresh decanter of brandy had been set. Waiting to be of service, I quietly absorbed as much as possible.

I was bombarded by information over the next hour—names and places I recognized from home along with others I didn't intertwined with words like *bomb*, *battle*, and *ambush*. Just enough to see them as a legitimate threat but not enough to determine their actual plans.

Two things became certain by the end though: Dax never would have allowed me to be a witness to this meeting if he suspected even in the slightest who I was. And he also wouldn't have let me be a part of it if I had any hope of going home.

The anxious pit in my stomach was growing big enough to swallow me whole. We were the sworn enemies of the Gaill, so surely this didn't bode well for us, which meant I had to get out to alert Father in time. Even if I wasn't exactly sure *what* I was alerting him of.

As the meeting wrapped up and people began leaving, I busied myself with picking up the glasses and napkins littered throughout the room.

I had just picked up an armful of trash when Romano approached. He handed me his empty glass, either not realizing my hands were full or not caring.

"I was surprised to see you serving tonight, Miss Lewis. Even more surprised than I was when His Highness let you keep your life in the throne room."

Power creeped from him, snaking its way around me as the feeling of dread wound its way around my gut. I swallowed audibly and fixed my gaze on the floor. Saying nothing seemed safer than saying anything at all. My only hope was that he'd leave quickly before I dropped what I was carrying.

"Seems you're… struggling."

My eyes flashed up to meet his hard blue gaze before he glanced down at the mess of cups and napkins I was holding. With that he shifted past me, nearly knocking the load from my hands.

I closed my eyes and inhaled deeply. When I opened them, Dax, the man he called Michail, as well as two other people I didn't recognize were the only ones left. They appeared to be having a tense discussion in the opposite corner. I couldn't make out what they were saying, and try as I might, they were too sequestered for me to get close enough without making it obvious that I was eavesdropping.

Moving my focus back to cleaning, I began to remove a spot of cigar ash from a very old section of upholstery, praying it would lift easily so I could leave as soon as possible.

But after two rounds with a wet rag, I sat back, pretty positive I hadn't made any progress. In fact, I was sure I'd made it worse. Setting the rag down, I got up, intent on finding actual cleaner when his voice sounded behind me.

"I assume that was General Watanabe's doing?"

Starting, I turned around to find Dax's assessing eyes on me. I hadn't realized the others had left the room. His bright green gaze was focused solely on me, its power filling the space around me like an electrical current, making my hair stand on end.

"I-I'm not sure, sir. I don't know who was sitting here."

"Sir?" He raised a brow before making his way over to a bottle of whiskey stationed next to the brandy. Turning his back to me, he poured a glass.

"Forgive me. *Your Highness.* I'm still acquainting myself to life here." I silently cursed myself for my slip-up and hoped he wasn't as cruel as the stories let on. I was sure he'd punished others for much less.

Turning back around and leaning against the table, he folded his arms over his broad chest and swirled the whiskey in his glass as he observed me with that same assessing look. But this time, it had a hint of something else… amusement?

"I hate the title anyway. Never did understand why Father insisted on our using it." He chuckled darkly to himself. But just as soon, the amusement was gone, replaced by the same mask of indifference I saw in the throne room.

I smoothed my apron before folding my hands in front of me. I wasn't sure what to do next, but I did know it wasn't my place to talk. Being a princess for eighteen years had taught me that at least.

"Tell me, Miss Lewis. Why are you here?"

I swear the lights flickered as he spoke, like a power surge, and I barely stopped myself from gasping.

He knew nothing, right? *Could* know nothing. But that didn't stop my heart from practically pounding out of my chest. It was so loud, I was sure he could hear it. Hell, I was sure the guards a floor down could hear it.

I willed my face to stay blank. No one knew what I looked like outside our palace. And like Kacey said, if he knew something, he would've done something already. Why give me access to all that information in the meeting otherwise?

I decided playing dumb would be the best route—make him see he was wasting his time with me.

"Madam Scarletti instructed me to serve you and the other Gaill leaders tonight, Your Highness."

Immediately seeing through my facade, Dax didn't address my statement but instead strode directly for me. I stepped back involuntarily, my legs hitting the chair as his power invaded my senses. He stopped a few feet away, crossing his arms over his chest again as he leaned back slightly, chin raised.

Now that he was closer, I got a better look at him. Towering above me, even from a few feet away, he was easily the tallest and still most devastatingly beautiful man I'd ever seen. His eyes were a jade green tonight, the color made richer by the deep tan of his skin. And his dark brown hair was loose and wavy—like he'd run his hands through it too many times. Up close, I could see it was streaked with amber throughout.

The sleeves of his simple black tunic—similar to the one he'd worn that first day—were rolled up to reveal the tattoos snaked over his muscular arms as they rested across his chest. Studying them, I recognized Celtic and Gaillic symbols, though I didn't know any of their meanings. And looking closer, I could see that the ink that curled up his neck was actually a series of broken chains woven around his throat. An involuntary shudder ran through me as I dragged my eyes up to meet his again.

Looking down at me, his eyes cold, he repeated his question. "Why are you here, Miss Lewis?"

I went for the same half-truth I'd told Lana.

"I was out with friends at a club close to the Wall. I was captured for no reason and brought here. I don't know why I'm here. And I'd like to go home," I added, looking down at my hands, instantly mad at myself for the nauseatingly high levels of fear I was feeling.

"Afraid we can't let that happen. Your life here is likely better than anything you had inside that prison anyway." He smirked as he turned and walked toward the nearest chair. "You're welcome," he added over his shoulder, sipping his whiskey before sitting down, lounging back and resting the glass on his knee.

"How do you figure?" I let slip, sudden annoyance taking over and making me forget my fear entirely. His arrogance and smug attitude were infuriating. *My* home a prison? Wasn't I the one not allowed to leave *his* palace?

Shock rang clear across his face before that smile slid back into place, but now it was laced with something else that looked dangerously close to anger.

"Here at least you're better cared for, actually have a bed at the end of the day, and meals you can count on."

Screwing up my face, I was suddenly confused. What was he talking about?

"Things aren't like that back home," I said with confidence, giving him a condescending smile of my own. Prince or not, two could play this game. "Everyone is positively welcoming."

"I'm sure. That's why we have refugees flooding the outer ward every month." He shook his head. "It's always the same story with you people from the interior. You're so close to the royals that you're brainwashed to the point of oblivion. Your life there wasn't normal, and it doesn't have to be like that."

Brainwashed? Interior?

What?

"I literally don't know what you're talking about. I was treated with the utmost respect," I said, losing my patience. "I lived on the land of the family I served in a similar way to what I do now."

And it was the truth. That is how we treated our servants at the palace.

Holding his glass to his lips and watching me, probably contemplating whether I'd told him the truth or was brainwashed, he took a sip and simply nodded, which was somehow even more aggravating.

"What do you mean, refugees?" I asked, not being able to help myself. Jacqueline the servant knew not to ask, but Jacqueline the princess didn't really care about the consequences. I had to know what he was talking about.

Dax sighed and leaned forward in his chair to rest his elbows on his knees, appearing to mull over whether he wanted to impart this piece of information.

"There are areas of your country, Calderone, and those like it that are not as nice. Other people who work in a similar industry or industries considered even less favorably are snubbed simply for the class they were unfortunate enough to have been born into." He took a long drink from his whiskey before continuing. "At best, they work in households for minor nobles or wealthy officials as servants and live in roach-infested housing. At worst, they're relegated to the government's labor camps, forced to work for free to atone for ridiculous crimes they didn't commit or a family debt they cannot possibly pay back."

My mind riffled through past memories, conversations, and policies I knew, but I couldn't remember ever being told of labor camps or conditions where people in my country lived like that. Biting my lip, I looked back at him, meeting his gaze and doing my best to hide what I'm sure was a mixture of shock and disbelief.

I obviously didn't hide it well enough, because Dax clarified, "You likely call the labor camps suburbs. That's usually what we hear them called."

No. That couldn't be.

I had toured a suburb near our palace a few times with Father, and it always was a pleasant, inviting place. People from our lower castes and those who had a debt or minor crime to answer for were able to live a comfortable life with access to food and healthcare. They even had their own stores, schools, and parks. I'd only been to one but had no reason to believe the other five in Calderone were any different.

No, he couldn't be right. Father never would have allowed it. I wish I could tell him more, prove what I had seen with my own eyes, but I couldn't do so without revealing who I was.

"Our king is true and just. He wouldn't do that to his people." I threw a smug smile back at him that I hoped looked more convincing than I felt.

Dax scoffed in return, shaking his head. "Your king is a tyrant, and his family, whatever heir they're now breeding, and his court are no better. Have you ever wondered why those who stage protests or speak out against the monarchies suddenly disappear, their movements gone in a flash? Where they go?"

I chewed my cheek to remain silent as my anger just about boiled over. Father was strict—ruled with a firm hand, yes—but he was no tyrant.

And neither am I.

It was true though I hated to admit it. We always had little dissenting opinion in the country, and what we did have was quickly resolved. I guess I'd never asked how, I just knew it was.

However, I also knew our people loved us. That was evident by the broadcasts of my parents' public appearances. I had watched the people's reactions on the TV for years.

But could it be possible that dissenters were forced to live in camps as punishment for using their voice? Was that the reason for the quick resolution to any problem? For Father always telling me not to worry?

"How much you bet we can get for this getup at one of the camps?"

The words of the woman in the cell echoed through my mind and sent me reeling. The *camps.*

I instinctively moved a hand to my chest as panic set in.

It could all be true.

Looking up, my eyes found Dax's, a grim smirk playing at his lips.

Damn him.

I did my best to regain my composure. Father and his advisors might not include me in everything, but they'd never be capable of what he was accusing them of. Dax on the other hand was known for his violent and manipulative nature. He reveled in it. And the fact that I let him get in my head for a second was just further proof that he was a very real threat.

I had to get out.

Clearing my throat, I decided to bypass his question and the discussion of Calderone entirely. "Is there anything else I can help with, Your Highness?" I willed myself not to fidget. He could not see me falter. I would not let him have that power over me.

Before I could breathe, Dax was standing in front of me. Too close for comfort. Pine and cold sea air invaded my senses as the power rippling from him froze me in place. My heart rate picked up, but my gut told me it was something other than dread that was making it pound. Unease rushed through me as I buried the feeling.

He looked at me with a sort of searching look in his eyes—they were a shade or two brighter now—but then he blinked and the mask was back in place. "That'll be all. Thank you, Miss Lewis."

Without another word, he turned and walked at a normal pace back to the large chair at the front of the room. I licked my lips, wiping my clammy palms on my dress as I picked up the rag and now-empty tray from the back of the room and made my way for the door.

I didn't dare look back, but I felt his eyes on me the entire time.

CHAPTER 5

ECLIPSE

"Look alive, Calderone."

I barely had time to lift my head from the table in the dining hall before Killian shoved a black coffee under my nose. Cream and sugar, two more things to put on the long list of what I missed about home.

It had been two days since my run-in with Dax. I'd been avoiding the group, partially because I wasn't sure how to handle the onslaught of information I'd been privy to at the meeting but also because I'd been using meal times to sneak back to the store room and look for the door that led outside.

I'd found it yesterday while most everyone was at dinner. It was locked, but a group of servants had approached before I was able to get a better look at it. I'd need to find another time to scope it out though because I was running on fumes at the moment.

"Thanks, Killian." Offering a sleepy smile in return for the coffee, I drank deeply, not caring that it burned on the way down. Lana walked up behind him, setting a tray full of food on the table in front of me—she'd taken the liberty of sneaking double portions. Guess I really did look as bad as I felt.

"Kace and Lana filled us in on serving Dax and the other leaders Saturday night. How'd it go? Any juicy gossip?" Killian wiggled his eyebrows, making me giggle.

"No." I sighed, not wanting to bring up the discussion Dax and I had for fear someone would pry too much. I'd already been up most of the past two nights as Dax's accusations against Father and the monarchy replayed in my mind, making me doubt everything I'd ever believed and in the next second hate myself for doubting. It didn't help that any spare time I had had been spent figuring out the logistics of how I'd get home. Even if I managed to get the door unlocked, I'd need food and water to survive beyond the outer ward, and I'd never make it without first finding a map of the area.

"Dax was as friendly and welcoming as he was the first time I met him—as was General Romano." I met Killian's eyes again as I recalled the general's look of disdain when he spotted me.

At the mention of the general, the Deviants exchanged looks.

"What?" I asked, after not one of them offered up any explanation.

"Dax is powerful and at times tough on his men, but Romano is cruel in a way Dax is not." Maverick looked at Lana and me both before continuing. "I know they both seem cut from the same cloth, but they're different. Dax has a heart, he's just good at hiding it. I can't say the same for Romano."

Lana started to nod, but I was in no mood to simply be told to do things. Blame it on the lack of cream and my increasing emotional instability. "What's so different about Romano?"

"Romano is King Aidoneus's most trusted general and oldest friend," Maverick began. "The two grew up together—"

"And that basically means Romano thinks like Aidoneus and can do whatever he wants," Kacey finished for him. "He's been known to get handsy with some of the maids from time to time. We defend who we can, but we can't be everywhere at once. It's better just to avoid him."

"Noted—avoid Romano 'cause he's a creep." Lana shuddered.

"Never would've guessed. It seemed like our mere presence disgusted him." I thought back on the two encounters I'd had with him. But the Deviants' tone and behavior completely changed when discussing him, so I trusted there was more than met the eye.

"Yeah, he's an interesting guy, that one. A little crazy, but guess you'd have to be to do what he does." Axel cut into his pancakes before taking a big bite. Washing it all down with a large gulp of coffee, he conspicuously changed the subject. "Anyway, was hoping you'd have found out if the rumor about the festival in a fortnight is true."

"What festival?" I asked, willing to let Romano go for now.

"Saturday night while the Devs were all together, there was some talk of a huge festival happening two weeks from now before the Eur leave. Apparently a celebration of some new alliance between them and the Nor Gaill." Kacey took a sip of her orange juice before dunking a sausage link in syrup.

The alliance—Michail's agreeing to be a prime whatever it was and to helping the Nor Gaill defeat whomever it was. *That must be what they're celebrating.* Two weeks. The Eur would be here for another two weeks, which meant two more weeks of increased security and people around the palace. How would I get out with this many people around?

"I hope they allow for a fight ring like they did last time." Killian interrupted my thoughts.

"They didn't *allow* that, Killian." Annoyance seeped into Kacey's tone. "You just did it on your own."

The boys laughed in response and began telling Lana and me

about Killian's antics the last time they held a festival. Apparently, he really couldn't say no to a bet.

As we left the dining hall to make our way to the guest rooms for the day, I'd almost forgotten about the two-week hold set on my escape.

By four that afternoon, my hands were sufficiently pruned and my entire body smelled like clean linen. But it had been a productive day and one day closer to the Eur leaders leaving. We still hadn't gotten word about the supposed festival, but most of the palace's rooms were occupied, so clearly our guests hadn't left yet.

Lana and I slowly made our way down to dinner as she told me about her conversation with Killian over the weekend. They'd discussed their favorite types of music. Not much was the same, but they did agree that they both loved any music they could dance to. I smiled, thinking about her having a somewhat normal conversation with a totally abnormal boy.

There was a massive group assembled outside the dining hall when we arrived with Scarletti and Pepridge at the front. They were saying something, but since we were so far back, I couldn't hear it.

Weaving closer, I caught Pepridge saying, "…and for two more weeks we are to show them the utmost hospitality and respect. Please continue to treat the Eur leaders as if they were our own royal family." He smiled down at us as if we were dumb enough *not* to treat them like that.

"And as most of you have already heard," he continued with a pointed glance to the front left where I noticed the rest of our group stood, "we will be hosting a festival on the final evening of their stay.

This will be a grand affair like we've had in years past for their leaders. It will take the full two weeks to prepare, so we'll begin tomorrow. Please rest up tonight. You're dismissed."

He stood to the side as the doors to the dining hall opened, and everyone began filing in. Looking around to where the group of Devs had been standing, I locked eyes with Tynan. A sinister grin appeared on his face before someone stepped in front of him, blocking him from view. Facing forward, I did my best to ignore the creeping feeling working its way up my spine.

Dinner was a whirl of activity. So much so, I soon forgot the look on Tynan's face and my visceral reaction to it.

Apparently festivals here were as extravagant as back home, where no expense was spared. Elephants, fireworks, full-scale amusement rides, casinos—anything was possible. We spent most of the meal talking hypotheticals over what might be there, and I found myself actually looking forward to the distraction the next two weeks would bring.

The next day, Kacey, Lana and I were assigned the task of dusting the libraries. They'd be used for the cocktail hour of the main dinner since their large glass doors opened out onto the terrace overlooking the gardens, providing the perfect view during twilight. Dusting would probably take the entire two weeks since the rooms covered most of the west side of the palace. But it wasn't all bad. If there were any place to find a map of the surrounding area, it would be there.

The first thing I noticed when we entered was the view of the gardens. I hadn't seen them until this morning, and I had to admit they put ours to shame. Somehow the plants here had flourished in the centuries since the War. Kacey said it was because for centuries no one touched anything, allowing nature to take its course and reclaim what was rightfully hers.

Thick green vines covered the palace walls along the garden, with large leaves sprouting in all directions, making the palace look more green than white on this side. White rose bushes with flowers the size of my head were in bloom at the start of the garden and lavender towered behind them. From where I stood inside the doors, I could smell the lavender on the summer breeze—it filled the entire library.

There was a large lake in the middle of the garden about a quarter mile away from the palace, and you could just make out a large fountain in the middle of it. A grove of old oak trees sat to the side, and tall rolling hills covered in more trees surrounded the palace on all sides as far as the eye could see. They were so tall they looked like mountains.

Not able to help ourselves, we had snuck out briefly to explore the gardens before getting to work. And because we were subsequently running behind, I was busy wrapping up dusting in one of the Renaissance rooms while Lana and Kacey had moved on to the next section.

Theoretically, I should've been working faster since we were behind or sourcing out the section that held the maps, but I found myself browsing the titles of the medieval books as I dusted them. We had libraries, but none were this large or this extensive. The collection of plays alone was the largest I'd ever seen.

I pulled an ancient copy of *Macbeth* from the shelves, and dust began billowing up as I paged through it. Slightly enraptured by the musty old-book smell, I paused, running my fingers over the words on the page, drawn into the plot to kill the king.

I was so lost in one scene, I didn't realize I was no longer alone until I heard someone clear their throat behind me.

Clutching my chest and whipping around, nearly dropping the book in the process, I locked eyes with Dax. He was leaning against a chaise a few feet away, wearing another black V-neck tunic, arms once again across his chest, his dark brown curls a wavy mess with nothing but that arrogant smirk on his face.

"My apologies, Miss Lewis. I didn't mean to interrupt you."

I could feel my cheeks heating as that familiar sense of power crept around me.

That was twice that I'd let him startle me. And this time, I was somewhere I shouldn't have been, doing something that I definitely shouldn't have been doing.

Quickly replacing the book I grabbed my rag and spray bottle and, with a quick curtsy, made to leave.

"What were you reading? It was clearly engrossing." Dax stopped me though he hadn't moved an inch.

"Oh, um… *Macbeth*." I turned to him, keeping my gaze on my hands and hoping he'd just dismiss me. After he didn't answer for some time, I looked up to find him staring at me, searching my face again—assessing, questioning, but not actually asking. He remained silent.

Exacerbated and losing patience, I rolled my eyes. Consequences be damned, I was tired of these games.

Either treat me like a normal servant and ignore me or ask me the questions you want to ask.

"You know, Shakespeare?" I raised a brow and did little to hide the irritation in my voice.

He chuckled. "I'm familiar. Do you often read the works of great playwrights in your free time? If so, maybe some in Calderone do treat their servants differently."

My breath hitched as I opened my mouth in a wordless reply. How did I explain my education without incriminating myself? Even my servants didn't have access to these type of texts unless they were with me.

Stick as closely to the truth as possible, I reminded myself.

"No, Your Highness," I said, recovering. "However, my lady is very generous and allows us free access to any of her reading materials." I looked him in the eye, hoping the lie would stick because it was mostly true—insofar as I did let Mir and Rachel have access to the few books *I* had access to.

"Your lady does indeed sound very generous. One of the few kind Calderonians I've heard of, if your story is true."

"There are many kind Calderonians, Your Highness." Annoyance streaked through me at what he was implying. "I know what you said about those in power, but the people, the citizens, are kind. And the royal family is also kind," I continued, because I obviously had a death wish. "I can assure you the heir has a good heart and would not knowingly support any labor camps if they do exist."

I sucked in my lips, willing myself to *shut up*. But then I remembered the plans he'd discussed with the Eur leaders. He was a murderer. A barbarian. And for the past few centuries, people had let him get away with it. I vowed then and there that my reign would be the one to stop him. The thought of the potential danger he could put my people in made me boil to such a degree that I suddenly didn't care about the consequences of defying him.

I opened my mouth to say more.

He watched me intently, one brow slowly rising in a challenge. Power surged toward me, reminding me that this wasn't just any enemy. I was greatly outmatched.

I slammed my lips shut as anger coursed through me. If he killed me, I wouldn't make it back to Calderone to warn them of a potential attack in time.

No, as much as I hated holding my tongue with a brute like Daxinius Da Luca, I had to. All I could do was toe the line of diplomacy—because I couldn't just do nothing. I had to say *something* in the hopes that it would change his view of Calderone and ward off any potential attack they could be planning.

His power receded as he lifted his hand to run his knuckle along his jaw. His brows furrowed. "How can you be so sure the royal family and heir is kind?"

"Word travels, Your Highness. Good deeds do not go unnoticed among us."

That answer seemed sufficient for the time being. He straightened and walked over to me, leaning past. My heart rate skyrocketed as the same woodsy mix of pine and the sea slammed into me, eradicating the lavender that had been there seconds before. I felt intoxicated from his scent, which wasn't helped by the electric power pulsating from him as his body shifted around mine.

Wait.

W*hat?*

Snap out of it, Jacqueline.

Before I could blink, he'd retrieved what he was looking for and handed me the book I'd just put back.

"For you. Undoubtedly, no one has touched it in centuries and won't notice if it goes missing. Maybe it'll help."

"Thanks… I think." I looked at him in confusion, not entirely sure what his cryptic answer meant but accepting the book nonetheless.

He nodded in return, dismissing me as he folded his hands behind his back, lifting his chin slightly, a tic in his jaw. I lowered my eyes, pocketed the small book in my apron, and made my way out of the library with my dusting rag and solution. Despite my better judgment, I looked back to find him deep in thought, staring at the row of books I'd just been perusing. I left before he could catch me looking.

The next week was a blur of stress and activity as we worked day and night to prepare for the festival in honor of the Eur alliance. So it was somewhat surprising when Kacey showed up to drag Lana and me to Mav's room about five days out from the festival for a night to "let off some steam" as she phrased it.

I quickly threw my hair up, removed my pearls, and changed into a weekend dress, which ended up being the V-neck version of our day dresses. Meeting Lana and Kacey in the hallway, we made our way upstairs. The two had also changed, and if I hadn't known any better, I'd say Lana was wearing some sort of lip gloss. No doubt Killian would notice.

We hadn't had time to meet up in the past week with everything going on. Everyone had been eating meals at odd times since our duties all required working different shifts, but tonight we had a few hours off, and I was excited to see everyone. I missed them. And it felt like the Deviants actually missed us too.

We could hear the boys shouting and laughing before we even made it to Mav's room. Smiling to myself, I realized how much I needed this. A group of friends who were just as happy to skirt their superiors as I was. It reminded me of home.

And then instantly, the guilt hit.

I shouldn't be enjoying my time here when I knew they were probably tearing themselves up with worry back home. I also shouldn't be getting close to any of these people. They were my enemies, even if they didn't act like it.

Even if it was starting to seem impossible to view them as my enemies.

I didn't have more than a few seconds to refocus. As soon as we entered the room, Kil shoved a flask of whiskey into my hands.

"Drink up, Calderone. We only have a few hours before we men have to be in the woods. You know we're in charge of supplying the firewood for all the bonfires this year? They're gonna be huge," he said with an arrogant grin.

"You? Men?" I pointed to the three Deviants in the room. "I only see boys here." I raised a brow, taking a pull from the bottle, resisting the urge to gag on the taste as the dark liquor burned my throat.

Killian gripped his heart like I'd mortally wounded him and fell back onto one of the pillows they'd already brought out. Giggling, Lana grabbed the flask out of my hands and promptly sat on the pillow next to his, her blond curls bouncing. "Yes, boys is right. Men wouldn't be hiding in their rooms drinking at the age of what, 103, 104?"

"Ouch, Lana, harsh." Mav pulled another flask from his jacket pocket and took a swig. "But if that makes us boys, so be it."

Laughing, the rest of us piled into the usual spots—a few on the bed, Axel leaning against the desk, me curled up next to Lana—and talked about the insanity of the past nine days.

"So do these festivals happen often?" I made my way to the desk to pour myself a cup of water.

"Ahh no. Every few years so we have time to recover. They're a helluva lotta work. But worth it for the night of revelry that ensues." Axel motioned for me to pour him a cup as well.

"Must be some alliance we're celebrating to go through all this effort," I said, as nonchalantly as possible, hoping the alcohol made someone's tongue loose enough to take the bait.

"You could say that," he said, raising his brows. "With the Eur at their side, Dax and his forces will be virtually unstoppable. There are a few more things to get in order, but once they are… it won't be good for Calderone." He gave Lana and me a grim look.

"When will that be?" Despite attempting to sound uninterested, my anxiety showed through.

"Hard to say. A war like that takes time to prepare for," Kacey answered gently. "And by Dax, Ax surely means King Aidoneus." Kacey threw a pointed glare in Axel's direction.

Clearing his throat, Axel only waved his hand. "Of course."

War.

So the Eur and Nor Gaill are planning a war against Calderone.

The realization settled in me like a two-ton weight. If I didn't escape soon, the consequences could be dire.

"So do we get to enjoy the festival at all, or do we usually work the whole thing?" Lana asked, lightening the mood as she handed me the almost-empty flask Killian originally had. I promptly finished it, wiping my mouth with the back of my hand before setting it down on the desk.

It dulled the dread only a little.

"We usually get to join, which means you two will too," Kacey replied with a wink.

"Wow, befriending the Devs has its perks," I said—like learning classified information that could be useful to my kingdom.

"Sure does, ladies." Killian jokingly stretched his arm out over Lana. "Can't tell me you're not impressed."

"Positively salivating, Kil." Lana smiled up at him.

From the way she looked at him, I wasn't sure she was entirely joking.

"All right, that's quite enough of that," Axel said.

Killian got up and playfully punched his shoulder but started putting the pillows away anyway. "S'pose you're right. It's nearing midnight, and alarms are set for 0330 tomorrow."

"Don't sound so glum. You're a man, remember? You got this." Kacey lightly shoved Killian on her way to give Maverick a kiss good night.

Killian laughed as he flipped her off while the rest of us started gathering our stuff to leave.

We all filed out and made our way back to our rooms, no one too keen on dallying considering the early wake-up call for half the group. Once inside in my room, I locked the door and collapsed onto my bed. Sleep once again seemed elusive as I sorted through thoughts and memories from the past few weeks.

And then a thought hit me, having me upright in an instant.

The Eur leaders visiting. The festival. This was my chance. This was it.

With the servants and guards all busy and the court preoccupied the night of, the lower levels, including the storerooms, would be virtually empty later in the evening. This could be my opportunity to access the door and get out. Cloaked by darkness, no one would see me if I wore the right clothing.

Turning over, I hugged my other pillow and smiled, truly excited for what felt like the first time in weeks. I was going home, and though I still needed to sort through all the details, it had to work. The timing was too perfect for it not to.

I woke up the following Friday morning having barely slept the night before—I could feel the excitement in the air.

At breakfast, the dining hall was buzzing with details about the festival that night, but I was busy running over the particulars of my escape in my mind.

I had spent the past few days using every spare minute alone to plan. I would be long gone before anyone knew to look for me. And though I felt slightly guilty that I'd have to leave Lana behind, I had to. It would be hard enough to get one of us out.

There was also the problem of not knowing what I'd encounter when I did get out. I couldn't endanger her like that. But I vowed to myself that I'd come back to get her. In the meantime, Killian and the others would protect her if she ever needed it.

Like they would me, if I needed it, right?

Try as I might, I couldn't ignore the voice in the back of mind telling me to trust the Devs. Part of me knew I could. But I had a greater duty to my family and my people—and I would fail them if I stayed here and let the Gaill destroy Calderone.

So my plan would begin as soon as the sun started to set around seven. At that time, the cocktail hour would start at which point my job duties would end, but Lana and Kacey's wouldn't for another three hours as they served into dinner. The boys were also booked into the evening. This time, I'd been overlooked and hadn't been scheduled for anything at night, a stroke of good luck. And I needed all the lucky breaks I could get.

A bag I'd taken from the extras lying in a storeroom was packed with enough food and water for five days. I'd also packed a map I found the day we dusted the geography section in the library. Though

I wasn't sure how outdated it was, I had planned out my route. The bag with everything lay hidden beneath my bed, and I'd use the extra time to grab it, my plan being to disguise it as dirty linens, and then make my way to the storerooms. I'd have to pass through several highly trafficked areas as people prepared for the dinner and the cocktail hour, hence the need for the disguise. I'd excuse it as a last-minute load of laundry to run down. Although odd, everyone would be too busy to question it.

I'd have to make my way unseen through the storerooms to the door that led outside. And once I slipped through, I'd have to find the exit. Considering I hadn't actually been through the door, I couldn't be sure if it led directly to the outside. My plan had been to pick the lock ahead of time and assess the layout, but there were always too many people around. I only hoped it was a clear shot to the outside and I'd be well on my way by the time they discovered I was missing.

A pang of guilt hit me again as I thought about what the Devs and Lana would think when they discovered me gone. And worse, discovered who I was without my explaining that I wasn't what they'd assumed. Because according to their prince, their assumptions weren't pretty.

But it didn't matter; I had to do this. I was safe at home, and staying here, knowing what I did know, wasn't an option.

Wrapped up in my thoughts, I hadn't noticed everyone breaking up to go about their final duties for the afternoon. Lana and Kacey were moving toward the back staircase that exited next to the throne room. We three were supposed to make our way to the libraries again to finish dusting. We'd been dusting almost every day since that first day. When Dax gave me *Macbeth*.

I gathered my tray, throwing out the trash and depositing it on the belt before joining them and making our way to the libraries for the last time.

Moving into the world history section, we branched out, each taking a side of the room to try to cover as much ground as possible. It was already noon, so we only had a few hours left before the servants were supposed to be downstairs for the final check-in before everything started.

I began dusting the books, going over my plan in my head for the hundredth time, when a title caught my eye. *The Eclipse: Now, Then, Forever.*

Looking over my shoulder, I was shocked to find myself still alone—Lana and Kacey continued to clean on the opposite side of the large room. Surely someone would be watching.

Nervously biting my lip, I turned back to check again and verified it was indeed *The Eclipse*—the most heretical text as declared by monarchies the world over. Although I'd been able to read some banned texts growing up, a copy of *The Eclipse* didn't even exist in Calderone.

Fumbling, my hand shook as I set down my duster and spray and reached out to grab the book. It wasn't big. In fact, it was rather thin and small for what it supposedly contained. I traced my fingers down the black-and-green spine. I was barely breathing as they grazed the author's name—Giovacchin Da Luca—ally to Calderone turned traitor and leader of the Gaill. To even speak his name or of his book was akin to treason back home.

I flipped it over, the now widely known symbol of the Nor Gaill, a circle with only a crescent of light—*fighting an eclipse*—the only thing on the front. I held my breath as I opened to the first page.

Dear Fighter,

The Eclipse is coming. The bombs that shook our Earth, shattered our lives, and set fire to our countries paved a way for a new life. But it is a new life unlike those the people in power have told you about. Their new life is an old life remade. One with shackles and chains meant to bring people back into a world we have been free from for decades. Their way of life is an everlasting Eclipse. Do not let it last forever. Rise up. Do what is right and fight for freedom, fight for democracy and our rights as humans. In order to be truly free, we must fight and rebel against those who wish to squander us and our vision for a just and equal future for all...

Knitting my brows together, I thumbed through the pages, looking at maps of early monarchies with locations I could recite in my sleep laid out, here from a Gaill perspective. I came across a map of Calderone in its early years, the palace and grounds marked out as were the factories, mills, farmland, and wharfs.

Six *x*'s dotted the map. Looking closer, I realized they were in the same location as the suburbs were now. Going to Da Luca's key, I felt bile rise in my throat as I read the word *camps* next to each letter *x*.

The camps. How?

Putting the back of my hand to my mouth, I closed my eyes briefly and fought a sudden onset of nausea, my mind racing as I desperately searched for a meaning. This book was hundreds of years old. Almost three hundred. It had been written soon after the Nuclear War. Either the camps had been around from the start, or this information was outdated.

And Da Luca could be lying. It was possible this was truly just Gaill propaganda written to spur others to their side.

Taking a deep breath, I looked around again and then quickly tucked the book into my apron without another thought. Swallowing my nerves, I knew what an idiot I was for stealing a book like that, but I cared more about what else was in it than I did about consequences in that moment.

I continued dusting as my vision blurred. Blinking back the tears, I willed them not to fall.

Angry tears. Shameful tears.

I wanted so much to believe the suburbs were just that—housing for those in need. But my gut told me something more was going on.

Even I wasn't allowed to read *The Eclipse*. Was it because of the damning information in there about what the monarchy had been doing to its own people for centuries? I mean, what other reason?

I knew my father and his advisors kept things from me, told me not to worry, and excluded me from meetings. I couldn't fully trust them because of that. But I didn't think they would be capable of doing something of this magnitude or keeping it from me.

Because even if the camps no longer existed, I was about to ascend the throne—didn't I need to know the truth about our history, the good and the bad, in order to be a just ruler?

And if they kept something like this from me, what else were they keeping secret?

This can't actually be happening.

I willed myself to stay calm while we continued dusting, locking away my feelings of isolation, anger, and shame deep in my chest as I'd done countless times over the past eighteen years. It was the only way I knew to survive.

CHAPTER 6

THE CORRIDOR

At around six o'clock, I was finally released and able to go back to my room. Unlocking the door, I made quick work of pinning the top layers of my hair back and then changed into a clean black weekend dress and packed Da Luca's book along with my old shirt and black jeans for when I got closer to Calderone.

Checking my appearance, I looked as I should, composed and neutral, nothing amiss. Inside I felt a war raging over Dax's accusations, what I'd seen and thought to be true, and my discoveries in *The Eclipse*.

I didn't know for sure what was happening in Calderone, but I needed to find out. In the meantime, I couldn't let Gaill forces destroy my people. I would get out—I *had* to—to save them.

Taking one last look around the room, I grabbed the black pearl necklace from my desk, almost forgetting it, and slipped it on. I was about to move into the hall when I hesitated and removed the book from my bag. Ripping the section about Calderone out, I tucked it as neatly as I could into my bra and put the rest of the book under the mattress. I was sure the whole book contained more valuable information, but the last thing I needed was to be intercepted by someone like Tynan or Pepridge and have my bag searched and a stolen, highly controversial book found.

The upper halls were virtually empty, another stroke of luck, everyone else having already moved on to their next tasks or the festivities. I saw a few groups as I moved through the lower floors, but no one stopped me—just a few smiles and nods my way as I passed by.

As I walked through the kitchens, I kept watch in my periphery but didn't spot any of the Devs. They shouldn't be here, but you could never be sure what any of them were actually doing at any given time. Killian in particular was the definition of a loose cannon.

I passed through the open hallway next to the courtyard, finally hooking a left into the area where the storage rooms were located. Looking over my shoulder and confirming that I was alone, I ducked into the middle room and headed for the door. Luckily, I had picked enough of my own palace locks to pretty much get anything open at this point. Removing the pin from my hair, letting it fall, I quickly worked the lock until it popped open. Steadying my breath, I took another look around to ensure I was still alone and heard the voices of servants making their way to me from the main hallway. I'd have to be quick. Quietly removing the lock, I opened the door and slipped through.

Breathing a sigh of relief, I ditched the sheet and lifted the bag onto my shoulders. Twisting my hair, I pulled it to one side as I found myself at a fork in the small damp corridor. The hallway to my left was barely lit by a few flickering lights while the one on the right was pitch-black.

Shivering against the chill, I wrapped my arms around me, quickly making my way down the hallway on the left. I had no idea if it was correct, but I didn't have much of a choice if I wanted to be able to see where I was going.

I crept along the corridor, doing my best not to stumble as I was thrown into shadows, seconds ticking by at a maddening pace. I couldn't tell how much time had passed, but my anxiety increased as I got no closer to an exit.

My breath quickened as I began to panic—turning down one hallway and then another, I passed through a door with a light above it. Turning a corner, I hit a darkened dead end and realized I had no idea where I was. In the dim light, everything looked the same, and apparently I had taken a wrong turn, or ten, and landed in this room. Wherever *this room* was. I turned around, intent on finding my way back to the storage room or at least somewhere recognizable when I heard them.

It couldn't have been more than five to six of them, but they were drunk.

And I was alone.

I moved into the shadows as much as possible as the voices neared, the group having paused in the doorway to the little room where I'd cornered myself. One voice instantly became clearer above the rest.

"So he said, 'Romano, I trusss you know what to do' and then left," General Romano said, slurring slightly. "So you wanna know what I did?" The others chuckled. "Broke them in, showed them what it means to disregard the rules."

I could hear the men laughing, exchanging head pats. It didn't take a genius—or someone with Mav's warning—to figure out what they were talking about.

"So Dax asked you to do that, Romano? Really? Asked you to do that to those maids?" One guy asked with a hint of incredulity.

"Nah, not like that," Romano answered. "He just said to take care of them. I determined the means of the uh, lesson."

I glanced around the corner to see him smiling cockily as he finished tying his boot, his blond hair shining under the light as the other men laughed with him. My blood boiled, disgusted by this group of so-called soldiers and angry for a group of Gaill maids I hadn't even met.

Mav had been right about staying away from Romano. There was no way this would end well for me if I was discovered. The only issue was I had no idea where to go. My only way forward was through the door they currently blocked.

I quietly moved back into the shadows, hoping to avoid discovery, but Romano must have spotted the movement.

"Hold on," he said, then laughed as if to himself. "Well, boys. Look at that. What do we have here?"

Taking a deep breath, I knew I only had a few seconds before they got to me. Turning quickly, I rolled my bag into the shadows behind me and made sure the sections of *The Eclipse* were securely hidden in my dress as I straightened. I might have been caught, but I'd be damned if they caught me running too. The consequences would be much worse.

I turned around, and a second later there was a rough tug on my arm as a man pulled me forward, sending us stumbling into the light near the doorway. Blinking against the sudden brightness, I found myself looking back at a pair of eyes I didn't recognize. He wasn't a Deviant as I didn't feel any power radiating from him. Just a regular man. With the same look of disgust for me as Romano always wore and was wearing now.

"Where ya going?" Romano asked with mock interest as he too casually leaned against the wall nearest me, hands folded in front of him.

"Nowhere," I answered quickly. *Too quickly.* "I was on my way to the festival when I got lost." I deliberately slowed, repeating the excuse I'd rehearsed for the past three days.

"Huh." Romano raised his eyebrows at his comrades. Straightening, he returned his stare to me. "Interesting. Miss *Lewis,* isnnit?" He slurred his words as he walked toward me, his power snaking around me the closer he got.

I backed up to find myself walled in by another body behind me as the other men closed around me. I licked my lips, willing my breathing to remain calm as my mind moved rapidly, trying to sort a way out of this.

Everything was *okay*. Everything was *fine*.

The brandy hung thick from Romano's breath as he closed in on me. "What was a servant going to the festival doing all the way down here in the lower south wing?"

My stomach dropped, and I tried to remain composed. Lower south wing—the military section of the castle. Where I'd originally been held prisoner, one of the places Romano had mentioned was off-limits the very first day. I somehow had gone the complete opposite direction I meant. Cursing myself, I stared straight into his chest, willing my words to come out slow and strong.

"My apologies, my lord." A few of the men snickered at that. I cleared my throat and repeated my earlier excuse. "I was going to the festival and got lost."

Gripping my jaw with bruising force, Romano pressed himself into me, forcing me to look up. I held my breath so I wouldn't have to smell the brandy, putrid on his breath, as his gaze perused my face. His eyes were a light glossy blue and shining with hate.

"This is one of 'em, one of the Calderonians we grabbed from that nightclub last month," he said to the others, his words suddenly becoming more lucid. "Funny we should find her down here, snooping around. I had my suspicions about you." Romano directed his gaze toward me, hate filling every corner of it. "A girl who clearly doesn't know her place, questions direction, lady's maid but hair loose like some wanton whore." He grabbed the end of my loose hair in one of his fists. "And a servant taken from the city closest to the palace."

My breath hitched, but he continued, too intent on what he had to say to notice. There was a glint in his eyes, like a hunter closing in on his prey… and I was the stupid mouse running straight for his trap. "So tell me, Miss Lewis, who were you a lady's maid for? Because I seem to remember a Lewis pretty high up in the Calderonian monarchy not too long ago."

I opened my mouth, but no words came out. I hadn't thought this far. *Fool.* I didn't think anyone would figure out where my name was from. But how could they *not?* I was in my enemy's court, and my maids were chosen from some of our greatest families. Someone was bound to figure out I was connected to the palace at some point when I used Miranda's last name.

Frustration and anger shifted across his face before he reached out and grabbed my throat. My hands flew to his as I tried to pry them away but could do nothing as his grip tightened.

"Tell me who you are, *Jacqueline Lewis*," he spewed out, saying my name with such venom.

I tried to speak, but the only word that I got out was *please*, which only seemed to anger him more because he squeezed tighter.

Tears streamed down my cheeks as my eyes watered from the pressure. My lungs felt like they were close to bursting—I was so desperate for air. I tried to concentrate, but my mind slipped as my body grew weak.

This was it. I knew it. I was going to die, alone. And my friends, my family… my country wouldn't even know.

And I won't be there to save them before the Gaill arrive.

As I felt consciousness leaving me, he let go, and I collapsed to the ground.

The world around me kept spinning as black spots covered my vision. I was so busy gulping air I didn't realize I was lying flat until they held my arms down.

Then I began to fight back on instinct.

Kicking, thrashing, screaming. But it didn't make any difference, I was nothing compared to them.

"Shut her up. We can't have her raising the suspicion of other guards." I heard Romano through the ringing in my ears.

There was a ripping sound, and suddenly a piece of cloth was shoved into my mouth. I tasted dirt and the metallic tang of blood. Gagging, I willed myself not to get sick, knowing none of them would care to remove the rag if I did.

And then I spotted Romano nearing me, dead in the eyes, ready to break me like he did those other maids. Only the stakes were higher. I had a secret he wanted, and I couldn't give it up no matter what he did.

My kingdom and my people need me.

Screaming behind the rag, I resisted harder, ignoring the damp coarseness of the ground as it tore into my dress. I attempted to kick the men holding me down when one elbowed me in the ribs, knocking the wind from me. The others shouted words of encouragement to one another as I coughed and choked against the rag, my eyes watering more.

A hand covered the cloth in my mouth, pressing down, silencing me completely. The pressure against my nose took whatever oxygen I had left, causing the spots to return.

I closed my eyes, focusing all my strength on transporting myself elsewhere—my terrace back home, mornings with Rach and Mir,

Mav's room with the Devs—anywhere but here. When I opened them back up, I saw Romano standing over me.

And that's when it happened.

Paralyzing, earth-shattering power erupted somewhere in the distance and plummeted toward us at light speed. Within a second, it filled the corridor like lightning, and I felt its electricity coursing through my bones, my very blood. I barely caught the look of terror exchanged between the men before they were all thrown back.

And I couldn't possibly keep up with what happened next.

The corridor became a blur of blinding light and movement, and I instinctively curled into a ball to keep the nausea at bay. Trembling, my fingers managed to remove the cloth from my mouth as my breaths came in ragged gulps. Closing my eyes, I focused on anything but the sounds of screams and splintering wood around me when that same electric power wrapped around me, calming me.

And then suddenly everything stilled, and the power receded.

When I finally sat up and refocused, Dax was holding Romano by his throat against the wall. Or what was left of it as most of it had been taken out along with the door that'd been splintered in half.

A few of the other men—I could see there were about eight now—were lying around either winded or unconscious. One had a sizable chunk of wood through his chest. I felt myself getting sick again at the sight of him—mouth hanging open, blood dripping.

Pulling my attention away from the dead soldier, I heard Romano straining to speak. "Your Highness. We were just playin' around. This is just a servant, a Miss Lewis, who says she was lost so—"

"Silence." Dax cut him off, his nostrils flaring in anger. "What were you trying to do, Romano?" A muscle twitched in his jaw as his tattooed fingers dug into Romano's throat. The sword with the Celtic cross at the hilt was strung across his broad back, and his hair was tied in a messy bun, some pieces fighting to escape after what he'd just unleashed on the small space.

A warrior who'd come prepared for a fight.

"Verify her intent here. Then teach her a lesson so she doesn't get lost round here again." Romano smiled like a drunken idiot. "But we didn't get that far."

At that, Dax threw Romano to the ground. The general doubled over, coughing while clutching his throat. Within a second, Dax moved behind one of the soldiers who had been by my legs. A look of terror flashed across the man's face for only a moment before Dax's long tattooed fingers wrapped around his neck and twisted. A sickening crack bounced off the walls of the room. Just as quickly, another crack sounded as Dax moved to the other man who'd been by my legs and did the same to him.

A small gasp slipped from me involuntarily as my mind worked double time to keep up with what was going on.

Weren't these *his* men? Was this how the Gaill doled out punishment for soldiers acting out of line? I looked at Dax, but he wasn't looking at me; instead, he'd turned his attention back to Romano.

Grabbing him by the collar, Dax slammed him into the stone wall again with such force debris fell from the ceiling. "The rest of you may live. But if any of you so much as look at Jacqueline Lewis in the wrong way, or in any way at all actually, I'll strip the life from you. Limb by limb. This goes for *any* Gaill. So consider this my one act of mercy. And your only warning." Dax's voice was low, laced with a cold fury that turned my blood to ice.

Eying Romano up and down, he let him drop before turning back to the room, looking at the remaining few soldiers in turn. Finally meeting my eyes, he strode directly for me. I felt the Gaill's eyes fall to me, but all I could do was stare at Dax as he approached.

His eyes were bright blue-green, almost white, and it looked like the ocean was churning behind them, they were so *alive*. The power of his stare rooted me to the spot. Not in terror, no, but sheer wonder at its beauty.

Deviant.

Before I could ask any questions or make any protests, Dax scooped me up in his arms and carried me out.

Too shaken to say anything, I remained silent as he swiftly carried me to the upper floors of the south wing. I didn't start to question things until he entered the main gallery of his apartments, at which point I struggled to get down, pushing off his chest, desperate to escape as the past twenty minutes replayed in my mind—the horror show I'd had a front-row seat to. I couldn't be alone with the Gaill leader right now.

"Relax, Jacqueline. I'm not going to hurt you. I promise," he said softly, locking me in to his gaze and tightening his grip on me. A few of his dark curls had fallen across his face, partially obscuring it, but I could still make out his eyes. They weren't quite as bright now, but the same aquamarine-colored current was churning behind them as well as unmistakable rage and concern.

We were too close right now. *Far too close.*

Nervously biting my lip, I looked forward as we entered his private chambers. I immediately tensed, but he quickly set me down on what I assumed was his bed and took a seat in one of the large armchairs by the fire across the room. Dark brown leather tried to envelop him as he sat back. Steepling his fingers before bringing them to meet his lips, he observed me in that way of his, the tic in his jaw the only sign of rage slipping through that mask that had moved back into place.

I could not take his scrutiny right now.

Looking away, I attempted to run my hands through my knotted hair, not realizing how dirty it had gotten. How dirty I *felt* after being down there.

Resisting the urge to run, I forced my mind to turn. I needed to get out of there and shower. I needed to be alone.

But suddenly the thought of being alone sent me spiraling, and the tears sprang to my eyes automatically.

Truthfully, I didn't know what I needed. Life had turned into a bad dream I couldn't wake up from.

I cleared my throat, ignoring the pain. "Will I be allowed back to my room soon?"

"No, not tonight. Tonight, you'll be staying here."

Wait, here? As in *his bedroom*? Was he insane?

"I'm perfectly fine to go back to my room, Your Highness."

Panic beat at my chest. *I have to leave—now.*

"I have no doubt, Jacqueline. Nevertheless, you'll stay here tonight." His tone of finality left no doubt the debate was done.

"Is there a bathroom I could use?" I stood suddenly, wringing my hands slightly, not able to keep still. I needed to make a plan of action away from him.

Dax looked at my hands, his eyes tightening before meeting mine, smiling almost sympathetically, and pointed to a door. "Feel free to shower, I'll call for an extra set of clothes."

I nodded, made my way across the room, and did my best to ignore the feeling of his eyes on me. Padding into the bathroom, I locked the door behind me. Having lost my shoes and ripped my stockings somewhere in the corridor, I did my best to ignore the cold of the marble floor against my bare skin. Scenes from what had happened no less than an hour earlier flashed across my mind, and before I knew it I had shed my dirt-covered dress and was naked, shivering uncontrollably in the middle of Dax's bathroom.

Turning the water on hot, I let steam fill the air before I stepped in, hissing when the scalding water hit my skin. But I welcomed it, wanting it to burn through every bit of the dirt that covered my body like a cloak of shame.

Finding the soap, a woodsy scent, I scrubbed. I scrubbed and scrubbed and scrubbed, attempting to remove the filth on me. That had become me. The filth of what had just happened, of needing Dax to come to my rescue, of needing my enemy in this moment.

Swallowing past the lump rising in my throat, I moved on to shampooing as I tried to keep my mind in the present. But it kept wandering back to the corridor.

Biting my lip to keep it from trembling, I attempted to calm my breathing as I closed my eyes, focusing on the hot water as I let it envelop me.

Why *had* Dax been there at that moment? And how did he know where to find me?

Inhaling a shuddering breath, I moved farther under the hot water as it poured down from the waterfall-like showerhead in the ceiling. Closing my eyes, I methodically conditioned my hair before tipping my head under one last time.

Something in my gut told me I could trust Dax not to hurt me. His gaze had been filled with a wrath so great the memory of it alone was enough to make me shake in fear, yet I hadn't in front of him. The only thing I remember thinking after he'd arrived in the corridor was, *I'm safe now.*

A sudden pang of guilt tore through all other emotions, engulfing me as I wiped the last dregs of water from my eyes. Feeling safe around Daxinius Da Luca? What would Father say?

I was supposed to be miles away, on my way home. And yet here

I was, barely having escaped with my life, in debt to the Gaill prince.

What would I do now? Say thank you to him for saving my sanity, my dignity, for saving *me* when I was supposed to be just a servant? When in reality I was still his enemy, and he was mine? Should I really be thanking him when he wouldn't allow me my freedom? When he would surely kill me on the spot if he found out who I was given his hate for my family? When he planned to destroy Calderone anyway?

Biting my lip again, I turned the water off. Reaching for a towel from the shelf next to it, I wrapped it around me and focused on the woodsy scent from Dax's shampoo and the feeling of my wet hair dripping down my back.

I couldn't think about my emotions—not here, not now. Tonight I had to survive in the company of my enemy. Tomorrow I'd deal with everything else.

Imagining hiding my emotions in a tightly locked box again, I took a deep breath, stepped out of the shower, and met my gaze in the mirror.

My blue eyes were bright, and my cheeks appeared flushed from the steam and adrenaline still coursing through my system. I had a small cut just below my left eye, probably from the guard who had his hand covering my mouth. I touched it lightly, wondering how I hadn't felt it sting in the shower. I had, however, felt the bump from when I'd dropped to the ground, hitting my head on the stone floor of the corridor.

And my black pearl necklace was still in place, intact somehow—the one solid piece of me left at this point. I tipped my head back as I fought a new onslaught of tears. Figuring I was already breaking every last rule by being in here in his chambers, I kept it on.

Sighing, I inspected other areas for any damage and noticed marks on my ribs and more on my arms.

Venturing toward the door, I suddenly wasn't sure what to do. I couldn't just go out there in a towel, but I *definitely* wasn't putting that dress back on. Swallowing, I slowly opened the door and looked around. Dax's back was to me. He stiffened before there was a clink of ice and the sound of a drink being poured.

A pile of clean clothes with a pair of thick socks was folded and waiting for me. I picked it up and slowly backed into the bathroom again.

After changing into the soft, cream-colored top and pants, I combed out my long, dark hair and towel dried it into messy waves the best I could. Grabbing the pages of *The Eclipse* from my dress, I neatly tucked them into one of the pants pockets before wandering back into the bedroom. My backpack was still in the destroyed corridor, but it would have to stay there. Given the amount of destruction Dax had caused, it was likely buried under rubble anyway.

Sitting cross-legged on the bed, because it was very apparent I still was not leaving, I stared at Dax who was now contemplating the glass of dark liquor in his hands. A palpable tension rolled off him in waves, and a few dark curls fell over his eyes as his thumb moved back and forth over the rim, the moons on his knuckles flexing with each movement.

"How did you know I was there?" It was the only question I could think to ask across the silence while I did my best to keep my emotions locked away.

"I was having you followed. When you disappeared and that door was found opened, I had a few people out looking for you. One heard you and alerted me to your situation."

I'd give him points for his honesty at least.

"Do you normally have the palace servants followed?"

"No, Jacqueline, I do not. You would be a first." He looked up from his glass and stared at me with a contemplative expression but didn't offer anything more.

I bit my lower lip, chewing over that new piece of information. Before I could start to question how much he knew about me or why he would have me followed, he stood, his gaze on my lip.

"Rest, Jacqueline." His gaze shifted from my mouth to the bed as he gestured toward it.

I frowned back at him. I would *not* be that woman for him. No matter how powerful he was. No matter if he had saved my life, I would not. "What're you going to do?"

"I'll sleep in one of my many guest rooms tonight. One close by. You'll be safest here. A guard will be stationed outside the hallway door as well as the one into the office." He motioned to a door I hadn't noticed on the other side of his bed.

Standing, he slowly made his way over to me, setting his drink down on the way. He stopped a good three feet away and put his tattooed hands in his pockets. The same ones he had killed with less than an hour ago. "Drink the tonic. Scarletti brought it up. It'll help heal you." He nodded to a cup sitting on the nightstand. "Jacqueline, you are safe with me. No one will touch you without your permission."

Again those green eyes searched mine. I wasn't sure if he found what he was looking for this time, but either way, he went into the bathroom and returned with my tattered dress.

"I'll dispose of this." His eyes connected with mine, the same bright fury from before pushing forward, and then he left through his office, closing the door behind him.

As the latched clicked, I let out a breath I hadn't realized I'd been holding. Turning to look at his room, I sniffed the tonic and took a hesitant sip, instantly feeling better as the warm, bitter medicine soothed my throat and entered my system.

Dax's private chamber was similar to the palace's guest rooms, although larger with windows that stretched from the floor to the top of the tall ceiling. And this room was darker somehow, with long, deep purple curtains covering the windows and pooling on the hardwood floors surrounded by walls that were such a dark wood they almost looked black. *Like a bruise*, I thought, recalling the ones already forming across my ribs. The entire room was a mix of dark mahogany and the same dark purple hues.

I noticed the Gaillic symbol of the Eclipse—the same one from the front of Da Luca's book—painted gold against a black ceiling. There weren't any portraits on the walls save the massive one of an older, matriarchal woman with long amber waves above the fireplace. She looked down on the room with a kind smile and loving eyes a shade of green identical to Dax's. I didn't even have to ask; I knew it was Queen Caragh Da Luca. Another recognizable face to anyone who grew up in the monarchies though she'd been dead over thirty years.

Sighing, I turned back toward the large four-poster bed. Every monarchical bone inside my body was screaming at me to use this opportunity to snoop through his belongings to gain an edge for the monarchies and my kingdom. Or at the very least not to sleep in the bed of my enemy.

But instead, as if on instinct, I slid between the black sheets. *I'm too exhausted*, I reasoned. *This night took too much out of me, and if this is how my life ends, so be it.* Though a part of me knew deep down I was safe here.

It wasn't until I was almost asleep that I realized he'd started calling me Jacqueline instead of Miss Lewis.

The morning sunlight hit my face before I opened my eyes. Keeping them closed, I fully rolled into the sun, not wanting to miss its heat upon my face or the smell of clean linens around me as I stretched.

I had missed this.

Wait.

I sat up so quickly the blood rushed to my head, momentarily disorienting me. I wasn't at home. Although it felt strangely familiar to my room in Calderone.

Rubbing my eyes, I realized I was still in the prince's chambers and the sun was up. My heart began pounding on high alert, and the emotions I'd locked away flooded through me as panic took hold.

How long was I asleep?

"It's ten," Dax said as if in response.

I whipped my head around, not having noticed him in the room. He was looking out the window, dressed as usual in a black tunic, expensive-looking black jeans, and a pair of heavy combat boots. No fighting gear. And his hair was how I saw it the first day—loose curls with braids in the front.

I pulled the sleeves of my shirt over my hands and kept my eyes down, wanting to disappear into the dark sheets after everything that happened. Shame was setting in and made it hard to breathe. "My apologies, Your Highness. For last night and overstaying my welcome this morning."

I was determined to leave as soon as humanly possible, but before my feet hit the floor, Dax was at the bedside with a cup of coffee.

"Cream?"

"Um… please yes. Thank you, Your Highness," I added as an afterthought, startled by both his offer and the fact he had access to cream.

Within a few seconds, he was stirring cream into my cup and handing it to me, the intricate web of ink on his hands seemingly in direct opposition to the delicate china of the cup. And the politeness of his offer.

Quietly thanking him again, I took the coffee, blowing on the steaming liquid and letting it warm my hands as I sorted through what to do next.

I made my way over to the windows Dax had been looking out, keeping an eye on him the whole time. He watched me from where he stood by the bed, an amused smile playing at his lips.

Through the windows, I watched palace workers tearing down the tent and carnival from the night before.

The festival. I had completely forgotten after everything that happened.

Turning around, I opened my mouth when Dax's piercing jade-green eyes met mine from where he now sat in one of the large chairs around the fire. "Don't apologize for that either. You weren't in the wrong last night."

I nodded and drank my coffee while taking in his answer. I mean, I was partially at fault for his missing some of the festival. A celebration and no doubt key political event we had just spent two weeks planning and preparing for.

And I felt worse than I should've. I should've been happy to upset his alliance with the Eur. Recognizing that only compounded my feelings of guilt.

Clearing my throat in an attempt to clear my mind, I turned back to the windows, looking out over the expansive view. Rolling hills and mountains were covered in rich evergreens as life flourished after three hundred years of waste. More workers tilled the palace fields in the distance, and still others labored in the library gardens to my right.

I suddenly felt the electricity of Dax's presence behind me and stilled as he drew closer, so close I could feel his breath on my neck, smell the ocean air on his skin.

I waited for the fear of him to hit, but it never did though the tension rippling from him was no less tangible than the night before.

"You know you broke the rules?"

My chest tightened as my heart pounded.

His touch felt like an electric shock as his fingers grazed the back of my neck, deftly slipping below the small strand of black pearls.

I smiled in spite of myself, knowing what he referred to. I turned to find him spinning my necklace carefully between his tan fingers. This time the black of the pearls seemed to compliment that of the ink which covered his skin.

Smirking, he raised a brow as if daring me to respond.

I reached back to unclasp the necklace. But he shot a hand out almost immediately, grabbing both of mine in one of his and sending more shock waves through me.

"No." He laughed lightly and shook his head. "It suits you. Don't take it off." He dropped my hands and stepped back, lifting his chin. "Hungry?"

A huge smile spread across my face. I never could hide my love for breakfast.

It's just breakfast. I was sure he was only being kind after what he caught his own men doing last night. He probably felt guilty, culpable, as I'm sure Phin or Father would had they been in a similar position.

Or maybe he was just plying me to get me to talk. Whatever it was, I did need to eat, and I had the feeling that even if I said no, he'd probably make me stay and eat anyway.

As Dax ordered the food, I stepped into the bathroom and found a new brush, a few different hair clips, and a toothbrush lying on the counter. I knew Scarletti was likely responsible for bringing these up since she, rather than any of the maids, served Dax. I tried not to dwell on it, but the fact she was aware I'd been here overnight set my cheeks on fire.

Making quick work to pull my hair back and splash cool water on my face, I brushed my teeth and finished up with some lotion I found on the counter—another woodsy, ocean-air scent that I was starting to think of as quintessential Dax. I hadn't had really good lotion in weeks, and I wasn't above using his.

I was surprised that I actually looked okay. The top and pants were chic but comfortable, my hair was half up—waves loose as I usually had them when I wasn't working—and the tonic Dax had given me had slowed some of the bruising and pain. My eyes weren't even bloodshot. I really must've slept well, which was a concerning thought considering I was under the eye of my enemy the entire night and had just been attacked by his men. Chalking it up to another emotion to sweep under the rug for a later date, I put the brush and spare toothbrush together on the counter and moved back into the bedroom.

Dax was on the terrace. The door to it stood open, a light breeze blowing in. I hadn't even noticed the door before because it blended in seamlessly with the windows looking out over the hills. Stepping out, I blinked against the sun.

It was so sunny. And actually warm.

A million memories of home hit me all at once like a train going a thousand miles an hour—the girls, my terrace, the pool, and all the days we spent out there, ignorant of everything else, including the future. Turning to face the rolling hills, I swallowed against the lump in my throat and tipped my head back to ease the burning in my eyes. Things would never be the same, *even if I do see home again.*

I turned to Dax and the breakfast that had shown up in the few minutes I was in the bathroom. He watched me from his seat with that same searching look as I approached. There was only one other chair immediately to the left of his. I bit my lip and made my way over to it, sinking down and slowly raising my eyes to meet his as one might do to an animal in the wild.

He was leaning to the side, one arm resting on the back of his chair, the other propping up his jaw, observing my every move. Before long, a small smile appeared across his lips, and he silently chuckled to himself as he shook his head and unfolded his napkin.

I did the same while looking over what he'd ordered—the whole kitchen apparently. Breakfast had always been my favorite meal, and although the toast or pancakes and dried-out scrambled eggs we received in the dining hall weren't bad, they couldn't compare to this.

My stomach rumbled as if in agreement.

"I wasn't sure what you liked, so I asked for a little bit of everything," Dax said as if in response to my thoughts, picking up his fork to dig into his pancakes. He had a weird way of knowing what I was thinking without my even having to speak. "Don't worry. We'll give what we don't eat to those living outside the palace."

"Thank you, Your Highness. This is all very generous of you." It truly was generous. We should be doing that at our palace with the leftover food. "But you didn't have to trouble yourself. You've already done more than enough for me—I could never repay you. And I won't say anything about what happened last night. I…" I was unsure of myself but felt the need to clarify that this could and should end here. Any attention from him would only make it harder for me to slip through the cracks enough to try escaping again.

I also needed to stay away from him. Every second in his presence made me question the vile stories I was raised to believe about him. Made me question myself and my judgment. That in and of itself was dangerous.

He is still my enemy.

And he was having me followed. An anger I was too numb to feel the night before bloomed in my chest. He'd been watching me, and I'd been ignorant of it.

He set down his fork and leaned back to look at me again. The power from his gaze, his eyes turning a shade of light green, ripped me from my thoughts and locked me in to him.

"Jacqueline. Make no mistake, I expect nothing from you. This world is different from the one you grew up in. You will not receive the same niceties from certain groups of people as you were once accustomed to as I'm sure you're figuring out. But," he continued, "that doesn't mean I will allow anyone to attack you. I protect what is mine as I've done with my people for centuries."

Centuries? Protecting what is his*?*

Like I was a piece of property to be guarded?

And what does he know about how I grew up?

I looked at my plate, my mind spinning from what he was saying. I had too many questions. So I asked the first one that came to mind. "Why did you have me followed?"

"Reasons."

I stared at him for a minute, waiting for him to expand on his answer. But he didn't. Instead, he fixed me with a blank stare.

The anger blooming in my chest blossomed into a full-blown inferno. He could be so cryptic. It was maddening.

I opened my mouth to ask more questions, but Dax spoke first. "Eat. And then we'll discuss your training. You need to learn to defend yourself against future attackers." He then shoveled a heap of pancakes into his mouth.

"Training? I wouldn't need to learn to defend myself if I hadn't been kidnapped and brought here," I snapped.

It was as if he didn't even hear me. He just kept eating.

I sat there staring at him until he met my eyes. "Your High—"

"Eat, Jacqueline." His fingers tightened around his fork before he went back to concentrating on the pancakes in front of him.

Another minute of silence ticked by before I released a huff. It was clear our conversation was over for now. And as much as I wanted to know more, I still had to play the role of the obedient servant. But that didn't mean I wouldn't ask more questions at the next opportunity.

I piled fruit, pancakes, and waffles onto my plate and began to eat.

The meal ended in silence.

CHAPTER 7

THE COALITION

I pulled the map closer, trying to match up Da Luca's drawing of twenty-second-century Siberia to my recollection of today's monarchy, the most powerful on the other side of the Atlantic. After breakfast, Dax had a guard escort me back to the servant wing and instructed me to take the day off. He told me to take tomorrow off too, but we both knew I wouldn't. I needed the distraction from my thoughts. And I couldn't feel helpless, even if it meant working for the enemy while figuring out my next move.

But today I willfully retreated, having spent most of the day reading and ignoring the knot of emotions in my chest.

Examining the map again, I realized it looked a lot like early Calderone—the palace, factories, farmlands, and ports all marked as well as the same *x*'s. Six of them. They were spread out around the borders of the country just as in Calderone. And the same marking on the key denoted them as camps.

I sighed, setting the book on my chest as I bit my lip, trying to figure out what to do. The camps clearly had existed outside Calderone, so they likely had served a greater purpose. The issue now was figuring out what that purpose was and if the camps were still around today. And if the conditions of them were truly as dire as Dax had implied.

The only way to know was to get home and discover the truth myself. And the sooner I got home the better—with the Eur gone, the plans for war were already in motion.

I made my way over to the desk and poured myself a glass of water. I caught my reflection in the mirror over the sink, set the glass down, and moved closer for a better look at the cut and bruising on my face and neck.

It had gotten progressively worse since leaving Dax's a few hours ago. Though the tonic had helped, it didn't stop the bruising entirely. Turning my neck side to side, I examined the deep purple marks obvious where Romano had grabbed me. Closing my eyes, a flood of memories hit me at once. I gripped the sink to steady myself, my lungs suddenly feeling void of air. Taking a few deep, shuddering breaths, I willed myself to return to the present—to the state of numb nothingness I'd inhabited for most of the day.

After a few minutes, I dragged myself back to bed. Tucking *The Eclipse* under my mattress, I lay back, my eyes tracing the cracks on the ceiling.

I didn't know why Dax was having me followed. It would make escaping harder, *much* harder, but not entirely impossible. The service entrance was no longer an option. Surely they'd be keeping a closer eye on it. But maybe during the next Full Moon, when everyone was busy partying, I could slip away undetected. It would be a risk, but I could likely use the woods surrounding the grove where Full Moon took place as extra cover.

And of course I still needed to figure out a way to get outside the outer ward that surrounded the palace grounds. There had to be a chink in the wall's armor somewhere. I needed a new map. Perhaps now, while Dax thought I was in my room resting, would be a good time to sneak into the library.

Starting with a shout, I sat up and my hand flew to my chest as sudden, loud pounding sounded against my door.

"Open up, Jac!" Axel's voice was urgent and worried as he pounded on the door again.

I needed to cover my bruises. The knocking continued, and I became frantic, looking around for anything to conceal the evidence of last night's attack and my escape attempt. After a minute, coming up with nothing, I undid my long hair and pulled it all to the front to cover my neck as best I could.

Walking to the door, I heard Killian's deep voice floating through. "Is she even in there? I told you we should've started looking for her last night when she never showed."

"Scarletti said she was fine."

Killian scoffed. "Oh, come on, if you believe that—"

But he never finished, stopping abruptly as I opened the door to five worried faces.

Killian instantly pulled me into a bone-crushing hug, eliciting an unintentional squeak from me as my sore muscles cried out.

Stepping back, he gripped me by the shoulder and looked me up and down, his hair a wavy black mess across half his face. I tucked my chin to my chest, attempting to hide the bruising and willing myself not to move even though being touched was the last thing I wanted right now.

The thought that I didn't even want comfort from one of my only friends here instantly brought tears to my eyes. I needed to get home. I was too weak, vulnerable in every way here.

With gentle fingers, Kacey reached around and lifted my chin, revealing the bruising and the cut beneath my eye. I kept my eyes downcast, willing myself not to get upset, but finally looked up when no one said anything after a minute, meeting Kacey and Lana's pain-filled expressions before turning to the boys. The murderous look on their faces had me taking an actual step back as Kacey's face filled my vision.

"What happened, Jac?"

Pulling in my lips, I turned around and walked back to sit on the bed. The group filed in behind me. Killian flipped the desk chair to face outward and sat down while the others leaned against the wall. Lana sat beside me, tentatively grabbing my hand as if she knew how I was feeling. No one said anything; they just waited for me to share what I needed to.

Before I knew what I was doing, the words spilled out. Everything Dax had told me about Calderone, what I had planned, what Romano did, how Dax saved me and kept watch over me.

Everything but my true identity and my discoveries in *The Eclipse*. I told them I was of noble birth and taken by accident that night, wanting to get home to warn my family and determine the extent of my country's wrongs. Lana confirmed my story, at least as far as what she knew.

By the end, Axel was pacing the room, hands folded behind his head as Killian sat, hands braced on his knees at the desk chair, rocking back and forth slightly, and Mav stood deathly still against the wall, arms folded across his chest. All three wore the same look of rage.

"This ends tonight." Killian stood and looked down at me before giving a hard glance at each of his boys.

At first, I wasn't entirely sure if they meant my being here or Romano's attacks.

Kacey, understanding Killian exactly, reached out to grab his arm.

"We do nothing right now." Looking at the boys slowly, she sat down on my other side. "Anything against Romano will be seen as an attack against the crown. You know he is like family to King Aidoneus. There will likely be repercussions for Dax for what he did," she said. "If we attack, none of us will make it out alive, and you know it."

We all knew she was right, although I didn't know what type of repercussions Dax could possibly face, or who could even punish him.

"So what? We do nothing? Let Romano think he can assault women? Assault Jac? He knows she's in our group. One of us. We've made that clear to the whole damn palace. We can't let his actions slide." Killian sucked his lip ring between his teeth and looked no less furious than he had two minutes earlier.

"No, of course we do something," Kacey said in a matter-of-fact, why-ask-me-something-so-dumb kind of way. "We further the Devs' cause. Put all our might behind it and help Dax in any way we can."

She let that hang in the silence for a minute as the boys mulled things over. Lana and I just looked at each other, having no idea what furthering their cause had to do with punishing Romano.

Axel nodded and slowly stopped pacing. "Help find the One, get the rest of the Devs and outlying Gaill to sign—anything."

"And put Dax where he should be sooner," Maverick finished, standing up straight.

Wait, *what?* I whipped my head to Lana who looked just as confused as I was.

Kacey turned to face us, eyes wide and freckled face flushed. "There are things you don't know about the Gaill. And the Deviants." She glanced over to the other three in the room. "The Nor Gaill cause with the Eur is really twofold." She leaned forward, resting her forearms on her bent leg to get closer to us as her voice dropped to a whisper. "You have our cause to defeat the monarchies, starting with

Calderone"—she glanced at me, eyes tightening, before continuing—"and then our cause, which only the Eur and some of the Devs know of, to overthrow King Aidoneus before we topple the monarchies."

"Wh-what?" My mind was turning too quickly for my mouth to keep up. "What do you mean?"

"The Eur have agreed to help us put Dax on the throne." Pride for her prince came through in her voice. "King Aidoneus, once fair, has turned cruel. It started long ago, but after Queen Caragh passed, things escalated. The stories you hear about the king, the nightmares you have of him, believe them. Because they're all true."

A shiver coursed through me at the same time I felt one go through Lana beside me. We'd grown up listening to stories of his savagery, his lust for blood, and need to torture even his own citizens. To think even some of it could be true made me sick.

"But Dax is different? He's better?" Lana asked, disbelief in her voice because the same stories we'd heard about the king we'd also heard about the prince.

"Aidoneus and Dax both hate Calderone to be sure." Maverick looked from Lana to me, his mouth set in a grim line. "But Aidoneus wants to end the monarchy even if it means eliminating those in Calderone who are innocent. Dax understands that most Calderonian citizens have no hand in the monarchy's corruption. He sees the innocent for who they are—victims in need of protection, both from the monarchy and his own father."

"Yeah, Dax knows that in order to save the innocents in Calderone before we attack, he first has to get rid of his father. Dax only wants to overthrow the Calderonian government to end their corruption. Aidoneus would be okay with completely destroying Calderone and every innocent person who lives there," Killian added.

Kacey nodded. "Dax was once like Aidoneus, although most

people think he was just doing his father's bidding. When his mother passed, everything changed."

"He is different," I interjected before I could stop myself. "I think Dax has a kind heart."

"A kind heart for you apparently." Killian threw me one of his cocky grins.

I narrowed my eyes at him. "Right, more likely embarrassed about Romano's actions."

"Which is totally why he had you followed," Axel pointed out, smirking.

"Right. So Dax is staging a coup." I diverted the subject.

"Yes, essentially." Axel settled into the vacated desk chair and pushed his blond hair out of his face. "Although is it really a coup if he's meant to inherit the throne eventually?"

"Yes," I said, a soft laugh escaping.

"Then yes, a coup." Axel grinned at me as his hair fell back over his brow.

"Anyway." Kacey pulled the group back to attention. "I think we should focus on getting all the Devs in the palace to enlist. Those who haven't already."

"So most of the Devs side with Dax then? I noticed Romano was a Deviant." I looked around.

"Yes." Anger passed across Mav's face at the mention of Romano. "Devs don't usually enlist in the Nor Gaill Army unless forced. Generally, we don't like our powers being used for warfare. Especially the type Aidoneus has planned. Romano is an exception. For the past few decades, many Deviants have supported Dax and his rise, a fair number of us having secretly enlisted in the Gaill Coalition—Dax's covert alliance with the Eur to overthrow King Aidoneus."

"Is the king not aware of the Coalition?" Lana asked.

"He's aware there's a growing division in court, we believe, based on how he's been acting in recent years. I personally think he knows his time is coming to an end and, like all adult children, he's been throwing temper tantrums—punishing Devs for no reason, keeping Dax on a tight leash when he's at the palace, blaming Dax for his own mistakes, raiding neighboring villages who are rumored to support the Coalition—"

"But the guy's not even here right now." Killian scoffed from across the room as he helped himself to a cup of water from the pitcher. "You'd think if he thought for even a moment that we were planning a coup with the Eur, he'd stay back to interfere."

Mav shrugged. "Unless he's trying to flex his power by saying that anything the Eur and Devs could be planning doesn't worry him."

"Or he's planning something else, something bigger. Something to keep himself in power." Kacey raised a brow, causing everyone to fall into silence for a beat as we contemplated this possibility.

"So the timeline's been sped up?" I said eventually. "The Coalition—they're trying to overthrow Aidoneus sooner because he's not fit to rule any longer?"

They all nodded back in confirmation.

"Romano is key to defeating the king because he's one of his top generals." Kacey looked between Lana and me. "If we get the rest of the Devs who haven't joined the Coalition to enlist, together with Dax, we could possibly defeat Aidoneus. That is, if we have all the other necessary things in place first."

The thought of what they could do, what I felt Dax alone do in the corridor, made the hair on the back of my neck stand on end. So maybe the question I asked next was dumb because I knew the type of power they could wield. Maybe I asked it because I was testing how far they trusted me. Or maybe I just wanted reassurance that I still belonged because what I asked next came out before I could even think.

"So since you all know why I was trying to escape, why are you not furious with me?"

"We'd be questioning you if you *didn't* take an opportunity to try to escape," Axel said as if it were obvious.

My face screwed up in confusion, and Mav jumped in, attempting to explain his best friend. "Given where you came from and that you've only been here a month, I don't think any one of us can blame you for trying to get out to warn your family of an attack. We'd do the same for one another."

"Yeah, we thought you were loyal, but now we know for sure," Killian cut in. "The problem is you're loyal to the wrong people, which is something that'll change with time." He grinned, sounding so sure of himself.

I only scoffed and shook my head in return. The arrogance of these three could be suffocating sometimes. But it was clear they didn't have it out for me because I attempted to flee. And they did have a point—any of them would've done it for the others.

"Not going to lie." I smiled in spite of myself. "I did think about you all as I left, and it made me think twice about going."

"There ya go, Calderone." Killian went in to give me a slap on the back before patting me gently, remembering what I'd just told them all. "Now where do you keep the booze in here?" He got up to rummage through my desk drawers.

"Ha, no booze, Kil. That's your job, remember?" I got up to grab my glass of water as the boys started joking around.

Lana approached as I took a long drink. "What're you gonna do about the bruises?"

"I'm not sure." I bit my lip. "There's no makeup anywhere. Maybe you could mix up some flour for me or something." I gave her a tired smile over my glass.

"We'll figure something out." She smiled back before turning to Kacey. "Hey Kace, you got a scarf or something Jac can borrow for the next few days for the, uh, you know..." She touched her neck.

"For sure. I'm pretty positive Scarletti will still let those neck scarves slide that were part of the uniform a decade or so ago. You'll be horribly out of fashion, but people will probably write you off as the hopeless new girl anyway." Kacey smiled teasingly from where she now sat on Mav's lap.

"Perrrfect," I said, drawing out the word sarcastically.

"Hey, Calderone." Axel picked up *Macbeth* from my desk and waved it around. "Did you have this on you at the club the night you were taken 'cause, uh, partying *and* Shakespeare? That's impressive."

"You're ridiculous." I laughed as Lana giggled next to me. "Dax gave it to me."

Immediately, everyone stopped what they were doing and turned to look at me. You would've thought I just grew wings from the looks on their faces.

"He just... well, I was in the library when I..." I felt myself turning red. I wasn't quite sure how to bring up the fact that their prince did *technically* give me a gift without making it sound like a gift. Because it wasn't a gift. As far as I was concerned.

"Wait, so he just gave that to you? Why?" Kacey asked, suddenly getting up.

"I don't know exactly. I was reading it in the library—I know!" I glared at Axel who had opened his mouth, likely to tell me off. "But I didn't exactly plan to. I just started. I know that sounds dumb—it *was* dumb. I didn't hear him come in until he started talking," I said, swallowing. "We talked about how I could read, and then when I was about to leave, he gave it to me, saying I'd find it helpful."

I shrugged in response to the look of confusion on their faces.

"Well, I guess it doesn't necessarily matter *why* he gave it to you. It's the fact that he did."

"Why's that?" Lana asked.

Kacey took the book from Axel, turning it over in her hands. "Servants are normally not allowed to use the library. It's for the courtiers."

"Plus Dax just doesn't give gifts. At all. He's pretty good at shutting out all emotion, so gift giving isn't really his thing. And to give a book this old—I mean… Wow," Axel said, seeming so sure.

"Oh well, I suppose it was probably another way of saying sorry for abducting me," I said feebly, all of us knowing it was a reach of a lie.

"All right, guys. Time to pack up." Lana suddenly turned to face the group, probably knowing I needed time to process what I'd just learned and revealed to everyone. "We gotta let Jac get some rest."

"Truth." Killian set his glass of water down on the desk.

"Let me know if you need anything. I'm just a few doors away, okay?" Lana said before gently drawing me into a hug. I was surprised to find the gesture soothing. An hour ago, the idea of anyone touching me had been nauseating.

"Thanks, Lan." I squeezed her back.

"Stay safe, Calderone. We'll be by partway through the night to be sure your door is still locked," Killian said matter-of-factly, coming up to put his hands on Lana's shoulders.

I gave the other three quick hugs before locking the door behind them and turning off my lights.

It was nearing dinnertime, but I was too exhausted to worry about food. Getting into the loungewear Dax had given me, I collapsed onto the bed and ran through what the Devs had said about him and the Coalition.

If Dax truly was trying to save the innocents in Calderone from whatever my government was doing, maybe that's why I felt so safe with him—why my gut instinct was to trust him even after he'd committed murder.

A sense of unease struck me. Could I ever fully trust Dax after hearing stories of his brutality for eighteen years? And if those stories were untrue... what did that mean for what my father and his administration had taught me of our enemies?

I wasn't sure how the Devs could know so much about Dax's personality—his lack of gift giving and his emotional unavailability—but they seemed confident. Maybe Dax's nature was common knowledge among the Gaill and the Devs. It certainly spread like wildfire anytime Phin gave me a lingering smile in the hallway back home. I could only imagine what centuries of rumors would do to a palace.

But that still didn't answer why he had singled me out. Why he had me followed. And why he let me take a book from the library when normally servants weren't allowed to. If word got out that he'd let me do that, it would only draw more attention to me—trying to escape again was going to be hard enough.

A sudden pang of guilt twisted itself around my heart and lungs. Even if I managed to escape, what was I going home to? I'd been so set on escaping that I hadn't thought about the true extent of Calderone's corruption. If I was able to get home and discover the truth, would I be equipped to handle it? Between what Da Luca had written in *The Eclipse* and the fact that the Gaill were planning a war to stop the corruption, I was no longer certain if it was something that I alone could fix.

Did it even make sense to leave before I knew the truth of what was happening in Calderone?

And before I know more about the truth of who the Deviants really are?

CHAPTER 8

ENCOUNTERS

"That thing is hideous," Lana said, trying not to laugh.

"Ugh, I know. It's like adding insult to injury, literally." I attempted to make light of the situation while I tugged at the white scarf around my neck.

After the past forty-eight hours, I was happy an ugly neck scarf was my biggest worry.

It isn't totally horrible. I tugged at the scarf again absentmindedly. Sure, it was big and white, but it did cover all my bruising, now an ugly deep black-purple, and I had managed to fashion it into something that resembled a bow.

Sighing, I looked up to find the four Devs waiting for us outside the dining hall. Lunch had just wrapped up, and we were all heading off to our tasks for the afternoon.

It had been two days since Romano's attack and waking up in Dax's room. I ended up taking yesterday off and spent most of it sleeping, but by this morning, I was getting restless. Nightmares woke me more than once over the past two days, and there was only so long I could be alone with the emotional firestorm in my head.

I knew I technically could take more time—I was still sore to my bones for one thing—but I was done doing nothing. At least if I got back to work, I could try to learn more about what was happening with the camps and within the Gaill ranks while figuring out my next move.

"You made it work," Kacey said as we approached, pointing to my scarf.

"You could say that." I laughed. "Thanks, by the way. I'll get it washed and back to you once all the bruising is gone."

"Don't even worry about it, Jac. Like I said, unless you start some new trend, the neck scarf had its day." She stuck her tongue out at me jokingly.

Smiling back, I turned to the group as we made our way up the staircase and out of the servant wing. "Thank you, guys, for bringing me meals yesterday too. If you hadn't, I probably wouldn't have remembered to eat, honestly."

"We didn't do that, Calderone. Technically not allowed to take food out of the dining hall, remember?" Killian lightly threw his arm over my shoulder as he grinned down at me and wiggled his brows. "But maybe you should ask your boyfriend."

I scoffed, shoving him away, which only caused him to laugh more.

The boys each hugged me, making sure I was really okay before we left them on the first floor and made our way up to the guest rooms where we'd been assigned for cleaning.

"All right, ladies, we have twelve rooms to get to this afternoon. I'll do the first six if you wanna divide up the last half?" Kacey said as we reached the top of the steps, her eyebrows raised in question. Whatever Dev powers Kacey had made her twice as fast as we were, so she usually took on more of the work.

"Sounds good," I answered at the same time Lana yawned her agreement, and we split up to clean our rooms.

I was halfway through my second room before I noticed that the sitting area had a perfect view of the gardens outside the library. Making my way over to the big floor-to-ceiling windows, I felt like I was floating, the room was so perfectly placed over the section with large hydrangeas and roses.

Looking out to the grove of oak trees in the distance and fields beyond, everything started to blur as my mind began to wander, not being able to keep myself from analyzing everything that had happened in the past few days.

My kingdom had a dark past. And potentially a darker present. One that was kept hidden from me, but one I had no doubt Father and his advisors were well aware of. My father would never assume the throne without knowing everything and anything about his country and the potential risks in being its king.

I still didn't believe my father was a true tyrant. His end goal was and would always be the betterment of his position and his power, but was he really capable of achieving that goal at the expense of his people's safety? I mean, our primary job as monarch was to protect our people.

What other secrets was he hiding? Were his soldiers—our soldiers—like Romano's too? An involuntary shudder went through my body recalling the other night. If I closed my eyes, I could swear I felt the cold of the corridor floor against my skin… the strain of the general's fingers as he gripped my throat.

Taking a deep breath, I focused my eyes on the horizon in an attempt to bring myself back to the present.

Would Father have treated a servant with as much kindness as Dax had me?

Dax.

My pulse quickened as I thought about his retaliation and what had happened after. I couldn't ignore that he did seem to be going out of his way to do things for me no matter how much I denied it to the Devs.

Saving me from Romano, letting me borrow that book, giving me time off to recuperate—he might not be the monster I grew up believing him to be. Which was further supported by the Devs' admission of their true goal to bring down King Aidoneus the other day in my room.

But he wouldn't have known *to save you from Romano had he not been following you*, I reminded myself, twisting my hair in my fingers. There were only a couple of reasons a royal had a person followed—either they wanted information or saw them as a threat.

No, he was probably a better man than I previously thought, but there were still questions. Ones that needed answers.

Just then the door closed, and the room became electric with a suffocating power. Goose bumps erupted across my skin as my hand paused midtwirl.

"You're back to work."

I turned slowly. Dax stood by the doors with his arms folded over the front of his black tunic, chin raised slightly, wavy hair undone like he'd been running his hands through it again and looking as breathtaking as ever.

His eyes, filled with concern, moved quickly as he looked me over, seemingly trying to figure out if I was okay. They came to rest on the scarf around my neck, and before I could move, he was towering over me, gently untying it.

Without thinking, I reached up and grabbed his hand, stilling him. We locked eyes, neither of us saying a word as his energy coursed through me, an electric current moving between us.

He already knew I was injured, so why did I care? Although the small cut on my cheek had all but healed, the bruises on my neck had dramatically worsened since leaving his room the other morning. And for some reason, his seeing the bruises made me feel more vulnerable. Broken.

I seriously could *not* be feeling this way around him.

"Jacqueline," Dax said, his voice a ragged whisper.

Empathy, compassion, and sorrow flitted across his gaze as his eyes moved between mine. I closed my eyes, feeling the last of my resolve melt away. I let go of his hand, and he lightly untied my scarf before stepping back.

When he didn't speak, I opened my eyes only to find his a shade so light they were almost the color of ice. It looked like a hurricane brewed beneath them.

If I thought the boys were furious at the evidence of Romano's hands on me, then I had no words to describe the look of pure murder etched across Dax's face, his only movement the slow clenching and unclenching of his jaw as he lifted his chin again.

And then he was back in front of me, not touching, just looking me deeply in the eyes, searching. From up close, I could see that his eyes were really the lightest shade of seafoam green with flecks of white and dark emerald throughout. They were shocking in their beauty. That power surged again from behind his gaze, but I didn't flinch as he lowered his face, bringing it level with mine.

"How much does it hurt?"

"Not too much." I shrugged and managed not to wince. "Only when I extend my neck, turn suddenly, lie down the wrong way, cough…" Trailing off, I closed my mouth, realizing I was only making things worse as his jaw locked again. "Your Highness is kind to check on me," I said finally, feeling extremely self-conscious again. His gaze unnerved me.

"Romano will pay for what he's done. I promise you." Dax straightened, anger and vengeance rippling through his tone.

"I know. I trust you," I replied, the words out before I could think twice as my eyes met his. I had no idea why I said it out loud, but the tightening in my gut made me realize that the feelings I had worked so hard to ignore persisted. I trusted him. And I wasn't sure if that made me an idiot or not.

Looking back at me, something passed across his face—sorrow and, maybe, guilt—before his gaze hardened, and he again crossed his arms over his chest.

"You shouldn't."

"Wh-what?" My mind as well as my speech sputtered. So I *was* an idiot.

But then I was angry. Irrationally angry. Angry at the whole situation, for being in this palace, for Romano, for being injured, for Dax's attention, and even more angry at myself for letting any of his attention get to me. For making me temporarily forget who he actually was, who *I* was.

How could I have been so stupid?

"And why shouldn't I trust you? Because you had me followed?" I stepped out of his immediate vicinity and matched his powerful gaze with one of my own. "Because technically I'm still your prisoner even though you claim to help refugees from Calderone? Or because some of the stories about you—the ones that gave me nightmares as a child—might actually be true?"

With this last sentence, he instantly stepped closer and lowered his face to mine again, his eyes practically electrifying the air around us as they focused on mine, silencing me.

"Because of all that, Jacqueline. And more."

His blinding gaze continued to burn into mine as I tried to feel fear at his words, at his show of power, at *him*. But all I felt was an intense pull in my gut telling me there was nothing—no one—in this room that I needed to fear.

As if to test that theory—or maybe thinking it would help me regain some of the control I'd lost over my life—I reached out and brushed away a stray curl that had fallen across his face. Even that little touch sent currents running through my body, settling low in my belly.

He turned his head slightly to look at my hand, so small in comparison to his, before his wide eyes turned back to meet mine again.

When he didn't do anything to stop me, harm me, or anything at all, I let a small smile slip. Pulling my hand away, I felt the electricity pull back with it.

"Whatever you say, Your Highness," I said, smiling bigger. I knew a victory when I spotted one, even if it was minor. Though I wasn't sure exactly why he told me not to trust him, I knew he wouldn't physically harm me. How I had known, I didn't want to think about—an emotional can of worms for a different time as was everything else in my life lately.

Scoffing and shaking his head, Dax straightened. But I saw through his farce. And he knew it. And we both knew he saw through mine straight to the mess in my head.

"You're done for the day, Miss Lewis."

"Your Highness?"

Dax didn't respond but turned on his heel to leave, his heavy black boots pounding the wooden floor as he strode for the door, instantly regaining the upper hand.

"The other maids will take over your duties." He turned back and ran a hand through his hair, his eyes tamer now, closer to their normal, bright jade green. "As with the rest of your shifts this week. You're still likely in shock from the attack. You need your rest. Your training starts Friday."

Before I could even digest what he said, he was walking out the door. "Oh, and feel free to use the library for the next few days should you need it," he said over his shoulder.

My jaw dropped, and I could have sworn I heard a chuckle as his footsteps receded down the hallway. Servants weren't allowed to use the library. So what was he playing at?

Scoffing to myself, I regained my composure and tied the scarf back around my neck.

Making my way out of the room with my rag and bottle, I picked over what he'd said in my head. I wasn't to trust him. I was to believe the stories I'd grown up hearing about him. And I knew he was capable of terrible things. But I also knew he could be kind. Hadn't he just proved that?

As I wandered down the hall, I nearly bumped into Kacey as she came out of her last room.

"Weirdest thing. Your boyfriend just stopped in my room and instructed me to help you finish your work for the day." She looked at me and raised a brow, her orange eyes shining with laughter.

"He would. And he's not my boyfriend." I scoffed, rolling my eyes. "Apparently he wants me to get healthy sooner so I can train."

"Like train as in learn to fight?" Kacey looked at me with an emotion I couldn't quite place.

I nodded. "That or just to defend myself in case Romano gets any more ideas."

"Ha, fat chance of that happening."

I raised my brows at her in question.

"Dax pretty much sent out a message that if anyone so much as breathes at you the wrong way, he'll string them up like he did to the soldiers who attacked you."

"String them up, what are you talking about? He snapped their necks, and the third he…"—the vision of the man with blood dripping out of his mouth flashed across my mind—"they weren't strung up."

"Well, their bodies are hanging outside the outer ward, near the prison wing. A decaying reminder for everyone else not to go near you." She closed her eyes as if the thought of the bodies nauseated her.

I opened my mouth, but I wasn't sure what to say. It was one thing for Dax to punish them, another to make such a public display of it.

"I don't even know what to say to that," I said finally, bringing my eyes back to her and finding hers just as unreadable as before. "He just told me not to trust him, then goes and does something like that? Why the games?"

"I have no idea, Jac." Kacey reached for my hand and gave it a small squeeze as she shook her head. "But like I said, Dax doesn't play games. And he's never done something like that before. Not for a servant, not for anyone." The orange glow behind her eyes pulsed then as she scanned me from head to toe, a look crossing her gaze.

Before she could say more, a guard appeared at the end of the hall and walked purposely for us.

I instinctively moved closer to Kacey. It wasn't until the guard was a few feet away that I felt her and saw the symbol on her uniform—a Celtic cross above her left breast rather than the slim crescent that designated all other Gaill soldiers.

A member of Dax's guard. And definitely Deviant.

"Good afternoon, Miss Lewis. I'm to escort you back to your room."

"Can't trust the guy. Right." Kacey snorted under her breath, nudging me forward gently.

Narrowing my eyes at her as she laughed, I started walking, turning to ask the guard her name as we made our way down the hall.

"Captain O'Leary, Miss."

"Captain?"

"Yes, Miss. I oversee His Royal Highness's personal guard." Captain O'Leary smiled down at me as we walked.

I simply smiled and nodded. Why were Dax's words telling me one thing but his actions another?

My small room became both my safe haven and personal prison. Dax had been right—the aftershocks of the attack wore off over the course of the following days, and all the feelings I'd tried so hard to avoid came back full force. They crept in slowly at first, but pretty soon shame as well as anger had taken up permanent residence in my bones.

The indignity with which Romano and his men had treated me, the guilt over what my country was potentially doing without my knowledge, and my rage at it all overwhelmed me. I felt cheated. And I wasn't sure what stoked the flames of my wrath more—Romano's clear violation or that of my father and his administration. Romano owed me no loyalties. But it was clear that my father had lied to me. Although I didn't know to what extent, my gut told me it was about something that could potentially put the safety of our citizens in jeopardy.

Even if it turned out that my father and the Calderonian government were corrupt beyond repair, I would never forsake my people. Not when they were innocent. To them, I would always remain loyal.

By Thursday, three days later, I had managed to gain a semblance of control over my emotions. My anger and shame were useless unless I took action—I needed to get answers and get home to start fixing things.

And the first place to go for information, where I knew no one could shrug off my questions, was the library.

For that reason, I found myself rushing through the back hallways of the palace around 0900 that morning. Rounding the corner into the library, I realized it was empty and breathed a sigh of relief. I let the scent of old books fill my lungs before setting off for history rooms.

I headed for the section where I'd found *The Eclipse* and browsed the other titles. It took me a bit, but I finally found a promising one: *A History of the Monarchies, Volume I, Years 2060-2160.* I reached for it but paused as the voices of two men drew near. My breathing stuttered as my heart took off at a gallop. If Romano were to find me here…

Two courtiers had entered the library and were talking animatedly to one another. I slunk to the corner where they were least likely to see me and watched as they continued on their way through the armchairs and bookshelves in the main room, then headed for the doors to the gardens.

An audible sigh escaped me as they exited, and silence once again descended on the library. Breathing deeply, I willed my heart to quiet now that the danger of being caught was momentarily over. I needed to grab the book quickly and go back to my rooms. But then I realized that I hadn't worn an apron or anything to hide the book in.

Dammit, Jacqueline.

Dax had given me permission to use the libraries of course, but I wasn't sure how widely known that was. And I had a feeling his version of using the library was to read fiction like he caught me doing the first time, not books that held highly sensitive information.

My body and heart wavered. Kacey had said knowledge wasn't kept for the few here, but did everyone think that way? Did that include servants? *Macbeth* was pretty harmless, but if someone like Romano caught me smuggling a history book back to my room, it would surely arouse suspicion. Especially since he made it blatantly clear servants were supposed to know their place and not question anything.

I felt pulled to the book by an almost supernatural force. I was sure it contained some of the knowledge about the camps I needed. But I also couldn't risk being caught with it. I'd have to come back for it.

The tang of regret was bitter in my mouth as I began making my way out of the library only to be distracted, again, by a different shelf in the Victorian fiction room I passed.

Rows and rows of dark books with golden detailing drew me like a siren's call. If there was any type of fiction I loved more than Shakespeare, it was a good Victorian love story. And those were pretty harmless, right? Dax had given me permission to be here, and a romance novel seemed like a safe option to read. I deserved a break from the real world, if only for a few minutes.

My hands glided along the bindings before I paused over *Jane Eyre*. Retrieving it, I immediately plopped down on the nearest oversized chair. It was overstuffed, so I easily got comfortable as I curled up, burrowing myself into the arm as I flipped through to Jane's arrival at Thornfield. If I ever needed an escape, a Brontë novel never disappointed. And Mr. Rochester and Jane's story was one of my very favorites.

I was so engrossed I didn't notice the passing of the morning light on the light cedar floors. Yawning and stretching, I focused my eyes on the grandfather clock stationed close to the entrance of the Victorian section.

1100. I still had more than an hour to read before lunch.

Smiling to myself, I tossed my waves up into a bun, knotting it around itself, and settled back in the chair. I had just found my page when I felt him over my shoulder.

"Reading again, Jacqueline?"

I turned, another smile spreading across my face as I met his playful gaze.

He was in a good mood, like he was trying to erase any remaining tension from our run-in the other day.

"How observant of you, Your Highness." I couldn't deny that I liked our banter even though I knew I shouldn't.

Before I could blink, Dax reached forward and grabbed the book from my hands.

"Victorian this time and Brontë at that? I would've taken you for more of an Austen girl." He looked at me, raising a brow. "Isn't Mr. Darcy every woman's dream man?"

"You mean pass up the brooding Mr. Rochester? I would never." I grabbed the book back and held it to my chest in mock offense.

"Ah, yes. Who could forget such a hero? One who effectively locked away his first wife and then chased another."

"That is not how it goes… exactly." I rolled my eyes at him.

Biting his lip and smiling, he only raised his brows. "You ready for tomorrow?"

"How exactly should I get ready?" I stood and placed the book on the chair as I walked around the back to meet him.

"I've had a few things dropped at your room while you were out. We'll start easy, just small defensive techniques."

"We'll?"

"Yes, you and I, Jacqueline." His jade-green eyes shone brightly at me as a small tug of electricity pulsed between us. How did his eyes change colors like that? How did someone get the kind of power to do *that* to their body?

Dax cleared his throat, and I took a quick breath, suddenly remembering myself.

"Your Highness, that is extremely kind of you to offer, but I..." I looked down, not wanting his gaze to shake my resolve. Spending more time with him, letting whatever *this* was progress, it couldn't happen. Not to mention his mere presence distracted me from asking the important questions—like how he'd known I was here.

"But nothing, Jacqueline. I am your prince. Accept my offer if for no other reason than it's an order."

Mouth falling open, I looked back at him only to realize he was being sarcastic. Scoffing, I playfully shoved him before I thought better of it.

It didn't matter though because he caught my hand before it so much as left his shoulder. Licking his lips, he kept my hand in his. His green eyes still sparkled, but something commanding lay behind them as he let our hands part.

Remembering my supposed place, I loosed a small laugh. "Of course, Your Highness."

At that, Dax took the opportunity to give me a closer look, tracing over the marks fading across my neck and cheek with his eyes before returning them to meet mine, a hardness now reflected in their emerald depths.

"So you're feeling better?"

"Yes, Your Highness. Better. Thank you. But... I had a question." Actually, I had millions of them, but we'd start with one for now and see what he was willing to answer.

Dax's expression remained unchanged though his eyes pulsed with that white glow again before settling back to their usual color.

"I heard about the men you strung up outside the outer ward. Why did you do that?"

A muscle twitched in his jaw, but his face remained as impassive as a stone wall. "Reasons, Jacqueline."

The anger that had lain dormant since I entered the library reignited as he gave me the same infuriatingly vague answer as before. "And what *are* those reasons, Your Highness?"

Dax sighed, looking up at the ceiling in apparent exacerbation before meeting my gaze again. "I'm skilled at controlling my temper until someone pushes me too far."

My heart rate raced at the thought that *I* had pushed him too far. I instantly shrank into the back of the armchair.

A flicker of something crossed his countenance before he continued. "I couldn't stand for the insubordination of those men. Not only did their corpses deserve no better than to be eaten by vultures, but others needed to know that defying my orders would not go unpunished."

His words were macabre—barbaric—but somehow the lethality with which he spoke only drew me to him more.

There was something wrong with me.

"Your orders to… stay away from me?"

He nodded slowly, his eyes never leaving mine.

His answer only provoked more questions. He was showing his loyalty to me, of that I was certain. What I wasn't sure of was why he said I shouldn't trust him. The countless conspiracies I'd come up with in the past few days came rushing back.

What if his attention, all of this, was really a ruse to get me to open up? Share who I was or some other secret they thought I held? But my gut again had me instantly forgetting that theory.

He didn't play games, right? Then why did this feel so much like an emotional whiplash?

Ugh, I'm a mess.

That questioning look of his once again appeared, but he didn't ask anything. "You look much better, and I'm pleased to see you down here." He motioned around the library.

"Why are you here?" The words left my mouth before I could stop them.

The emerald of his eyes danced as he slowly cracked an arrogant smile. Running his hand through his loose curls, he lowered his face to mine for a second before reaching around me and the back of the chair to grab *Jane Eyre* from where it sat. The power rippled from his body in palpable waves as he came within an inch of touching me, not breaking eye contact the whole time.

Dax handed me the novel, and the scent of pine and ocean air washed over me.

"Servants will be walking to the dining hall for lunch soon. You'll probably want to drop that in your room beforehand." He smirked down at me.

I glanced at the book in my hands, and when I looked up to ask why he was giving me another gift, the room was already empty.

Biting my lip, I tucked a stray hair that'd fallen from my bun behind my ear. I'd smiled more in the past twenty minutes than I had in days. And Dax had been the one to make me do it.

I made my way back to my room to hide Dax's latest gift while ignoring the small voice in the back of my mind that told me I was teetering on the edge of something that looked very akin to treason.

My morning alarm came far too early. I'd returned from the library to find a pile of fighting gear and a note to be ready for training by 0500 sharp.

Dragging myself out of bed and wandering over to the mirror, my bloodshot eyes stared back as I once again wondered what the hell I was doing. Training with the enemy was most certainly a bad idea.

But did I really have a choice? After all, I was a prisoner—servant at best. If Dax said jump, I jumped. Jacqueline the princess would question; Jacqueline the prisoner could not.

Shaking my head as I began to brush my teeth, I knew I could tell myself I didn't have a say in what happened to me here all I wanted, but that wasn't the case. Not anymore. And that was perhaps the most concerning fact of all.

Things were starting to shift, and I was on perilous ground.

I washed my face, then weaved my dark waves into a side braid and pulled the clothes on—a pair of black leggings, long-sleeved black tee with loopholes for my thumbs, black combat boots that somehow fit me perfectly, and lastly, a dirk that I strung through a holder around my waist.

I looked like a soldier. A Gaill soldier.

Just then, a knock sounded. I gave myself another once-over in the mirror, tucking in my pearl necklace as I opened the door.

"Ready, Miss Lewis?"

"Yes, thank you, Captain O'Leary."

We made our way to the training center in silence. I breathed a sigh of relief as we ascended the stairs to the upper levels of the south wing. I wouldn't have to train in the lower military levels, which I hadn't been in since the night of the attack.

O'Leary paused next to a set of double doors, letting a panel to the right read her eyes before going through. I recognized the Celtic insignia above the door, signifying Dax's apartments. Should've figured he'd have his own private training center.

Moving through another set of doors at the end of the corridor, we entered a large room with equipment and hundreds of weapons lining the walls. Swords, guns, machetes, tomahawks, grenades—I couldn't tell what most of them were. There was a ring in the middle set up for fighting, but it was Dax in the far corner, working on a punching bag, that caught my attention.

His shirt was off, curls back in a messy bun as he worked through a series of moves. His skin was slick with sweat, the tattoos covering his upper body glistening under the fluorescent lights.

He turned and grabbed the bag to steady it with one hand, wiping away the sweat from his brow with the other. Tipping his chin in thanks and dismissal to O'Leary, he stalked toward me as O'Leary turned on her heel and left the way we came.

Dax's muscles strained under his skin as he moved, broad shoulders swaying and tapering into an impossibly toned chest—a warrior's body chiseled after many years of training and battles. He was even more built than he looked with his signature black tunic on. But it wasn't only his body that I noticed; it was the ink tattooed across it. Swirling Celtic knots and Gaillic symbols were etched across his body like a map, covering everything except his face and making his already-tan skin appear even darker.

Having only a limited knowledge of Celtic culture, I didn't know what most of the knots meant. Except the cross, same as the one on the sword he sometimes wore, which was inked clear as day above his heart.

Looking up to him as he neared, I found his eyes raking me over, a look of approval on his face.

"The clothes suit you. If I didn't know any better, I'd say you were born a Gaill," he said, his signature smirk appearing.

"Let's not get too carried away."

Ignoring my response, he grabbed a towel to wipe himself off. Picking up his shirt, a more fitted version of his usual tunic, from where it was strung over the ropes lining the fighting ring, he shrugged it on before he walked through our plans for the day.

"We'll go over basic self-defense techniques to start. Am I correct in thinking you've never had any sort of instruction on this before?"

I nodded my head. As much as I probably should've, physical training wasn't one of the lessons I was granted as heir. At least not as the *female* heir as it was always implied I'd have a man or some other security around to protect me should the need arise. Not that Mother would've gone for it anyway. She could barely stand my reading, so any physical activity beyond dance lessons for the past decade had definitely been out of the question.

"I'll start easy, no weapons or anything. If it gets to be too much or you just need a break, you let me know, okay?" He inclined his head slightly.

I nodded. "But are you sure you should be the one training me? You must have more pressing matters to attend to." Being in close contact with him would only serve to make us more familiar with one another. Which couldn't happen. I was the future queen of the kingdom he wanted to destroy.

This couldn't happen.

"I have trust issues, Jacqueline." He said gruffly. "I'll be the one doing the training." And with that he moved around me so we could begin.

We spent the first hour going over ways to immobilize my attacker from the front. Dax stood a few feet in front of me, and I had a feeling he was putting a damper on his power so that I could concentrate.

It took me a bit, but toward the end I was able to keep both my feet solidly planted in a staggered position while either throwing an elbow or punching up with the heel of my hand to theoretically break my attacker's nose or damage their throat. After I'd practiced so much my arm felt like it was about to fall off, he finally seemed satisfied.

"All right. We'll move on to some other forms of attack." He moved behind me then, and I stiffened, instinctively on high alert. "Is it okay if I put my arms around you?"

I nodded, relaxing at the softness in his tone.

He wrapped his arms around me from behind, and an electric warmth engulfed me. I seemed to mold into his body like a puzzle piece as he pulled me close, hugging my arms and small frame to him. Even though his power wasn't as intense, I still felt that same magnetic current pulsing from him through to me.

Was this normal—this magnetism? Was it a Deviant thing?

"All right, this is a bear-hug attack. One where your attacker has immobilized you from behind." He cleared his throat slightly, the sweet scent of pine, ocean air, and sweat swimming around me. "Your instinct will be to lean back, but you mustn't do that; it'll only give your attacker more power. Lean forward, as low as you can go, destabilizing your attacker. This will give you leverage to throw an elbow or two in order to escape."

Leaning forward, I felt his body shift as his shoulders encircled mine.

"Okay. Now turn in to me and throw an elbow or two."

And I did exactly that, only moving proved to be much more difficult than I would've thought. I couldn't even turn.

"Try harder, Jacqueline. Breathe, relax, control your body. I'm attacking you, and your life depends on your escape" came Dax's low command.

Letting out a very unladylike grunt on an exhale, I threw more momentum behind my move, envisioning Romano as I channeled all my rage, twisting and throwing an elbow into Dax's side, causing him to jerk back slightly.

He let go of me then, a small smile playing at his lips as he rubbed the area I just hit. "Better."

"Hopefully I didn't do too much damage." I smiled back, slightly proud of myself.

"I think I'll live." He chuckled.

"Do you really think I can do this? Learn to defend myself?" The questions rushed from me before I snapped my mouth shut. It was obvious I was vulnerable, but I didn't need to point that out. Especially to the Gaill prince.

Dax's brows crashed together. "Of course you can. You've already survived so much by being here. Learning to defend yourself is as much about physical strength as it is about mental fortitude."

His answer sent shock waves through me. *Was that a compliment?*

Dax glanced at the clock on the wall. "It's almost seven. Let's call it a day. I'll have O'Leary escort you back to your room. Breakfast will be waiting. Rest today, Jacqueline." He fixed me with a look like he knew I would argue otherwise. "You still need time to recover. You can resume your work Monday after we get in an hour of training in the morning. From now on, you'll train four days a week, continuing with the basics next week and moving on to weaponry after that."

My eyes widened. *Weaponry?*

Coming in close, Dax's eyes locked on to mine, and of course I was powerless to look away. "You need to master the basic skills with and without weapons. I won't always be around to protect you,

Jacqueline. It's imperative you learn to protect yourself."

Nodding slowly in stunned agreement, I looked to the right to find Captain O'Leary waiting to escort me back. I turned to Dax, but he was already retaping his hands and moving back toward the punching bag.

Having no choice, I turned to follow O'Leary out, wondering if one of the people Dax wanted to protect me from was himself.

CHAPTER 9

A DECISION

The following week passed in a blur. Between training, getting back to work, and peppering the Devs with questions while trying to appear like I wasn't fishing for too much information, I was exhausted, asleep before my head hit the pillow most nights. By the time the weekend came around, I was more than ready for our day off.

Dax was there every morning even if he himself wasn't the one instructing me. On the mornings he had to step out, Captain O'Leary took over.

I told myself it didn't matter who was training me—I was there to fulfill Dax's order and maintain an image so that it'd be easier for me to escape. And if I learned a thing or two along the way, I wouldn't be the worse for it. But I'd be lying if I said I didn't look forward to mornings when Dax took over. Something between us just felt easy, natural.

Even thinking that felt like the worst type of treason.

Laying my head on the table during lunch Saturday, I was almost asleep when Lana set her tray down and put a coffee in front of me.

"I could kiss you right now." I gripped the warm drink, letting the aroma flood my senses and bring me back to life.

"Killian talked the kitchen staff into making some for us. Gonna need our strength for tonight." She winked and pulled her hair back into a low bun as she sat down to eat.

Tonight was the Full Moon Festival. So much had happened in the four weeks since the last one, it was hard to believe it had almost been a month. I was still sourcing information about Calderone and had postponed my escape until next month's Full Moon. Any hope of leaving flew out the window when Kacey mentioned that not only were openings guarded at all times, but the outer ward itself was protected by some sort of Deviant power to keep everyone safe inside and random intruders out.

It dawned on me that even if I had managed to go the right way through the service door, I would've triggered the protective wards anyway.

It seemed I was back at square one. I was at a loss at how to leave. But that was a worry for another day. Because I needed a night to let loose and forget everything.

I deserve it, I reasoned.

Drinking from the steaming liquid, not caring that it was black as tar and burned my throat, I looked to the Devs who were just sitting down. "So what's the plan for tonight?"

"Well, we're meeting in the grove at eight. Sun sets a bit before nine, and then the real fun begins." A mischievous grin appeared on Killian's face as his hazel-brown eyes cut to the other boys.

"Are we making the same drinks as last time?" Lana took a sip of her coffee before picking up her sandwich.

"Yes, and actually," Kacey said, holding her fist and fork to her mouth to finish chewing before she continued, "Jac, you can pick up the bottle from Scarletti's, right? She's still gone, so no one will be around."

"For sure," I said. I'd agreed to grab the liquor this time. It had come to light in the past six weeks that Scarletti was the source for the group. Whether she was aware of this or not wasn't entirely clear.

Typically the palace provided beer and wine for the festival—a gesture of good faith to the Devs. But if we wanted something stronger, it was up to us to bring it. And since Scarletti had been gone since the previous weekend, I had little risk of getting caught.

The group had tried to convince me not to do it; everyone worried after what happened with Romano. But they also knew Romano never came to the servant wing, as he made pretty clear to Lana and me that first day. So the real risk was relatively low. And plus, I was the only one left to actually sneak something out, and I refused to be treated differently because of what happened. I was the future queen of Calderone.

Even if no one here knew that.

"Perfect." Kacey smiled, putting another forkful of pasta in her mouth.

"Yeah, it should be a fun time assuming Tynan doesn't try anything again." Killian grunted, tossing his head slightly to move his hair out of his eyes.

"I swear if you three take another bet or start something, we will leave." Kacey's fiery orange eyes glared at each of the boys in turn.

Axel raised his hands in surrender. "Hey now, that was all Kil's doing the last time. But really, who bets on how far you can throw the kegs? Amateurs." He snorted into his drink, which caused all the boys to snicker.

"The boy was wasted, had to put him in his place." Killian grinned, causing Kacey to roll her eyes.

For as old as the Devs were, their playful sides reminded me so much of the boys Phin hung around with back home. The thought crossed my mind before I could even process it, leaving me with a sudden pang of guilt, which I promptly buried.

The rest of the afternoon and early evening passed quickly enough, and the coffee at lunch seemed to help me wake up at least a bit. Before I knew it, I was back in my room pulling a fresh weekend dress from my wardrobe.

I combed through my waves, which had become much more pronounced having been braided most of the day, and caught sight of my black pearl necklace, clearly visible with the V-neck of the weekend dress. Should I take it off? Dax had already seen it, hadn't he? Who else would care if he didn't? Plus Scarletti was gone, and I hadn't actually seen Pepridge all day.

Deciding to leave it on, I glanced at the clock, and my heart started to race as I realized it was already half past seven. I had to leave now if I was going to make it down to Scarletti's office where she kept the alcohol and out to the oak grove behind the gardens by eight.

Grabbing a satchel Kacey had lent me for the night and stowing away the fake liquor bottle full of water—apparently Deviants used the same tactics for tricking authority that we did in Calderone—I left my room and made my way to Scarletti's office.

Everything was eerily quiet as I moved through the lower levels of the servant wing, most servants either in their rooms or already at the festival if they were a Deviant. Stopping in front of Scarletti's door, I picked the lock as quickly as I could, worrying the entire time someone would catch me. Her office wasn't exactly in a discreet location, off the open corridor that ran next to the storeroom hallway.

But no one passed by, and soon the door swung open into a pitch-black room. Resisting the urge to shudder, I fumbled for the light switch, flicking it on to find a small wood-paneled office, lined with books and journals. There was a modest desk centered along the back wall behind which were two barred windows facing the woods outside. There was a tall-backed chair in front of the desk as well as an overstuffed armchair off to the side, piled with more books.

Spotting the liquor cabinet in a corner behind the desk, I closed the door behind me and made my way to it, making sure to avoid the stepping stool left by the desk, which was no doubt how Scarletti's stout frame reached the topmost books. I picked the lock and found several bottles of liquor, cigars… and a gun.

I looked through the bottles to find the clear one with a red VODKA label and grabbed it, replacing it with the dummy bottle I brought. The stolen bottle was thin, so luckily it wasn't as obvious after tucking it into the satchel.

I closed the cabinet and relocked it, then peeked out into the corridor to make sure it was clear before making my way out of the kitchen hallways.

I didn't want to think about what Romano or any of his men would do if they caught me. Dax had given the order to stay away, and they had. So far. But I didn't want to risk a confrontation, so I pressed the satchel to me and quickly moved through the darkened servant wing, up the back staircase to the main section of the palace.

I only had to make it across a short hall to get to the exit nearest the gardens and grove. From there, I could run through the gardens if I had to and quickly be within sight of the Devs.

My heart raced as I crossed the open foyer, the soft thud of my black boots on the marble stones the only sound save my breath, now coming in shorter and shorter bursts the nearer I got to the doors. As I reached out to push the glass-paneled door open, a throat cleared behind me. My heart felt like it was in my throat, threatening to choke me as I turned slowly, practically frozen in fear.

Dax.

Leaning back with his ink-covered arms folded across his chest and that typical smirk on his face, he eyed the satchel before moving his gaze back to me.

"Going somewhere?"

Stammering, I tried to piece together a coherent thought as my mind raced to catch up with the fact that I wasn't in imminent danger.

Why didn't I feel him? Is he putting a damper on everything again?

"I, uhm… I'm just heading to the grove for Full Moon. The Devs, you know…" I nervously pulled the satchel closer before his face broke out into a knowing smile.

Walking up to me, his jade eyes were full of amusement as he slowly pried my hands away from the satchel so he could look inside.

"Hmm. Scarletti's?" He looked down at me through his dark curls, eyebrows raised.

Not knowing what to say, I just nodded. He didn't exactly seem angry, or surprised, that I was stealing from his housekeeper.

"They never change, do they?" He shook his head, smiling slightly before taking the satchel from over my shoulder—so fast I didn't even feel it—and tucking it under his arm. It was far too small to fit him as it normally should.

"Come." He pulled in his bottom lip and motioned with his head to follow him out toward the gardens… and the grove.

I had no choice but to follow him. I just hoped he wouldn't make a huge deal about everything once we reached the group.

Daylight was fading as we made our way through the rose garden, the slanting rays of the sun casting a magical golden hue on everything. The flowers were now in full bloom, and the sweet scent that surrounded us as we moved along the path temporarily dulled my anxiety. The light took that moment to bounce off the amber in Dax's curls, making them shine even more than usual.

No.

No, Jacqueline.

You don't care what his hair looks like.

Blinking hard, I instead focused my attention on the sword he sometimes carried, strapped across his back. It was even bigger up close. I'd never noticed the intricate engravings on the blade and hilt until now either. Of course the large Celtic cross that made up the hilt, identical to the one tattooed on his chest, was unmistakable. But there were smaller crosses and symbols carved into the entire sword. I had no idea where he'd been before, but for some reason I didn't think he'd been planning to intercept me.

As we neared the grove of large oak trees, I drew in a quick breath at the sight. Everything looked so magical.

Hundreds of floating lights added to the glow from the setting sun. And there was an assortment of random tables from the servant wing, along with various overstuffed leather chairs and antique couches scattered throughout the small clearing between the trees, which themselves cast a rich green tone over the whole crowd below.

Tables of food lined the opposite side of the clearing from where we approached, and a stack of dented kegs—presumably the ones the boys had thrown—sat at the end of one of the tables. Music was playing softly, but I couldn't tell from where. A makeshift dance floor had been created near the food and drink area, but no one was dancing right now, the night having just begun. Everything looked so peaceful, and everyone seemed so happy it made me smile involuntarily. It was beautiful.

I caught site of the Devs, *my Devs*, and the obvious looks of shock on their faces as they caught site of Dax holding the satchel.

"'Bout time you showed up!" Killian recovered first, walking up to *Dax* and clapping him on the shoulder as we reached the group. "We were about to think you forgot you were one of us."

Dax cracked a smile at him—a genuine, true smile—before playfully punching him in the ribs. "How could I forget, brother? You wouldn't be who you are without me." Which only earned him a chorus of jeers from the boys.

Brother?

Kacey walked up with a drink and a plate of food in her hands. She only looked between Dax and me, then turned to sit down, smiling and shaking her head of strawberry blond hair.

Okay, what's happening here?

I could tell Lana was just as out of the loop as I was. I couldn't make sense of why the group almost expected Dax to be there. My mind, naturally, went into overdrive imagining the worst-case scenarios.

Because what if this *was* all a game? What if Dax and the Devs *had* plotted something? And I'd fallen for their trap.

Why else would they know each other so well? It had to be bad, right? They were all Gaill, so it was bad. I mean, if nothing else, they had lied by omission, right?

Right?

Snatching the satchel from the random chair where Dax had put it, I held it out as leverage, knowing full well how ridiculous I was acting and how nonsensical my line of thinking was. I didn't even make sense to myself. But I was so tired of the games and holding in all my emotions, I couldn't think straight if I tried.

"Okay, tell me what the hell is going on here." I willed my voice not to break or show the emotion and feelings of betrayal beneath it as the Devs looked at me in blatant shock.

My mind raced as Kacey walked up, compassion in her eyes.

"Chill, Jac. It's not what you're thinking."

"And what am I thinking?" I spit back, my emotions raw despite my trying to hide them.

"That... I don't know." She gave a shrug. "Obviously something bad! But you know who *we are*. You know we wouldn't do anything to either you or Lan. Believe this."

I looked behind her to see Killian walking toward Lana, who was looking at Kacey like she wanted to believe her words, badly.

My eyes wandered over to Ax and Mav who were looking reassuringly at me, and then to Dax, who had his bright green eyes glued to mine.

Dragging my eyes back to Kacey, I swallowed. Why shouldn't I believe them? So far, they'd treated me with unfailing kindness. And besides Max, Miranda, and Rachel, they were the only people in my life who hadn't lied or betrayed me in some way. And I'd known them almost six weeks. My own parents could barely go an hour without lying or belittling me to my face.

But they were Gaill. What was I to them? They could have anything planned. And hadn't Dax *told* me not to trust him?

Sucking in my lower lip, I tried to keep the tears at bay as the emotional toll of the past few weeks hit me full force. Maybe it was the happy atmosphere surrounding us, the fact that my two Gaill worlds were colliding, or that I myself was falling apart from the inside out, but suddenly I could barely breathe. The pressure on my chest was so severe, I felt it caving in.

I knew I could trust them—even after Dax's remark, I knew in my gut I could. And I knew I was bordering on irrational. But the magnitude of what it meant to trust them—to trust the people I spent the first eighteen years of my existence thinking were my enemies, to trust *Dax*—made me physically sick. Because how could people like this—this good, this kind, this funny—want to destroy my home? How could I sit here and effectively let them? What was I doing?

I felt powerless as my breathing quickened and the ache in my chest worsened. Panic was setting in. But before I could take another ragged breath, I was fifty feet away, next to a darker section of the grove not illuminated by the lights.

The wind was stronger here, blowing my hair off my shoulders and out of my face behind my back. Cold ocean air and pine filled my senses at the same time that Dax tipped my chin up with his knuckle, forcing me to meet his gaze. His eyes were bright as they searched mine.

He was so close I could feel his electricity coursing through his fingers, warming my skin.

"Jacqueline."

At the sound of my name, an involuntary tear escaped the corner of my eye, falling down my cheek. I reached up to wipe it away, but Dax was quicker, gently swiping it with his thumb before looking back at me.

"Kacey is right. It isn't what it looks like." He waited for me to look at him again before continuing. "I haven't been to one of these, or spent time with any of these Deviants in fifteen years. We haven't even talked; we're just old friends."

"But they're fighting for you," I blurted out before I could stop myself. "Or at least they plan to," I finished, quieter.

At that, he pulled in his lips and nodded, removing his hand to rub it along his jaw, seeming to understand that I'd been filled in on the true state of the Gaill court.

"It takes years to forge the type of alliances we need for the Coalition. I couldn't risk exposing our actual purpose by associating with the Deviants here. That's why they work as servants—to throw my father off. They know I'm loyal to them. I've proven that over decades."

I nodded slowly, understanding his reasoning. "But you're back here now."

Tucking a stray curl behind his ear, he smirked down at me. "That's right."

"Aren't you concerned this is dangerous? Being here?"

"Things change." He gave me a noncommittal shrug in return. "Worried about me, Jacqueline?"

Putting my hands on my hips, I quirked a brow in response. His arrogance instantly made me remember myself.

Sighing, I patted him on the chest, forcing myself to ignore the wall of muscle my hand collided with, and made my way around him. "Don't be silly. You've been around for decades. I'm sure you can take care of yourself."

"Don't know about that. I might need some help." He turned, whispering in my ear as I passed and causing an instant tug of electricity between us.

Whipping around, my gaze met his, a smile once again on his lips as he tipped his head back, waiting for my response.

"Okay, old man. I'll grab your cane." I smiled smugly before turning and starting to walk the fifty feet or so back to the others.

Seconds later, a wind whipped past me before Dax appeared again with the group, leaving only a faint chuckle in his wake.

Sighing, I trudged on. This being-only-a-human thing was getting *really* old.

Reaching the group, I beelined it for the bottle I stole from Scarletti now sitting open on a nearby table and immediately took a swig. The liquor burned my throat at the same time it dulled my senses. Just what I needed to temporarily forget the past few weeks and the totally screwed-up situation I'd landed myself in.

"Ooooo Calderooonee!" Killian shouted, dragging out my nickname, causing Lana and Kacey to giggle into their drinks, the tension from earlier forgotten. Laughing, I could only shake my head as I made my way over to where the rest of them were standing.

"We knew you'd fit in at Full Moon." Axel threw his arm around me, messing up my hair with his hand and causing it to become a tousled mess of waves and curls.

"Gee, thanks Ax," I replied sarcastically, playfully shoving him away. He stuck his tongue out at me before he moved back to chatting up his latest crush: Sean, the stable master.

I shook my hair back to repin the top layers, feeling the pull of Dax's gaze on me the entire time. He inclined his head, so I made my way over to where he sat on the arm of a nearby chair and handed him the bottle without saying anything. He held up a flask instead, silently toasting me and taking a pull. Before I could even take mine, he handed me the flask, removing the cheaper vodka from my hands and setting it on the end table nearest him. I could tell it was whiskey from the smell alone. *Really* good whiskey. And putting it to my lips, I took a small drink.

The dark liquor didn't burn quite as much going down, and the taste briefly reminded me of home—in a good way, like nostalgia. Licking my lips, I handed the flask back to him.

Grabbing it, he watched me as he ran a hand through his loose curls, sending a wave of pine and cold sea air over me again.

Great.

Biting my lip, I looked down and scuffed my shoe on the grass in an attempt to distract myself.

"Don't do that."

His eyes were on my lips, and his mouth twitched at the corners into a crooked smile. I'm pretty sure my insides melted at that moment.

"Oh, Daxinius Da Luca." I sighed, shaking my head.

"Daxinius?" His bright green eyes slid back to mine, brows raised.

"Oh, I—"

"Dax, brother, you gotta see what Axel can do with his eyes now," Killian called out from across the open circle before turning back to the others.

Dax stood and looked down at me through his curls, unworried.

"Nothing." He shrugged. "I like it when you say it."

Still smiling, he jogged passed me to the group, leaving me in an utter state of shock.

Did the Gaill prince really just tell me he liked it when I said his name?

Lana sidled up to me then, nudging me slightly. "So you two came together or…?"

"No," I said quickly, turning to her and cutting a quick glance over to see Dax watching Axel but only partially. Anyone looking couldn't miss his occasional glances in our direction. "He stopped me as I was walking out the door to the gardens. He does have me followed, remember?" I scoffed, but it came off sounding more like a lighthearted laugh.

"How could I forget?" She laughed herself, absentmindedly twirling one of her blond curls with her fingers. "If it's any consolation, I really don't think the group had any idea he was going to show up tonight. From what Killian and the others were saying, it sounds like they haven't talked to him in years. And I can't think of why they'd all be plotting against us."

Thinking back to their reaction, the shock on their faces, and Dax's own story, I had to admit she was probably right. It was easy to trust them no matter how hard I tried not to, no matter what crazy excuses I dredged up.

"I can't deny I feel at home here," Lana continued, seeming to read my thoughts. "But I also can't deny that I wish you had escaped." She turned to me. "At least one of us, so we could warn people back home about the war to come."

"I know, me too." I took in her worried expression before pulling her in for a hug. A thought dawned on me. "Lana, back home, how were things really? Did you live comfortably like we do here or was it… worse?" I moved back to look at her. She might very well be more comfortable here in our enemy's kingdom than my own.

Her eyes filled with pity, and I had a feeling it was for the truth she was about to bestow on me rather than for her situation. But before she could speak, Mav walked past to grab the vodka from where it sat on the table.

"Might wanna check on Kil, Lana. He's about to bet his power against Dax's, and we all know that's not gonna end well."

Sure enough, I glanced over to find a playful Killian in Dax's face and an unmovable Dax, arms folded, shaking his head back at Kil. For how built Kil was, even he looked somewhat small compared to Dax. Though the tattoos covering their bodies made them both pretty imposing either way you swung it.

Shaking her blond curls and sighing, Lana turned back to me, grabbing my arm. "We'll talk more later, 'kay?"

"Sure, Lan." I put my hand over hers while we walked back to the group.

As we neared, Killian suddenly sped away from Dax, in a move so fast he was just a blur of black shadows until he reached a large oak tree on the edge of the grove. He was hardly visible given the sun had set, and the strings of light only brightened the area we were in.

But it didn't really matter because within a second he had ripped the entire tree from the ground, spun it around and launched it, javelin-style, into the distant fields. A few seconds later, I felt a rumble beneath my feet as it connected with the earth, landing upright.

Turning around and grinning, Killian sped back to the group, dusting off his hands as if he hadn't just ripped a full-size tree from the ground and thrown it into a field one-handed.

I turned to Lana whose expression mirrored my own—mouth open and eyes wide.

Devs were powerful, but seeing it and hearing about it were two entirely different things. And I had no idea our group of Devs was like *that*.

"You've moved on to the one-handed throw, Kil. I'm impressed," Dax said as Killian approached him, his tone ripe with sarcasm, clearly having seen this move from Killian before.

Killian just screwed up his face and flipped Dax off in return.

With that arrogant smirk of his, Dax moved to the edge of the clearing and reached behind him. Even from here, I could see his tattooed fingers as they curled around the hilt of the sword across his back before he unsheathed it in one fluid motion. Holding on tight, the Celtic cross shining in the moonlight, he circled it once above his head. White pulses of electricity shot up through his arm, illuminating the engravings along the blade, before he quickly knelt, bringing the sword down at the same time that he struck the point into the ground.

The electrical current rippled from him across the earth like lightning. Its power washed over all my senses and shook the ground beneath our feet as it hurtled toward the tree, bathing everything in its path in light and tearing apart the ground before it like an earthquake. Within seconds, the whole tree was engulfed in flames. And in only a few more, the entire thing was nothing more than ash to the wind.

Immediately, the boys and every other Dev present started

shouting.

"The man is BACK," Axel shouted above them all, air toasting Dax with the bottle as Dax threw his head back and laughed.

Glancing over, Dax made eye contact with me, a look in his eyes like he was both waiting to see if I was impressed and making sure he hadn't frightened me.

Shaking my head, I managed to close my mouth before looking down, not wanting him to see the effect he'd had on me.

I remembered his power in the corridor, against Romano, but the night was such a blur that I couldn't quite know if what I'd witnessed was real or not. And I hadn't wanted to think too hard on it for fear of what it might mean.

But I could never forget *this* type of power. He didn't seem fazed that he'd just lit an entire tree on fire with his own electricity. I mean, he practically generated his own lightning.

And I would be the worst liar if I said I wasn't impressed.

Turning away from the guys now encircling Dax, my gut immediately twisted as another thought hit me. If he could do that to one tree with minimal effort, what could he do to my armies? My country? *Me?*

Sighing, I wandered over to Kacey and Lana, grabbing a cup of water on my way.

"I swear, if Mav attempts to show one of them up, I will kill him," Kacey said as I walked up.

"Can he shoot out sparks too?" I joked, hoping to make light of what had just happened if only in my own mind.

"No." She sighed in exasperation as she tossed her long hair over her shoulder. "They all *wish* they could do that. Only Dax has that ability. No, Mav is the fastest among them, so I guess the worst he could do is challenge them to a race of some sort."

"Better watch out Kace, sounds dangerous," Lana replied as we both giggled.

Kacey rolled her eyes before smiling back. "Yeah, guess you're right."

"So what do we do here exactly?" I asked.

"Eat, drink, and forget everything else, Calderone!" Killian responded from behind us as he walked up to Lana, his dark arms coming to rest around her milky-white shoulders. His eyes momentarily came to rest on my black pearls, and a look crossed his gaze I couldn't quite place before he refocused on Lana. "Music is on. Care to join me?" He smiled down at her, his cocky grin gone for once, replaced by the most genuine smile he reserved only for her. She nodded, completely smitten, and the two walked off to the makeshift dance floor as Kacey went to find Mav.

Looking up, I made eye contact with Dax who'd been roped into chatting with a group of Dev girls I recognized from the dining halls. A sudden pang hit my gut that felt an awful lot like jealousy. Biting my lip, I buried the feeling, determined to ignore it as I turned to the food, suddenly in need of a distraction.

Walking along the spread, I piled my plate with fruit before moving to the cheese, keeping one eye on the buffet and one eye on Dax and the girls, attempting to appear casual.

I was so wrapped up in my spying that I didn't even notice the person standing beside the brie before it was too late.

A loud grunt sounded in front of me as I collided with a body twice my size and as hard as stone. I might as well have run into a brick wall. Almost losing my footing, I barely kept my plate from falling while I attempted to regain my composure.

"I am so, so sor—" The words died on my lips as my eyes met Tynan's.

Tension zapped between us as the gray of his eyes gradually lightened.

I cleared my throat, determined to play nicely. "Sorry."

I had just begun to move around him when he gripped my arm. His fingers dug into my skin, but I refused to let him see me flinch. "You think I want an apology from *you?* We're long past apologies."

Annoyance bloomed in my chest, all thoughts of placating him forgotten. "I have done nothing to you personally, Tynan. Holding such a prejudice is a sign of weakness," I hissed before I jerked my arm away.

But there was no shaking him; I was no match for his Deviant strength. Instead, he dug his nails in deeper. So deep, I knew they'd leave a mark.

I was about to shove him when I felt a power surge at my back.

"A pleasure to see you again, Tynan. It's been a few years, hasn't it?" Dax asked as his hard chest pressed into me, not a hint of friendliness in his cold tone.

Tynan straightened and immediately dropped my arm, fear evident in his eyes as he cleared his throat. "It has, Your Highness. I'm happy to be here for your return."

"I'm sure you are," Dax replied, his tone sharp enough to kill. Lightly touching my low back, sending sparks up my spine, he reached around me. I tensed, waiting for him to do something to Tynan, but he only grabbed the plate from my hand and turned, leaving me to follow.

Suddenly my mind cleared.

Even if I was in danger, I could handle things myself. I *needed* to.

Maybe it was the caveman levels of testosterone swirling around me in that moment, because the realization dawned on me that somehow in the past six weeks I had become a *follower* and not a *leader.*

The Gaill prince, a known enemy to my kingdom, expected *me,* the future queen of Calderone, to follow *him.* And I had been.

I turned on my heel to catch up with Dax who was thankfully walking at a normal pace back to the others.

"Hey—HEY, Dax, stop right there."

I'm not sure if it was my tone or the use of his nickname, but whatever it was, he froze.

Catching up with him, I snatched the plate from his hand before whipping around to face him, not even flinching when his white-green gaze hit mine with lethal force.

"Listen. I don't know what master-of-the-universe complex you have the need to fill, but I can assure you I don't need saving." I held up my hand as he opened his mouth to reply, ignoring the gasps from a few random Devs standing nearby. Lowering my voice, I continued, "I will forever be grateful to you for what you did for me in the lower south wing. But I *am* strong. And I don't need anyone coming in to dictate my actions or my life. Not anymore."

I was done with being directed, told what to do, how to think and who to listen to. I'd been blindly following my whole life. Here or back home, what was the difference? Those in power told me what to do, and I followed orders.

I had forgotten I *was* power. *I* was the sole heir to the throne of Calderone, a future *queen.* And I couldn't let anyone, including the Gaill prince, tell me what to do, especially when my people's safety lay on the line. Because in the end, though he and the Devs had cared for me when no one else had and though they claimed to want to help my people now, they had until a few decades ago victimized them. And what was a few decades against hundreds of years of hate and anger?

So I would decide if I could truly trust them. I would decide if they had truly changed. How they'd factor into my life. And what my next move would be. On my own. Without their influence. And then maybe if I could trust them, they could help me save my country when the time came.

Steeling my resolve, I stared him down, willing him to defy me, tell me how wrong I was or order me to back down.

Closing the gap between us, Dax lowered his face to mine, the churning energy behind his gaze burning a hole straight to my soul.

"I know you don't need saving, Jacqueline. You're one of the strongest people I've ever met. You proved that to me the first time I saw you, when you comforted the other Calderonian captive in the throne room. And again when you didn't let Romano's attack stop you from living," he said. "If you felt like I was trying to dictate your actions, I'm sorry for that. I wasn't trying to. I know what it feels like to live a life that's not yours to control."

Screwing my face up, I opened my mouth to ask him what his last sentence meant. But before I could, he leaned in to whisper in my ear, his words creating a warm energy against my skin.

"There's a war coming on two fronts as you know. After the other week, in the corridor, you've been marked. My father knows you're associated with me. He knows you… *matter*. And I wouldn't be able to live with myself if something happened to you."

He refused to meet my eyes as he straightened.

So I reached up and gripped his chin, looking him in the eye and asking the question I'd been dying to since he spared us that first day. "Why *do* I matter so much to you, Dax?"

"I don't know, Jacqueline," he answered immediately, looking at me then, his eyes open, honest, and slightly confused, like he truly couldn't figure out why I did matter that much. As if I was still that puzzle he couldn't solve.

Sighing, I remembered myself and immediately removed my hand. This had to end. *I* had to end this. Whatever this was with the Gaill prince could jeopardize everything.

"Okay, well, I appreciate the extra explanation. However vague it might be. But if you're going to feel the need to hang around, I have some ground rules, okay?" I leaned back and crossed my arms.

"Okay, *Calderone.*" He leaned back, mimicking me but with that playful smirk back on his lips, the uncertainty from moments earlier nowhere to be found.

Taking a deep breath, I began, knowing his mood would undoubtedly change once he heard what I had to say. But I had to say it.

"I want no different treatment than any other servant—I want no extra attention or concessions. The trainings can continue," I said quickly before he could speak, "but only if Captain O'Leary or one of your other guards are the ones to train me. And third," I barreled on, training my eyes on the ground because I was sure my resolve would crumble if I looked at him again, "you will take back the books you lent me. It was very kind of you but unfair to the other servants who aren't afforded the same luxury."

Finishing, I took a deep breath and met his eyes to find them white again. He was fuming.

He blinked, and the mask of indifference, the one I hadn't seen in weeks, slipped into place.

"All noted, Miss Lewis. Training can continue, and I will have Captain O'Leary officially take over from here. Keep the books, I will open the libraries to everyone." His voice was suddenly hard and unfeeling. My chest tightened. He hadn't moved, but I could feel him pulling back. And the feeling made it difficult to breathe.

Before I could say anything in return, he walked around me.

Except for shaking a few hands with people I didn't know, he left immediately. I remained standing in the middle of the grove with everyone partying around me, ignorant of what had just happened. What I'd just done.

Rubbing my chest, I tried to ignore the growing ache. I knew I'd made the right move by putting distance between myself and Dax, by putting an end to whatever *this* was between us.

There would be no more banter in libraries or chance encounters in corridors. No more opportunities for his very presence to distract me or single me out as different. I couldn't risk it. My feelings had already clouded my judgment enough. And I needed distance to decide what my next move would be and then act on it.

The Calderonian people came first. My *duty* to them had to come first.

But the tightening in my lungs was getting worse by the second.

Leaving the grove without saying goodbye—everyone was dancing anyway—I practically sprinted back to my room.

No one followed; no one even noticed.

Entering the servant's quarters, I rounded the corner by the dining hall, intent on using the closest staircase, when two people talking against the wall stopped me in my tracks.

Tynan's unmistakable figure was speaking to someone, partially blocking them.

I tried to quiet my labored breathing and moved as quietly as possible, but it was of no use. I only made it a few feet down the hall when Tynan turned around. And Romano was standing right in front of him.

My next breath caught in my throat as I tried to sort out the pieces of what was happening. Because the two of them together had to mean something. And whatever that something was, it wasn't good.

They looked at one another, then Tynan shifted for the stairs and Romano shifted right to me.

I wheezed and a cold sweat broke out as that familiar smell of brandy infiltrated the air.

"Seems you've angered the prince, Miss Lewis." Romano clucked his tongue before he leaned into me. "I do wonder, would he come to your defense now? When you've so publicly humiliated him?"

I raised my chin slightly, hoping I conveyed a bravado I certainly didn't feel.

Romano's hand twitched at his side before an ominous smile appeared on his face. "Have a… *safe* night, Miss Lewis."

He shifted. A second later, I was standing alone in the hallway with nothing but sweat pouring down my neck and a set of lungs struggling to function. Dread consumed me as I rushed up the stairs.

I flew down the third floor hall, trying my best to regulate my breathing and not caring a bit that my black boots echoed off the corridor's walls. Glancing behind me, I confirmed I was alone, but it still felt like *something* was chasing me.

I barged into my room, the door slamming against the wall as I whipped back around, barely able to lock it before running to the bathroom and heaving up everything I'd just consumed.

After a few minutes, I sat on the cold stone floor and pulled my knees up. Resting my head against the wall, beads of sweat collected on my forehead as I worked to steady my breathing.

The threat Romano and Tynan posed separately was hard enough to overcome, but together? I shuddered.

It didn't matter though. I had to face it on my own. Because tonight I'd done what was right for my country. I couldn't be getting too close to them, to *him*—I had a greater purpose. My feelings didn't matter when I was the heir. I knew that. I had to do what was *right*, what was *needed* to save my country by doing the only thing I could to move forward. It's what was right.

So then why does this all feel so wrong?

CHAPTER 10

REVELATIONS

I made it to Wednesday and my second trainer of the week before I got up the guts to mention Dax's absence. Luckily, none of the Devs asked about him or where we'd both gone on Saturday. Then again, I'd been avoiding most meals by spending them in my room. I knew I couldn't keep it up forever, but I told myself it was good to pull away from everyone now.

Lana was right; one of us needed to get out. And it made sense for it to be me. She obviously didn't know I was the one destined to run Calderone in a year.

"Keep your elbows raised, Miss Lewis. It'll help support your weapon," Captain Davis commanded, interrupting my thoughts.

Raising my elbows higher, I blocked his sword with my own. We were going through slow movements with wooden weapons after mastering some basic fighting techniques last week. I couldn't help but think I was a lost cause when it came to all this, but I wasn't about to pass up some training. If there was a war coming, I planned to fight for my people—both on and off the battlefield. Father would never agree to training women to fight when I made it home, so this was as good as it was going to get.

"And you're sure we were given the okay to move on to weapons from Dax?" I hedged, hoping my mention of him seemed natural as I blocked another slow blow from the left.

"His Highness"—Captain Davis not so subtly cleared his throat—"laid out a very clear training plan for you. We are to follow it exactly while he is away."

"Away?" I lowered my sword and straightened, forgetting my pretense of disinterest entirely. "Where has he gone?"

"He's away on Gaill business, Miss Lewis. Now if you will?" He raised his brows at me as he lifted his sword again.

Mimicking his movements, I let muscle memory take over as I mulled over that little bit of news.

So Dax had left. Apparently sure enough of my safety to leave, even though he'd been so concerned just a few days ago. Or maybe he really didn't care after all. Maybe this was all part of the "don't trust me" side of him.

I reminded myself it didn't really matter. He was gone. *Now* was the time to learn what I could and work out an escape.

"That's it for the day, Miss Lewis. We'll pick it back up tomorrow morning," Captain Davis said, interrupting my thoughts again.

Wiping my brow with the back of my hand, I only nodded as I caught my breath. He gave me a reproving look, clearly knowing my head was elsewhere, before grabbing a towel from the nearby pile of clean ones and wiping his brow. Without another word, he exited through the door to Dax's apartments.

I'd never asked, but my guess was that they were pretty extensive and likely a lot bigger than the few rooms I'd seen so far. And if the servants' quarters and guest rooms were any indication, they likely rivaled if not outshone my apartments back home.

Sighing, I placed the wooden sword back on the table next to a slew of real ones. I wasn't fool enough to try to steal an actual sword, especially when I still had the small dirk.

Grabbing the bottle of water I'd opened, I made my way back to the servant wing.

Dax was true to his word. I didn't get an escort and received no special treatment outside the trainings. And although I knew I should've been okay with it, being without his protection left me feeling vulnerable. Part of me hated myself for it.

Showering and getting dressed for the day, I was knocking on Lana's door before she'd even put her hair back. Grabbing a small ribbon, she wove a braid as we made our way down to the dining hall, finding the others already digging in.

Midweek was always busy, so I avoided any questions about my missed meals as everyone ate quickly though I knew I'd face the firing squad eventually.

As we made our way to our morning assignments, I found myself actually looking forward to the deep clean of the main foyer we were beginning today, figuring it'd be a good time to sort out a new escape plan. And a way to keep my mind from wandering to *him*.

The project in the foyer took the rest of the week and, before I knew it, we were at dinner Friday night.

"I almost feel bad it took the three of you all week to clean the foyer except for the fact that Romano had us cleaning the armory, which is *so* much worse," Axel grumbled while pushing his rice around his plate.

"Just you three?" Kacey looked at Mav.

"Us and the rest of the Deviants who aren't with Dax," Axel answered, twisting his fork in his hands as he rolled his tongue against the back of his lips, his agitation palpable.

"Yeah, he's all powerful now that Dax isn't here." Killian scoffed.

"Not here?" Lana looked at me briefly before fixing her eyes on Killian.

"Yeah, not here. Left earlier this week for some special Gaill mission. Not sure the reason—only a few know—but he hasn't been here since Monday morning."

Relief flooded through me, and I bit my lip to fight against the almost overwhelming guilt that followed. He wasn't just avoiding me; he'd been away on duty this whole time. I knew it shouldn't matter, but of course it did.

"What happened between you and Dax on Saturday anyway, Calderone? Scare him away? You've been avoiding us for a reason," Killian joked from across the table, earning him a playful shove from Lana.

I'd filled the girls in a bit on what happened as we'd worked in the foyer, doing my best to make it clear there was not and never had been *anything* between Dax and me. I'm not sure how much they believed me, and in truth, I wasn't sure how much I believed myself.

"Please, isn't the guy like hundreds of years old?" I fixed him with a sarcastic smile. "I'm sure what I say doesn't matter to him."

"Oh, so you *did* say something!" Axel was suddenly full of energy as he cut a quick conspiratorial glance around the table.

"Stop, you guys." I widened my eyes at them in warning. But everyone remained silent, waiting for me to continue. "Okay, what if I did? I wanted him to know where I stood. My true feelings. So I told him not to treat me differently from the other servants and gave him the books back. Well, I tried to."

Killian suppressed a grin as he nodded his head, his black waves bobbing. "Right, so you scared him away." He laughed as Lana actually shoved him this time, catching him off guard and causing him to fall out of his chair.

"Lay off her, you guys. It can't be easy having the attention of the most gorgeous person in the world on you at all times." Kacey stuck her tongue out at me, but I knew she was really joking, probably trying to save me from having to explain my feelings any further.

I shook my head and smiled back at her, sighing.

"Anyway, who needs books or the attention of a prince when you have this lovely group to keep you company?" Mav motioned to the group, laughing.

"That's what I was going to say." Axel punched his shoulder.

"Hey, what's up with Sean? You two make it official on Saturday or what?" I asked, desperate to change the subject.

"Eh, no. He's clingy as hell, and it's grating on my nerves."

"Ah clingers, the worst sort of person." I laughed.

"Got that right." Axel matched my sarcasm, flashing me a grin. Almost instantly, it was replaced by a pair of furrowed brows as he pushed himself to standing.

The others quickly followed, and looking around, I realized almost every Dev in the hall appeared to be listening for something.

A feeling of unease carved a path through my chest. "Wha—"

Axel met my eyes, his glowing blue, and shook his head.

I didn't know what was happening, but something in his eyes had my heart stuttering.

Just then a barely audible rumble met my ears.

"MOVE, NOW!" Killian bellowed across the hall, and suddenly everyone was shifting.

Kacey shifted, grabbing Lana before the two appeared right in front of me. Dragging me to standing, she looked between Lana and me—unmistakable worry on her face. "You two need to follow the other non-Devs to the storage rooms *now*."

"What's hap—"

"There's no time to explain."

"I'll take them." Axel was at her side a moment later.

"But we'll need you, Ax."

He shook his head. "They'll need you more. Your fire will be more effective if it's them."

They held each other's gaze for a few seconds, and understanding passing between them before Kacey shifted away, Mav and Killian following.

Axel ushered us into the crowd of people streaming toward the storage rooms. I attempted to keep up, practically tripping over my feet at the pace he was forcing on us. The first room was already full, but we found space in the second and sat along the wall with everyone else.

As we sat down, there was an even louder rumble and dust fell from the ceiling. A few people screamed. Then a bright blue light flooded the doorway from the windows that lined the ceiling in the hallway.

My heart pounded in my ears. "Axel, what's happening?"

Another rumble sounded, and then a flash of orange light mixed with blue.

An explosion followed, and screams erupted around us. We ducked as dust fell from the ceiling.

Everything sounded so muffled through the ringing in my ears. I opened and closed my jaw, attempting to regain my hearing.

Were we being attacked?

He licked his lips, keeping his eye on the doorway. "Calderone."

His eyes moved to meet mine briefly, unmistakable rage swimming in their aqua blue depths. "They're attempting a raid."

"A raid?" Lana's question echoed in my mind like a bell.

He nodded, nostrils flaring.

Calderone was *here?* Suddenly it felt like I was swallowing sandpaper. Were they here for the Gaill... or for *me?* I stood without a second thought. If they were here for me, I needed to get to them before they destroyed the palace and everyone in it.

Before I could move, Axel reached out and grabbed my arm, yanking me back down. "What're you doing?" His voice was a low growl.

"Stopping them!" I rushed in a panic.

"Noble or not, Calderone won't stop, Jac. This isn't the first time they've done a raid. Just the first in a few decades. They're probably doing it now because both Dax and the king are gone. Someone might have tipped them off." He bit the inside of his cheek as his bright eyes again moved for the door.

I bit my lip. Of course... *of course* that's why Axel thought they were here. Calderone had never sent a rescue mission for nobles taken in the past, so why would they now? Most people here knew me as a Calderonian servant, and the Devs thought I was a noble. Not the future *queen*. Making a scene would only cause more people to ask why I thought I was special enough to be saved.

And it was entirely possible Calderone was here because the prince and king were gone. It'd been seven weeks since I was taken—and Calderone didn't even know who took me. And if they did, wouldn't they have staged a rescue mission already?

They would've... *right*?

That same feeling of unease grew exponentially.

Nodding at Axel, I remained where I was as Lana's hands found mine.

It was as if everything was moving in slow motion. Another round of orange and blue light filled the doorway. The boom of the explosion echoed throughout the room as more sizable debris fell. A scream rang out from my right, and I swiveled my head to see a servant with a river of blood trailing down her temple being held by another.

Axel pulled us to him. I wasn't sure if it was me trembling, Lana, or both of us.

More rumbles. More screams. More blue and orange light. More breathless moments. More falling debris. More times when my heart almost gave out.

Until the light stopped. And it felt like time stopped with it.

A somber feeling hovered around the palace the next day. Kacey, Mav, and Killian had returned a short while after the light stopped, largely unharmed. Mav had his arm around Kacey, supporting her; she'd used most of her fire power to bring down the Calderonian plane. I was stunned to hear it was Kacey alone creating the orange glow that matched the Calderonian plane's blue one.

A small part of me felt guilty that those in the plane had perished, but an even bigger part that I didn't feel as badly as I should. I found myself more relieved that no innocent Gaill were killed, then sad for the few Calderonian soldiers that might have lost their lives. Especially if they had a hand in or were sent to defend Calderone's corruption.

The destruction at the palace was mostly nonexistent. Some areas of the ceiling needed repairing, but the Devs explained that the whole place was outfitted to withstand a bombing. And the fighting had occurred outside the outer ward, so what we felt were aftershocks.

I tried not to think about how large those aftershocks were and what that meant for the destruction a war would bring.

Dinner that night was a rather silent affair, and we all parted ways after—everyone going to their separate rooms. A layer of ominous grief hung over all of us, even though no Gaill had lost their lives.

So I was surprised when there was a knock at my door shortly after eight o'clock. I answered it only to find Kacey, Lana—and a bottle of wine.

Kacey cracked a tired smile. "Figured we deserved it after last night."

I returned her smile. "I can't argue with that." Although Kacey deserved a lot more than a bottle of wine.

The girls filed in as I grabbed a few extra cups. Filling them to the brim, we cheersed before sitting together on the bed.

"How are you, Kace?" Lana eyed Kacey worryingly over the rim of her cup.

"I'm fine, promise. Honestly, just tired."

I gave Kacey's arm a reassuring squeeze. "Any news on why they might have attacked last night?" Not knowing if I was the cause of the raid or if it was Dax and the king's absence had been eating at me for the past twenty-four hours.

Kacey shook her head. "Normally we don't know. And every time we've brought down the plane before they even get access to the palace. They just attempt to bomb it from afar. I don't know why they keep trying. It's been decades since they attempted to breach the outer ward, and I honestly thought they'd given up."

A thought occurred that had somehow gotten buried in the craziness of the past day. "So Calderone knows where the palace is and how"—I struggled to find the right word—"developed it is?"

"Oh, they know where we are. Though I don't think they've ever truly seen the palace. The protections around the outer ward distort the palace's image to anyone outside. It's part of our defensive strategy. It's better if they believe we're the uncivilized people from their stories. I think that's why they've mostly left us alone—because they don't really see us as a true threat."

Lana nodded because what Kacey said made sense. What didn't make sense is that if Father knew where the Gaill were, why hadn't he ever told me? A pang zapped my heart that I tried to drown out with another hefty gulp of wine.

"It's been a while since I've had a girls' night like this." Kacey took a long drink from her cup and then smacked her lips.

"I can imagine. Has it always been just you and the guys?" Lana asked.

"For the past few decades, yeah." Kacey nodded, setting her drink down on the nightstand before continuing. "Before that, Scarletti and Dax used to be around, but then everything changed after Queen Caragh passed."

"Wait, Dax and *Scarletti*?" I choked, almost spitting my wine across the stone floor of my small room.

"Oh no." Kacey laughed lightly, clutching her chest. "Not *that* Scarletti. Violetta Scarletti—Madam Scarletti's daughter. She was a Dev like us and was in our group. She, Dax, and Kil all grew up together in the palace. Mav, Ax, and I all came to court as teenagers."

She looked up and caught my eye, her tone turning somber. "Violetta was a Gaill soldier for Queen Caragh's guard when they were ambushed by a group of Calderonian militants on the coast. Only a few of them made it back to the palace, and Queen Caragh never recovered. She was in bed for a week before her injuries took her life. Although it wasn't Violetta's fault, King Aidoneus had her executed for it. And he did it when Dax was gone. By the time he got back, it was too late. I know Dax still blames himself."

Lana gasped, her hand flying to her mouth as I felt an overwhelming anger take hold for a woman I had never and would never meet. First attacked by *my* government, then shown no mercy by her own. And I couldn't imagine the effect the killing of his childhood friend had had on Dax.

"What mistakes did she supposedly make?" Lana asked.

"She let the queen die," I replied, knowing full well that a soldier's most important job was preserving the life of her monarch.

"That is awful." Lana shuddered as she reached for the wine. "No wonder you all hate the king so much."

"And that's only a bit of it. After her execution and the queen's death, everything changed. Although suspected before, it became obvious after her death that the king was no longer the merciful leader he once was—one determined to lead the Gaill and innocents from the monarchy to a better future. He'd become hardened to the world and its treatment of the Gaill, seeking vengeance where he should've been seeking peace." Kacey shook her head, looking down as she played with a fray in her pillow.

"Dax was once like that too," she continued, looking up at me curiously. "Full of vengeance. Sometimes I think he might still be, but their deaths changed him. I mean, I think he was changing before, but it's as if their passing woke him up—made him realize that the path his father was taking would only lead to more destruction or something."

I chewed my bottom lip as I thought over this information. The portrait of Queen Caragh Dax had hanging in his room suddenly flashed across my mind. Just Queen Caragh, not them as a family. Not even her and the king. His love for his mother and his distance from his father, even decades later, was clear.

"So is that when Dax started working with the Eur on the Coalition?"

"It was a while after that, but yeah, I think their deaths were the final straw for him." Kacey sighed as she stretched her legs out. "Dax started working to overthrow the king as soon as he realized the true nature of what was happening. But he knew he couldn't do it right away. Aidoneus still had too much influence and power. So he slowly worked away at his base. Today there aren't many who'd side with Aidoneus if the two stood head to head."

"Well, if that's the case, what's Dax waiting for?" The monarch in me didn't understand the wait. It seemed negligent for Dax *not* to step in and take over.

"Although he doesn't have as many people on his side, Aidoneus is still extremely powerful. And not every Dev has agreed to fight… yet. Without every Dev, more of the outlying Gaill clans who live beyond the outer ward, and the One, there's no chance. And since every other Dev and Gaill clan is pretty much waiting on Dax to find the One before they enlist, that means we're all waiting on the One."

"The One?" I raised my brows. The Devs had mentioned the One in passing before, but it had always seemed like an afterthought. Not an integral part to their war effort.

"Yes, *the One.*" Kacey looked between Lana and me like we should know what she was referring to. "We really haven't told you two about this yet? Not even when we discussed the Coalition?"

Lana and I looked at each other and shook our heads. Racking my brain, I couldn't think of any time in all our conversations where the Devs had explained what the One meant or alluded to the fact that Dax was waiting on something called the One.

"Okay." Kacey's voice cut through my thoughts as she scooted closer to us. "Before Queen Caragh passed, she left a prophecy of sorts regarding the future of the Gaill. Some say it was a prophecy for the whole human race, but most think it was just for the Gaill. I personally think it applies to everyone."

"Kace."

"Sorry, getting off topic. Okay, so the queen grabbed Dax's hand when it was just him and Madam Scarletti in the room and told him, 'One day, a Gaill will come into your life unlike anyone else you've ever known. They are *the One*. The One who will unite us. The One who will save you, save our people, save us *all* if only you let go of the hate in your heart to see it.'"

Kacey sat back as she finished, folding her legs beneath her, clearly waiting for the impact of her words to hit us.

Lana and I glanced at each other, exchanging identical looks of disbelief.

"I mean, this is nothing against Queen Caragh; she seemed like an amazing woman. But you have to admit that sounds kind of ridiculous. You mean you're waiting to go to war against someone as horrible as King Aidoneus all because *Dax* is waiting for some mystery person to walk into his life and act as savior?"

"Trust me," she replied, rolling her eyes, "I know it sounds crazy. King Aidoneus and his supporters think it was just delirious muttering. Even Dax wrote off the prophecy until recently. But as he distanced himself from the king, he started to believe there might be some truth to it. Especially since the king has been so insistent that it's nonsense. The fact that Aidoneus won't even look into the prophecy at all makes you wonder if there's some truth to it." She grabbed her glass, downing the last of the wine before waving the empty cup in the air. "I personally think that the king knows if Dax found the One, their combined powers would be enough to overthrow him and put an end to his war plans for good."

"So this One person could really be anyone? Old or young? Man or woman? Anywhere in the world?" Lana set her glass down before reaching for the popcorn.

Kacey nodded. "Anyone—as long as they're Gaill born. And I mean, Queen Caragh did have extraordinary powers. So it's not totally unreasonable to think that she might have had the power to see the future in some way or another."

"Well, if there's anything being here has taught me," Lana said, looking at both of us with an eyebrow raised while swirling her wine, "it's that anything is possible. So maybe there *is* someone out there who'll save us all. Would be nice." She sighed before taking a sip.

"Kace you in there?"

A sudden pounding at the door caused all of us to jump, and Lana spilled her wine down the front of her dress.

Kacey, recovering first, rolled her eyes and huffed jokingly before getting up and walking over to open the door. Flaming red hair was visible even before Mav poked his head around her, a grin on his face as he waved at Lan and me.

"All right. Girls' night is done. It's Maverick time now."

"You're insufferable," Kacey said, but I could hear the smile in her voice.

Turning back to us, she gathered her small bag, tossing her long reddish-blond hair behind her as she lifted it onto her shoulder. "Sorry ladies, can't leave this one on his own too long. He's like a child. I'll leave the wine with you though." She winked at us before turning to follow Mav out.

"You better not have finished that game we started last night," she said as they shut the door behind them.

Sighing, Lana put her wine on my nightstand before flopping onto the bed.

"This week was utterly exhausting."

"Yeah, if we ever have to scrub the foyer again, I will literally volunteer to chop wood with the boys instead."

Laughing, Lana sat up on her elbows. "I second that. I know they complain, but it can't really be *that* bad. They're such babies."

"Seriously though."

"And actually, cleaning the foyer wasn't that awful either. It was really just having to redo it to Scarletti standards so many times," Lana said. "I'm sure we've both done worse things. Well, I guess I can't speak for you." She stuck her tongue out at me jokingly before lying back down.

A sudden pang of guilt hit me even though I knew Lana didn't mean to make me feel bad. Her words reminded me of the differences in how we grew up. And how different her life was here compared to back home.

"So things back home were…" I waited for her to elaborate and hopefully pick up our conversation from last weekend in the grove.

"Different." She sat up fully, folding her legs beneath her and turning to face me.

I looked at her, waiting.

Sighing again, she just shrugged in response. "Some things were definitely worse. Well, a lot of things. To be honest, being here kinda feels like a vacation. But Calderone is where my family is, however fragmented, and ultimately where home is so… yeah. It's a weird feeling, you know?"

Nodding, I did know. "If you got out, would you go back? To Lord Duvay's?"

"Hell no. Are you kidding me?" She laughed, but it was a hallow sound. Shaking her head, she looked down and continued. "I'll never go back there. I'd rather be King Aidoneus's personal attendant than work for that man again."

"What happened?" I asked apprehensively, both wanting to know but not wanting to make her relive it.

"Look, Jac." Lana met my eyes, her expression unreadable. "I'm only saying this because I know who you are—a true lady, one of the good ones. But most of the Calderonian nobility are complete scum. They trade humans like we're livestock and don't treat us much better either. We essentially work to survive. Luxuries like education, healthcare, and just general freedom don't exist for us in the way it does for the nobility. And although I didn't have to sleep in the camps, my bed at Duvay's was usually no more than a mattress on the cold stone basement floor, and I went to bed hungry more often than not."

The camps.

I felt the air go from my lungs and the world fade away as all my worst fears were actualized in that one tiny phrase. Were they really so casually referred to like that?

Tears began building behind my eyes as the reality of what was happening, what *had been* happening, unfolded before me.

The issues in Calderone are so much bigger than I imagined.

Moving to sit next to her on the bed, I reached for her hand. "I didn't know about any of this or the camps—or I guess I knew about the camps; I just didn't realize what they *actually* were. I had no idea. And if I had, Lan, I swear I would've done something to stop it. If I do get back home, I *will* put a stop to all this." I was rambling, needing to make a promise out loud, if only to her, that I would do what I had to and make things right in Calderone. Clearing my throat, I continued after a pause. "So is it ever any better or is that how it is for everyone?"

"Everyone outside the palace. I hear the palace servants have it okay, but I can't say for sure, never met any of them. They keep them on a short leash 'cause of the whole 'keep the heir's identity a secret' thing." She made air quotations with her fingers. "I'm guessing things were different in your household?" She tipped her chin at me as she took a sip of her wine.

"Yes, very." The guilt again ate at me for the lie I was perpetuating. Polishing off my wine, I got up to put it on the desk before wandering back to sit next to Lana on the bed. "Did you know anyone who lived in the, uh, camps?"

Lana nodded. "Yeah, only a few. That's where my dad is too, assuming he's still alive."

A deep sorrow bloomed in my chest. "Have you ever, you know, lived there?"

"No, thankfully. But from what I hear, there's no electricity or running water, and you're just as likely to wake up murdered as you are hungry. There's no shortage of petty crime either. When someone goes to the camps, you give them a year before they're either dead, in some sort of prostitution ring, or a druggie."

My mouth opened and closed involuntarily as I attempted to process everything she was saying.

Murder? Starvation? Prostitution? In *my* country? Lana acted like it was all normal. A simple, everyday fact of life for people like her.

A fact I'd been ignorant of until I'd arrived at my *enemy's* court.

Reaching for her hand again, I willed myself not to cry. "I'm sorry, Lan. Truly sorry. I had no idea things were like that." I blinked back more tears. "Maybe we need to rethink who the enemy is. I'm not sure if it's who we were brought up believing. I'm not really sure of a lot of stuff right now. But I do know that if we get home, I will never let you suffer again."

"I know, Jac… I know," Lana replied softly, gently squeezing my hand and giving me a small smile.

Drawing her in for a hug, I could no longer stop the tears as they fell silently down my cheeks—tears of mourning for Lana, for the life of heartache she'd led, for my country, and for what I'd been ignorant of for so long.

"We'll get through this together," I said. My voice was surprisingly steady, an unmovable resolve evident beneath my words.

"Yes, we will," she replied before squeezing me back.

We wrapped up the night polishing off the bottle of wine and telling each other happier stories from home before I let Killian escort Lana back to her room shortly after midnight.

Turning the light off and curling up on my side, my mind wandered back to our conversation from earlier. And as much as I tried, I couldn't keep the tears at bay as the true nature of Calderone, the place I called my home, started to reveal itself in full.

The country I was raised to believe had triumphantly risen from the ashes of a fragmented and corrupt society might in fact be more corrupt than the country it replaced. What had they done? And who was going to stop those in power, those controlling things, while saving the lives of my people if it wasn't going to be me?

CHAPTER 11

HOMECOMING

"We'll have you start serving at dinner from now on," Scarletti told me the following Monday morning. "As long as you don't have any prior engagements." She raised her brows at what I assume was the look of disbelief on my face.

They really wanted me, the Calderonian servant, to wait on the palace courtiers? Usually that job was reserved for tenured Gaill servants.

"Of course, madam." I nodded, not wanting to ask why she was giving me orders when usually it was Pepridge doling out our duties.

"Okay, everyone, on your best behavior while it's just Master Pepridge. I'm off to visit my nephew again. Poor thing is so ill." She shook her head before busying her short frame with her bag as a few servants moved forward to help her.

Axel turned around to the group of us assembled near the bread oven and cocked a blond brow. *Nephew?* He mouthed.

Kacey gave him a look like "not now" before turning and heading toward the back staircase. The lot of us followed her before breaking off to our own individual duties.

Since I was serving dinner, my shift didn't start until after lunch. The courtiers all ate lunch in their own apartments, so a different set of servants handled that meal, thankfully. It was all I could do to learn the motions for serving one meal let alone two or three.

Kacey had been assigned to serving too, so the two of us made our way back to our rooms to pass the time before we had to work.

"Why did Ax question Scarletti's nephew?" I asked as we made our way down the third floor hallway, pausing at my door.

"Because we know she doesn't have one. My guess is none of the other servants are aware of that."

"But you are because of Violetta?"

"Right. Scarletti's sisters didn't have any children, and her husband's relatives have all been killed in service." She looked down. "She's up to something, but I can only assume it's something that Dax is involved in. She, along with Kil's mother, were Queen Caragh's closest friends and confidants. Scarletti loves Dax and Kil as if they were her own."

I nodded. It made sense if the three grew up together that their mothers had been close. The same could be said for my mother when it came to Rachel and Miranda's.

"Anyway, I'm gonna shower. Slept in *way* past my alarm today." Kacey shrugged one shoulder at me before pulling her hair out of the braid it'd been in.

"That actually sounds amazing."

"Doesn't it? Come over when you're done!" she called over her shoulder as she walked the rest of the way to her room.

Serving turned out to be fairly easy. With Kacey's guidance, having served many times over the decades, and my experience *being* served in a palace, it actually turned out to be rather instinctual for me. And I considered it no small victory that I managed to drop only one glass my first night and none my second.

The days and nights passed quickly as I trained every morning and served well into the evening, packing the between times with reading various history books I'd taken from the library and hanging with the Devs—who I was trusting more and more after Lana's confession supported everything they'd ever told us.

The history volume I'd found a few weeks prior was massive. With how busy our schedules were, it would take me weeks to complete it. And though I grappled with what to do about the corruption in Calderone and whether escaping or allying myself with the Devs was the best route forward, I at least could feel myself healing from my run-ins in with Romano as I got stronger, both mentally and physically.

It wasn't until Kil and Ax began to chat about planning the next Full Moon at lunch a couple of Fridays later that I realized not only had it been over a month since the attack, but it had also been almost two weeks since Calderone's failed raid. Not many mentioned it, but I supposed that was because it wasn't the first time it had happened. Plus Calderone never did get past the outer ward. Something about the timing of it all still plagued me. But as everyone else seemed to have brushed it off as a typical act of aggression from the monarchy, I tried to do the same.

The upcoming Full Moon also meant it had been three whole weeks since Dax left.

Not that I hadn't thought about him or missed him. I had, constantly. And to say that unsettled me would be a gross understatement. I didn't know why I missed him. Because when I really thought about it, I knew little to nothing about him.

"Look, it's Friday. Let's make a sample and settle this at Mav's tonight," Killian said matter-of-factly, tossing his black waves out of his face with a jerk of his chin and leaning back so his chair was balancing on two legs. "That way we have a week to place an order with the kitchen for what we need."

Our current topic of debate—whether to include a kegged cocktail in addition to the regular lagers and wine. I didn't bother asking how they planned to get a kegged cocktail. I knew by now the Devs could do just about anything they set their minds to, especially when it involved a night of partying.

"Calderone." Killian nodded at me. "Think you can get the alcohol and ingredients before tonight since you'll be working? I assume Kacey will be too, but she's probably not up yet, the lazy bum."

Ever since getting assigned to serving, Kacey had taken to sleeping in until our afternoon shift, usually missing breakfast and most of lunch.

"For sure." I laughed, nodding back at Killian.

Scarletti had gone on one of her mysterious trips again so there would be little risk in getting the alcohol. It was my turn anyway, my last liquor run being three weeks ago when I'd had my run-in with Dax.

"I can't believe it's almost been a month since the last Full Moon," I said in disbelief, shaking my head.

"Yeah, speaking of which, when is Dax gonna be back?" Axel wiggled his brows.

"Ha ha, Ax. Funny." I rolled my eyes at him. "I wouldn't know. Remember, he's no longer talking to me?"

"Riiiight," he replied, dragging the word out with extra sarcasm.

The truth is now that I'd spoken with Lana and Kacey, I was

seriously questioning icing Dax out. King Aidoneus was my enemy, without question. But Dax? He fought against tyranny and injustice so much so that he was going against his own father. I was getting the feeling Dax wasn't the monster history and the monarchies had made him out to be.

"Well, let's just hope these next few hours fly by 'cause your boy needs a night off. These last few weeks with Romano and his men have aged me at least a few decades," Killian complained, venom in his voice as he pulled his lip ring between his teeth and rubbed a knot in his shoulder.

Leaning over, I patted his hand. "If it helps, I'll grab your walker when I head upstairs."

Spinning to get up and scoot away next to Lana, we both squealed as Kil jokingly made a grab for me before clutching his shoulder again and laughing.

"Ah, and Calderone just added another few decades right there. I'm tapped out, kids. I'll be upstairs icing and having a tonic before dinner," he said, laughing, before getting up with his tray, kissing Lana on the head and making his way to the return line before leaving the hall.

"I should be off too." I sighed as the three of us started getting up. "Gotta get to those kitchens in time for Pepridge's orders."

"Right. I should get back to cleaning too, and you"—Lana pointed her finger at Axel—"don't want to be late for Romano."

"Ugh, don't remind me," Axel moaned, tipping his blond head back. "With any luck, a sword will accidentally find its way into his heart soon."

His eyes were a brighter blue when he tipped his head back down, giving us a knowing look before turning and heading to the south wing.

The kitchens were virtually silent as I walked through late that afternoon—most everyone was enjoying the few hours' respite before dinner. Knowing just the primary cooks would be left and they'd be very busy, I wasn't too worried as I weaved through the various countertops and cook spaces, grabbing ingredients we needed as I made my way to the corridor that led to Scarletti's office.

Steadying my hand, I expertly picked the lock again until the door popped open. Rushing in and quickly closing it behind me, I locked it on instinct and beelined it for the liquor cabinet. We might have been in the afternoon lull, but I knew I had to be in and out before anyone saw me. Otherwise, I risked punishment from Pepridge or worse, Romano. He hadn't reappeared since he confronted me after the Full Moon Festival a few weeks ago, but his presence always seemed to hover like a demon I couldn't shake.

I was so focused on getting to the cabinet that I didn't even register Scarletti's stepping stool in my path. Before I knew it, I was hurtling forward. Flinging my arms out, I caught myself on the desk but not without scattering her numerous books and papers across the tabletop.

Pausing and looking around, making sure I hadn't made too much noise, I straightened and hurried to right the stool.

Walking to the other side of her desk, I tried to remember how she'd had her papers. It didn't take me long to realize I had no idea where they'd been, so I began to gently nudge things back into place, hoping she wouldn't look too hard.

I didn't plan to read anything—but then a label on one of the leather-bound books caught my attention.

YEARS 2210-2350

It could've been nothing, just a ledger of stock numbers. Or it could've been something more.

I glanced up to make sure I was indeed still alone before I let curiosity take over and gently flipped it open to a random page.

1/2/2225

Vivi and the boys were gone all day again. I'm worried they'll soon face repercussions for their rebellious behavior though I can't say we don't encourage it sometimes. Caragh and I often relive our own childhood through their eyes. But I'm worried. After Dax came back with that cut last time, we knew they were no longer just staying around the palace. And Vivi's explanation didn't make much sense either.

From what I gathered, they'd run into some trouble near the coast. Whether with other Gaill or Calderonian soldiers, they avoided answering when asked. Either way, we determined that Dax stepped in to save Vivi from an altercation she was sure to lose, though her hotheadedness had convinced her otherwise. It must've been some group he fought to be able to wound the boy.

Either way, she was lucky he was there. I knew I liked him and little Killian ever since they taught that Tynan a lesson when he picked on Vivi because of her size. Dax insists she'll be the best Gaill soldier, regardless of her height, and I have no doubts.

But had we been unlucky enough to have the king home when they got back, there would've been hell to pay. Not because someone hurt the prince, of course, but because the prince failed to properly defend himself regardless of the number of people he fought. The shame of it would be reason enough for punishment in the king's eyes.

Hopefully they'll return soon without issue because the king is in court today…

Closing the book, holding the page with my thumb, I bit my lip. This was wrong, so wrong. But I was getting a look into a side of Dax's life that I somehow felt the need to know more about. I needed to know my assumptions about him were one hundred percent false.

Chewing my lip, I reopened the book, flipping through the pages until I found another mention of him.

9/25/2335

We had a little celebration for Vivi's promotion today. Of course Dax and Killian were there as well as a few of the other Devs whose names I can't recall offhand. One with red hair and another with a mop of blond hair.

I'm about to head over to Caragh's for a glass of wine and dinner. We figured a ladies' night was in order to celebrate the kids. I only wish Kitty were joining us. She'd love to see the man Killian has become. And Dax—Caragh is so proud as she should be. He will make a fine king one day. I know she worries he will become too like his father, but I think his disposition is different. He has his faults, especially when it comes to his feelings about the enemy, but a lot can change over the years. King Aidoneus himself is an example of that.

Letting go of my lip, I scanned farther down the page and, finding nothing, skipped farther ahead.

3/14/2340

It's been almost four months since they passed. It feels like yesterday. But in some ways, it feels like I've lived another hundred years.

Dax stopped by my office again this afternoon. His guilt over their deaths has consumed him. He looks as if he hasn't eaten or slept in weeks. It's as if because his father feels nothing, he feels everything for the both of them. I keep telling him there's nothing he could've done, but he is far from forgiving himself. Or his father.

The king will pay for what he's done.

Looking up again, feeling like I could be caught at any moment, I went to close the book, when a flash of gold caught my eye.

Pulling the book underneath it out, I ran my hand over the cover—a dark rich brown with gold handwritten lettering.

YEARS 2350-

Intrigued what recent information this new journal might hold, I flipped to the middle, finding myself within a decade of my appearance at the palace.

5/29/2369

They rehoused more refugees today. The king has continued to express his disgust, but he and Dax reached an agreement: the refugees who made it to the outer ward can live as long as neighboring villages take them in and give them work. In exchange, Romano and his men will continue their raids into Calderone to gather intel on how the country functions. If they capture regular citizens, the king's men will be allowed to question them using… any means necessary. The king has it in his mind that everyday Calderonians know more than most of the nobility, and I, unfortunately, can't disagree with this assessment. Citizens like servants work for their country day in and day out, they hear things others think they don't, and they're not secluded like most of the nobility. I hate that some of those questioned come from the despicable places the Calderonian government calls the suburbs. Absolute pigs to house people in such conditions. Those citizens have already suffered enough. I'm sure it killed the king to compromise with his son, just as it killed

Dax to concede to Calderonians being questioned. But I think Aidoneus also knows that Dax would likely defy his orders and keep saving refugees regardless, so such a compromise gives him more control.

This time we were able to rehome ten Calderonians, mostly women and children. Five more than last time, so we're improving.

I think this has been good for us both, Dax especially. I always knew he had kindness in him, even if he did lose his way for a while by following his father. Aidoneus has been far off course for too long—punishing all Calderonians the same even though some endure worse fates than we have and live within their borders. It's incumbent upon us to step in if we can, having also dealt with their king, his officials, and their predecessors.

But this is good. I know it is. We both seem to have a renewed sense of purpose these last few years—Dax with the Coalition and then the two of us with saving the refugees and our goal of finding the One.

We haven't spoken much of the One these last few months, but I know Dax feels it too. Whoever they are, they're out there now. And it's only a matter of time until we find them. Or they find us.

I bit my lip, digesting the new information about refugees while turning through more pages until I found my arrival. My breathing picked up as pressure descended on my lungs.

6/26/2374

Romano and his men brought in more Calderonian captives from the raid they led three nights ago. Mostly civilians though one was a military member dressed in plain clothes. The Calderonian military is in charge of defending and running the day-to-day operations of the suburbs. They're also known to be fiercely loyal—almost as if Manasseh brainwashed them himself. I didn't see it, but heard that Dax killed the man on the spot. His vengeful streak, though tamer in the past decade, still gets the best of him at times.

What's more surprising, Dax spared the two women who were brought in with the group. This isn't the first time Romano has captured women. But it is the first time Dax intervened to stop them from being questioned. And he assigned them to work in the palace—something he never would've gotten away with had Aidoneus been present. But since the king left earlier in the week, it's as if Dax is testing the limits of his authority.

Or perhaps he knows something about the women we don't. I met the two briefly while giving them their room assignments. Both claim to be Calderonian servants, but the one called Jacqueline is noble born. I'm sure of it. And Dax is risking—

Just then there was a noise at the door, and I watched in horror as someone attempted to turn the handle. My heartbeat thudded in my ears, and the pressure on my lungs intensified tenfold. Something scrapped against the door, the sound of metal on metal reverberating throughout the room, as if someone was attempting to pick the lock. I froze as the handle again twisted back and forth.

I wasn't sure who was out there, but I was almost certain my heart was beating loud enough for them to hear it. Looking around, I realized I had nowhere to go. The only windows had bars on them. Suddenly the turning stopped, and after a few more seconds, footsteps receded down the hall.

It was then that I felt the burning in my lungs because I'd stopped breathing altogether. I inhaled a shuddering breath as a shiver ran down my spine, and I immediately closed the book. I was desperate to read more, but I had to get out in case the person came back and managed to get the door open.

Slipping the journal below the other, I tidied the papers, barely paying attention to what I was doing, before picking the lock to the liquor cabinet and quickly finding what we needed.

Tucking the bottles along with the other ingredients into the satchel I had grabbed again from Kacey, I double-checked the office before inching open the door. There wasn't a soul to be seen, but that didn't stop the hairs from rising on the back of my neck. Hurrying out, I quickly locked the door behind me before attempting to walk at a normal, unsuspicious pace back to my room.

Once inside, I slumped against the door as blood rushed in my ears. My heart was still pounding, and the tightening in my chest was making it increasingly harder to breathe.

Scarletti knew, or at least suspected the truth of who I was.

And Dax—Dax was good. He was trying to save my people. The Devs were being truthful.

What's more, the One was out there.

Everything is already in motion.

I feigned a headache to get out of prepping for dinner. Pepridge was displeased, but he begrudgingly approved the time off. It was the only thing I could think of to help me make a sizable dent in *A History of the Monarchies.* My gut told me this book, more than any others, was key to filling in the holes of everything I'd just learned.

So I passed the hours before dinner pouring over it. Dissecting the pages and crosschecking them with the maps and entries in *The Eclipse*, I hunted for more clues into our history and that of the Gaill we'd exiled.

Three hours later, I sat back in my chair, rubbing my eyes; I was exhausted, but utterly certain of a few things.

One, the labor camps were indisputable and had been in existence since shortly after Calderone's birth. Not only had they been around since the beginning, but they were essential to the economic backbone of the kingdom, ensuring cheap labor and peak production of our most precious export—artillery.

It was decided in the early days of the monarchies that each kingdom was to supply a different export. Ours was artillery. Siberia, for example, produced petroleum, and Vidalivre, in what was once South America, supplied most of our food. Growing up, I as well as every other child of the monarchy was told this was to ease the burden on our flailing planet and to ensure all kingdoms were dependent upon one another. Without such interdependence, Father said, our countries would suffer, and we'd fall into civil and world war as we did before.

But I knew better now.

The kings used this system and the monarchies themselves as simply a way to keep their power and instill fear in the public.

By the year 2100, a little over twenty years after Calderone's inception, King Richard and his advisors had completely dismantled the public education system. Those that couldn't afford private education often could only find work in the camps where they labored long hours in poor conditions only to go home to worse.

The king, his court, and their descendants, on the other hand, profited. High taxes, maximum production, and a low minimum wage for those in the camps meant more money for them. And the pervasive lack of any education for the lower castes meant that the gap between rich and poor remained defined, never changing for the past three hundred years.

The fact that my opulent upbringing was largely a result of the money made from the camps made me physically ill. I couldn't be sure who all knew of or had a hand in their current operation. My father and his advisors did, no doubt, but Mother or Phin? I didn't know yet. Though the fact that both Scarletti and *A History* had mentioned the military's involvement in the camps made me think Phin, at least, knew. A weird fissure formed in my heart at the knowledge that my childhood best friend could be involved in something so heinous.

Standing from the desk, I moved to my tiny window, looking out into the courtyard below and mountainside beyond, thinking through what else I'd determined.

Da Luca's book did indeed expose the lies behind the monarchies, which were only supported by *A History of the Monarchies. The Eclipse* essentially acted as a call to arms for others to join a movement against the monarchies, to rebel. But it was written before his exile, so I didn't glean any new information about the Gaill's lives after they were banished beyond the Wall—how they'd earned their name or reputation.

Lastly, steeling myself as I met my gaze in the reflection of the window, I had determined that in order to reform my country, to save it and those innocent people in the camps, I would have to go against those that I loved. It was becoming increasingly obvious there were enemies within Calderone that needed to be weeded out. And maybe I'd wait until I ascended, or maybe I'd fight with the Deviants, but whatever the case, this could only end one way—with the destruction of the current monarchy and everything it stood for.

News arrived right before dinner that Dax and his men would

return early Sunday, and it sent everyone into a frenzy. Things got so chaotic that Pepridge ordered everyone to return at 0600 for work the following day to further prepare the palace for their arrival. Madam Scarletti, he informed us, would return in the morning to help finish the preparations.

There was much debate over the necessity of the drink tasting scheduled for Mav's later that night, but in the end, all the boys reconciled to the fact that we could do it Sunday evening and still place our order in time for Full Moon.

Somewhat put out by this change in plans but more excited for what news Dax's return would bring, the six of us made our way upstairs after our duties and said an early good night. I spent the time reading the other history texts I'd managed to grab and attempting to ignore the fact that Dax was consuming my every thought.

I had been wrong, and I'd set it right. I would.

I didn't know what he and I had or if it was anything at all. It was probably nothing. The weeks apart had made me doubt what I thought was there. And, I mean, Axel and Kacey made it pretty clear he was emotionally unavailable. All his energy was spent on saving refugees, the Coalition, and searching for the One, who I now felt I needed to find too.

But even if it was all in my head, I was convinced more than ever that we needed to be allies to survive this fight. I would make him see that just as soon as I figured out a way to tell him who I was without totally breaking the Oath of the Heir Proviso and getting myself or my people killed.

Having been assigned an extra shift to help ready the palace, I was making my way through the largely deserted kitchens around ten the following morning, determining exactly how I'd get Dax to forgive me for blowing him off, when I found myself pausing next to the freshly made pastries.

They were still warm; steam gently rose in the air above where they sat, carrying with it the sweet smell of hazelnut and chocolate. My mouth watered. It had been so long since I'd had good breakfast food.

Would anyone really notice if I take just one?

Looking around, I reached for the chocolate croissant closest to the end when a pleading voice rang out from the storeroom corridor not twenty feet away, stopping me in my tracks.

"STOP *please*!"

Looking around again to ensure I was alone, I withdrew my hand.

"Please, I beg you. I escaped. They told me it was safe here. I can't go back."

The girl's accent was the same as mine—Calderonian. And something in her tone had me moving into the hall, edging closer to the entrance of the corridor. I stopped immediately though as another voice joined hers.

"Well, the funny thing is, you don't have to go back… if you do what we say."

Romano. Here.

A shudder racked my body as instant nausea roiled through my gut. Pressing the back of my hand to my lips, I focused on steadying my breathing and forced myself to swallow the saliva suddenly pooling in my mouth.

Another shudder racked through me involuntarily as a cold sweat broke out on my brow.

I willed my feet to move. I needed to run. Alert Kil, Mav, Ax,

Kace—anyone who could help. But fear rooted me to the spot as images from that night, the ones I'd tried so hard to suppress, started to replay on autopilot in my mind.

The clammy touch of his sweaty palms. The overwhelming stench of brandy on his breath as his spit flew in my face. The black evil in his eyes as his men held me down on the cold dirt floor.

"No!" The girl's heart-wrenching scream tore through my memories, erasing every thought except one—*I have to save her.*

Anger and an overwhelming power coursed through me, immediately replacing my fear, and I rushed forward, rounding the corner and bursting into the hallway.

The girl was struggling, Romano had a firm grip on her elbow, and Tynan was making a grab for her other arm, his eyes hard with hatred.

My anger intensified at the sight of the two men together.

"Stop right there." An undeniable voice of power rang out, and it took me a second to realize that it belonged to me.

Turning in shock, their expressions became a mixture of hatred and fury as they realized who had commanded them. Tynan broke first, stalking toward me, that smile of his quickly turning to a sneer.

"What do you think you're doing here? Always where you're not wanted... or needed." He closed the space between us.

I automatically got into my fighting stance, feeling oddly confident.

"What? You gonna fight us or something?" He laughed. "We heard Dax, for whatever idiotic reason, had you in training. Should we test out what you've learned?" Within a second he was at my back, and in another he was grabbing me from behind.

I struggled, not used to his speed or strength. With Dax, everything was slow and methodical. The fact that we hadn't done any real fighting in training was painfully clear as I wriggled ineffectively in Tynan's grasp.

Try harder, Jacqueline. Dax's voice forced its way to the forefront of my mind.

Then, as if on instinct, I exhaled and threw all my weight forward, hinging at the waist as quickly as I could, throwing Tynan off guard. He loosed his hold and didn't see my elbow coming before I thrust it into his face. Reeling back and roaring in pain, he automatically doubled over, his nose gushing blood. Spinning out of his reach, I turned to face Romano only to realize he'd gone, taking the girl with him.

"No!" My shout echoed off the stone walls of the chamber.

Feeling a steel grip on my arm, I whipped around to find Tynan, almost fully recovered thanks to his Deviant powers. A small twisted smile appeared on his lips as they parted to show me teeth coated with the blood from his nose. But he was so intent on my face, he didn't see my knee as I drove it up, connecting it with his groin. Instantly releasing me again, he fell to the ground, moaning.

Apparently, deviating couldn't save men from one thing.

"Touch me again, and you'll wish you were dead."

"She's right. Either she'll kill you, or we will."

I turned to find Axel and Kacey standing in the doorway. The trio held eye contact for a few more seconds before Tynan got up and disappeared, heading in the direction of the side corridor.

"They took her. They *took* her," I practically screamed, my voice coming out rushed and frantic.

"Took who, Jac?" Axel was at my side, taking my hand, concern clouding his bright blue eyes.

"A refugee, I-I think."

"A refugee here, in the palace?" The shock in Kacey's voice was palpable.

I nodded. "She was here. They were going to force her to do something. Romano and Tynan. I stepped in. Tynan got to me. Romano escaped with her." I could feel the panic rising in my chest the more I spoke. We were losing time.

At the mention of Romano, a look of icy fury entered Axel's gaze, and he turned to Kacey.

"Why was Tynan with Romano?" I asked, not waiting for either of them to speak.

"There's a reason we don't trust Tynan besides his blatant prejudice against anyone from Calderone." Axel's voice was sharp as a blade.

"Jac, go to Scarletti's. We can grab you later. It's going to take both of us if Romano is headed to the south wing, and if he's not, he might be looking for you. With Dax gone…" Kacey's face filled with worry before she pulled me in for a quick hug. "I am so proud of you," she whispered before kissing me on the cheek.

They watched from the entrance to the storerooms as I ran to Scarletti's office, which was a clear shot down the hall. I was in front of her door and knocking before I knew what I was doing.

"Jacqueline." She opened the door a crack. Taking one look at my face, her usually austere expression softened, and she ushered me in. Gesturing for me to sit on the chair in front of her desk, she walked to the small table in the corner and poured me a glass of water, then set it in front of me.

Taking a few big gulps, I slowed my breathing enough to truly recognize where I was and realize I definitely *should not* have come here. Just yesterday, I'd committed the most brazen violation of Madam Scarletti's privacy and read her most personal thoughts. She also knew, at least in part, who I was. I didn't know what to say now that I knew that and more of her past, her daughter's tragic death, and her involvement in the refugee process. And her thoughts on *him*.

My skin crawled with awkwardness as she drew nearer to me, leaning on the front of the desk and folding her hands in her lap.

"Tell me child, what's going on."

Taking a deep breath, I raised my eyes to meet her gray ones. So like Dax's in their depth, so alive, despite her apparent age. I wasn't sure what to tell her or not to tell her, but for some reason I felt the need to tell her everything. So I did. Everything about Romano, the Devs, and Dax. Even going so far as to tell her I was a member of the Calderonian nobility, since she'd already guessed it anyway, but leaving out my true identity as heir.

Nodding like she already knew everything I was saying, she simply stood and put her hand on my shoulder when I was finished. Looking down at me, her gray eyes crinkled with kindness as she gave me a reassuring smile. "Dax will forgive you and will understand why you distanced yourself, Jacqueline. You are a very strong young woman. Do not underestimate yourself. The two of you together would be an unstoppable force, I am sure of it. In whatever capacity you decide to… work together." She paused as she said the last two words, then gave my shoulder a small squeeze before walking around the back of her desk.

"As for Romano, it won't be long now until he's taken care of." Gathering some papers and a clipboard, she moved for the door, turning back to me before she opened it. "You are welcome to wait in here until Axel or Kacey comes to get you—I'm sure it'll be soon. There's a lock on the door that cannot be picked by anyone who I would consider an enemy." She winked at me before walking out and securing the lock behind her.

The dining hall was abuzz the next morning, everyone eating

quickly to be ready for Dax's return at 0800. We'd spent most of the meal discussing my run-in with Romano and Tynan.

Kacey and Axel had found the girl, unharmed, in one of the back corridors. They suspected Romano didn't want to deal with the repercussions from Dax since he'd already been caught by me. The irony being that I don't think Dax would've done anything since I had literally told him to stay away from me.

And stay away he did.

When he wasn't at dinner Sunday night or the following day, or at any of my trainings, I got the sinking feeling that everything I'd felt between us was all in my head.

Come Tuesday afternoon, my thoughts had become increasingly negative, going from complete apathy to anxious extremes without notice. By the time I went to the kitchens to prepare for dinner, I had convinced myself that Dax was purposefully avoiding me and that my opportunity to form an alliance with him and truly save my people would never happen.

Kacey gave me space as we prepared the trays for serving, only approaching me immediately before dinner was to start and dragging me into the pantry for an intervention.

"What's going on, Jac?" She propped her hip on the pantry shelf. "What is with you these last few days?"

Refusing to meet her eyes, I instead focused on a loose thread in my bodice, not answering right away. I was acting like a child, but it was like I had no control. The weight of my country's future mixing with the foreign feelings pressing on my heart had me not knowing how to act.

"Let me guess. It has something to do with Mr. Da Luca?"

Sighing, I looked up to meet her gaze and nodded. "I know I'm being dumb. You don't have to tell me."

"No, I don't think you're being dumb. I think you're both being stupidly stubborn."

She had a point. Was he being stubborn, or was I truly just a charity case he no longer felt responsible for?

Ugh, I'm a mess.

"Look, I don't know if he'll be in there tonight. It's not like him to miss meals. If he is, just act normal. And if he isn't, act normal. What's supposed to happen will happen, Jac."

"I know. You're right, Kace. I'm just, I don't know." Shaking my head, I loosed a breath and grabbed her free hand in one of mine. "I'll be fine, promise."

Walking into the Great Hall, I went straight for my section at the back. I was still relatively new, and although I'd gotten better, I clearly lacked the experience of those who'd been serving on and off for decades. Everyone had been very welcoming and nice, but it was generally agreed that it was best I didn't serve in the front lest I drop a tray near the prince.

Standing with the other servants who worked the back sections, I watched as the courtiers wandered into the hall, talking animatedly with one another as they found their way to their usual tables based on their rank in court.

The hall itself was bigger than the throne room. The towering cathedral ceilings and large windows lining the top of the walls helped add to the grand feel of the room. The windows themselves were etched with intricate webs of Gaillic iconography. And early evening summer sunlight flooded through them creating patterns on the tapestries and floor below. The tapestries, which covered portions of the light stone walls from floor to ceiling, contained more iconography as well as Celtic symbols I didn't recognize.

The courtiers were almost finished being seated among the assortment of modest wooden tables that filled the space. About seven round ones were scattered in the back where I served with maybe five large bench-style tables in the center. One massive table, with two large chairs in the middle, was located in the front of the room. Though they'd never been in attendance, I knew that's where Dax and King Aidoneus sat. The two chairs were flanked on either side by various top Gaill officials and military personnel.

So far, Romano hadn't been in attendance at any of the meals I'd served. I didn't know if that was because King Aidoneus hadn't returned to court or because he knew his every move was being watched by the Devs while he was around me. Either way, I was thankful for his absence. Though my gut told me it was only a matter of time before he reappeared.

Grabbing a tray, I moved along the circle of now-seated courtiers. I had just started filling glasses with wine and setting hot rolls on plates when a loud bang sounded at the front of the hall. Starting and working to steady my tray, I stepped back to see one of the guards at the front move forward as the large oak doors behind him were thrown open.

"His Royal Highness, Daxinius Antonio Giovacchin Da Luca, Prince to the Gaill Forces, Defender of the Innocent and Ruler of the Deviants."

At that, the guard pounded his large cane on the floor, and everyone stood, eyes fixed to the front.

My mouth instantly went dry as I watched the doors. I felt him before I saw him, and the thrumming of his power became more intense as he approached, causing goose bumps to erupt down my arms and my hair to stand on end.

As he appeared, the entire room moved into a collective bow, and I quickly followed suit, dropping into a curtsy, keeping my head down but watching him through my lashes as he moved along the head table.

How could it be that he was even more stunning than when I last saw him? Like a Viking stolen from some legend, he was cut from stone—every angle of him chiseled, harsh, and unrelenting. He was beautiful in his brutality.

Half his dark brown curls were pulled back, some in the front fighting loose while others were braided. He wore a richly woven black tunic, open at the chest to reveal his tattoos, slim black pants, and heavy black boots, per usual. But this time a thick cloak of dark evergreen hung about his shoulders, held together by an intricate gold chain. It flowed behind him while he walked, moving as if on its own wind. His sword appeared as he moved along the table, rotating on its axis next to one of the two chairs at the center.

He stopped to shake hands with a few advisors as his power continued to radiate and ripple across the room, washing over me in waves, practically drowning me. I fought back the butterflies taking over.

Sauntering over to one of the two chairs at the head of the table, shoulders swaying, he paused before sitting, eyes scanning the room. I could've sworn they hovered in my direction, but he quickly looked forward again, taking his seat and giving a nod to his court that they could do the same.

The mood instantly lightened with the prince's arrival, and multiple courtiers gave speeches wishing him, the king, and the Gaill alliance against Calderone well. By halfway through dinner, groups had started to mill about the head table, wanting more details about where he went and what he did on his latest excursion.

I hung back in my corner, silently witnessing how Dax interacted with his court as I served the dinner and refilled drinks. Given I'd only been around him a few times with other people present, I had missed how much his people really loved him. And how much he loved them back.

He spent the better part of the main course speaking with an elderly couple before being commandeered by a group of school-aged children. But he never once looked exacerbated. In fact, he looked like he'd rather be chatting with them than eating the meal he'd come for.

Pushing the stray curls out of his eyes just then, he pressed a tattooed finger to his lips, leaning over to grab a cookie from the plate on the table and handing it to one of the younger girls, who couldn't have been more than three or four. Giggling, she managed to curtsy and take a quick bite before setting off at a run, cookie in hand. Straightening, he laughed lightly, his face the picture of happiness, his green eyes shining.

Biting my lip against a smile, I looked away, not wanting to be caught spying, and made my way to where Kacey was currently serving a group of young privates.

"Ah, Jacqueline. Won't you tell Kacey here how having three glasses of red is actually good for me?"

Smiling, I recognized the man as Private O'Connell, a member of Dax's guard who frequented the training center.

"Well, I mean, that's what twenty-first-century doctors said. But I'm pretty sure they meant one glass, and I'm also pretty sure that theory was debunked in the twenty-second century."

"Nonsense." He scoffed, tossing his head and holding out his glass for a refill.

Shaking my head, I filled it halfway. "You get half, Private

O'Connell."

"Whatever you say, boss." He winked.

"You're ridiculous, O'Connell." Kacey laughed, rolling her eyes at me before we split up to check on our areas. The last of the desserts had arrived from the kitchens, which meant the final push from us servers.

Grabbing a dessert tray, I was momentarily distracted by a loud laugh from the front of the room. One of the younger courtiers had her hand on Dax's bare arm. He'd taken off the cloak and rolled the sleeves of his black tunic up to reveal his maze of tattoos. Leaning back in his chair, he smiled at her as she spoke from the chair to his right. The one the king sat in.

Red hot jealousy tore through me, burning through every rational bone in my body. I continued watching them as he leaned in to say something to her, causing her to toss her head back and laugh again, long, straight blond hair cascading behind her. As she looked back at him, he fixed her with another smile, one that made me feel like I'd been sucker punched.

Who is she? I couldn't place a name to her face.

Is he into her? She was gorgeous. The perfect match for him—Gaill and obviously a member of their nobility.

Has she been here the past few weeks or did she go on the expedition with him? Why can't I remember seeing her?

"What kind of pies are these?"

Starting, I looked down to see one of the elderly courtiers inspecting the pies on my tray.

"Um." I cleared my throat. "They're apple. Made from the trees that line the grove."

"Ah," was all the woman replied, wrinkling her nose as she swiped a plate and moved to the nearest table.

I looked back to the front, and my heart instantly sank—both Dax and the woman were gone.

CHAPTER 12

CONFESSIONS

Groaning, I rolled out of bed at ten minutes to five the next morning, simultaneously turning my alarm off and scrubbing a hand down my face. I'd barely slept the night before—the images of the blond with her hand on Dax replayed over and over in my mind. And the fact that I should be more worried about the fate of my country and the world rather than my overwhelming jealousy only made me feel worse.

I brushed my teeth at the small sink and splashed cool water on my face before pulling my hair half back, the front layers inevitably slipping forward. Blowing them out of my face, I slipped on my fighting gear, a black formfitting vest the newest addition to my uniform, and put the small dirk in the holder that now hugged my thigh.

I looked slightly haggard and definitely ready to do some damage. I had no idea what the plan was for today's training, but I was looking forward to breaking a sweat and letting out some of my pent-up emotions. I only hoped Dax's men were ready.

No longer having an escort, I hurried to Dax's apartments where the guards let me into the training center. Looking around for one of my typical trainers, my breath caught in my throat when that familiar pulsating power hit me, and my eyes connected with *him*.

Dax sat on the edge of the fighting ring, arms resting on the ropes, emanating energy like a forcefield. His curls were loose and messy, and he'd pushed his tunic sleeves up to his elbows, revealing that maze of tattoos and muscles. The stubble on his jaw was more pronounced, as if he hadn't shaved in the past week, blurring the hard line where the ink on his neck met the brown skin of his face.

We stared at each other for a minute before I let pride get the best of me.

"Where's Captain O'Leary and Captain Davis?"

Ignoring my question entirely, he continued to stare at me, his eyes ocean green and bright—like he finally had me figured out, like he was waiting for me to realize what he already knew.

He slipped beneath the ropes and was in front of me before I could blink. "Have you been talking to Private O'Connell?"

What?

"Private O'Connell? You mean the member of your guard, Private O'Connell?"

He nodded, looking down at me, chin raised and arms folded.

"No. Well, yeah." I attempted to order my mind—a useless pursuit in his presence. "Last night, when he asked for a refill of his wine and made a joke about it being for his health."

He turned and grabbed his sword off a nearby stand. Walking to the nearest dummy, he began to strike it with such force I thought he'd break the wooden figure from its post.

"Who's the blond?" I asked before I could think.

He turned to look at me through his curls and ground out, "What blond?"

"From last night, at dinner." I raised a brow and crossed my arms, not bothering to hide my annoyance. "The one who had her hand on you. You know, the one you *left with*."

Scoffing, he turned back to his practice. "I didn't leave with Lady Daniels. I left right before dessert was served; I have no idea where she went."

"So you *didn't* spend the night together?" I hated myself for wondering, let alone saying the words out loud.

"No, Jacqueline. Contrary to what you might think, I'm not like that."

How could he *not* be like that when he looked like he did? I mean, at both Full Moon and at dinner, courtiers were practically hanging from him. It would take a unicorn of a man to resist that.

"Oh right, *Daxinius Antonio Giovacchin Da Luca*," I muttered under my breath. "Chaste virgin of the Gaill court. You likely have a different woman in your bed every night."

A loud clanging sounded, and my eyes flew forward to find Dax striding for me, his sword thrown on the ground.

On. The. Ground.

My heart started hammering as I took an instinctual few steps back, hitting the wall. I knew I could trust Dax not to hurt me, I *knew* he wasn't Romano, but the power thrumming from him was near to suffocating, and his white-hot gaze was so intense I couldn't look away if I tried. His muscles rippled beneath his tunic as he neared, every step more intimidating than the last. I held my breath, bracing for the impact.

Had I gone too far? Insulting his honor… insulting *him?*

And suddenly he was in front of me holding my face between his large callused palms. Sparks of electricity ignited from his touch while he pinned me between him and the wall. Ocean air and pine crashed into my senses, momentarily dulling the pounding of my heart, while power snaked from his hands down my spine, throughout my body, rooting me to the spot. My hands automatically flew to his but paused when his green eyes locked on to mine.

It was only a second, but it felt like forever. Longing, heartache, and overwhelming desire flitted across his gaze.

Then he kissed me.

And it obliterated everything else.

Passionate, hungry, *soul-shattering.* As if he couldn't get enough but didn't want to miss any second of it. Like he was memorizing this moment, my lips, *our kiss* forever.

Breaking away as suddenly as he began, he rested his forehead against mine, palms moving to the wall on either side of my head as our breathing came heavy and ragged.

"Jacqueline, there is *only* you. There has *been* only you since the moment you walked into the palace." His voice was a low rumble, his accent thick as he moved back to look at me.

I held my breath as my eyes searched his, seeing the reassurance that everything between us hadn't just been in my mind.

"I will respect your boundaries, but I'm done keeping my distance from you." The energy behind his green eyes began to churn again, his gaze burning into mine like a brand. "These past three weeks away nearly killed me."

Dax hardly showed affection or interest in anyone—he kept most of the world at an arm's length. Yet he'd given me a place in his household, had kept tabs on me, had given me gifts, including the gift of knowledge, before he even knew me. He'd saved me without a second thought, then took care of me, bringing me meals, medicine, and teaching me how to defend myself. Even giving me a weapon to use against him, yet trusting me not to.

He cared for me. Perhaps more than anyone else did. He might not have gone about showing it the right way, but he had done it the only way he knew how. And he was willing to learn, to live within my boundaries, to respect my wishes. To respect me.

Staring into his bright emerald gaze, I knew then.

There was no more guessing, there was only knowing. Like light into darkness, everything clicked into place.

Him. Me. Us. The Coalition. Calderone.

This.

Any second apart was another second too long. Another second wasted.

Nodding then, I reached up, cupping his cheek and pulling him to me as I let his eyes set my soul and heart ablaze.

"Then don't keep your distance."

At that, his lips crashed into mine.

White light burst around us, encircling us like a globe. I felt it claiming me, wrapping around my heart, penetrating my very blood.

And in that moment, I swear time stopped.

Dax's light pulsed, drowning out everything else so I didn't feel a thing… only *him*—his hands as they gripped my hips, possessive and claiming. His lips as they took mine without mercy. His silky curls as they brushed my face. The heat of his chest against mine as our heartbeats merged so I couldn't tell where his stopped and mine began.

He let out a small moan as I gently pulled on the curls at the nape of his neck and kissed me deeper, pressing his body into mine so that I was sure every ounce of my being was ready to explode beneath his touch.

"Dax," I managed to whisper, my voice raspy and raw.

His eyes flew open at mention of his name, and he gazed headily down at me through his dark curls. A smirk slowly took over his face as he squeezed my hips and, pulling me impossibly closer, put his lips to my ear, sending more sparks ricocheting down my spine.

"Hungry, Jacqueline?"

Leaning back, he bit his lip against a smile before reaching for my hand. Walking us to where he'd discarded his sword, he stuck his free hand out, letting the sword shoot up into it before he set it back on the stand by the door, never letting go of my hand the entire time.

"Sorry for making you throw your sword." I grinned as we walked out, making a mental note in my haze to ask him if magnetism was another one of his Deviant traits.

Looking back, he fixed me with a playful look.

"I guess that was your fault, wasn't it? I'll have to come up with a suitable punishment." He winked at me, turning back around and simultaneously sending storms of butterflies through my stomach.

We didn't meet anyone except a few guards while we moved up through Dax's private apartments to his living quarters on the top floor of the palace.

I'd never seen them like this, in the daylight. All the hallways were the same dark wood as his bedchamber, unlike the light stone in the rest of the palace. But the color was a definite rich mahogany now in the glow from the morning sun, whose rays streamed through the large windows that towered from the floor to the tall ceiling above. Windows covered the entire top floor, even the hallways we passed through, so it felt like we were practically floating above the gardens and hills below. And each window was framed by intricate moldings made from the same mahogany as the walls. Celtic as well as Gaillic symbols etched in gold leaf were everywhere—the walls, the moldings, the floor, even the black ceiling.

We eventually turned in to a small breakfast nook that stood open to a large terrace that I immediately recognized from the only time I'd been there.

"Breakfast is your favorite, yeah?" He turned, smiling down at me while he walked backward into the room.

Smiling back and nodding, not bothering to ask how he'd figured it out, I moved past him to the table positioned near the terrace, realizing there was already a full spread of five different types of waffles and pancakes as well as bacon, various fruits, and coffee waiting. A blush heated my skin when I noticed that he'd remembered my favorite foods, the ones I ate the most the last time, and had ordered only those.

Turning to thank him, I ran directly into his chest.

"You're welcome." He chuckled before I could speak. Smiling, he leaned down and pressed his lips to my cheek.

I did my best not to act inebriated from the contact.

Smirking as he straightened, fully aware of the effect he had on me, Dax walked around to pull my chair out, the one to the left of the head, and let me settle in while he grabbed my plate. Picking up a set of silver tongs, he motioned to the plates of steaming food, raising his brows in question.

"Um, two chocolate chip waffles and a banana pancake. With syrup. Fruit with bacon. Oh, and coffee please," I added, doing my best not to drool as I took it all in.

"My girl likes chocolate and banana. I can respect that." Dax nodded slightly, setting my plate down and filling my cup from the coffeepot stationed at the table. Grabbing his own, he started to load it with pancakes, waffles, and fruit, putting his bacon on a separate plate when he ran out of room.

Laughing, I shook my head and quirked a brow at him as he sat down. "*Your* girl?"

"Yes, *my* girl." Raising his brows at me in an obvious challenge, he popped a forkful of waffles and syrup in his mouth, that arrogant smile of his slowly appearing on his face as he chewed. "Something wrong with that?"

"No." I shrugged, ignoring what that smile did to my insides. "I guess I like it when you say it."

He just shook his head, his gaze turning a few shades lighter and more intense.

"Eat, Jacqueline, before I lose all my control and you lose the opportunity." His voice came out a husky command while his eyes drifted to my mouth—to the lip I hadn't realized I'd been biting.

"Whatever you say, Your Highness." I smirked as he looked away with effort, refocusing on his food.

We ate in silence for a few minutes, with only the sound of our clinking silverware filling the room.

"Where did you go these last few weeks? The others mentioned you were away on Gaill business." I waited to see if he wrote me off again or if things really had changed between us and he was willing to answer my questions.

Dax looked up from his plate and cocked his head slightly. "I was." Wiping his face with a napkin, he leaned back in his chair never breaking eye contact with me. "The others told you about my plans with the Coalition, correct?"

I nodded.

"Did they inform you of everything we needed to have in place to make it a success?"

I nodded again. "They mentioned the alliance with the Eur, other Gaill clans who lived outside the palace, and… the One."

The green of his eyes pulsed white. "I see the Devs have been busy filling you in on everything."

He didn't seem angry that they had, more surprised that I had ascertained that much about his plans in my weeks here. "They have, but to be fair, I pushed them for answers any chance I got."

"Why am I not surprised?" He shook his head and gave me a crooked smile. "The past few weeks I've been out courting the northern Gaill clans, if you will, to see if they'll join the Coalition as well as looking for the One."

"Do you think the One is a member of one of the clans?" I met his gaze as I sipped my coffee.

"It's a theory we're working on. We know per the prophecy the One will be Gaill born, but we've been searching for years with no results. It's also possible they're somewhere else, like in Eurasia. That's part of why it's essential we have the Eur's help. They can search there while we focus here."

"Are there Gaill anywhere else?" I wiped my mouth as I set my cup down and pushed my chair back slightly.

"Of course." He cut into his last waffle. "But I hope we don't have to search outside our two continents. Most Gaill in other areas of the world are very spread out. It would be next to impossible to find the One if we had to search every continent."

"I want to help," I blurted out. I had planned to approach the situation in a more eloquent way and only after I was sure he knew me well enough to know the truth of who I really was. But the words just rushed from me.

He cocked his head again, like it would help him understand me. "I'll think about it."

My mouth dropped open in surprise. Though I'd asked, I assumed he'd shut me down right away. But perhaps this was another sign that he took what I said at Full Moon seriously and that he did truly think I was strong enough to handle myself.

"But there's more you need to learn." He finished his last bite and set his fork down. "And more training you'll need first. As strong as I know you to be, you don't possess the powers of a Deviant, which already makes you greatly outmatched against most in this fight. I'll be dead before I put you in harm's way without the proper training to take on a Deviant."

"I can agree to that." Any further training and knowledge I had of how the Gaill worked and their plans would only better my position.

"Good. Now no more talk of the One or the Coalition. I've been thinking about that world for the better part of the past decade. And right now"—he moved my chair suddenly, grabbing hold of me and setting me in his lap—"the only thing I can think about is…" His long fingers wrapped around the back of my neck as he brought my lips to his, instantly devouring mine with a rabid hunger. It was all I could do not to drown in his embrace.

"Okay, you don't have a choice; you have to tell us."

My eyes moved from Lana to Kacey as the three of us huddled together at lunch. The boys were busy discussing news from Dax's expedition, so I found myself cornered, unable to dodge the expectant looks on their faces.

"We're a hundred percent serious." Kacey followed up. "Lucy saw Dax walk you back to your room and go *in*. She's telling everyone he was in there for a few minutes, Jac." She fixed me with a look that said everything without actually saying anything at all.

It was true. I had let Dax escort me back, but nothing had

happened—besides another earth-shattering kiss. But surely that hadn't taken a few minutes.

Had it?

Shaking my head and looking between them, I tried to hide my smile. "Well, yeah. He was at training this morning... if you can call it training," I gushed.

Both of them promptly squealed.

"Hey, pipe down, ladies. Some of us are discussing important matters."

"Shhh, shh." Lana waved her hand at Killian and the boys. "Don't interrupt." She looked back at me, raising her brows and gesturing for me to continue.

"Okay, well, I'm not really sure how it happened to be honest. Everything happened so fast. One minute he was asking if I liked Private O'Connell."

"Private O'Connell?" Lana shouted, brows furrowed, before she slapped a hand over her mouth and looked around, remembering we were in the middle of the crowded dining hall.

Laughing, I just shook my head, expecting nothing less. "Yeah, O'Connell. I know! And I asked him about a blond I saw him with at dinner—Lady Daniels or whatever. I basically accused him of being a playboy and told him he probably had a different girl in his bed every night."

Both the girls' mouths dropped open in shock.

"I cannot believe you said that to Dax Da Luca," Kacey said after a beat, shaking her head. "Bet he wasn't happy."

"No." I laughed, remembering his reaction. "Not at all. He actually threw his sword on the ground—you know the big one he carries on his back?—and then proceeded to storm over and, well, kiss me." I smiled, blushing despite my efforts to keep my cool. "A lot.

Like several times. And, well, I kissed him back. It was actually really amazing…"

I trailed off as Kacey and Lana both stared at me, mouths agape and eyes wide. They seemed utterly transfixed by the news for a few more seconds before Axel's laugh snapped them back to reality.

"Holy. Hell," came Lana's response.

"Mav. Boys!" Kacey shouted, causing all three to whip their heads in attention. "Dax and Jac. It happened."

There was a slight pause before a mad dash as all three moved their chairs to be closer to our side of the table.

"What does that mean, exactly?"

"Okay, so you both came to your senses then?"

"Details. Now."

"Okay. Hold on, boys, slow down. One at a time." I laughed, taking in their excited expressions, having had no idea they were so invested in my love life. "First, we kissed. And I guess he called me his girl."

"He what?" Kacey shrieked.

Okay, so this was kind of a big deal.

"Yeah, uh… h-he, uh…," I stuttered as I took in her stunned expression. "So uh, yeah, he did… And I guess we both did come to our senses." I flipped Killian off as I answered his question.

"Wow, this is insanity." Axel shook his head. "In a good way," he followed up, giving me a huge grin as he tossed his hair out of his eyes with a flick of his chin.

"I hope." I smiled back, looking down, suddenly shy with the exposition of it all.

What were Dax and I? We hadn't clarified anything yet. And he was the prince. I was no one here… yet. Maybe I shouldn't have said anything…

"Think Dax will be at Full Moon again Saturday?" Lana asked no one in particular between bites of her fries.

I shrugged in response.

"Absolutely," the boys answered simultaneously.

CHAPTER 13

FULL MOON

Turns out they were right.

Five minutes before I was set to meet Lana and Kacey to walk down to the grove, there was a knock at my door.

I gave myself a quick once-over—my eyes were bright, and my skin had that natural glow that comes from a regular routine of healthy eating, exercise, and good sleep. I ran my hands through my almost dry hair to separate the waves, having decided to leave it down on a whim. Usually I put it up or half back, but tonight was a special occasion. Plus it was a good hair day, so I decided to roll with it.

Straightening the black skirt of my weekend dress, I moved to the door, instantly feeling Dax's magnetic energy on the other side. Smiling involuntarily, I opened it to find his towering form leaning against the frame. His eyes were a swirling viridian as he smiled back at me.

Although he'd been at my trainings the past few days, Captain O'Leary or Davis had led me as I'd requested. He'd kept his distance except for walking me back to my room where he'd never even asked to come in after that first time.

He hadn't mentioned Full Moon either, and I hadn't brought it up. I wasn't exactly sure what we were and didn't want to press it. Obviously he'd called me his girl, but what were we really? He was a prince, and I was a servant in his court.

However, if he showed at Full Moon, I vowed to myself that I would clarify what we were, and what I wanted.

Which was everything.

Crowding into me suddenly so I was forced to step back, he reached behind himself to close the door. His presence immediately filled my small room, overpowering everything. I bit my lip to keep an involuntary groan in as I looked up at him—a rugged mess of tattoos and dark curls in all black.

How could one person be so utterly intoxicating?

"Thought I told you not to do that?" He pulled at my bottom lip with his thumb.

"Thought I told you not to tell me what to do?" I scoffed slightly, playfully raising a brow.

He quickly lowered his head to mine, pressing his lips to my ear. "Don't you know you're a guest at the Gaill court? It's not in our nature to do what we're told." He nipped at my ear as he finished, a husky laugh escaping when it sent a shiver down my spine.

Stepping back, he let out a low breath, his eyes filling with a sudden indescribable energy as they slowly raked over my face, my hair, over *me*.

"Do you know how absolutely radiant you are, Jacqueline?"

"Stop." I swatted at him before looking down in an attempt to hide the blush setting fire to my cheeks as his eyes continued their perusal.

Grabbing my hand before I could pull it back, he held it while his other tucked my dark brown waves behind my ear, lifting my chin when he finished. "You are. Truly. The most beautiful woman I've ever seen."

He leaned forward and lightly kissed my forehead, nose, then lips before stepping back, my hand still in his. "So you have a date for Full Moon tonight, or is it not too late for me to step in?" He raised his brows.

"Well, I was going with Kacey and Lan, but I *guess* you can join us." I smirked up at him.

Sighing, he just shook his head at me, a small smile on his lips. "I suppose that'll do."

"You suppose?" I smiled back, standing on my tiptoes, and reached up to grab his chin, pulling him down for a kiss. He let out a low guttural sound as he wrapped an arm around my waist, pulling me closer to him, fingers splayed on my hip. Breaking away suddenly, he grabbed my hand and started backing toward the door, a look on his face like he knew there was a strong chance that if we didn't leave now, we likely wouldn't make it to Full Moon at all.

Kacey and Lana managed to keep their cool on the walk to the grove—insofar as they managed to only make faces and obscene gestures when Dax wasn't looking.

"I will murder you two." I shot daggers at them behind Dax's back just as the lights from the grove came into view.

"You love us." Lana stuck her tongue out, causing Kacey to burst out laughing. The two took off then, running ahead before I could reply.

"Don't ask." I looked up at Dax as he turned to look at me.

"Wasn't going to." He smirked before looking forward and

wrapping my hand in his.

The setup was similar to last time—lights strung up between trees that were now dark green in the setting summer sun. A wide array of food was set out along several tables with even more kegs than last time since we hadn't been able to decide on just one drink after our taste test at Mav's.

We weaved through the groups of people already partying, Dax seemingly unfazed by the looks of shock thrown our way, and made our way toward our group, which had congregated near the food and drinks. Naturally.

The candied smell of maple syrup and pastries hit me as we passed the buffet, and I zeroed in on a separate section of breakfast food that definitely hadn't been there last time. Was I just imagining things, or had he really done that for me?

Looking to Dax, I met his gaze, and watched as his lips turned up in a smile when he realized where I'd been looking.

"Did you… was that… did you do…"

"Dax! Two months in a row? You lookin' for a rematch or what?" Killian was immediately at our sides then, slapping Dax on the chest. "What's good, Calderone?" He threw a wink and a nod in my direction, the setting sun refracting off his brow piercing.

"You looking to embarrass yourself again, Kil?" Dax laughed, playfully punching him in a way that would probably break a normal human's ribs before we followed him back to meet the rest of the group.

"And to answer your question," Dax said, slowing down and pulling me in to kiss the top of my head while we walked, "breakfast is my girl's favorite food. Can't really call it a celebration then without chocolate chip or banana pancakes."

Looking down, I bit my lip in a poor attempt to keep what was now an idiotic smile from taking over my entire face.

"Breakfast twice in one week, Mr. Da Luca? You spoil me," I said.

"Get used to it, Jacqueline," he murmured in my ear.

Clearing my throat, I looked up to find our group and the rest of the Devs in the grove watching us. In silence.

Doing my best to focus only on the faces of our friends, I followed Dax as we walked the last few feet to the group.

"You done?" Dax asked as we reached them, seeming to snap everyone out of their haze and causing the entire grove to move into action at once.

Axel busied himself pouring the group a round of drinks to celebrate Dax's return, or so he said, while the rest of us found a spot to sit. Everyone else in the grove did their best to look occupied while not so subtly stealing glances in our direction.

I couldn't tell if the general shock was because Dax was actually giving someone attention or because the person he was giving it to was a member of the staff. And a former Calderonian prisoner.

It was probably both.

Before I could start seriously second-guessing myself, I felt Dax's hands on my waist as he tugged me down onto his lap. He was already sitting back in one of the larger armchairs with his legs spread out in front of him. Because of his height, my feet dangled below me while his free hand came to rest on my stomach, holding me to him before it began making lazy circles, sending chills throughout my body. Looking down at me over my shoulder, he brought a beer—a bottle he must've just grabbed from who knows where—to his lips with his free hand and looked at me as if to say "what're you gonna do about it" before taking a swig.

Laughing, I narrowed my eyes at him, instantly feeling at ease as I deftly swiped the bottle from his hand after he took his drink. Raising a brow, I took a swig. He only shook his head as he watched me, his eyes sparkling with amusement as he gave me a rare crooked smile before turning his attention to Mav, who was speaking to the group.

"—Queen Caragh herself said the One is Gaill born. Their being anywhere besides here or Eurasia is incredibly unlikely."

The debate as to the present-day location of the One had been going on since Dax's return. Some Devs believed the One was on New American or Eurasian soil given those continents held the greatest concentration of Gaill. Others were convinced the One was on a different continent since no one had been able to locate them yet.

"That's all wishful speculation." Dax's low voice came from behind me, causing everyone to look our way. "There's a reason neither we nor the Eur have found the One."

"So what you're saying is… that we're not sure where the One is?" Kacey asked, sipping her wine slowly, hazel-orange eyes looking innocently at us.

"Not exactly," he said. "But like Mav said, there's a greater likelihood they're here or in Eurasia. The theory that they'll be from one of the northern clans is still the dominant one. Though all our searching there has yielded nothing as of yet."

Kacey nodded. This was clearly common knowledge among the Gaill.

"Why do you think the One's likely of northern decent?" I asked quietly, turning to Dax as the others carried on about more news from Dax's expedition.

"It turns out that in the years before she passed, my mother did extensive research into the identity of the One. She wanted to be absolutely positive her vision was correct in every way before telling me, which is why she was out the day she was attacked. She was on her way home from a library farther north when Calderonian soldiers ambushed her caravan."

An involuntary shudder ran through my body as I remembered what Kacey had told us about the attack and what had happened after. Although he did his best to hide it, the guilt and anguish now swimming in his eyes was enough to drown me with him.

His guilt over their deaths has consumed him.

Scarletti's words from decades earlier rang in my mind.

Reaching up, I pulled him toward me as I tipped my head up to place a soft kiss on his cheek. "Your mother sounds like an amazing woman. I wish I had been lucky enough to meet her."

"Me too, Jacqueline." He gave me a small smile, loosing a low breath before he continued. "There's… a lot to her research we're still figuring out because she didn't have time to finish it before her death forced her to tell me of the prophecy. It wasn't until a few years ago that I even stumbled upon her notes in a hidden drawer in her old office." He took a long swig, polishing off his beer. "From what we can tell, there's evidence that the One was likely born after 2345 and to those of at least partial northern decent—north of even my kingdom. Though her theories could all be incorrect. She didn't have time to verify much. Whoever they are, we likely haven't encountered them yet, or else I would've been aware of it."

"Aware of it?"

"Girl. Bathroom, now."

Before I could hear Dax's answer, Kacey yanked me out of his lap, and we were halfway across the grove to the bathrooms set in the garden pavilion.

"Kace!"

"Sorry, Jac. Girl time takes precedence!" Kacey smiled back at me as Lana caught up to us and shot a conspiratorial glance in Kacey's direction.

"Yeah, we just want the inside scoop." Lana pursed her lips on the last word and looped her arm through mine.

"And I think we deserve first dibs, right?" Kacey held open the staff door for us, and we piled into the bathroom. Walking over to one of the mirrors above the small porcelain sinks, she flipped her reddish-blond locks behind her before giving herself a quick once-over and looking back at us in the reflection.

I laughed, looking between them. "What am I going to do with you two?"

Kacey shrugged, smiling. "So spill it, Jac. What's going on with you and Dax?"

"Okay." I laughed again, then shook my head. "Well, actually I don't know. I guess I haven't clarified things with him, but I feel kind of stupid asking. I mean, he's been at all my trainings this week, and he picked me up tonight. I know there's something between us, something more, but I haven't clarified exactly what we are."

Meeting Kacey's teasing look in the mirror, I let out an exasperated sigh, piling my hair on my head. "The guy is hundreds of years old. You can't expect me to act like this is a normal thing! I mean why does he even have an interest in me? He could have someone who can actually do something cool. Like shoot fire out of their eyes or something—I don't know! All I can do is serve dinner, and I can only do that moderately well."

"Stop, Jac." Lana met my eyes in the mirror as she walked to my side. "You know that's not true. Stop doubting yourself. You're strong, kind, and loyal, not to mention a host of other things that magical Dev powers can't give you."

"And let's not forget how you single-handedly kicked Tynan's ass." Kacey winked at me as I met her reflection again in the mirror. "I mean the guy hasn't even shown up tonight, probably still embarrassed."

Letting my hair fall, I loosed a low sigh. I *had* defeated Tynan, hadn't I? Even in that small way, a victory was a victory. And despite the fact that I'd landed myself in this totally messed-up situation and had had more than a few setbacks, I *was* getting stronger. I felt it in my bones.

I gave them a grateful smile. "Thank you, ladies. Truly."

"Anytime, Jac." Lana blew me an air kiss. "So you gonna ask Dax what's going on tonight?"

"Yes, at least that's the plan."

"Good." Lana nodded before pulling out her lip gloss and reapplying.

"Ooh, you know you're gonna let me use some of that, Lan."

"Of *course*, Kace." Lana rolled her eyes as she handed the lip gloss over to me to reapply before I passed it to Kacey.

Exiting the bathroom, we made our way to the kegs to grab some mixers. Apparently, Kacey and Lana weren't the only Devs looking to confirm the rumors that were now undoubtedly swirling about the grove since we were practically swarmed the moment we stepped up to the buffet.

Some of the Devs I recognized from work, some were members of Dax's guard, but most I had never exchanged more than a few words with. When you're one of two prisoners turned servants, prisoners from the hated monarchy at that, most of the other servants view you as someone worthy only of their pity.

But since I had managed to at least momentarily snag the interest of their elusive prince, they were all much more interested in getting closer. It wasn't every day that someone tied down Daxinius Da Luca. I assumed the big question on everyone's mind was the same as the one on mine—*Why her?*

Though no one would ask that of course. Some things were the same across all kingdoms. Court flattery was most definitely one of them.

"Jacqueline, you look stunning tonight."

"Is your weekend dress different than ours? Yours is so much more flattering."

"Are those your natural waves? How do you get them to fall so well?"

Although I was used to the typical comments, I was surprised to find that they didn't affect me like they usually did back in Calderone. Smiling at each of them in turn, I thanked them, letting them know I was in fact wearing the same dress as all the other women and they had caught me on a good hair day.

Taking the opportunity when there was a break in the conversation, I gave the assembled group another smile and walked the short distance to grab the drink Kacey was pouring from one of the kegs. As I reached for the cup, the hairs on the back of my neck stood on end, and goose bumps erupted across my outstretched arm. I didn't even have to look; I knew Dax's eyes were on me as my body reacted in the way it only did for him.

"Loverboy is staring." Lana giggled as if reading my mind.

Not able to resist, I pulled my waves to the side and peeked over my shoulder, instantly connecting with him across the dimly lit clearing. Even in the low light, I could make out the swirling intensity behind his eyes, and an involuntary shiver ran down my spine. He lifted his chin slightly in that way of his, like he knew exactly what I was feeling as I felt it. I let out a nervous laugh as I turned back to the girls.

"Yeah, he has a habit of doing that." I laughed again though it came off more like a hoarse cough as I bit my lip and looked between them.

"If I didn't know any better, I'd say that boy is smitten with you,

Miss Lewis." Kacey smiled into her drink as she took a sip, holding my gaze over the rim with a knowing look.

Tucking my chin, I did my best to hide my smile and my blush at her words while we walked back to the guys. I only hoped he was as smitten with me as I was with him. Or else I was in for more trouble than I already was.

By midnight, most everyone was on the dance floor. Well, floor as in the area in the middle of the grove that had been cleared and strung with more lights. The DJ stationed at one end was playing a mix of music that had been popular when I left Calderone with music I didn't recognize. It sounded faintly Celtic, but all of it somehow had the same hypnotizing electronic beat.

Not realizing how much I'd missed the freedom brought from dancing and truly feeling a rhythm as it moved through me, I let the pulse of the music vibrate in my chest as it reverberated throughout the grove. The last time I'd danced had been the night I was taken. Though suddenly that night didn't seem as bad as it once had. I still missed my friends back home, but surrounded by Kacey, Lana, and a few of the other Dev girls I knew from serving, I'd never felt more at home.

Until he found me.

Feeling him approach from behind, I was in his arms like a magnet before my next thought. His hands found their home on my hips as his head dipped and he kissed along the top of the black wool lining my shoulder before his hands moved my waves to the side so he could place a small kiss on my neck.

Shuddering, I felt him smile against my skin as he relished the undeniable power he had over my body. Electricity sparked at the base of my spine before slowly winding its way up and out across my whole body as his hips expertly rolled in time with mine.

Little surprised me anymore, but Dax being a great dancer? That… *that* surprised me.

"Where you been, beautiful?" His voice was a husky whisper as his lips moved against my ear, intensifying the magnetic energy already coursing between us.

"It's been a busy night." My voice came out rushed, not at all the strong and sultry I intended.

"Mmm." His chest vibrated against me as he kissed along my jaw.

Not being able to take more of his teasing, I turned in his arms, and my hand came to rest over his heart, feeling the beat of it, fast but strong beneath that wall of stone. The ocean churning in his eyes was almost white as he looked down at me through his lashes.

"You're not so good at hiding your emotions, are you?" I asked, smiling slightly as his gaze only brightened more.

"Usually I am." He leaned down to press his forehead to mine. "It's only around you that I can't seem to find control."

That made two of us.

He bit his bottom lip then, causing my eyes to momentarily break from his as I became distracted by it. And what it did to me.

Suddenly his knuckles, the ones with the moons tattooed across them, tipped my chin up as he leaned back. Running them along my jaw and cheek, his eyes drank me in. "I've never seen something so stunning."

"Hmm?" The only sound I was capable of in that moment.

"You. Everything about you. Your eyes, I can see the moon reflected in them, the stars—everything. Simply beautiful…" He trailed off as his words became a jumble. He bit his lip again, and if

I didn't know any better, I'd say a blush was creeping up his tan skin though it was hard to tell through the stubble and tattoos in the dark.

The smile taking over my face froze as his body went rigid against mine and his gaze shifted, just as bright but the passion replaced by something worse than hatred. A wrath so deep I couldn't begin to comprehend what could've happened to make him change so suddenly.

Turning in his arms, I was surprised to see a small aura of white light surrounding us, like we were in a bubble. I was so captured by it that I almost missed Tynan standing across the grove—watching us. Making no effort to hide his disgust.

I shivered involuntarily. Images of when he grabbed me flashed across my mind before I reminded myself I had no reason to be afraid of him. I had left him crumpled on the floor.

I could handle this.

I felt a slight movement as Dax started to make his way around me, lethal power rolling off him in waves. Whipping back, I gripped his arm, giving him pause.

He looked down at me through his dark curls, eyes ablaze, teeth clenched, and nostrils flaring. "He put his hands on you," he rumbled as a muscle twitched in his jaw.

I could've killed the guys for telling him about my run-in with Romano and Tynan. The last thing I needed was for him to go all caveman on me again and potentially screw up our plans against the king.

"I handled it," I reassured him, doing my best to stand my ground as my resolve melted under the intensity of his gaze.

Looking over my head at where I assumed Tynan was still standing, Dax was deathly still except for the muscle still twitching in his jaw. After what seemed like an eternity, he licked his lips and loosed a breath, meeting my gaze again as he nodded. "For you,

Jacqueline, I won't do anything. But I can't deny the fact that every fiber of my being wants to go over there and hammer his face in."

It really wasn't fair for him to be so good-looking *and* say things like that.

"Well, it might not have been his face, but he definitely didn't leave without getting the message to not touch me again." A small smile took over my lips as I remembered Tynan cowering in pain after his thwarted attack.

"So I heard." Dax's crooked smile reappeared as he looked down at me, his mood lightening as he tipped his chin back. "Good thing a devilishly handsome prince started you on that training program."

"Devilishly handsome and exceedingly modest." I rolled my eyes at him.

"You two ready to head?"

Both of us turned as Kacey and Mav walked up from where the rest of the group was gathering.

"Yeah, you good?" Dax looked down at me.

I nodded at him as he took my hand, and we made our way through the rest of the Devs still dancing.

Chancing a glance back, my eyes found Tynan—he hadn't moved, and his eyes were now trained on our intertwined hands. Quickly looking forward, I suppressed another shudder, a creeping sense of foreboding coming over me as I felt Dax glance back at me. Looking up at him, I saw that same look of death cross his face, and he tightened his grip on my hand like he knew exactly what I'd been feeling.

CHAPTER 14

ULTRAVIOLET

Not having stayed until the end of a Full Moon yet, I didn't realize the group typically assembled for an after-party of sorts in Mav's room. Leaning back, I sat on the floor between Dax's legs as he sat on one of the pillows. I tried not to laugh at the sight of his huge frame on the comparatively smaller pillow. Especially when the group started exchanging stories from their childhood and teenage years, which apparently spanned decades when you were a Deviant.

"Caragh was so pissed at you that night." Killian snorted into the beer he was still nursing from the grove. "'Cougars, Daxinius Antonio? Have you lost your mind?'" The group doubled over laughing at Killian's imitation of the queen.

Where I sneaked out of the palace and partied, apparently teenage Dax had parlayed with cougars.

Dax let out a deep chuckle. "Yeah, well, Kitty wasn't too happy when you decided you wanted one for yourself."

"Oh, Ma was on the verge of killing me that day. Pretty sure she would've too had Caragh not talked her into letting us keep them."

"You actually keep cougars here as pets?" I raised my brows as I looked back at Dax, shaking my head in disbelief.

"Kept." He raised his as if that was enough of an answer.

"Yeah, this was what, the 2270s?"

A hundred years ago. Unreal.

Shaking my head again, I was momentarily dumbfounded. It always managed to slip my mind that Lan and I had befriended a bunch of Deviants who were centuries old. It was easy to forget when most of them didn't look or act a day over twenty-five. Usually.

I looked to Lana for some camaraderie but found none—she'd fallen asleep. Drool was dripping from her slightly open mouth as she lay with her head slumped against Axel's shoulder.

"So if you are all so old, why do you act like overgrown teenagers most of the time?" I asked before thinking.

There was a slight pause before the entire group burst out laughing, again causing Lana to start as she wiped the drool from her cheek and looked around in a sleepy haze.

Pulling me up into his lap, Dax's loose curls tickled my neck as he leaned down. "Because we can," he said, his voice low.

"Yeah, what he said." Killian grinned before grabbing the flask they'd been passing around from Mav's hands and taking a hearty swig.

"We have our moments," Mav said. His smile was joking, but a seriousness lay hidden behind his gaze. "Don't worry though; we do have a more mature side. One you haven't had to see much of yet because, right now, everything's at peace."

"And hopefully it stays that way a while longer," Kacey said.

"Mmm." Dax's reply came from behind me. An agreement but acknowledgment that the peace we were experiencing now was likely the calm before what could be a catastrophic storm.

A loud yawn came from Lana then, although she did her best to stifle it behind her hand.

"All right, bedtime for Lan," Killian said, standing and picking Lana up in his arms as he turned for the door.

"That's us too." Dax stood and righted me with him before I could blink.

Leaving Kacey and Mav, the five of us piled out and headed to the lower floors. We parted ways with the boys and Lana at the start of the girls' wing. Lana waved sleepily from Killian's shoulder as the three made their way to the boys' rooms. And then it was just me and Dax outside my door.

I turned to look up at him before going in, feeling the effects of his power as it curled around me.

In all honesty, I felt him all the time. Even when he wasn't near me. But times like this? When we were alone? His presence consumed me in an instant.

Tucking my waves behind my ear, Dax ran a tatted finger along my jaw before sticking both hands in his pockets. "You tired?"

"Not really," I said quickly, shaking my head.

Call it adrenaline or the hammering of a thousand butterflies that had taken up permanent residence in my stomach, but it felt like Dax's own energy was coursing through my veins. I didn't want the night to end, not yet at least.

"Good." His only reply before cracking a smile and scooping me up, lifting me onto his back in one fluid motion.

"Are you giving me a piggyback ride, Your Highness?" I laughed as I attempted to wrap my legs and arms around his large frame.

"You could say that." He smirked at me over his shoulder. "Though I don't think you've had one like this before."

That was all he said before we were flying through the palace.

A blinding white current of energy enveloped us again, and it's as if everything moved at the speed of light but in slow motion at the same time. When I looked forward, I could barely make out where we were going everything moved so fast. But looking to the side, everything was frozen in time—the few night servants we passed weren't even moving. The water one was pouring into a large vase of roses was paused, cascading in midair. And before I knew it, Dax was setting me down on one of the large, richly colored Persian carpets inside the main gallery of his apartments, grinning at me.

I let out a breath I hadn't realized I'd been holding as it occurred to me that likely no more than a few seconds had passed between the time we were standing outside my room to when we'd arrived, there in his apartments, clear across the palace. I attempted to speak, but nothing came out while my mind scrambled to keep up with the fact that I'd essentially just teleported.

"Since you can't shift, I wanted you to experience it. It's the most common Deviant trait, along with better hearing, strength, intelligence, wit, charm..." He threw a playful smile in my direction at the last few words.

"Is there a trait you *don't* have as a Deviant?" I fixed him with a teasing stare as I cocked a brow.

An indiscernible look crossed his eyes, but just as quickly, he flattened his mouth, pretending to be stumped. I huffed a sigh, rolling my eyes at him, which only caused him to throw his head back and laugh, a deep rumbling sound that echoed off the mahogany wainscoting, making the entire gallery somehow more intimate.

"Come." He grabbed my hand again before pressing on the wooden panel next to him. On his touch, the panel turned transparent revealing a dimly lit hallway leading to his private apartments.

As we passed the little room where we last ate breakfast, a thought hit me.

Groaning, I stopped and scrubbed my free hand down my face. "I never had any breakfast tonight! I can't believe I did that. I mean you went to the trouble. And I just... such an idiot," I moaned, half-joking, half-serious, because I never passed up an opportunity for a good meal, especially when it only came once in a full moon.

"I thought as much." Dax looked back at me, the corners of his lips turned up, then kept walking, opening the large door at the end of the hall that I remembered led to his bedchamber.

As soon as it opened, the familiar scent of maple and powdered sugar hit me, and I let slip an excited gasp when I realized what he'd done.

A smaller version of the breakfast from the grove was set before the overstuffed armchairs in front of the fireplace, which was currently crackling with a few large birch logs.

I turned, launching myself into Dax's arms before planting a kiss on his lips. It was only breakfast, but for some reason, the gesture felt like the nicest and most sincere thing anyone had ever done for me.

Taken by surprise, he quickly recovered, smiling against my lips before setting me down and brushing the loose waves out of my face.

"So how often were you watching me, Mr. Da Luca, to know that I hadn't eaten?" I grabbed his hand and ran my finger over the moon etched on his thumb before I slowly led him back toward the chairs.

"Often enough," he said, his voice low.

I turned to the food in an attempt to hide the blush and foolish smile spreading across my face.

"And you're not an idiot." His voice came in my ear. "What you are is a really good dancer."

Inhaling sharply, I whipped around to find him eye level with me. The green in his irises was getting whiter by the second as the electricity between us intensified.

"I..." I stopped myself. I'd had dance lessons since the age of three, but what Calderonian servant could say that? A new sense of guilt started to take hold. Keeping my true identity a secret might have helped me keep my oath, but it required more and more lies to the people who meant more and more to *me*.

His thumb pulled at my bottom lip, bringing me back to the present—to the lip I was perpetually biting out of habit.

Fixing on his questioning gaze, I gave him a small, teasing smile, evading the subject the best I could. "I've had practice. Your men did find me out at a club, remember?"

Something like guilt crossed his eyes before he smiled playfully. "How could I forget? What was it... You were out with friends at a club close to the Wall... captured for no reason and brought here. You're not sure why, and you want to go home?" Ending the last sentence like a question, he raised his chin and brows at me.

Laughing lightly, I shook my head. He'd remembered verbatim what I'd said to him the first night we'd ever been alone together—when I'd thought he hated me and wanted me dead.

When I still thought of Calderone as home.

"I thought you hated me that night—the night I served you and the Eur leaders. I was so scared." I laughed nervously, looking down, suddenly taking a great interest in the intricate weavings of the rug beneath our feet. I didn't know why I was telling him this, admitting my fear and self-doubt. There was no reason for me to do it. It had to be my inner masochist.

"I know." He laughed as he reached down to tip my chin up. "Dev hearing, remember? And unlike a Dev, as a human, you have no way to block us out so if we want to hear everything, we can. Which I did. Your heart rate and your breathing, not to mention your energy, were all off the charts. It's why I was so taken aback when you challenged me. That type of strength in the face of such fear is unusual."

"Wait, what do you mean, *my* energy?" I met his gaze while his own energy sparked and coursed from my jaw down my neck to my spine and back to him again.

"Your energy." He moved his hand to my neck before dragging it down the side of my body as he shifted past me to sit on one of the chairs. "Everyone exhibits an energy. It can change depending on how the person is feeling or thinking. Some, like a Deviant's, are more pronounced than others. Yours is particularly noticeable, which is unusual considering you're fully human."

"Well, what does that mean?" I walked around to sit down on the chair next to his.

Leave it to me to stick out like a sore thumb when I needed to blend in the most.

"I'm not really sure to be honest." He looked at me thoughtfully. "It's one of the many things I've been trying to figure out about you."

Another involuntary blush crept up my cheeks.

Okay, and what did *that* mean?

"So you could tell how scared I was that night. Is what you are saying?" I asked instead, not ready to know exactly what he'd been trying to figure out about me. Especially if it had anything to do with my identity. I did have to tell him who I was eventually—I knew that—but it had to be at the right time. And two in the morning after being out all night definitely wasn't it.

Nodding at me, chin raised again in that arrogant way of his, he shot me a lopsided grin. "Oh yeah. As if you had told me your thoughts out loud."

"So then you could also tell how scared I was that first day in the throne room?"

His expression instantly changed to one of… respect? "Yes."

"What're you, impressed I put that together?"

Chuckling again, he smiled back at me. "Yes, actually."

"You know you come off like a huge dick to people when you first meet them?"

Several seconds passed while he held my gaze before we both started laughing.

"I know," Dax said eventually, heaving a sigh. "I know I do. But when you and your people have been persecuted for centuries, you learn that you have to be a certain way in order to survive."

"I don't think you're really like that though… the villain the world believes you to be."

My words hung in silence as he looked at me then, a rare vulnerability evident behind his eyes like maybe I was one of the only people who truly saw him for him.

Another minute passed before the air became impossibly thick. A subject change seemed like a safe bet. "Uhm, so"—I cleared my throat—"what does my energy look like?"

His gaze turned lighter, the energy between us intensifying. "It's ultraviolet."

Like that should mean something to me.

"Okay, so—"

"It's the most intense energy someone can display," he said. "Most humans can't reach it, and if they do, it's at the expense of something great like their heart. And even then, it's only for a second or two. But your energy is ultraviolet more often than not. It has been from the first time I saw you in the throne room. I could feel it before you walked through the doors."

I tried to sort through what he was saying. People display an energy? Ultraviolet? Wasn't that invisible?

"I don't... I'm not understanding," I said slowly. "So I can't see it, but I'm still showing it? All the time? I thought UV light was invisible. And if mine is so intense, why has no one else said anything?"

"Because my mother and I are the only Gaill, at least in this hemisphere, that have—or had—the ability to see someone's energy. And you only display it when you're particularly... emotional."

Well. That's great.

"What does it look like?" I did my best to not go back and analyze every interaction we'd ever had.

"When you're calm, next to nothing, a small glow—you almost look like everyone else. But when you're excited, energetic, or insanely happy? You shine—your light is the brightest blues and violets I've ever seen."

"What does it look like when I'm scared then?" I was extremely curious as to what I looked like, what the *world* looked like, through his eyes.

"It looks the same no matter how you feel. The more energy you expend on any emotion, the more you will exhibit it to the outside world. It's not that this is new. You've always done this, had this type of energy and power. Others just can't see you like I can."

I paused as his words made something deep within me shift. And looking at him, I wasn't sure if they meant anything different than what they did on the surface, but I couldn't help but feel like he was right. It did feel like he saw me, actually saw me *for me*, when no one ever had before.

Just like I see him.

Clearing my throat, swallowing over the unwelcome lump that had suddenly appeared, I attempted to move the conversation forward. "So others, other humans and Devs, what do they look like?"

"It varies," he said, thankfully not noticing or just ignoring the emotion in my voice and undoubtedly in whatever ultraviolet force field I was exhibiting. "Most Devs are black, a neon color, or white, as I am. Most humans have a dull yellowish glow to them that rarely brightens beyond their most pivotal life moments, and even then, it's barely discernible unless you really look for it."

"So my whole ultraviolet, bluish-purple thing is pretty out there then."

"You could say that."

"Okay, well, wait. If you're the only person who can see me in all my ultraviolet splendor, how come I can see your white light-power-whatever." My arms flailed as my words failed to explicate the indescribable manifestation of his powers.

"Oh that." A sad smile passed over his face. "That's a story for another time."

Something about his tone and the look on his face pulled at my heart, but I nodded, not wanting to push him too far too soon. Instead, I decided to ask if my light was the reason he'd first had me followed. But as I opened my mouth, he popped a piece of bacon into it—his actions so quick they made me jump.

"Food's getting cold," he said, the sadness from moments earlier forgotten.

Chewing, I smiled against the rumbling in my stomach. I was hungry, and it was late. My questions could wait. For now.

Morning light poured through the floor-to-ceiling window panes, creating slanting squares on the wood floor. Everything was still; even the dust swirling in the faint sunbeams seemed to hover, waiting for the day to begin.

I buried my face in the feather pillow, relaxing into the scent of fresh sheets mixed with ocean air and pine. Opening my eyes after a few minutes, I slowly rolled over, stifling a yawn when I realized I was nuzzled against a sleeping Dax.

We'd fallen asleep talking. The last thing I remembered was his giving me a kiss on the nose before my eyes closed. Looking at him now, I drank in the sight of him. How many people had been able to watch him sleep? Not many, I'd bet.

His beauty was even more striking when he was sleeping, fully at ease. My eyes traced the light as it refracted off the amber in his messy curls where they lay across the pillow, undone from the bun he'd thrown them in last night. His tan skin was marked by that same stubble he always had, the stubble I had now grown to love, and his full lips were slightly ajar, his jaw slack, relaxed for the first time in what was probably a long while.

How had this happened? How I had let myself start to fall for the fabled Gaill prince?

And as soon as the thought entered my mind, I realized it was true. I was falling and had been for a while.

Rolling onto my back, I stared up at the golden Eclipse on the ceiling and did my best to ignore the tightening in my chest as panic started to take hold.

We still hadn't clarified anything. I still had no idea what I was doing. And I suddenly felt like I was out on an emotional limb, alone, with nothing to hold on to.

A sudden pang hit me deep in my gut. Not only was I falling for him, I was doing so when he thought I was someone else.

Even if I did go against my oath and tell him who I was, how could I be certain he would help me?

I knew Dax was a good man. I knew he wouldn't physically harm me no matter how angry he would be once I finally revealed the truth. But I also knew that though he wished to save the innocents in Calderone, his hatred for the monarchy was unwavering.

My government was responsible for his suffering and that of his people, of so much loss and destruction, and the death of his own mother. And the fact that I'd been untruthful thus far about my identity and my complicity in that suffering... would he even believe my true intentions once he found out I'd lied about something so great? Would he take out his anger on me? On my people? My government didn't have the best track record with being truthful. I mean, they were still attempting to attack the Gaill as evidenced by the raid a few weeks ago. And Dax wasn't exactly known to be merciful to those he thought were loyal to the monarchy.

A lie that great wasn't something I was sure I could forgive if the roles had been reversed. But not confessing wasn't an option. I couldn't live a lie forever. Not if I wished to ally myself with Dax and the Coalition to truly help my people.

My old enemies fear and self-doubt quickly took hold, and only one thing came to mind—I had to get out of here.

Moving the covers, I slowly sat up and swung my legs off the side of the bed. But I shrieked as I was immediately ripped backward by my waist. A second later, I was on top of Dax, my legs straddling him as he lay back on the pillow.

"Going somewhere?" His voice was gravelly with sleep.

"Um, no?"

He smiled then, a shy sort of smile that made me realize that maybe he was feeling just as strongly for me as I was for him. "Mmm, good." His only response before his hands moved over the wool material that covered my thighs to my waist. One hovered there as the other moved up my back to press me to him.

If his smile hadn't been enough to convince me, his kiss was.

We connected with such automatic intensity it was like I was oxygen, and Dax needed me to breathe. Like I was his very key to existence. I felt the power beneath his fingertips like a brand in my back and hips as it marked my skin before shooting through my body. I didn't have to look; I knew his energy mixed with my own, creating that same bright light around us. Our own supernova.

Moving my hands up his chest, I traced along the various knots and symbols visible from where his tunic lay open before dipping my head to kiss along the chains going up his neck.

"Jacqueline." His voice was low and gruff before he turned us around so that he was on top, between my legs, his arms caging them in on either side.

Pulling himself up on his elbows, his bright white gaze connected with mine as the scent of the sea invaded my senses.

"You're intoxicating." The words were out before I could stop them.

Smiling suddenly and lowering his gaze, he just laughed. "If I'm intoxicating, Jacqueline, you're absolutely addictive."

Biting back a smile, I propped myself up and reached out to lift his chin. "What're we doing here, Dax?" I asked before I lost my courage.

"I'm not sure." And to my surprise, he smiled bigger before resting his chin on his fist. "But I do know that I want you, Jacqueline. Only you. And I don't want anyone else to have you either."

My stomach somersaulted as I grinned back at him. Why was it my insides practically melted when he said my name?

"Well, I want that too." I shrugged a bit in an attempt to play off the fact that I'd just agreed to be exclusive with Prince Daxinius Da Luca. The prince that up until two months ago I'd feared above just about everything else on Earth.

It was Dax's turn to tip my chin up. Leaning forward, he kissed me possessively, making it clear that his words were no mistake. Backing off me and pulling me with him in one smooth motion, he carried me into the bathroom before I could say another word.

Setting me down gently on the marble countertop, he moved to the large porcelain claw-foot tub across the room and turned the hot water on. I'd been in such a daze the last time I was there that I'd missed it entirely, along with the big bay window covered in gauzy curtains behind it. The view was breathtaking; you could see the mountains to the north, the rolling hills directly ahead and the coast beyond. The sun was deep orange, having just begun its daily ascent over the water.

Yawning, I realized it was still early, and we likely hadn't slept much. My eyes continued to wander sleepily as Dax pulled a glass jar from the shelf that ran along the outside wall of the shower and dropped a few champagne-colored crystals in the tub. Replacing the cap, he moved back the way we came and out a separate door I hadn't noticed before.

Curiosity took over, and I hopped off the counter. Walking to the door, I peeked in.

What the…

Rows and rows of clothing, almost all of it black, accompanied by shoes, belts, jackets and weapons—mostly swords, knives and guns—filled the spacious closet. There were perhaps more weapons than anything else.

Dax reappeared in the doorway, his eyes questioning the surprise in my own as he handed me the fluffy white robe he'd been grabbing.

"I've just never seen someone collect weapons like they're shoes, Your Highness."

"I like to have them on hand. Just in case." He shrugged like it was no big deal.

I didn't ask what the "in case" referred to, but I had a feeling King Aidoneus had something to do with it.

"If you have access to guns, not to mention your inherent powers, why all the swords?" It was a question I'd had since I arrived. I was pretty sure no one in Calderone even owned a sword. At least I'd never seen one on our military members or anyone else.

"Any fool can shoot a gun, Jacqueline, but it takes a true warrior to swing a sword."

"You realize how arrogant that sounds?"

He chuckled. "But it's true, at least as far as the Gaill are concerned. Plus there are advantages to using swords, especially for Deviants—we can channel our powers through them. Though we can use our hands, a sword is a more powerful conduit."

"Why's that?" I wasn't very adept at matters of science, but it seemed odd a regular sword could do that.

"It's the type of steel we use. Our swordsmiths are particularly skilled in making them."

I nodded, backing out of the closet doorway as Dax followed me into the bathroom. Walking over and turning off the still-running tub, I stood and inhaled deeply, letting the aroma of lavender and vanilla wash over me.

Dax's touch sparked across my skin as he moved my waves to one shoulder and bent down to wrap his arms around me, his frame quickly dwarfing my own as he spoke against my ear. "Relax, Jacqueline. Take a bath, read." He nodded his head to the little stool next to the tub and the copies of *Jane Eyre* and *King Lear* on top.

Smiling, I bit my lip as I turned my head to his, my eyes settling on his lips that were mere centimeters from my own. "What're you going to do?"

"I have some work I have to attend to. You threw me off my typical schedule," he said, his expression playful.

"That's lame." I rolled my eyes.

"Indeed." He chuckled as he straightened and hung the robe on the hook nearest the tub. "Robe is here, and I'll have Scarletti send up a few more sets of clothes. Come find me in the study when you're done. You good?"

I nodded back as I turned to him, and he was immediately in front of me, cradling my face between his large hands as he tipped it up to meet his. "Don't be too long. We're spending the day together."

And before I could respond or even register the surge of energy coursing through me at his words, his *touch*, he kissed me and was out the door, lightly closing it behind him.

The bath was sorely needed and one of the most relaxing I'd ever had. Back home long baths were a regular occurrence. Here I was lucky to get in a quick two-minute shower before the water turned freezing cold. And before I had to go draw someone else's bath for them.

After becoming sufficiently pruned, I rinsed off using Dax's shampoo and conditioner again, reveling in his scent before I hopped out. Wrapping my hair as I moved for the counter, a glint of gold on one of the center drawers caught my eye. My fingers traced the gold letters etched into the drawer.

Mo ghrá, I mouthed silently.

I was sure they hadn't been there before. And I also had no idea what they meant or even what language they were in. My curiosity piqued, I opened the drawer only to find my brush and toothbrush from last time inside, along with a hair dryer and various ties and clips.

Smiling to myself, I grabbed the brush and set about getting ready.

Finding a small pile of loungewear outside the door again, I changed and towel dried my hair before padding back into Dax's room and through to his study—a spacious room with a tall ceiling and more windows stretching the length of the outside wall. They wrapped around the northern corner of the palace, providing a beautiful view of the snow-capped mountains. The walls to either side of me were covered in books.

Dax was sitting at his desk, facing the windows, speaking with a member of his guard. Holding his finger up as if to say "just a minute," he returned to making a note on the ledger in front of him before leaning back and listening, one hand resting on his knee, the other propping up his jaw.

His desk was otherwise clutter-free, which wasn't surprising. If there was one thing I'd learned from the few times I'd been in Dax's apartments, it's that he didn't do clutter. Everything seemed to have its proper place—even my hair accessories in the bathroom had their own drawer.

"How was your bath?" Dax asked, dismissing the guard as he got up and walked over to me.

He'd changed into a dark fitted long-sleeved shirt—the fabric pulled tight across his chest as he moved. His black pants, soft cotton, hung low at his hips, tapering down to a pair of his standard black boots. His hair was fully pulled back off his face, and a small smile played on his lips as he got closer.

So. This was Dax. All dressed down.

Licking his bottom lip and pulling it in, he tipped his head back, waiting for my answer.

It look me a second to remember to stop looking *at* him and respond *to* him. "Um good, it was good. Great actually, I haven't had a bath like that in ages."

"The servant bathrooms sound rather luxurious in Calderone," he said after a beat, fixing me with a questioning look.

I blushed, realizing my mistake. "My mistress's doing. She would sometimes draw them in her name and then let us take them instead. After a long day or something."

Shrugging, I looked away, embarrassed to be lying again when I had to tell him the truth sooner or later. The weight of it all had been on my mind the entire time I was bathing. I'd come to the conclusion that I could forsake my oath and reveal my identity to him but only when I was sure that he knew in his heart who I was. And only when I was certain it wouldn't endanger my plans to ally myself to the Coalition in order to help my people.

I was falling for Dax, but my oath to rule Calderone and protect my people superseded all, including my feelings. I had to be sure that when I told him, it would be after we'd had enough time together to convince him I was different from my father and those before him. He had to know for certain that no matter who I was that I wanted to help my people and do right by them. And showing my loyalty to him through actions would carry more weight than words alone.

"Tell me something, Jacqueline."

Holding my breath, I met his eyes, seeing nothing but genuine curiosity behind his gaze.

"Are you comfortable here? If I gave you the option to leave, to go home as you called it, would you?"

"No," I answered instantly. "I wouldn't leave, not now."

Nodding, he closed the distance between us and took my hands in one of his, using his other to brush my waves out of my face and behind my ear. "Good. No matter what happens, you'll always have a home here."

He turned then and, not saying anything else, led me out a glass side door that seemed to blend seamlessly into the windows surrounding it. We wound our away around the large terrace to the same table we ate breakfast at the morning after Romano's attack. Except now it was set for lunch.

"I hope you don't mind, figured we already ate breakfast this morning." Dax threw me a wink over his shoulder.

As we neared, I noticed the table was set for a traditional American lunch: cheeseburgers, fries, hotdogs, potato and pasta salad—the whole nine yards.

"Breakfast might be your favorite, but I can't say no to a good burger."

"Who can? Especially if there's cheese on it." I raised a brow and threw him a teasing smile before we both dug in, eating our weight in burgers and fries.

Two hours later, we were sprawled on his bed, recovering from food comas. We'd spent the past few hours reliving stories from our childhood, from Dax's and the Devs' misadventures on the coast to my sneaking out to the clubs or theaters to see shows that women were banned from in Calderone.

It felt like we were in a bubble, just us two, cut off from reality. And that for once maybe we weren't a prince and princess destined to fix a crumbling world but just two ordinary people. A part of me wanted to hold on to that feeling for as long as possible.

"What is it about a burger and fries?" Dax moaned next to me.

"I'm still full, but I want more."

"I know." I rolled onto my side to face him. "There's this little burger place back in Calderone. We went weekly at one point. Max and Phin used to eat so many fries we'd practically have to wheel them out."

"Max and Phin?"

Another slipup. And I'd been doing so well leaving all their names out too.

Sighing more at myself than anything else, I met his gaze. "Max is my cousin, and Phin is… a friend."

"Mmm." His deep voice rumbled. "What kind of friend?"

"Phin is nothing to me. Not like *that*, Dax."

"Was he at one point?"

"Why are we even talking about this?"

He threw me a look that made it clear the conversation wasn't up for debate.

Flopping back on the pillow, I heaved another sigh. His possessive side was equal parts aggravating and wildly attractive. "Phin was one of my first friends. He was there when no one else was—when my parents forgot they had a daughter to care for." *Because they were too busy hoping for a son*, I silently added. "We grew up together, and he's one of my best friends. But that's all he'll ever be."

"And he knows that?"

I shrugged because the truth was, though I'd tried to distance myself from Phin in the past year, I'd never explicitly told him how I felt. It was the coward's way out, and I knew that now. Phin deserved to be with someone who loved him. The true kind of love. The kind of love that changes you, leaves you radically different but evermore yourself.

"If you haven't told him, the man is likely in love with you."

"Okay, well, that's a little extreme."

"Trust me, it's not."

I raised my brows.

"You don't need to be able to see ultraviolet to see how you glow, Jacqueline. You brighten any room you enter. Any day I have is instantly made better by having you in it, and any man would be utterly blind in all ways not to fall for you."

Wait. Is he saying what I think he is?

Just then a loud pounding came at the door. I bolted upright, but Dax was already answering it before I could take my next breath.

His massive body and the door blocked my view so I couldn't see who he was talking to, and I lacked the Dev hearing necessary to understand what they were saying from my position on the bed. After a minute though, he closed the door and shifted across the room, entering the closet attached to the bathroom.

Wandering in after him, I found him layering on the last of his fighting gear.

My gut sank instantly. "What's happened?"

He picked up his Celtic sword, secured it to the sling strapped across his back, and was in front of me a second later. "Nothing of concern." He brushed the hair out of my face as he'd grown accustomed to doing. "There's a passing group of Gaill who have yet to swear allegiance to my father. And there's always the hope that they know something of the One. We need to intercept them and gain their loyalty before my father has a chance to."

"May I join?"

A pained look crossed his face. "Not this time. I haven't spoken to these Gaill before… so I'm not sure how they'd react to a Calderonian being in our ranks."

My gut sank even farther, but I understood his reasoning. "Will it be dangerous?"

"No, it shouldn't be. Although safety outside the palace walls is never a guarantee."

Sighing, I pulled my bottom lip in. I refused to be *that* girl. The annoying girl who begged the man she was falling for not to run off into danger.

"Worried about me again, Jacqueline?"

My emotions must've been obvious, and they were mirrored by the distress in his own emerald eyes—he clearly didn't want to leave either.

"I'll be fine. Promise me you won't go looking for trouble while I'm gone?"

"Will you be gone for a long time again?" I did little to hide the desperation in my voice and hated myself for it all the same.

"No, only a few hours." He couldn't hide the smile in his voice. "I'll let you know when we're back and safe."

Nodding, I watched him gather the rest of his fighting gear as he prepared to meet his troops in the lower south wing. And before I knew it, I was back in my room, staring up at my plain white ceiling, watching the afternoon light turn to dusk while it filtered through the bars on my window. I drifted off to dreams of war, the Coalition, and a dark Gaill soldier in all black.

CHAPTER 15

THE WOMAN IN BLACK

Falling. Falling. Falling.

Gasping, I sat straight up in bed as beads of sweat pooled on my forehead and ran down the nape of my neck. Goose bumps erupted all over my clammy flesh, and I shivered beneath the sheets though the night was warm.

Working to steady my breathing, I looked around and gathered my bearings. I was in my room, alone, and it was still dark out. I squinted at the clock—0330. Closing my eyes, I tried to piece together what had awoken me.

Bright violet light rushing past. A windy coast. Gray skies void of color. A gaunt woman with dark hair dressed in all black turning to stare at me.

My eyes flew open.

Shivering again, I lay back down and pulled the duvet to my chin.

A nightmare. I hadn't realized how much better they'd gotten since starting training. They'd been more frequent after my abduction and Romano's attack, though I'd been so exhausted most of the time the dreams themselves were a blur. But perhaps all the talk of Deviant powers and Gaill history this weekend had pushed those old thoughts to the surface.

I buried myself deeper, but there was no escaping—the woman's face was burned behind my eyelids. Every time I closed my eyes, I saw her.

She looked so forlorn, so worried, like she was about to tell me something of life-altering importance. And she was familiar. I had the creeping feeling I should know her, but try as I might, I couldn't place her face.

I rolled to the wall and willed myself back to sleep. But it never came, and my 0445 alarm went off what felt like a few seconds later.

Dragging myself from bed, I forced my legs into my tight training leggings and shrugged on my long-sleeved tee and vest. It had dawned on me in the hour I lay awake that Dax had never come to let me know he'd returned. So either they hadn't come back last night, or he'd been wounded.

Or he's just changed his mind and doesn't feel the need to update you on his whereabouts.

No, stop.

I couldn't allow myself a moment of self-doubt. I had enough on my mind between the dream last night, Dax's safety, and how I was possibly going to tell him who I was without his hating me. Last night's call of duty couldn't have come at a worse time.

Sighing, I faced the mirror. Bloodshot, puffy eyes stared back.

Great.

After brushing my teeth and french braiding my hair half back, I quickly picked up the rest of the room, everything having been scattered from where I left it before Full Moon, then opened the door and ran directly into the solid wall of muscle and tattoos standing on the other side.

"Cutting it close, Jacqueline. It's five till." Sarcasm dripped from

Dax's voice as he looked down at me through his curls. He was dressed in his regular black tunic, his sword and fighting gear nowhere to be seen.

I took my time looking him over but didn't find a scratch.

Loosing a sigh of relief, I brought my eyes to meet his, finding nothing but amusement looking back at me. "What? I was worried, okay?" I raised my brows and only got a chuckle in return.

"I know, and I'm flattered." He put a hand over his heart, a cheesy grin spreading across his face as he started walking backward.

Sighing again at his arrogance *and* the effect it had on me, I locked the door, and we began the long walk to the south wing. Dax filled me in on the results of their mission along the way.

They'd apprehended the group of nomadic Gaill but had been unable to get any information on the One or convince them to join the Coalition. Apparently, this hadn't been the first group they'd approached and been rejected by. Luckily for us though, no group was looking to support King Aidoneus either.

"Groups like this often only make a move when they're sure of a victory; there's too much at risk otherwise. They've all suffered at the hands of my father, so they have cause to go against him," Dax explained as he held open the door to the training room for me, nodding to the guard as I walked through. "But they likely won't join until they know we have contact with the One or until the One has joined our side. The same can be said for the groups I met on the last expedition. Most are waiting."

"Do most Gaill know about the One then?"

"Yes. The prophecy spread after my mother's death. She was very well-known and equally well respected, especially among those who believe in the prophetic abilities of certain Deviants. And our searching has only helped spread the prophecy."

"So it wasn't just your mother who could see the future? Other Devs can too?"

"There are other seers, although rare, and most come from the same region she did in the far north, where they were exposed to a greater level of radiation than those farther south."

Nodding, I tried to absorb this new information. "I guess I hadn't realized powers differed that much depending on where you were from."

Dax gave me a curt nod. "It used to matter more, but now that radiation can be harnessed and controlled to expose people as needed, it doesn't matter as much."

I shuddered as I remembered what Kacey had said about Dax's being overexposed to radiation. And if his mother had been a seer, he likely had far greater powers than I could even imagine.

Shaking my head clear, I walked over to where Captain O'Leary was waiting in the center of the ring, her sword drawn and ready. Apparently, it was a weapon's day. We'd moved from wooden swords to dulled *actual* swords last week. I was still intimidated by them.

Drawing my new training sword from a nearby stand, I entered the ring as Dax walked to one of the punching bags for his usual warm-up, slipping off his tunic and taping his hands on the way. My eyes involuntarily wandered from the moons and letters that dotted his knuckles up his muscular, veiny forearms to the chains woven along his neck and chest. He truly was sculpted like some old Norse god.

"Miss Lewis?" Captain O'Leary cleared her throat behind me, causing me to start.

Sighing and turning to face her, I brought my sword into position. It really wasn't my fault there was a massive distraction in the room.

We started out slowly but pretty soon were going through the motions full speed as I felt myself physically expending all my emotions from the past twelve hours—as if I could get rid of all my self-doubt and guilt with each hit.

"Agh!" I let out a guttural sound as I swung my sword back toward O'Leary's. The second they connected, an electric shock ricocheted through my arm and violet light exploded around us, throwing me backward.

There was shouting and rapid movement, and everything was slightly blurry before I blinked a few times to find Dax leaning over me. O'Leary and a few of the other captains were right behind him, their faces all blanketed in concern.

"Jacqueline." Dax's voice was full of worry, and I realized he was actually holding me, having caught me before I hit the ground.

"Wha— What was that?" My heart raced as my mind plodded. I'd been ten feet from where I was now in Dax's arms. *How?*

"I'm not sure." Looking behind him, he corrected himself. "*We're* not sure." He turned back to me. "I'm going to pick you up, okay? Get you out of here."

"I'm fine, really." I held a hand up to stop him from helping me.

I'd be fine as soon as I got some water in me and maybe a coffee. But looking around, I realized everything was much more distorted than it looked lying down.

Wait, am I lying down again?

"That's enough." Dax scooped me up as my body made its way back down to the mat through its own volition.

Holding me tight to his chest, he ducked below the ropes that encircled the ring and strode for the doors that led to the rest of his apartments, giving commands over his shoulder on the way. "O'Leary, have the men put the room back in order. The one who does the least amount of work has to stay and do rounds. Davis, you will be overseeing the new recruits this morning on my behalf." Dax then lowered his voice to speak to a guard stationed beside the door as we walked by. "Have Scarletti send up a goji tonic."

"A goji tonic, Your Highness?" The guard's voice was filled with shocked.

Dax's body went rigid against mine. Turning back, he met the guard's eyes, and the man instantly shrank into the wall behind him.

"My apologies, Your Highness. Of course," the man mumbled, quickly averting his gaze.

We were inside Dax's bedroom before I could take my next breath.

"Did you have to scare him like that?" I asked, suddenly annoyed—at the situation, at Dax's behavior, and at myself for being unable to handle this on my own. Whatever *this* was.

"Yes. To question me is to question my authority, my power, my position."

"He questioned you about a *drink*." I raised a brow, making sure to emphasize the last word to let him know just how ridiculous I thought his behavior was.

"It's not just a *drink*, Jacqueline." Dax sat me down on the bed and walked to the fireplace. Holding out his hand, he placed it on one of the birch logs, instantly bringing a roaring fire to life where previously there'd been none. "It's a medicine which you currently need."

I screwed up my face. I had no idea what he was talking about; I wasn't injured. "A medicine?"

"What just happened to you in there? The purple light, the explosion that shot you backward—all that?"

"Yeah?"

"That's what happens when someone starts to deviate. But you"—he pointed at me, up and down like I was some other species—"can't deviate. You weren't born with Deviant blood or on this side of the

Wall. You're fully human."

"So how did what just happened... happen?" I stared at him, dumbfounded.

Just then there was a knock at the door. Dax answered it and was in front of me with the tonic before I could even think to ask who it was or what they wanted.

"Here, drink this. It'll help. As for the rest of it, I have no idea... yet. But we'll figure it out." He looked at me reassuringly as he handed me the glass of steaming liquid.

The bubbling water had a slightly sweet smell that did not at all jibe with the sour taste. Gagging, I wiped the back of my mouth.

"Yeah." He laughed. "It's not generally something most of us drink by choice. But it'll help restore your vitamin and antioxidant levels, which are likely depleted from exerting the type of power you just did."

Nodding, I sipped the tonic, feeling my senses gradually return as the warm taste of berries and herbs trickled down my throat and pooled in my belly.

"Better?"

"Much, thank you."

Nodding once, he moved to one of the big chairs by the fireplace. Turning it to face me, he sank down with a sigh, steepling those long fingers in front of him and observing me as I finished my drink.

Squirming under his gaze, I distracted myself by studying the various Celtic and Gaillic symbols that decorated the walls, pausing as my eyes landed again on the portrait of Queen Caragh over the fireplace.

"Your parents. They've lived in Calderone their whole lives?"

"My parents?" I looked back at him—he hadn't moved.

"Yes. They were born there, I assume?"

"Yes, they were. I think." I added as an afterthought. Truthfully, it had never crossed my mind. I just assumed they'd both been born in Calderone. My father was the king. Where else would they have been born?

"You think? Do you have reason to believe they were born outside the Wall?"

"No. I'm sure they were both born inside Calderone."

Nodding in response, Dax looked at me speculatively.

"What?"

"Nothing." He shook his head. "Simply ruling out all possibilities for what just happened."

"Oh… wait. You think one of my parents might have been born a Gaill? Outside the Wall?"

He didn't move, just looked at me, waiting for me to connect the dots. And at that I burst out laughing. It was comical to think that my father, king of Calderone, could've been born a Gaill or married one.

"No, no definitely not. My parents are loyalists. Staunch supporters of the monarchy. There is absolutely no way they were born Gaill." And although I couldn't give the exact reason I knew neither were Gaill born, I hoped the conviction in my voice was enough to convince Dax not to look into my parentage for a potential explanation as to what had happened. "Maybe it was just a freak occurrence? Maybe my weird ultraviolet whatever was all worked up and came out like that?"

"Why would it be all worked up?"

"Well, I don't know, Dax. I spent half the night worried you were in danger because you were gone, and then there was that dream with the woman in black…" I trailed off, shivering involuntarily as I remembered the look on her face immediately before I woke up.

"What woman?" Dax's brow furrowed, his expression turning more serious.

"It was a nightmare. I don't know who she is—just a woman with jet-black hair, dressed in all black, standing on a coastline. She was turning to look at me, I think to tell me something, but then I woke up."

Nodding his head, his expression didn't change.

"Do you think that means something?"

"Not sure." He shook his head slightly, deep in thought. We fell into silence for a few minutes, both trying to find a logical explanation for what had happened.

"Take the rest of the day off." He stood suddenly and made his way to me. "That's an order, Jacqueline. You need to rest, and I don't want a repeat of this morning happening when I'm not around."

"I told you I am fine, Dax," I said through gritted teeth.

"I know what you said. But neither of us knows how this happened or if it could happen again. You could be a danger to yourself or others," he said quietly as if to soften the blow of his words, knowing full well I'd never put others in danger.

"Oh, you're right." I nodded sheepishly, suddenly embarrassed by my childishly stubborn behavior.

"I'm right? Might need you to put that in writing for the future." He bit his lip on a grin.

"Ugh." My only response as I got up and playfully shoved his shoulder. Of course he didn't budge.

Taking my small hand and folding it in one of his, he turned, leading me toward the door. "Let's get you back to the servant wing. I do have work to attend to today, and you need to rest."

We swung by the library on our way to my room and stocked up on books before I settled in, giving him a hundred reassurances I had no plans to move for the remainder of the day.

And I truly meant to keep those promises until Kacey and Lana stopped by at the end of the day to see where I'd been and convinced me to take a walk in the gardens before we were set to prepare dinner. Well, until Kacey was set to prepare dinner. Pretty sure Dax would kill me himself if I showed up ready to serve.

"So it just came out of nowhere? And he's not sure what caused it?" Kacey's face was taught as she too tried to make sense of my ultraviolet episode from earlier.

"No idea." I shook my head in response and kicked a pebble out in front of me as we walked down the path between the roses. "He asked about where my parents were born, but there's no way they're from outside the Wall. Just no way. It's actually kind of laughable to think about."

"Yeah, that makes sense." Kacey nodded slowly. "His asking about your parents, I mean. It's not like I have a ton of experience interacting with people from inside the monarchies, but I do know that what happened to you only happens to Deviants."

"So Jac is deviating?" Lana asked. We paused by the little white gazebo in the middle of the gardens, and she began picking flowers nearby to bring back to her room.

"I mean, it would appear that way. But like Dax said, unless you have Deviant blood in you already, you can't really deviate. The radiation out here isn't strong enough anymore to trigger a deviation on its own without the added help of genetics. It just doesn't really make sense." Kacey scuffed her shoe on the ground as if doing so would help her uncover the answers we all desired.

"What about being overexposed to it somehow? Like how Dax was exposed to it longer to make him stronger than the rest of the

Devs?"

"Oh"—a knowing smile appeared on Kacey's lips as she turned to me—"you haven't been exposed like that. First, you would know 'cause they'd put you in the chamber. Second, you wouldn't survive it. There's not many who've survived the levels of exposure you get in the chamber. Dax was forced into it repeatedly but only survived because he'd already deviated so much on his own."

"Oh." My only response because what do you say to that?

"Yeah, your situation is..."

"Odd?" I offered up.

"Yeah, something like that." Kacey smiled back at me. "Try not to worry about it, Jac." She took my hand. "If Dax says he's figuring it out, he is. If he thought it was something really bad, he wouldn't let you out of his sight."

She had a point.

"You're probably right," I said, squeezing her hand. "Thanks Kace."

"Anytime, Calderone. And on a lighter note, I am happy you two established that you're now exclusive, even if that was pretty obvious to the rest of us," she added with a wink.

We'd gotten so tied up in discussing the details of my ultraviolet display that I'd almost forgotten I'd told them Dax and I had decided to be exclusive—that *I* had decided to be exclusive with a centuries-old Deviant who used to be my worst enemy.

Life was weird right now.

"Let's head back; I wanna get these in water." Lana walked up then with an armful of peonies and roses she'd taken from the surrounding bushes.

"Yeah, let's get out of here before we're caught with the evidence." Kacey laughed, taking in the various stems lying on the ground.

Making our way back to the palace, I tried to immerse myself in the conversation—the topics being what was for dinner and whether Axel's new love interest was worthy of his attention—but my mind was absorbed elsewhere.

Once everything had seemed so predictable, so in control, so *easy.* And now? I wasn't even sure who I was anymore.

CHAPTER 16

THE TAVERN

Much to Dax's dismay, I was back to work the following day. And much to everyone's relief, I didn't have any more ultraviolet incidents.

I immersed myself in my duties over the following days to keep my mind as busy as possible, but my anxieties were never far away. Even though I was learning more about the Coalition from Dax and the Devs, and Dax had promised to include me more, I still felt like things were taking forever to progress. And my people didn't have forever if they were suffering now. Plus the fact that I was now apparently deviating for who knows what reason and that Dax still didn't know who I really was made it feel like my anxieties were eating me from the inside out.

I was certain the Devs could tell. Everyone was approaching me with excessive caution like they were afraid one word would send me over the edge into a nervous breakdown. Then again, they were probably just concerned for their own safety given we had no idea what powers I did or didn't have at this point.

"If you keep dusting that spot you might rub the varnish right off." Dax's voice came over my shoulder Thursday morning. I'd been so wrapped up in my thoughts that I hadn't registered his presence in the small guest room I'd been dusting.

I turned to find him smirking down at me through a mess of dark curls.

Running his hand through his hair, sending a wave of pine and ocean air my way, he leaned back and folded his ink-covered arms across his chest. "Seems like you need a break."

"I'm fine."

Admitting something was wrong was almost as bad as the fact that there *was* something wrong in the first place.

"Right. That's exactly what a not-fine person says."

Rolling my eyes, I picked up my duster and solution and made my way around him. But his arm slid around my waist as I walked past, holding me in place.

"It's okay not to be okay right now, Jacqueline," he murmured, concern clouding his eyes like an impending storm.

"Is it though?" I asked without thinking. "Aren't we supposed to always have the right answers? The next steps figured out? Know what to do?"

I posed the question servant to monarch, but there was no denying, for me, the question was asked from one future monarch to another.

"Would be nice, but based on my experience, you never truly have the next steps figured out. And even when you think you do, things are sure to change, so your plans will likely fall apart anyway." He was looking at me like he wanted to ask what was on my mind, but I knew that wasn't his way. Dax wasn't one to ask or beg for information; he'd let me come to him when I was ready. "Come. We both need a break." One of his hands slid to the small of my back, pulling me to him, as the other moved my braid out of the way so he could whisper in my ear. “And I have some Coalition business to attend to south of the palace.”

“South? Like outside the outer ward?”

“Yes, *outside* the palace.” He smiled playfully as he mimicked my excited tone.

My mood instantly lightened at the thought that I was about to make my first big move in supporting the Coalition. “What about my work? Pepridge gave me five rooms today.”

Taking my free hand, he led me toward the door and threw an unconcerned look over his shoulder. “Already handled.”

Turns out Dax’s business was with a small Gaill stronghold about a half-hour’s ride from the palace. He insisted on taking us there himself to save time, but I really think he wanted to see my reaction after shifting twenty miles at light speed.

“Never again, Mr. Da Luca,” I said from my current position—doubled over with my hands on my hips, eyes closed, trying to catch my breath as the world spun around me.

His deep chuckle sounded nearby, and I opened my eyes to find his shining down at me.

Swiping a hand across his chin, he let out a sigh. “That reaction will never get old.” He then motioned with his head to the decrepit fortress behind him. “Shall we?”

Throwing him a death glare, I walked past him toward the little castle, willfully ignoring another deep chuckle as it echoed off the tall pines encircling us.

Our meeting with the Gaill clan lasted most of the afternoon. Dax had introduced the group as longstanding friends of his mother’s family, and after updating them on the current status of the Coalition, he attempted to persuade them again to help us overthrow Aidoneus.

And though the Gaill verbally supported the Coalition, being yet another group well acquainted with Aidoneus's cruelty, they told us repeatedly that they couldn't justify raising their small number of forces until they were sure we had the support necessary to take him down once and for all.

"So they're waiting for the One too?" I asked after the meeting while we loaded the small loaves of pumpkin bread and apple juice the caretaker's wife had prepared for us into the backpacks Dax had brought.

"Yes." Dax sighed, a heavy, burdensome sound like the weight of the world was on his shoulders. "The Eur are vital to our cause. But we also need the support of the Deviants and remaining Gaill factions in Old America if we're to have any hope of taking down my father and then Calderone. Support which we have no hope of getting if we don't find the One." He straightened then, a faraway look in his eyes. "My father isn't as powerful as he once was, but his age gives him a certain… advantage. He has a recklessness to him. I think he truly believes that at this point he has nothing left to lose."

I chewed over his words in my mind. Everything I'd ever been told about King Aidoneus pointed to a man who valued power over morality at any cost.

Shivering despite the warm summer evening, I concentrated on buttoning the bags to keep my mind from wandering to my ever-growing apprehension surrounding the future.

"So are we no closer? To the One?" I lifted the bag onto one shoulder, adjusting my braid.

Dax shook his head, that faraway look still in his eyes. "We're getting there."

"Getting there?" If we were closer to finding the One, that was news to me. I tried to ignore the feeling that I'd been left out of important developments.

Dax regarded me, a knowing look in his eyes. "I have a theory of where we can find them. It'll just take time to see if it's worth pursuing."

"I can help you." I did my best to keep the desperation from my tone.

"You already are, Jacqueline." His lips tilted into a small smile. "Being here today was a big help."

A big help? The Gaill we'd just met with refused to join the Coalition. Before I could ask for clarification, Dax pointed down the road.

"Have you ever been to a tavern before?"

I screwed my face up in confusion, but he didn't give me time to respond before he began walking.

"I thought so. Come." He motioned to follow him in the opposite direction of the palace.

We—thankfully—continued at a normal pace along the tree-lined dirt road. The late afternoon sun was low on the horizon, casting long shadows where it shone through the tall pines. As we walked, a thought gave me goose bumps. "Is it safe being out here, especially after Calderone just staged another raid?"

Dax looked down at me, his playful countenance totally at odds with what I considered a very dangerous situation. "You think I'd bring you beyond the outer ward if there was any real threat to you?"

I loosed an exacerbated sigh. "It's only that the Devs made it very clear how risky being out here is."

"They're right; it is dangerous. That is, unless you're with the head of the Deviant forces." He looked down at me through his curls, his lips curving into a smirk before looking forward and taking my hand. “Moreover, Calderone has been known to do raids, but it’s rare. They usually wait a couple of decades between attempts to breach our boarders. And given Kacey absolutely demolished their last plane, I suspect it’ll take them a while to figure out another way to approach us.”

“Have you always been so conceited when it comes to your abilities?”

His eyes slid back to mine. “I’m sure there was a time when I wasn’t. Perhaps before my tenth year.”

I narrowed my eyes at him. “I’m secretly hoping someone jumps out at us and catches you off guard if only to take you down a peg or two.”

“Now Jacqueline, don’t wish for that. I’m not in a killing mood today.” He squeezed my hand, the playful smirk back on his face. “Ah, here we are.”

A little tavern set back in a small clearing came into view.

It had to be at least a hundred years old. The building itself looked like a log cabin—it was cedar-colored with a green tin roof, and smoke billowed from the crumbling chimney despite the fact that it was early September. It was two stories, and I speculated the second was reserved for the inn advertised on the sign outside, which read VACANCY.

Two rough-looking men lingered in front of the tavern, smoking what looked like old cigars though they were far more rudimentary than those I often saw Father and his advisors smoking. Next to them was a small shed with its door slightly ajar, revealing a mess of construction and gardening tools inside.

As we approached, the men turned to greet us, recognition sparking in their eyes when they saw Dax. Immediately dropping their cigars, they bowed deeply.

"Your Highness, it's been years."

"Your Highness, an honor."

"Gentlemen, the honor is mine." Dax's deep voice was filled with gratitude as he pressed a hand to his chest. "I've brought Miss Lewis here to experience the finest tavern this side of the Wall." His eyes twinkled as he glanced down at me. "Is there room for us inside?"

"Of course, Your Highness. You'll find your table ready and waiting."

With a nod, Dax took my hand in his, giving it a squeeze before leading me toward the door. Offering the men a shy smile, which they kindly returned, I followed Dax into the tavern.

Squinting against the darkened interior, I was shocked to find it filled with people. All of whom barely spared us a glance, maybe a nod in Dax's direction, before returning to their conversations.

"There he is!" A voice bellowed from behind the bar as a stout woman with short, wiry gray hair threw her bar rag down on the counter and made her way around to greet us. Smiling wide, she pulled Dax into a hug and then quickly drew me in as well.

"Who's *this*, Daxinius?" The woman asked through a thick southern accent as she raised her brows, looking between us.

I blinked rapidly as I stared back. I had never heard anyone use his full name to his face so casually. Especially someone who wasn't a Dev. Well, besides me.

"Jacqueline"—Dax turned to me—"this is Dolly, the keeper of the Cape Inn and Tavern." He motioned around him to the small bar we'd just entered.

"Pleased to meet you, Dolly." I gave her a small smile to which she pulled me in for another bone-crushing hug.

"'Bout time ya brought a girl round my boy. Only been waitin' for this day my whole life." She gave me a knowing smile before moving back to the bar, picking up her rag and throwing it over her shoulder as her other hand came to rest on her hip. "What can I grab ya two? Couple o' pints?"

"Better make mine a double." Dax nodded in response, and Dolly set to work pouring our beers, motioning for us to find a seat.

Dax walked to a nearby booth, putting his backpack and sword in, then immediately removed mine from my shoulders and placed it next to his as he sat down.

Taking the seat across from him, I rested my chin on my folded hands as I took in the rest of the tavern. It was small, made even smaller by the crowd of people. And even though it was a warm day, it wasn't unpleasant inside. The atmosphere itself was homey, almost cozy. It seemed everything—the stools, chairs, tables, and booths—was cut from a similar wood as the logs that made up the tavern walls. All of it reminded me of the cabins on the edge of Calderone we sometimes vacationed at when I was younger. Only this place was much older.

Men and women milled about, most sitting on the benches that lined the tables in the center of the room with a few groups congregating in the booths along the side or on the stools in front of the bar where Dolly was now pouring our drinks. There was a particularly rowdy group in the middle, where a woman with a bow and arrow strapped to her back took hold of the man next to her and brought his head crashing into the table with such force he was knocked out cold. Everyone around her cheered and laughed, and the man himself sprang up from the bench a few seconds later.

Stunned, I looked at Dax for his reaction only to find him watching me. He laughed as soon as he caught sight of my face.

"How are you laughing? Did you see what just happened?" I

practically shrieked, not bothering to keep my voice down; the room was so loud with the cheering I could barely hear myself think anyway.

"It's fine, Jacqueline. The man is okay." Dax smiled at me, eyes crinkling with amusement. "He's Deviant. He's already healed."

Right.

"I forget your special powers include that." I motioned back to where the man was already downing a pint with the woman who'd just knocked him out.

"If I had to guess, he just lost a bet or they were playing some sort of game, which is why she knocked him out." Dax nodded to the pair with his chin as he leaned back in the booth and crossed his arms, practically taking up his entire side.

"That's absolutely barbaric."

He was silent for a moment before he looked at me. "Any less barbaric than keeping people prisoner in labor camps?"

"Here ya are." Dolly arrived then, setting down two beers, empty plates and a platter of cheese, crackers, and sausage before giving Dax and me another smile and walking back to tend the bar.

I leaned forward, grabbed a cracker and stacked it with sausage and cheese. Obviously, Dax was right. A silly bar game seemed like child's play compared to the monarchies. They were truly the barbarians—committing the most atrocious crimes against their own citizens on a daily basis and covering it up from the rest of the world.

The irony of our two worlds suddenly seemed so clear to me. Whereas all the modern trappings and weapons of Calderone exuded civil advancement, the Gaill were the far more advanced ones—even though they lived in a palace better fit for a medieval court and fought almost exclusively with swords.

"I feel like my life has become one big joke. I mean the fact that I had to enter the enemy's court to figure out the truth about my own country, I just…" I trailed off, suddenly aware that I was more than likely saying too much. Shoving the cracker in my mouth, I concentrated on chewing in a desperate attempt to keep myself from talking.

Dax didn't say anything, didn't move from where he sat back in the booth—just watched me through his curls with those piercing green eyes of his, waiting for me to continue.

"You know how you told me about the suburbs, the *camps*, when I first got to the palace a couple of months ago?" I asked across the silence a few minutes later.

He nodded, his expression unchanging, revealing nothing.

"I believe you now. And I'm sorry I didn't before."

Nodding again, he appeared to consider what I'd said before responding. "What changed your mind?" Finally sitting up, he ran his hand through his hair and took a sip from his beer before piling a plate with crackers, cheese, and sausage.

"It was a lot of things," I said, happy to have the tension broken. "Getting to know you and the Devs, talking to Lana, and reading some books including… *The Eclipse*." I held my breath as I said the last two words, hoping he wouldn't be angry.

He didn't even blink twice.

"Oh. The copy in the library?"

I nodded.

He simply put a cracker in his mouth and washed it down with a healthy gulp of his stout. "Should have guessed you'd find it, bookworm that you are." He smirked at me through his dark curls, eyes teasing.

"You're not angry?"

"Jacqueline, this isn't the monarchy. You're welcome to read anything you find in the library—or my apartments for that matter.

Nothing is off-limits, especially for you."

"Especially for me?" I raised my brow at him in response.

"Yes, *you*." He stood and in one swift motion was sitting next to me on my side of the booth, inclining his head to meet mine as I turned to him, bringing my leg up to rest in the area between us. "I'll give you any resource you need to free yourself from the tyranny of the monarchies."

His words left me temporarily stunned, not because he'd said them—because he'd said similar things to me in the past—but because I now recognized the truth behind them.

The monarchies were tyrannies. My father was a tyrant.

"So tell me, what did the original Da Luca teach you?" Dax leaned back, looking down his nose at me.

I rolled my eyes in response to his smug attitude, causing him to throw his head back and laugh—a belly laugh so deep I couldn't help but join in with him.

"A lot actually." I recounted for him what I'd pieced together regarding the five monarchies' trade agreements and how those agreements were intricately connected with the labor camps and the extreme wealth of the noble families.

"What I can't figure out is—well, two things." I took the final sip of my beer before putting it down and folding both my legs beneath me, pretzel-style, to face him. We'd been discussing the history of the monarchies and the camps for the better part of a half hour, and time was going quickly as was my drink. I figured now was as good a time as any to not only inquire about the Gaill's history after exile but also verify my father's involvement in the camps. A small part of me was still holding out hope he was somehow not involved.

"One, how much does the, uh, current king in Calderone know about what's going on? And two"—I busied myself with stacking another cracker to avoid eye contact because I was sure he would sense how emotionally invested I was in his answer—"what exactly happened to Da Luca? I know he was exiled for treason and was the first leader of the Gaill—everyone in the monarchies knows that—but what happened after he was cast out? How did the Gaill form their own monarchy?"

Dax lifted a finger while he stacked my now-empty glass into his long-empty one. He barely had a chance to move them to the front of the table before Dolly took them, leaving us with two fresh drafts.

Handing me mine, Dax lightly toasted me. "To the One."

"The One." I smiled at him as I took a sip of my beer before setting it down.

"Well, those are two loaded questions, Miss Lewis." He fixed me with a crooked smile through his messy curls, having no idea what a blow to my gut it was when he used that name.

Swallowing back against the sudden lump in my throat, I made myself stay in the present.

I seriously need to drink more for this.

"My apologies, Daxinius." I sighed as I reached for my pint and brought it to my lips with a smile, suddenly forgetting everything as I focused on his playful expression. The electric chemistry between us was enough to cause immediate amnesia. "I'll try to keep my questions easier in the future to accommodate your simple mind."

"Oh, is that right?" He scoffed, reaching out and pinching my side, causing me to squeal and spill my beer as I attempted to wiggle away.

"Look at what you did!" I laughed between gasps of breath.

"Nah, that was all you, Jacqueline. An insulted Deviant can't be held liable for their actions."

"Oh, is that right?" I asked mockingly. "I'll keep that in mind." I raised a brow before exchanging my beer with his, forcing him to take the smaller, less filled one.

He only shook his head as he folded his arms across his chest and leaned back against the side of the booth. "Always distracting me, Jacqueline. You had two questions?"

I couldn't help but smile at the sight of him—all tall and broad, nothing but a mess of curls and tattoos, wearing his typical black tunic and pants with those big boots on like he could go off to war at any time. All folded into one side of a too-small booth in the middle of Nowhere, Gaill Country. *My* Gaill in Gaill Country.

"Jacqueline."

"Oh yeah. Sorry."

His eyes flared a bright white before returning to their usual jade green—he wasn't dumb. He knew I'd just been ogling him.

"Shall we continue then?"

I nodded, and he took a swig from the smaller pint before beginning.

"The king knows. Of that I'm sure. Besides the fact that a man like Manasseh Livingston wouldn't be so daft as to let an industry like the labor camps run undetected under his nose—that man loves money and power—there's definitive proof he's involved."

"What proof?" I asked before I could stop myself, hoping my anticipation over the answer didn't come through in my voice.

Dax ran his tongue over his top teeth before rolling his lips as if the next piece of information was physically difficult for him to share. "We've spoken with refugees who are his and his advisors' victims. We have photographs and videos of them in the camps, directing executions among other things. Similar things to what Romano does here." Dax clenched his fists as he said the last part, and I felt my gut twisting in a sickeningly similar manner.

"You mean, he's done… what Romano's done? What he tried…" I trailed off, my voice barely above a whisper, not trusting it to remain steady if I spoke any louder.

Thinking of my father doing that, or anyone in our government doing that to our own citizens…

I focused on a spot on the table as the nausea building in my stomach threatened to rise up.

Although I'd hoped, I hadn't been foolish enough to actually believe my father had no involvement in what was going on at the camps. Even Dax pointed out his need for money and power were too great to ignore such an opportunity. But to go this far? I pressed the back of my hand to my mouth, concentrating on my breathing as I tried to keep it together.

Dax reached across my lap, taking my other hand and completely covering it in the Celtic and Gaillic imagery etched across his callused ones. "We're not positive if he's done *that* exactly, we just know he's been there when it has been done and hasn't done anything to stop it. And has condoned it on more than one occasion as a means of punishment." Dax's eyes held mine, showing me nothing but compassion and understanding as he continued. "I know it's hard to hear this about your king, especially when you thought him to be honorable. But it's true. He's corrupt, just as my father is. The sooner we find the One and unite with the Eur, Deviants, and other Gaill to overthrow them both the better."

Blinking back tears, I looked down, hoping to play it off as pure shock at the deceit by a man I thought to be a just king. The confirmation of my father's true nature coupled with my mounting feelings of guilt over the whole situation was too much.

But I needed to get a grip.

Dax still didn't know who I was, and I sure as hell wasn't going to have him find out the truth when we were talking about my monster of a father and his government.

Taking in a deep breath, I blew it out slowly, making eye contact with Dax again. He leaned forward slowly, holding my gaze as he bent down to kiss the top of my nose.

"Your second question about what happened to Da Luca and the Gaill then?" He leaned back.

I reached for the larger glass of beer and took a bigger sip than I probably should've. I wiped my mouth with the back of my sleeve as I set the glass down. "Giovacchin wrote about those first few years—the warfare in the countryside and journey north from the land that used to be Georgia. But what about the radiation?"

"Well, by the time he and his followers were exiled, the War had been over for forty years. Radiation existed of course, as it still does given the amount used during the War, but it was considerably lower than in the 2060s. Many succumbed to the effects, but a few survived. It wasn't pleasant either way." Dax brushed his hand through his hair, his forehead creasing like the thought of it all physically pained him. "Those that did survive eventually adapted, but most had little to no control over their powers. Mix that with their anger over being exiled, and it was a bit… chaotic." He finished with a cock of his brow.

"Chaotic?"

"Let's just say there was a time when the stories about our baser tendencies were more fact than fiction."

I just nodded at him before taking another sip from the larger stout. "So what happened after Giovacchin passed away? How are you a Da Luca when he had no children?"

"Oh. That." Curls fell across Dax's face as he reached for the beer I'd just put down, exchanging it with the smaller one while he took a swig, raising his brows at me in a challenge.

I narrowed my eyes in response.

"My grandfather, Antonio Reyes, was a young, up-and-coming Gaill and Da Luca's right-hand man. There had been talk of establishing a Gaill monarchy just for some semblance of order, especially as Da Luca declined in health around 2115. My grandfather, who himself had been deviating but had gotten control of it, seemed like the most logical choice at the time and was endorsed by Da Luca in his final days."

"Okay, so your grandfather assumed the what, throne? What's with the Da Luca name then?"

"Yes—the surviving members or family members of the group Da Luca brought from Calderone voted to instate a monarchy the day Da Luca passed and unanimously upheld Da Luca's final wishes for my grandfather to take his place as de facto king. In a show of support for the Gaill cause and because Da Luca's name was so tied to the movement, he changed our last name to Da Luca."

My jaw practically hit the booth between us. I tried to move it but couldn't seem to remember how.

You mean THE Dax Da Luca is actually Daxinius *Reyes*?

"What?" Dax popped a cracker in my open mouth, causing me to laugh as I closed it to chew.

"I'm just in a bit of shock, I guess. It's hard to picture you as anything but Daxinius Da Luca."

"That's because I *am* Daxinius Da Luca. We've held this last name for over two hundred and seventy years, before the time I was born. Reyes has long been a name of the past. And"—he grabbed the last cracker from the plate and proceeded to pile it with cheese and sausage—"if my name was Da Luca or Reyes, I'd still be the same Dax, wouldn't I?"

I nodded because he was right. I knew now what I didn't a couple of months ago—that I wasn't Jacqueline *Livingston* or Jacqueline *Lewis*. I was simply Jacqueline.

"So what happened after your grandfather assumed the throne?" I asked.

"We prospered. And we also learned the value in the monarchies thinking we didn't, so we exploited that. I was born about a hundred years after the War ended. Well, a few years before that, actually," he corrected himself. "And—"

"Wait, a few years *before*?" I held up a hand.

He nodded, his smile growing bigger with every passing second until he was full-on grinning.

"You're saying you were born in the year twenty-one-fifty-what? Seven, eight, nine?"

"I'm not *saying* I was born then. I was born in 2158."

"Right, okay." I licked my lips, suddenly feeling parched beyond measure. Or maybe it was normal to see spots when the guy you were dating told you he was over two hundred years old. "It's 2374 right now. That's two hundred years ago, Dax. You mean you've just been wandering around for two hundred years doing what exactly? Sitting on your throne and pouting? What have you all been doing if some of you are that old?"

I knew the Devs were old. But somehow hearing out loud that they were born closer to the War than present day was too much for me to wrap my mind around.

"You're feisty when you don't know the answers to things." He picked up a fry from the basket of burgers Dolly had just dropped off and put it in his mouth with a smirk.

Grabbing my cheeseburger, I took a bite and widened my eyes at him half glaring, half waiting for him to answer.

"You're right, I am on the older side," he finally conceded, looking down at me, his full lips pulling up into a small smile as if he hadn't just uttered the biggest understatement. "There are others as old, if not older, though I'm the oldest alive in our faction besides Scarletti and my father."

Nodding, like this somehow made the news of his age more palatable, I waited for him to continue.

"In 2200, my father assumed the throne upon the death of my grandfather. I was young—relatively speaking." He shot me a look like I should give him a break, which I did just this once. "And because of my age, I didn't question some of the circumstances surrounding his death that I should've. Had I, I probably would've realized that even if my father hadn't poisoned my grandfather himself, he was instrumental in planning his death."

At that, Dax loosed a sigh and hung his head. Reaching forward, it was my turn to hold his hand in mine.

"You are not your father, Dax. You could never be him."

He gave me a look then, like there was something more he wanted to tell me, but the look passed, and he took my hands in his, bringing them to his lips. "Thank you, Jacqueline."

With another deep sigh, he brought his basket of food to the edge of the table, preparing to dig in. If nothing else, this trip had solidified that Dax did indeed have the appetite of a human teenage boy.

"After my father took control, things moved pretty quickly from a quiet economy, just surviving, to a booming one, dependent only on itself. But we always operated in secret. And we always had the mission of undermining and eventually destroying the monarchies. It wasn't until my mother was murdered and"—he searched for words he ended up not finding—"a few other things, that I realized my father's mission was much more catastrophic in nature."

"Catastrophic?" Of course I knew what he meant, but I couldn't really confess that I'd casually browsed Scarletti's journals. And admitting that I'd discussed him at such length with the Devs just seemed awkward. Plus part of me wanted to hear it from him directly.

"My father views all inside the walls of the monarchy as a threat to the Gaill and even more so to him and his power. But that's not right. There are people suffering inside those walls by the same hands that we have. It's our duty to save them as we did ourselves all those centuries ago." There was a faraway look in his eyes as he leaned back, legs wide, one foot on the floor and the other up on the booth with his arm resting on his knee, swirling what was left of the double pint.

The distant din of rain could now be heard on the tin roof, and I had a faint sense of other people around, time passing, and life happening, but as I looked at Dax all I saw was him. He utterly eclipsed everything else around me.

How was I so blind before to who he truly is?

Reaching over, I took his glass from his hands and placed it on the table, feeling his eyes on me the entire time. His hand stayed resting on his knee as I moved closer, fitting like a puzzle piece between his legs. Grabbing hold of his tunic, I pulled on it to bring him eye level with me, willing him to see himself as I did—compassionate, brave, and honorable. A true prince in every sense of the word.

His eyes held mine for what seemed like an eternity before his hand came up to grip the back of my neck, bringing me to him as his lips collided with mine with a passionate ferocity. That now familiar glow instantly pulsated around us, but it wasn't until we broke that I realized there were now streaks of violet where there'd previously been only a blinding white light.

Letting his hand fall to my low back, the other to my thigh, Dax observed me while I took in our light. Reaching out, I tried to touch it, but all I felt was an intense surge of energy before it finally dissipated.

"You feel that electricity when we touch? When I touch you?" Dax's low voice was gravelly, like I had the same effect on him that he had on me.

Looking back up at him, I nodded, momentarily lost for words.

"I feel that too," he said, pulling in his lips, a sudden uncertainty in his eyes, and I wondered if he'd ever felt anything like this. Or if he'd always been the only one with this kinetic power.

Before I could think twice, I reached out, using my fingers to trace along the stubble that covered his jaw and chin, outlining the ink where it met the tan skin of his face. Within seconds, small purple-blue sparks shot from my fingertips.

Gasping, I pulled my hand back, both stunned by what I was capable of and worried I'd somehow hurt him.

Laughing, he drew me to him again. "It's okay, Jacqueline. It doesn't hurt. Just as it doesn't hurt when I touch you, yeah?"

Nodding, I tried to put into words what his touch felt like. "No, it's like an electric shock you get from static… only bigger. Much bigger. So big it touches my heart, my soul, becomes part of my very blood and, I don't know, binds me to you all at the same time."

"Exactly." He nodded, biting his bottom lip and smiling down at me.

"Is that what it feels like when you touch everyone?" I was suddenly irrationally jealous of anyone else who'd ever had the privilege of Dax's proximity.

"No." He barked out a laugh. Then taking in my expression, he laughed harder. "Jealous now, Jacqueline?"

Rolling my eyes, I went to shove him, but he expertly dodged it, already predicting my next move.

"See, learning." He tapped a finger to his head. "It all depends on my mood at the time and my intentions behind who I'm dealing with. Most of the time, there's nothing, but if I was in battle, looking to inflict pain, I would." Taking my hand in his then, he rubbed a tattooed thumb over the white of my knuckles. "And when I'm with someone I love, the feeling is much different."

"Oh." The only thing I could think to say before pulling in my lips and awkwardly looking away.

Smooth, Jacqueline.

"You know you've gotten more out of me than anyone has in decades. I'm not usually so... open."

I looked back to find his eyes doing that stare again—like they saw to the very bottom of my soul.

"So," he continued, "when are you planning to tell me who you really are, Jacqueline Lewis? Because I know you didn't grow up working as a servant."

My breath hitched, and I forced myself to blink against the sudden spinning in the room.

He didn't seem angry. No, his tone was definitely more jovial. And his eyes weren't white, *yet*, so he couldn't be mad, right? But how did he know? And did I admit the truth to him? Or at least some of it?

Now was my opportunity. He clearly trusted me with how open he'd been. And he needed to know who I was in order to help me when the time came.

"H-how did you know?" Was all I could think to ask while I sorted through what to tell him and how best to do it.

He only laughed in response, fixing me with a look that basically said, *Are you kidding me?*

"Okay, okay." I laughed, putting my hands out in mock surrender, deciding to roll with his joking attitude. "So I'm not the most convincing housemaid out there. I'll give you that."

"Hardly." His deep chuckle resounded off the small walls of the tavern as I rolled my eyes again. "And," he continued, his eyes still playful, "you carry yourself like someone born of noble blood. The way you speak, the way you move, the way you act are not at all like a typical servant."

"What's so different about how I act?" I practically shouted. I had bent over backward to ensure I blended in, especially since Romano pointed out my shortcomings in the corridor all those weeks ago.

"You forget I've had centuries to observe how nobility behave and am myself one of the highest ranking members of my court. After a while, it becomes easier to distinguish those who are born *being* served from those that are born *to* serve. Although it might be harder to discern now, at the start, it couldn't have been clearer than if you'd been wearing a bright light-up sign."

My cheeks instantly felt aflame at the realization that he had known, at least in part, who I was all along and had let me act a fool anyway.

Embarrassed was an understatement.

"Why didn't you say anything sooner? Try to get information from me?"

"I did."

I raised my brows in question. "You never interrogated me."

"There are many other ways to get information besides interrogation."

"Like…"

"Like how I had you serve the Eur leaders so soon after you arrived. You tried your best to keep a neutral face, but I could see it in your energy, hear it in your heart how afraid you were once we began discussing war plans. I knew you'd put two and two together that our plans were likely directed, if not solely at Calderone, then the monarchies in general given they are our enemies. Your reaction showed me that Calderone likely had no idea a war was coming."

His answer made sense, except for one thing. "Women in Calderone aren't privy to war plans though."

"True, but if your men and country had been preparing to fight a war this big, it would be hard for even a Calderonian woman not to notice. There'd likely be a conscription or at the very least, an uptick in training for those already enlisted."

I nodded because although there'd never been a war fought in my lifetime, there had been wars between the Gaill and Calderone in the past. And every history text I'd read as heir mentioned conscription.

"Plus," he continued, "we've captured and interrogated enough Calderonians that we know rather intricately how their society works. And women, noble or not, are barely treated better than how they treat people in the camps." He scoffed, polishing off the larger pint before putting it down on the table with a heavy thud. "After that first meeting, it was clear that not only were you loyal to the monarchy, but there was a high likelihood you had no information we still needed seeing as you didn't even know something as integral as the camps existed. But I understand. Like I said, I know how they treat women in there."

I nodded, recognizing now what I hadn't in our first conversation. And a part of me was angry, but a larger part had known the truth all along. Because heir or not, I'd always been kept in the dark back in Calderone. I knew now it wasn't some subconscious move because, as a woman, I wasn't inherently weaker or less than. Though that's how my government had made me feel. No, this had been deliberate. Like those in the camps, I'd been kept ignorant so the power could remain in the hands of the few.

"Why follow me?" I asked. If he knew I could give him nothing, following me seemed like a waste of time.

"I had my reasons." Dax raised a brow. "But to put it simply, I was waiting to see if my assumptions were correct or if you did know something of import. Nothing cropped up until that night with Romano."

It was impossible to miss the clenching of his fists or that his gaze became five shades whiter as soon as Romano's name left his lips. Grabbing his arm in an attempt to calm him, I held my breath against the energy that poured from his gaze as the full force of it hit mine. I only hoped that whatever rudimentary power I had was enough to quell that building in him at least for now.

"You're right. Women aren't treated the way they should be in Calderone. And I didn't know everything then that I do now about the way my country works. But I want to change Calderone. I want to change the monarchies," I said, the churning intensity in his eyes both mesmerizing me and giving me the strength I needed to admit what I had to next. "Dax, there's something more I have to tell you. Something I think will change everything, but hopefully for the better."

The entire tavern grew silent. Pausing, at first thinking they were listening to us, I slowly realized they were actually listening to the faint sound of an engine outside.

Looking back to Dax, I found his eyes an even brighter white. I opened my mouth, ready to ask him what was going on, when he pressed a finger to his lips, indicating for me to remain silent.

My gut dropped as it dawned on me what was happening.

Just then the engine grew louder.

The sound unmistakably belonged to a large aircraft. And considering the look of concern on Dax's face, my guess was that it wasn't part of the Gaill fleet.

Within a second, everyone in the tavern was in motion.

Dolly swept an arm over the bar, throwing all the glasses within her reach into the sink as people started to shift at light speed.

Dax stood, throwing a hand out toward the nearest lamp, immediately casting the entire room into darkness save the glow through the window from the streetlight outside. "No one moves until they're gone. No one utters a word."

His voice was a clear command slicing through the chaos, causing everyone including me to stop abruptly and more than a few nearby to flinch as if the words impacted them physically.

I'd gotten so used to my Dax that I'd forgotten who he was to the rest of the world.

He grabbed my hand and lifted me from the booth in one swift motion. Reaching for our bags, he handed me mine as he strapped his sword to his back.

"They're about a quarter of a mile to the north but quickly approaching." His voice was calm and collected as Dolly appeared at our sides. "Dolly, the bunker?"

Nodding, she moved for the door. We followed through the crowd of Gaill, most of whom were too preoccupied with the threat of a Calderonian raid, or with avoiding eye contact with Dax, to pay us attention.

Exiting the side door of the tavern, we entered the small alley next to it. My eyes were instantly drawn to the planes circling directly to the north, spotlights of the brightest blue engaged as if they were hunting for something. Or *someone.*

It was still raining, so they were low to the tree line, some dipping down to the road, and they were definitely searching.

"Ya know the way." Dolly nodded with her head toward a shed I'd noticed when we first arrived—the one that looked like it belonged in a hoarder's nest.

We made our way to it as quickly as possible, Dax walking ahead, his big boots splashing in the mud as I did my best to hold my skirts up from total destruction though I knew it'd be a failed effort. We'd both be soaked.

The door to the shed swung open noiselessly as Dax pushed against it. He stepped back, allowing me to enter first. My eyes quickly adjusted to the darkness but not enough to make out any reason to be in here other than its relative anonymity compared to the tavern next door.

"Can you hold this?" Dax's whisper cut across the hum of the monarchy's planes in the distance.

I grabbed his backpack from his outstretched hand as he moved a pile of rubble on the floor and revealed what appeared to be a trap door. He held his hand over the door, and it slid open. Taking the backpacks from me, he helped me down the small ladder into the pitch-black cellar and then jumped down himself. Once inside, he latched the door before lifting a hand again, igniting the small lamps on the surrounding walls.

The bunker reminded me of those I'd seen in photos from the War. Built in the ground, with thick metal walls to withstand nuclear activity, they were often outfitted with enough food and supplies to last a year. This one appeared no different.

Shivering, I hugged myself. I was still in my wool day dress, warm enough for a summer's night, but the bunker's dampness mixed with the dire reality of our situation suddenly had me freezing with fear.

Until I felt him. Wrapping his arms around me, Dax's electricity mixed with mine, creating our own type of heat as I turned in his arms to face him. The enemy might have been right outside, but I knew my best chance of survival was here in front of me.

"You're safe, Jacqueline. They can't detect us, and there were no other Deviants in that tavern by the time we left. They have no need to look further."

"So they *are* looking for something? For Deviants?" Including myself in that group still seemed wrong somehow.

"Typically. Though I haven't seen them do multiple raids so close together like this in a *very* long time. It's… unusual." His bright green eyes clouded with concern as he looked down at me.

"Unusual." I repeated the word, thick and heavy on my tongue, as a new fear started to take hold.

Are they coming for me?

My anxiety must've been obvious because he only pulled me closer.

"Jacqueline." He kissed my forehead before lowering his face to bring it level with mine, hands coming up to cup my jaw, locking me in. His eyes were as bright and bottomless as the arctic as they stared into mine.

"Lewis. That's a member of King Manasseh's Advisory Council. Is this who you're related to?" His eyes searched mine, and the energy from his touch intensified as if he could extract the truth from me through it alone.

I couldn't tell him. Not *here*. Not *now*.

Not like this.

Not when he was so on edge, ready for a fight, or before I knew how my reaction would play out. And not before I knew what the monarchy was actually searching for. No, I had to control this. We had to have more time.

But we didn't.

Planes roared overhead, and I crouched to the floor with Dax on instinct. He pulled me to him so that his larger frame shielded my smaller one as the walls around us rumbled. Dust fell from the ceiling as everything shook, and it felt like the planes were right on top of us.

Dax gently stroked my hair, his cheek resting on my head, while I stayed tucked beneath him. There were no explosions like last time, no bombs, and no screams like in the footage from the War—just the deafening thrum of the engines. I desperately hoped that meant they were only searching for Deviants, as Dax had said, and when they couldn't find any, they'd leave everyone else in the tavern alone.

Slowly the planes receded until there was nothing but absolute silence surrounding us.

We waited a few more minutes, then Dax stood in one fluid movement.

"Stay here." He instructed, unsheathing his sword, the symbols along the blade instantly alighting, before going to the hatch, unlocking it and lifting himself out with his other hand.

I sat there, crouched for what seemed like an eternity, immobilized, until Dax finally poked his head through the door.

"It's safe. Come."

Taking a deep breath, I stood, my legs and hips groaning beneath me for staying in one position so long. Hobbling over, I took Dax's extended hand, and he lifted me from the bunker. Shutting and locking the door behind me, he moved the pile of rubble over the entrance again, and we made our way back to the tavern.

CHAPTER 17

MO GHRÁ

“Monarchy didn’t find anythin’ to their likin’.”

I started as Dolly appeared, bar rag over her shoulder and hands on her hips again.

“I suggest you two find a room. Monarchy’s likely to be out all night.” She nodded toward the small, rickety staircase that led to the inn on the upper floor before turning to a customer who’d been waving her down.

“She’s right.” Dax looked at the stairs, then back to me, his gaze growing whiter at whatever was on his mind. “I won’t risk running into them on the road. Not with the technology they have and your powers being what they are.”

“So that means we stay here tonight?”

He looked down at me, his lips curving up in a smile. “You okay with that?”

“Yeah.” I shrugged like it wasn’t a huge deal.

I mean, we’d already slept in the same bed. Whether it was here or the palace, what difference was there? I could resist him. It wasn’t like I was worried about *going there* with him because I’d already done that with Phin. And I knew whatever I'd had with Phin was nothing compared to what I had now with Dax.

But there were still a hundred reasons not to actually sleep with Daxinius Da Luca… yet.

The biggest one being that if I wasn't already in love with the Gaill prince, sleeping with him would certainly seal the deal. Another equally massive reason being that he still didn't know the truth about who I was. The urge to tell him swept through me like wildfire. Though it was quickly quenched when I remembered what had just happened.

Would he believe me if I told him I had nothing to do with the raids? Especially when both had occurred exactly where I just so happened to be?

No, I wouldn't tell him tonight. But sleeping with him while keeping that secret seemed like a whole new level of deceit. One I didn't think I was capable of reaching. And one I knew I shouldn't regardless.

Dax took my hand and led us up to a back room on the second floor. Keeping the lights off, he set our bags down on the bed, swiftly moving to the windows. After a few seconds, presumably when he'd made sure there were no planes in sight, he closed the blinds and turned the lights on with a wave of his hand.

"The suite." He gestured around him.

If this was their version of a suite, I wondered as to the size of a normal room.

This one was small, quaint even, tucked into the back corner of the log cabin with a fireplace on one wall and a large bed that appeared to be made from the same logs as the cabin on the other. Various blankets were strewn across it as well as along the back of the old, overstuffed armchair that sat in front of the fireplace. A desk with various books stacked on top hugged the wall next to the chair. And there was a small bathroom outside of which was a porcelain sink with a tiny, speckled mirror positioned above it.

Moving to the mirror, I undid the tie around my braid, running my fingers through my wet tangle of waves as I inspected myself in its reflection. My skin was slightly flushed from the events of the evening, and my hair and clothes were soaked through from the rain. But my *eyes*. They were far brighter than usual, so much so I had to look away as if I'd caught the eye of a stranger.

"We should be safe. They appear to have left the area for the time being. And I'll know if they return." Dax's calm, deep voice sounded from behind me. I looked up to find his worried gaze assessing me in the mirror. "How do you feel?"

"Relatively okay." I turned to watch as he slowly started to unpack what little we'd brought with us. "Excepting the scare of the past hour, it was actually a great night." A small smile started taking over my lips when I remembered our conversation, *our kiss* from earlier. "I'll be happy when we get back to the palace and are safe inside the outer ward. But I can't say I'm too upset we're stuck here for the night."

My smile only grew as I watched him pause, midmovement, at my words. Returning my attention to the mirror, I occupied myself with combing out the last of my waves. Tossing my hair over my shoulder and gathering it in both hands, ready to knot it into a bun, I turned to find Dax staring at me from across the room, still frozen.

"Wha—"

But he was gently removing my hands from my hair before I could even finish the word, letting them hang as he brushed the now-falling layers out of my face. With every movement, he sent a heady wave of pine and cold ocean air washing over me, completely numbing my mind and all my senses except those that responded directly to his touch.

"Leave it down… please," he said, a hint of a smile on his lips as he tipped his chin back.

Biting my bottom lip, I looked up at him. Though my mind was cloudy from his presence, I was vaguely aware that he'd just let slip a weakness of his, at least when it came to me.

"I thought I was going to lose you tonight." His hand moved down to cup my jaw as his thumb stroked my cheek, deep in thought.

"But you didn't." I shook my head at him in response, knowing then that my next words were the truest I'd ever speak. "You'll never lose me. They'd have to physically drag me away from you."

"Not gonna happen." He lifted my face up to meet his and bent down, kissing me possessively. "You're mine," he practically growled against my lips.

I smiled against him. "I'm yours. And you're mine."

His eyes flew open at that, a bright white, but I could see the storm beneath them, the storm that raged only for me.

I knew then that I didn't need to sleep with Dax to fall for him. I already had. Long ago.

Turning, but keeping my eyes locked on his, I pulled my hair over one shoulder.

"You sure?" His voice came low in my ear as his chest pressed into my back.

Nodding, I smiled. "A thousand percent."

I felt his smile on my ear before he proceeded to nip at it and kiss down my neck to the wool fabric that covered my shoulders and back up again.

"I don't know how you make these dresses look so damn good."

"You flatter me, Mr. Da Luca." I shook my head at him, biting my lip as my smile grew wider.

"I speak only the truth," he said, gently pulling down my zipper. Taking his time, he let his fingers skate down the bare skin of my spine, igniting a spark that shot like lightning through my bones. The cool air rushed against my skin only to be quelled by the fire of his touch as he moved his hands higher. Slipping my dress from my shoulders and letting it pool at my feet, he loosed a low breath.

As I turned to face him, I expected to feel self-conscious—this was Daxinius Da Luca after all—but I only felt that ever-present magnetic tug between us. The one that was making goose bumps erupt across my bare skin though internally I was on fire. The one that made me certain this wasn't just some crazy impulse—this was forever.

"You are the most beautiful woman I've ever seen." His eyes raked over my body at a tortuous pace before coming back to rest on mine. They were now so bright it almost hurt to meet his gaze, but I couldn't look away if I tried. "Truly, Jacqueline. Everything about you, everything you are… simply radiant."

Reaching up, I cupped his cheek, not daring to break eye contact. "I'm yours, Daxinius."

And it's like those words caused something within him to snap, because in the next moment we were moving in fast and slow motion all at once.

Gripping my jaw in his hands, his touch was hard and claiming as it sent a surge of electricity through my body. He kissed me deeply, mercilessly, and I wrapped my arms around his neck, pulling him to me, wanting more, *needing* more—as if I could kiss him for eternity and it would never be enough.

Almost immediately, I was in his arms, legs wrapped around his toned waist as one of his hands moved to grip the hair at the base of my skull, pulling tight, and the other moved beneath me, holding me in place. And before I knew it, Dax threw us, as if we were weightless, into the wall on the opposite side of the room, sending out a blinding halo of light in all directions but never breaking our connection. Like we now existed in zero gravity, I didn't feel the impact; all I felt was the combined effects of our electricity as it coursed through Dax's veins to mine and back again, the tangible heat between us intensifying with every second.

He broke away, breathless, eyes searching mine, making sure I was okay, but I was already lost again in his gaze. It had become a swirling green-and-blue vortex—a hurricane I was drowning in, Dax himself my only lifeline.

I didn't say anything. Instead, I showed him.

Wrapping my hand around his neck, feeling the violet light spark from my fingertips, I marked him as mine. Pulling him to me, he smiled against my lips before expertly kissing me back.

And if two hundred years on Earth had taught Dax anything, it was how to be a good lover.

He let me have control for all of a second before he took over, moving so quickly I didn't have time to react. Ripping his tunic over his head, his muscles rippling with the effort, he took both my hands in the same movement and placed them above my head so he could kiss me how he wanted. His hips pressed into my very core, a heat spreading through me like never before as his other hand held my jaw in place again.

Nipping at my bottom lip, he kissed the same spot, then slid his tongue between my parted lips, staking his claim to me, body and soul.

Lifting me from the wall, he moved us to the large bed, and I let my arms come to rest around his neck as he lowered me down onto the sheets. He looked at me through heavily lidded eyes as he straightened, letting his head fall back slightly so that his curls covered his face while his tatted hands slowly began to unbutton his black jeans.

My eyes roved over his chiseled frame, taking in the maze of dark tattoos covering his body before coming to rest on his hands.

There were moving so slowly. *Too slowly.*

Getting on my knees, I reached forward, growing impatient, when his hand tipped my face up to meet his.

Our eyes met for what I'm sure was the briefest of seconds, but for the first time I felt like as much as he saw to the bottom of my soul, I could finally see to the depths of his.

He kissed me then, keeping his eyes locked on mine the entire time, and that's when I felt it.

The moon collided with the sun.

The planets aligned.

And like two currents coming together, swirling to create something much more powerful, our energies combined to fuse our souls, as if we had known all along we were destined for this connection that was nothing short of perfection.

Not wasting another moment, he pulled me to him, and we were quickly lost in one another again, a blur of rapid movements and blinding light, and I was only sure of one thing after that. Neither of us would ever be the same.

"What're you thinking?" Dax asked a while later, nudging my nose with his.

Our movements had become slower, more languid and unhurried. And he currently had me caged in—both arms on either side of my head where he was holding himself up with his elbows, looking down at me, his curls falling across my face.

He held me in, but I'd never felt more free.

"That I feel free... like I can be myself with you." Gazing up into his eyes, I bit my lip as the words left my mouth, realizing how cliché they sounded.

A small smile crossed his lips, and he leaned down, grinding himself into me as he kissed my forehead, nose, and finally my lips, making me forget my embarrassment entirely.

"Want to know what I'm thinking?"

"Hmm?" I asked.

"That I love you, Jacqueline."

My mouth dropped open. He'd alluded to it before, but to have the Gaill prince actually admit he'd fallen for me... I mean, I'm pretty sure the world stopped turning.

"I love you, Daxinius," I said without another moment's hesitation.

The light around us grew stronger, more vibrant, spilling in all directions and eradicating the darkness as our connection floated between us.

I loved him, as he loved me. I'd do anything for him, for his people. As I knew he'd do for me and mine.

"*Mo ghrá*," he murmured as he kissed me then—slowly, deliberately, like he was sealing our words with his movements, making sure the imprint of his kiss would last on my lips and heart forever.

I reached up to stroke his cheek before my next thought, my movements coming quicker. Smiling, I met the look of surprise in his eyes with one of my own before I brought his lips down, once more, to meet my own.

A tiny sliver of light fought its way through the curtains around seven the next morning, slowly moving across the bed before resting on my face.

Blinking sleepily, I yawned as I opened my eyes.

The room looked ancient, decrepit, in the daylight, half of it still cast in deep shadows. But the man next to me never looked more beautiful.

Lying on his stomach with arms bent under his pillow, he looked like a medieval Viking from one of my history books—a hard and striking kind of beauty beneath a wild tangle of curls. A rugged warrior whose size alone practically dwarfed the small wooden bed we'd slept in. And gave ourselves to each other in.

We'd fallen asleep not having bothered to get dressed. I guess neither of us felt the need. Things just felt so natural between us.

I didn't try to conceal my smile as I let my eyes have full perusal of Dax. Unguarded, vulnerable, and *mine.* I'd never seen him so at ease except when he was with me.

Intricate webs of ink covered every inch of his back, like almost everywhere else. It was hard to miss the large tree detailed in a circular pattern in the very middle with Celtic knots surrounding it. But what was more intriguing were the chains. I thought they'd only been around his neck and chest, but looking closer, I realized they were actually intertwined throughout his back as well.

Resisting the urge to shudder at the brutality of them, I traced a finger along one.

Small, bright violet sparks ignited the second my finger touched his skin.

Gasping quietly, I quickly pulled my hand back.

Looking to Dax, making sure he was still asleep, I put my finger back down. I didn't want to wake him, but my curiosity was getting the better of me.

As soon as I touched him again, sparks began to fly.

"You know I'm awake?"

This time my gasp was much louder. "Dax!"

I could only see part of his responding grin, half his face still buried in the pillow, but he reached up and grabbed me before I could move, pulling me to him and smothering me in kisses.

"Good morning, *mo ghrá*."

"Good morning." I smiled back at him. "*Mo ghrá*… That's what was written on my bathroom drawer, wasn't it? What does it mean?"

"It means, *my love* in Irish." A shy look took over his face.

"Oh." A blush creeped up mine, and I fought back my grin like a schoolgirl.

He smiled back before gently kissing me on the nose. Rolling on his back, he sleepily scrubbed a hand down his face, yawning in the process.

"It's the Crann Bethadh—the tattoo on my back. The tree of life. Surrounded by Celtic knots and Gaillic symbols of varying meanings," he said, a hint of pride in his voice.

"Why Celtic?" If Dax's father was a Reyes by blood, the Celtic symbolism and words didn't make much sense.

"The Gaill have always been heavily influenced by those who settled in White Point. It was one of the barely inhabitable areas when we were first banished. Those who settled there are some of the most powerful in the Gaill. Even the word *Gaill* comes from the ancient Irish word meaning foreigner."

I nodded in response because Dax didn't need to say anything further. It was common knowledge that most Gaill from Ireland and the United Kingdom had settled in northeast New America, specifically White Point, since their countries and most of those in what was once Europe had been decimated in the War.

"My mother, Caragh Da Luca, was born Caragh MacIvor, daughter to the Lord of White Point at the time that my parents' marriage was arranged," Dax continued.

"So the Celtic knots are for the Gaill and for her?" I lay on my side next to him and propped my head on my hand.

Nodding he stared at the ceiling, lost in thought, his expression unreadable. Then suddenly it lightened as he remembered something.

"She was so mad at the first one I got. I was very young, only about fifty. She thought I was ruining myself. 'You have your whole life ahead of you to make dumb decisions. At least wait till you're a hundred.'" He laughed as he mimicked her scolding.

I laughed at the absurdity of time in his world.

"Let me guess. Killian talked you into it?"

"Something like that." He cut me a glance out of the corner of his eye before laughing again, one of his deep chuckles that sent sparks through my body without his even touching me. "That kid was always getting us into trouble. And I was always getting us out."

"Sounds about right." I laughed, shaking my head. Killian was much older now, so I couldn't imagine what he'd been like when he was a kid and deviating.

"So what was your first one?" I brought us back to the topic of the tattoos that covered a majority of his body.

"The tree." He grinned again, and we both laughed. "Yeah, Mother was not happy with me."

"But she got over it eventually, right?"

"Within a few years." He shrugged jokingly. "Nah, she was fine with it after a while. The Crann Bethadh is powerful Celtic image. It symbolizes perfect harmony—the roots planting themselves in the ground as the branches stretch to the sky. It's the ultimate sign of life, longevity, strength, and wisdom."

"It's beautiful," I said. And it was. I'd never heard of something so beautiful captured so perfectly by a single image.

"As are you, *mo ghrá*." He reached up, pulling me to him and kissing me gently.

"You are so sappy sometimes, you know that?" I giggled. It might have been sappy, but we both knew I loved it.

"Only for you." He kissed me again before lying back to face the ceiling. "After that first one"—getting back to the topic of his tattoos—"it was easier to get the others. I came to like the feel, the needle on my skin. It became a form of release for me. And Mother eventually gave up the good fight and actually took an interest in what I'd do next."

"Do all the Celtic knots have different meanings?"

"Mmm." He nodded. "Some symbolize unbreakable bonds while others translate to the forces of nature—earth, fire, water, and air." He placed a hand over his heart drawing my attention to the large Celtic cross tattooed above it and the small knots surrounding it. "The Celtic cross is the symbol for hope and faith and Dara Knots for strength. These surround the Crann Bethadh as well. They're hidden all over along with Gaillic symbols I'm sure you already know."

His eyes searched mine, and I nodded in response; an eclipse, a comet, even the words GAILL and ONE were tattooed on his knuckles along with the phases of the moon. And then there were the chains.

"What of the chains?" As soon as I asked, I noticed that the ones from his neck did indeed infiltrate his entire body, extending beneath the sheets that sat low at his hips.

"It's obvious, isn't it?" His eyes slid to mine, open and honest with not a hint of hostility.

"The monarchy?"

He nodded in response. "And my father."

"I'm sorry, Dax." I'm not sure why I said it or what I was apologizing for. But I felt like I needed to apologize. Maybe for his evil excuse of a father. Or for my country's role in his suffering. Probably both.

"Don't be, Jacqueline." His hand came up to cup my cheek. "His fate is sealed, as are the monarchies'. They will pay for their wrongs."

Nodding, I leaned into his callused palm and said the next words without hesitation. "I trust you."

My eyes flew open the moment they left my lips, looking for reassurance in a stormy ocean as his eyes locked onto mine.

I *did* trust him. Regardless of what he had once said, I knew in my bones that I could.

And much to my surprise, he smiled as he leaned forward to kiss me again.

"So this means you're letting me trust you? No 'Don't trust me, I'm a bad guy, Jacqueline?' No 'I'm the man of your nightmares, Jacqueline?'" I smiled teasingly at him.

Leaning back, he let out another deep chuckle. "No, not this time." Then drawing me to him, he pressed his lips to my ear, creating the static electricity only he could. "Though I don't think I have to tell you twice that I am the man of your nightmares."

Scoffing, I went to shove him, but he caught my hand instead, pulling me back to him.

Looking in his eyes, so vibrant and fully alive, I knew I should've seen the man from my nightmares—the one they warned us about and told us was the worst sort of Gaill. But all I saw was a man who embodied everything I knew a perfect leader should. He was compassionate but unyielding when needed, ruling everything with a strong hand but a kind heart so that even those outside his walls knew he was good and could be trusted. And he had spent the better part of the past thirty years guilting himself over actions his father had forced him to commit.

My father and his advisors had lied about many things, and I knew now and had known for weeks that Dax was yet another thing they lied about.

Lying on his chest, I intertwined my fingers with Dax's as I bent my other hand beneath my chin. His fingers lazily stroked my knuckles.

"I know why you don't think I should trust you. Or didn't at least. And I want you to know that I don't think you're a bad person for what happened in the past. I know who you are *now*. And I think you're one of the kindest, most compassionate people I've ever met. I feel lucky to have met you." His fingers stilled their movements as I spoke, and his gaze searched mine as if he could determine the validity of my words if he kept looking long enough.

"Do you really believe that?"

His self-doubt broke my heart in two. How could he not see himself as he truly was? The man who risked his very life to go against his father? The one who saved refugees from his enemy? Who persisted in finding the One to save his people, to save us all, even when his own father called him crazy?

"With every fiber of my being."

He looked at me then, his eyes burning with an admiration and love so deep it knocked the breath from me.

"I'm the lucky one, Jacqueline—*you* are kind. And smart. Not to mention incredibly brave, strong… and a little stubborn at times." He chuckled, pulling my leg over his so I could settle in the nook between his arm and chest.

Laying my head down, I got lost in the steady beat of his heart.

"I've waited a very long time for you. Did you know that?" he murmured into my hair a few minutes later.

I hadn't. But I was starting to get a very good idea.

"How do you say I love you in Irish?" I asked.

He stilled before responding, and the emotion was evident in his voice when he spoke next. "*Tá grá agam duit.*"

"*Tá grá agam duit*, Daxinius."

In an instant he was over me, eyes of the brightest green searching mine as I lay beneath him.

"Say it again," he commanded, his voice low and rough, like he had to work to get the words out.

"*Tá grá agam duit*," I repeated, doing nothing to conceal the smile spreading across my face.

And then we collided like never before, light shooting in every direction as he kissed me all over—my neck, my jaw, my collarbone, claiming every inch before he moved his lips to my ear.

The electrical current thrumming between us reached an almost unbearable level, and I wasn't sure how much more my body could endure without combusting.

"*Tá grá agam duit*, Jacqueline. I have forever. You were always meant to be mine and I yours."

Nodding, I looked up at him because I knew what he meant. Even if it didn't make sense. Nothing had ever felt so right as the two of us together.

Brushing my hair from my face, he resumed his kisses. They slowly turned more passionate as we lost ourselves in each other again, letting our light become one in that small room in the Gaill tavern where our whole world changed.

CHAPTER 18

THE KING

"Why don't I carry that for you?" Dax attempted again to take the small leather backpack from my shoulders as we made our way to the palace a few hours later.

The rain had stopped, but the sky was still a dark stormy gray like it wasn't quite sure if it was noon or night. He had agreed to let us walk at least part of the way because I didn't know if I could handle shifting after the breakfast we'd just inhaled.

Of course Dax would be the one doing the shifting either way. Apparently, it took years to learn how to travel like he and the other Devs could. And considering my powers had been relegated to touch—and outside of one instance, touching Dax in particular—I wasn't yet up to the task.

I truly wondered if I'd ever be.

We'd discussed my powers a bit more over breakfast, but Dax was still stumped. Without Deviant blood, it was impossible for this to be happening. The radiation out here just wasn't strong enough otherwise.

Which meant one of two things. Either I was some one-in-a-billion-type person who deviated for no reason, which, knowing my luck, was a possibility, or there were secrets in my past that needed uncovering. And based on how things in my life were unfolding lately, I'd say the latter was more likely.

Whatever the case, the powers I had weren't nearly as strong as a typical Dev's and were still relatively unknown. Shifting and the expert hearing they all seemed to have weren't currently in my wheelhouse.

"Stop it, seriously!" I swatted at Dax's hands as he attempted to take the bag again. "What? Suddenly you're a Gaill in love, and you've gone all soft on me?"

It was just a backpack, but I did appreciate the act of chivalry nonetheless.

"Something like that, Jacqueline." Glancing down at me, he smirked before looking back at the road, grabbing my hand in the process and bringing it to meet his lips.

He'd put his curls half back, and the front few pieces hung forward in a messy way, partially covering his face, but I didn't miss how the smile stayed as he pressed his lips to my skin.

If he'd let go of my hand in that moment, I was pretty certain I'd float up to join the clouds, never to come down, my heart felt so full.

"There you two are!" A breathless voice sounded from in front of us, instantly drawing us both back to reality.

I looked forward to find Maverick doubled over, wheezing and out of breath, his fiery red hair stuck to his pale forehead with sweat. "You didn't send word. I've been searching all morning."

Dax scrubbed his jaw with this free hand. "Mav, brother, I'm sorry. I didn't mean for you to be out like this. It's usually not an issue. The monarchy has never attempted two raids so close together."

"That I get. But that's not the problem. Your father's returned."

Minutes seemed to tick by as I stared at Mav, willing my brain to comprehend his presence and the words he'd spoken.

The fastest runner, Kacey had said—the one who could get to us before anyone else could.

My heart kicked into overdrive as the reality of what was happening hit me. The king was awaiting us back at the palace. Dax and I were out of time.

I was out of time.

Dax's grip tightened on my hand as he turned to me, bringing his face level with mine. "Nothing will happen to you, Jacqueline."

"Dax, I have to tell you something."

"Jacqueline, I know you're a noble from Calderone. It doesn't matter what he says."

I opened my mouth and willed the words *I am Princess Jacqueline Louise Livingston, future queen of Calderone* to come out, but they were lost, stuck in my throat from the very real threat to my safety his father posed. Being a member of the Calderonian nobility was bad enough, but being the future queen? That was unforgivable.

If I had fooled everyone, including Dax, into thinking I was simply a member of the nobility, not a member of the royal family, couldn't I fool King Aidoneus as well? And then, when it was safer, I would figure out a way to tell Dax my true identity. Once we were free from the king, which would undoubtedly be soon.

Dax kissed me then, and I responded fervently, knowing we likely wouldn't be able to touch once we reached the palace, knowing even doing so here was a risk now that his father was close.

Pulling away, cocooned in our web of light, he let the full power of his gaze fall over me.

"I love you, Jacqueline."

"I love you too, Dax."

He kissed my forehead, and then I was on his back, his sword moved to his chest as we shifted across time and space, back to the palace. As we neared, I moved to Maverick so that he and I could split off to the tunnel that led to the servant wing. The one I'd been so unsuccessful in finding that one fated night all those weeks ago.

The moment I entered the palace, I felt the difference in the air. It was more confined, cramped, anxious even, like someone had arrived and zapped the entire place of its happiness.

Mav shifted us to the servant wing, where we parted at the girl's corridor. I assured him I'd be fine for the short walk back to my room, but as I neared, I decided to try my luck with Lana first, figuring she might be in since it was nearing lunchtime. Something was going on, and I wasn't about to just sit around and wait for the other shoe to drop.

I quietly knocked on her door, licking my lips as I looked around, making sure I was alone in the small hallway.

Even knowing King Aidoneus was in the building sent a chill through my body.

Opening her door a crack and peeking out, Lana quickly pulled me in.

"Where have you been?" she whisper-shouted as she closed the door, locking it behind her and double-checking to make sure it was secure before turning to me. Taking in my rumpled dress, loose waves, and warm glow, her eyes grew wide.

"Lan, what's going on in the palace?" If the atmosphere in the castle wasn't enough, Lana's disheveled appearance—blond curls wiry with hauntingly dark circles under her eyes—made me genuinely concerned.

We'd only been gone *a day.*

"The king is back, and he's just as vile as everyone says, Jac. Just as vile." She shuddered as if the thought of him made her physically ill. "He arrived soon after you two left yesterday." She cut me a glance, her brown eyes suspicious, clearly questioning his timing. "They ransacked your room before any of us could get in, put the entire palace on lockdown so no one could get out to warn you, and just waited for you two to arrive home, unsuspecting. Killian and Axel helped Mav sneak out while they were chopping wood this morning. I assume he found you?"

Nodding, I sat on her bed, sorting out the chaos we'd come back to. Twenty-four hours ago I'd been in perfect bliss with Dax. And now?

What did it all mean? The monarchy planes last night? The king's sudden arrival home? His waiting for us and searching my room? A pit of dread filled my stomach as I remembered the books and the copy of *The Eclipse* I'd hidden under my mattress.

Dax said it doesn't matter. About the books, or who you are.

"Lana, I have something to tell you." I stood suddenly, adrenaline coursing through my veins.

She looked at me expectantly, like she too knew I was about to say something of life-altering importance.

"I'm not Jacqueline Lewis. I'm Jacqueline Louise Livingston. *Princess* Jacqueline Louise Livingston, future queen of Calderone."

The words hung in the silence between us as Lana stood there, stunned.

"Ho-holy hell, Jac," she stuttered after a minute. "I mean Your Highness. I-I mean, wait—"

"Just Jac, Lan. I'm still Jacqueline—the same person."

"Well yeah, except for the fact that you're heir to the most powerful throne in the world."

"Except for that."

Lana slapped a hand over her mouth as the realization of what had actually been happening these last ten weeks unfolded before her. "They don't know, do they? That they took the heir? Your identity hadn't been revealed when we'd been taken… That's how you've gotten away with using the name Lewis. But wait—can't only boys be heir?"

I quickly moved to her, taking her trembling hands in my own. "My mother only had me so they changed the law. Lan, I am *not* the same girl I was that night I left the palace and then got taken. I know things now that I would've never known had I not gotten out. I know that I have to become queen so I can change Calderone and make it better. Do away with the camps and the injustices so many face." I held her gaze, hoping my eyes conveyed the weight and truth of what I was saying. "But I can't do it alone. My father and his advisors are too powerful as Dax is aware. I need the help of him, the Devs, and the Coalition."

"Does Dax know?" She asked after a beat, slowly nodding as if what I'd said made perfect sense to her.

"No." My heartbeat picked up again as my anxiety kicked in. *I should have told him.* "I was going to tell him, but Calderone's planes arrived before I could. And after… I was just… I feel like a coward for not telling him. And I need to tell him myself. He has to know from me that he wasn't some pawn in the monarchies' game. That I might have Livingston as my last name, but I am not nor will I ever be my father."

"He'll know, Jac. Anyone who really knows you knows the truth of who you are."

Pulling her into a hug, I let slip a shuddering sob. For the family of Gaill I never expected to gain, for our present situation, and for my overwhelming sense of foreboding as I thought about our future—hers, mine, Dax's, and my people's.

I didn't hear from Dax all afternoon or that evening. And being too scared to leave Lana's room, I didn't dare venture out, so there I stayed. Lana snuck one book to me from the library—a teen romance novel. So I filled my afternoon with the drama of a twenty-first century high school in the hopes that I would forget my own.

It didn't work.

By the time Lana returned from dinner with news that Dax hadn't been in attendance, I felt physically nauseated from my anxiety, the knot in my stomach churning endlessly.

Around 2300, Killian stopped by but was just as disappointed as we were that Dax hadn't been to the servant wing once all day. Apparently, no one had seen him since our arrival home earlier that afternoon.

I slept in Lana's room that night, not feeling safe enough to sleep in my own. But my worries continued to eat me alive regardless. I tossed and turned most of the evening, alternating between fear of what the morning would bring and what was happening to Dax.

Falling. Falling. Falling.

There's a roaring in my ears, bright violet light rushes past me, and then my vision clears. I'm on a cliff. One I recognize—but from where?

"Who are you?" I shout at the woman. Her long, straight jet-black hair whips about her face as she fully turns to me. A gray and bleak ocean lays behind her, her eyes a haunting violet in comparison.

"Who are you?" I shout, and it isn't until the second time that I realize my words are a voiceless nothing. Shouting into the void, I try to speak again, but nothing comes out.

My voice has been reduced to nothing.

Her face is still somehow familiar as she reaches for me, her features holding that same look of desperation they had the last time.

I extend my hand to meet hers. Only a few inches more.

I feel my energy taking hold; ultraviolet sparks ignite from my fingertips as I close the gap between us.

But she disappears as I near her and fades into the nothing surrounding us. And I'm moving too quickly toward the edge.

Then I'm falling again, someone's screaming, and the sea is rushing up to meet me from below.

"Jacqueline!"

I blinked against the light from Lana's desk lamp as I came to. I was sitting straight up, screaming.

The screaming was coming from *me.*

I stopped then, panting, beads of sweat breaking out along my forehead and neck as I focused on the room around me. Kacey and Killian were crouched at my side, Lana hovered behind them, and all three were looking at me as if I'd just been an inch from death.

"What in the hell was that?" Kacey asked the question on everyone's mind.

Shaking my head, I felt a fire in my throat. *How long was I screaming?*

Momentarily unable to speak, I wiped the sweat from my brow with a trembling hand.

"I have no idea, but we need Dax. Jac needs Dax," Killian ground out, sucking in his lip ring and running his black nails though his hair. "Where is he? He can't just leave us in the dark like this."

"He always has his reasons, Kil. For now we need to make sure you're okay, Jac. Until Dax can do it himself."

Nodding, I accepted the cup of water from Kacey's outstretched hand, audibly sighing when no light erupted from my fingertips. I took a sip, but it barely quenched the scorching in my throat.

Seriously, what was happening to me? I shuddered as flashes of the dream flickered across my mind.

"I'll stay in here the rest of the night with you and Lana." Kacey took my hand as she spoke.

I nodded in reply, my words still missing.

"Let's hope Dax returns soon," Killian muttered as he looked warily around the room, like he thought better of leaving us. But he finally did, heading back to the boys' wing.

The three of us curled up on a makeshift bed we'd made on the floor. Kacey snuggled up beside me as Lana bravely took the other side. Together, we three made it through the final hours of the night, but I never fell back asleep.

At 0440, I was back in my room. Or what was left of it.

Kacey and Lana had tried to insist I stay in Lana's room, but I was done hiding in fear. I doubted my training would continue with the state of the palace being what it was. But part of me—and it was an admittedly desperate part—held out hope that maybe things would be more normal today and that Dax would be picking me up at 0500 like always.

The entire room had been overturned. They'd taken all my fighting gear as well as my dirk and my books, including the copy of *The Eclipse*.

I told myself none of it mattered. They could never stop the conviction I felt pulsing through me that I would put an end to what Calderone was doing.

I slipped on a fresh day dress, one that hadn't been ripped to shreds, and quickly washed up using what Dax had packed in the backpack. My usual toiletries were nowhere to be seen.

Weaving my hair into a single french braid, I brushed the front layers out of my face and gave myself a level stare—I could do this. I'd been training for weeks—my whole life really—to stand up to situations of intense pressure. These next few days might test us, but Dax and I would come out ahead. We had to—our love had to be stronger than any adversity we'd face.

The knock on my door came at 0455 exactly, making me smile. It was so *him* to be unerringly punctual after not seeing me for a day.

I opened the door, already making excuses for my lack of fighting gear. "I know it's unusual, but you have to admit, the petticoat will likely soften the blows I'll ta—"

I'd hoped to lighten the dire mood as well as my own anxieties but stopped when I realized it wasn't Dax in front of me but a rather grim-faced Captain O'Leary flanked by two Gaill officers I didn't recognize. Both had matching crescents on their uniforms and dark eyes that turned more deadly the longer they looked at me. Willing myself not to shrink beneath their gaze, I looked to O'Leary.

"Miss Jacqueline, your presence is requested."

"Of course, Captain. Training, right?" I willed her to make eye contact with me, but she kept her stare straight ahead, somewhere over my shoulder.

"If you'll follow us, miss."

I had no choice but to follow as we weaved our way through the deserted halls of the servant wing. And as much as I tried to keep it at bay, panic slowly took hold again as not one of the officers bothered to tell me what was going on.

A knot of anxiety spread its talons, sinking its claws into every ounce of my being and bringing with it the fear I'd had during my first days here. That creeping, sinister fear that invaded and immobilized all my senses. Only now it was impossibly bigger. Like my body knew what my mind was desperate to deny—this time, I was getting no special passes.

We saw no one as we passed from the servant wing to the main section of the palace, which only caused the knot to tighten.

The cooks are always in the kitchens by now.

And when Captain O'Leary passed the hallway that led to the south wing, I knew my fate was sealed. I was being taken to the king.

Where is Dax?

My heart began beating erratically as the air became heavy with fear, and I was certain it wasn't all mine. Like a physical weight, it sat on my lungs as we drew nearer to the throne room.

I did my best to regulate my breathing, but my chest physically ached from the weight. My lungs struggled to function as my breaths came in shorter and shorter bursts. I could taste the fear, feel it entering my bloodstream, turning my body into its own enemy. Sucking in a shuddering breath and holding it, I desperately tried to keep the outside world from closing in on me as I blew it out.

Do not spiral, Jacqueline. Do not.

I swallowed against the lump of fear clogging my throat and willed my heart to slow against the mounting pressure snaking its way through my body. My mind clawed for some semblance of control over my emotions, but it was tenuous at best.

I was faintly aware of our presence being announced as the mammoth black oak doors swung open to the throne room. Though I hadn't been in here since that first day, the day I first saw *him*, nothing had changed.

The tall walls ending in Gothic-style arches were just as intimidating, made even more so by the fact that there were no courtiers filling the space or sunlight pouring in from the windows that lined the ceiling. There was absolutely no warmth to be found.

There was only a small group assembled at the very front with two thrones on the dais, Gaill guards flanking them on either side.

King Aidoneus, who I immediately recognized from photos and his striking resemblance to his son, was sitting in the throne that sat vacant last time, hatred emanating from every pore of his being.

Whereas Dax was pure light, the king was pure darkness. Hair black and speckled with gray, his jaw was hard-set, and the age lines in his face disappeared into the shadows that seemed to pour from him. His dark eyes reminded me of my nightmares as he watched me approach. And he was dressed entirely in black, a matching cape designating rank draped across his shoulders ended at his feet where a sword stood, rotating on its axis.

Dragging my eyes from the king, I forced myself to look at the person sitting to his left. And when I did, I forced my knees not to buckle.

He was staring at me. Hair pulled back, sword strapped behind him, the throne somehow accommodating for it, and eyes white with a rage that knocked the breath from me completely.

It was Dax. But it wasn't *my* Dax.

No, this was the Daxinius Da Luca of the legends—far worse than the man I'd seen sitting in the same throne that first day. This was the man known for mercilessly slaughtering whole villages and obliterating his enemies without so much as blinking. The man who'd been born hating me and the family I came from.

I didn't have to guess. I felt it as my chest, my very heart, cleaved in two. My Dax, the man who only twenty-four hours before had professed his love to me, was gone.

"No," I groaned, not being able to hold it in as I stopped in my tracks, my hand flying to my chest, sure I'd be able to feel the physical effects from the blow I felt reverberating throughout my entire body.

"No," I repeated as I took in the hatred flowing from his eyes. The hatred that was directed solely at me. I felt it then, that terrifying power the stories described. He held nothing back, the once cosmic magnetism between us twisting into something malevolent before my very eyes.

And I could do nothing to stop it.

One of the two men stepped from behind O'Leary then, apparently growing impatient, and roughly grabbed my upper arm, his long nails digging into my skin as he jerked me forward, causing me to stumble.

Regaining my footing quickly, I didn't miss the fact that O'Leary instinctively reached out to steady me. Neither did I miss the fact that Dax did nothing. His old mask of indifference had slipped into place, his face emotionless as he looked over my head while I approached.

Swallowing my tears, I tried to find my breath, but my chest keep constricting as my very lifeblood was ripped from me. Stopping a few feet in front of the dais, I was told to curtsy. And when I did, I was forced to my knees.

Keeping my head down, the tears fell from my eyes as the cold stone floor cut into my skin through my wool dress. I willed myself to stay strong, but to do that I couldn't look up. To look at *him* would shatter what was left of *me*.

Working to steady my breathing, I flinched as a deep voice filled the hall, slithering its way into every nook and corner, seeping into that knot of fear in my stomach, making sure its message was heard.

"The girl who thought she'd single-handedly bring down the Gaill court, *my* court. And I'm ashamed to say she almost succeeded."

My head shot up at his words. It took me only a moment before I realized where I'd heard something similar. Heard that tone before. *My father.*

"I wasn't trying to bring down the Gaill court," I spit out through gritted teeth. I would bring *him* down, but his court was my home. I wasn't about to jeopardize that.

"You will speak when I say, Calderonian scum."

Several of his officers, including Romano, who stood behind him, laughed at that. It made my lip curl. Dax remained emotionless next to him, eyes fixed straight ahead.

"You. You thought you could get away with it, didn't you? Jacqueline *Lewis*." The king laughed, but it was a hallow sound, his cold black eyes dancing with a type of sinister amusement as they rooted me to the spot. "Or is it Livingston... Your Highness?"

And at that, I did stop breathing. My eyes locked onto his, and the outer world became a blur as he uttered his next words.

"Jacqueline Livingston, future queen of Calderone, and guest at our court." He put his hands out, eliciting a chorus of jeers and laughter from his officers.

"You see, my son should've been suspicious of you from the start. Instead, he let your looks cloud his vision." He waved a hand over my body as if it were the only thing I had to offer a man. "If he hadn't, he'd have realized you were trying to escape that night my officers found you in the corridor, undoubtedly to go tell your family of our plans." He threw my bag, the one I'd forgotten the night Romano attacked me, at my feet.

My heart lurched as I realized how it must've looked to Dax.

"No, he didn't realize then," King Aidoneus continued, "or even when you offered your body to him after he fed you priceless Gaill information at that tavern. The fool."

I felt nauseated at what his words implied. What had happened between Dax and me was anything but that. It had been sacred. Dax *had* to know that.

My eyes were drawn to the tightening of Dax's fists on the arms of his throne. His eyes might have still been vacant, mask in place, but I held on to that small bit of emotion. Even if it was hatred, showing something was better than nothing.

Doing something is better than nothing.

Turning back to the king, I drew myself up. I was standing before my next thought, fixing him with a stare so powerful it felt like an actual electrical current was passing through it.

Slowly but surely my anger was becoming stronger than my fear.

I wasn't about to let him speak like that to me *or* to Dax. And I certainly wasn't going to let everything I'd come to love be ripped from me without a fight.

"You will show more respect, sire, when you address the future queen of Calderone. My name is Jacqueline Louise Livingston, and I am a guest at the court of your son, Daxinius Antonio Giovacchin Da Luca. And it is with him and him alone that Calderone will make peace with in the future, under *my* reign. Not because I have had a plan all along—I assure you I have not; *your* guards captured *me*, if you recall, before my identity was known and brought me *here*—but we will do so because your son embodies all that is good and right in the Gaill cause. He is a model for Calderone to follow for reform in the future."

The king stared at me in blatant shock as my voice, the indisputable voice of a monarch, rang out across the hall, leaving a tangible silence that only those that are truly commanding can deliver in its wake.

I looked to Dax then to find him staring at me.

"I'm the same Jacqueline, Dax. My last name does not define me." I met his gaze, finally seeing the blue-green maelstrom of emotion within his eyes as I willed him to hear and know the truth behind my words.

"Grab her!" the king shouted somewhere in the periphery.

And I watched a look of fear pass in front of Dax's eyes before I felt a pair of hands on me again. Then violet light exploded as I instinctively sent my power out in all directions, throwing the guards surrounding me back and causing me to land on the floor ten feet behind where I'd been standing.

There was more shouting, then a scramble. I was on my feet again, but so was the guard who had originally grabbed me.

And so was Dax.

I didn't get a good look at his face before the guard ran for me, stabbing a needle in my neck as he shifted past, not having touched me in the process.

"What was that?" Dax roared from the front of the hall.

I felt the medicine take hold of my senses, numbing everything so that my limbs became heavier, so that *I* became heavier with every passing second.

"Dax!" I shouted, but the words came out a hoarse whisper as my vision blurred, and I realized then I was slipping into unconsciousness.

Within another second, everything went black.

CHAPTER 19

THE ONE

Coughing, I blinked back against the water in my eyes as I came to in a prison chamber. There was a dull throbbing at the base of my skull, and I was only vaguely aware of something crusted against the left side of my cheek. My entire body, my *mind*, felt heavy with numbness.

I sputtered as more water splashed in my face.

"Wake up!"

I immediately recognized the voice from my nightmares.

Romano.

Coughing again, my eyes stung as I forced them open and searched for the source of the voice. Not finding it, I attempted to stand, but my movements were agonizingly laborious. And the more I moved, the more I felt a burning sensation in my wrists. It wasn't until several more seconds passed that I realized they'd been tied behind my back to the wooden chair I was sitting on.

My heart rate picked up only slightly as I realized I was trapped. I should've been afraid with that rush of adrenaline coursing in my veins, but I felt next to nothing except the haze clouding my mind.

I attempted to catalog my surroundings while I was still somewhat conscious. The room was so dark I could barely make out the door in front of me, and the only source of light was a small window with bars on it about fifteen feet up against the ceiling.

Just then a sharp object collided with my cheek, whipping my head to the side. I gasped against the pain that tore through my numbness. Romano gripped my chin, forcing me to face him as blood poured down the back of his hand from where his ring had cut my skin. From the looks of it, this wasn't the first blow I'd taken.

"I'll ask again," he said, the smell of brandy rancid on his breath. "What do you have plotted?"

"Nothing," I croaked out, which evidently wasn't what he wanted to hear because his hand struck my other cheek in another heavy blow.

I could feel the warm blood trickling down my face as I gasped for air, trying to stay alert though I felt my body slipping into unconsciousness from the pain. I had no idea how long he'd been at this. Or how much of a beating I'd taken.

"Give her another dose," Romano commanded to someone behind me.

A needle pricked my skin, and the fog over my mind thickened. I desperately tried to send my power out but felt I had nothing inside me. My body was hollow, free-falling into oblivion.

The chamber was dimmer when I awoke next; the small cracked bulb that hung from the ceiling barely illuminated the room, and the window above revealed a starless night.

The numbness had somewhat worn away, enough for me to feel intense pain radiating throughout my body. Romano was sitting across from me on a chair identical to the one I was still strapped in, watching me. Waiting.

"Your plans."

I shook my head, too weak to speak. He stared back, his eyes cold and unfeeling, their black depths mirroring the bleakness slowly coming over me.

It had been hours, at least, since I'd been taken. And if Dax hadn't come yet, I knew he wouldn't be.

As if hearing me, Romano echoed my thoughts. "No one's coming for you, *Jacqueline Livingston*, especially not our prince. I hear he entertained Lady Daniels after dinner this evening." His smile was smug as he sat back and waited for my reaction.

I willed my face not to betray me though the crack in my heart grew exponentially bigger.

That wasn't possible. My Dax wouldn't do that.

And then I reminded myself, *my* Dax no longer existed.

"And none of your other Deviant friends seem to care much either, not even your human friends. Not even your own father," he continued. "Can't say I'm surprised. You truly are worthless. Just a pawn. Who would care to save you?"

The words echoed through me as I felt my world crumbling. No one was coming. And if all the Devs, even my own father, were willing to let me be captured without a fight, maybe I was as worthless as he said.

Tears slid down my cheeks, but I barely felt the sting as the salt hit my open wounds. My mind began its retreat, locking away every emotion and leaving me as mentally numb as I was physically.

"So even if I do this"—Romano was suddenly in front of me, driving his fist into my stomach—"no one will care."

I lurched forward as he knocked the breath from me but didn't have time to recover before he punched me again. A shooting pain ricocheted through my ribs, and my vision swam through my tears as I gasped for air.

He began to back away, fading into the darkness of the cell as I felt myself fading into the darkness within me.

A warm liquid hit my lips as my head was forced back. Swallowing on instinct, I began to choke when the cup was held there a little too long. The moment it was taken away, my body slumped forward involuntarily.

I'd been moved, strung up between two intersecting wooden poles. A small glow of light was visible from the window above. A new day was dawning.

And I couldn't feel… anything.

Why can't I feel my hands? My feet? My legs?

Wait, *who the hell am I?*

I screamed, but only silence filled my ears.

"Oh look. She's trying to say something." I heard someone say from miles away as a body appeared in front of me. A hand, in jagged motions neared my face, wiping away the drool that had fallen down my chin.

I looked up with effort as Tynan's face swam before mine. Gasping, reality returned at warp speed.

All of a sudden every bone, every fiber of my being, screamed in pain. My head felt like it weighed a million pounds as I rolled it to the left, the effort alone exhausting me. My wrists were raw from the ropes, and my muscles ached from how long I'd been tied.

"Better give her more." The command came from Romano nearby.

"She'll bleed out from the cuts if we're not careful."

Another body moved in my periphery. It was impossible to tell how many of them there were as I fought through the pain to remain conscious. Someone tilted my head again and forced the same liquid down my throat. Gagging on its bitter taste, I recognized it as one of the tonics Dax had given me—the one that helped with healing.

I coughed as I tried to swallow but instantly cried out against the resulting pain in my stomach. Looking down, I was filled with dread as I realized I'd been cut in multiple places. Blood poured through the tattered fabric of my dress. I licked my dry, cracked lips, swallowing against the iron taste filling my mouth, while I concentrated on the sound of my own ragged breathing.

"Can't have you dying on us just yet, *Princess.*" Romano's venomous voice prickled in my ear. "Don't give her any more of the tonic unless I say. Tynan, inject another dose now."

A needle then pricked my neck, and I welcomed the familiar nothingness that washed over me.

Falling. Falling. Falling.

Bright purple light surrounds me. Goes through me. Becomes *me.*

"Remember, Jacqueline. Remember."

Her eyes are as violet and alive as the light surrounding us. But they're quickly covered by black hair when her hand reaches out to grip my unmarred cheek. Fire shoots through me at her touch.

"You know."

Confusion infiltrates my mind at her words.

"Know what?" My hoarse voice cracks.

Her eyes round with pity. "Your destiny. Who you are. Who you were always meant to be. It's always been here." She moves her hand from my cheek to cover my heart.

Heat spreads from her fingertips like wildfire as an inferno engulfs my heart, incinerating any trace of who I thought I was and leaving the one I'm meant to be.

Coming to with a start, I attempted to control my breathing despite the erratic beating of my heart. Sweat was pooling on my forehead, and I could feel a drop slowly making its way down my temple. The burning in my chest only intensified as my eyes slowly refocused on my surroundings.

I was in the same chamber, but everything had changed. Through my barely conscious haze a new realization dawned on me. The one truth I'd been ignorant of this entire time, my entire life, but had known in my heart all along.

I thought my purpose was to be queen when all the while I was, in fact, meant for something much greater.

"How?"

"Broke into the king's chamber. Him and that damn Killian Carver." Romano's voice was filled with fury as he addressed Tynan. I had no idea what they were discussing, but I closed my eyes and kept my breathing steady, hoping they wouldn't notice I'd regained consciousness.

I no longer felt so numb—the pain in my abdomen and along my wrists intensified with every breath I took, but I willed myself to stay still.

"And the king?"

"Gone. Instructed us to finish the girl before leaving. We likely have no more than a few minutes."

My heart rate picked up as I realized what he was implying. I tried to summon my powers, but they'd either dampened them too much, or I was still too weak. Beads of sweat trickled down my face from the effort, causing my loose layers to stick to my skin and shivers to rack my body.

I needed to survive. What I knew now was too important for me to perish in this dark cell.

I gathered the last of my strength, willing my powers to manifest, and it was in that moment I felt it. Not my power. But one that was much more intense. One I recognized in an instant.

It detonated like an atomic bomb in the distance, shaking the walls of the chamber and hurtling toward us at the speed of light.

I felt the guards start to race around me, some shifting, others shouting orders. But it was of no use. Seconds later, a blinding white light filled the room as the door and wall around it burst open.

The light flooded past me with such force my head whipped back. And it was only then that I dared opened my eyes.

They instantly found Dax as he shifted into the room, sword drawn, his gaze a blinding ray of light as he spun and struck the first guard who appeared, gutting the man from navel to nose in one fluid motion. He wasted no time, advancing on the other guards who were now ready, weapons drawn on the right side of the room.

My eyes then caught the movement of more people entering through the wall as Killian, Mav, Kacey, and Axel all shifted in.

Deadly as a nightmare.

But not my nightmare.

Kil was a blur of black smoke across my vision as he threw a guard against the wall, the sickening crunch of bone doing nothing to stop him as he rounded on the next one who was poised to attack. Axel and Maverick worked in tandem, each shifting around one another in a blur of blue and orange as they fought with the Gaill guards on the left side of the room. Kacey worked behind them, setting fire to the stragglers. I almost felt sorry for them as their screams reached my ears.

Just then energy exploded all around me, creating an impenetrable tunnel of light to the door, and a figure came into view. She was running for me, blond curls wild, brown eyes locked on mine.

"We're here, Jac. We're here." Lana rushed out as she reached me, holding my face in her palms, eyes shining with tears as she took in my injuries.

"H-how?" I struggled to form words against the cocktail of drugs in my system.

"Dax figured out the truth just minutes ago. He knows Aidoneus lied about *everything*. And when he figured out what his father was doing to you, not even Kil could control him. Hell hath no fury like a Da Luca scorned." A small smile flickered across her face as she moved to the ropes binding my hands.

She fumbled with one only a few moments before Killian was at her side. His eyes were as black as the shadows surrounding him while he took me in, but they were comforting, like the warmth of shelter on a winter's night.

"I'm so sorry, Jac," he said, his voice a mix of rage and sorrow.

Not bothering to stop my tears from falling, I forced myself to speak, needing to tell him and Lana what I'd discovered. "Sskay, you came. I—"

"Killian!" Lana shouted, and it was then that I saw Gaill guards, all with crescents on their uniforms, moving toward us down the tunnel, weapons drawn. More were behind them, flooding in through the open wall, some shifting, others running to the sides of the room.

Too many. There were *too many.*

Killian broke away, unsheathing his sword from his back as the black smoke thickened around him. And then he was shifting, slicing through skin and bone like he was executing a lethal dance choreographed specifically for him. A blaze of red sped toward us as Kacey ran up behind the guards. Extending her sword, she ignited those closest to her, running through the flames before launching herself over the growing group Killian was fighting.

She was to me a second later, her orange eyes as bright as her flames as she incinerated the ropes holding me to the poles. The moment they were gone, I collapsed, my legs too weak to hold. But Kacey caught me, moving under one arm as Lana took the other.

"Dax!" She shouted across the room, and the tunnel of light immediately lifted.

A savage roar sounded somewhere to my right, and I knew then that Dax had seen me for the first time. His responding rage consumed the room, adding fuel to the fire for everyone inside. I looked up as he shifted to Tynan, raising his sword with the movement and striking Tynan's head from his body before doing the same to all the other guards in his immediate vicinity.

My heart clenched as I watched. Not for Tynan. Or the guards. But for Dax.

I knew Dax hated this. Killing. Hated ending another's life no matter whose it was. No matter what they'd done. I knew it killed *him* to do it. And I knew he would avoid as much carnage today as possible because of that. But I also knew the palpable fury flowing from him could only be quenched by one thing.

Showing no mercy.

"Quickly." Kacey nodded to the door where there were still more Gaill guards entering. It appeared Aidoneus had wasted no effort. I was sure his goal today was to end not only my life, but his son's as well.

Kacey turned us toward the back of the chamber and a second door I hadn't noticed. We began hobbling to it but made it only a few feet before I almost collapsed, the pain unbearable.

"She's not going to make it unless I heal her!" Kacey shouted over the fighting.

In the next second, I was on the ground, staring at the ceiling. And in another, Kacey had her palm pressed to the cuts across my stomach, sending what felt like fire through me.

I screamed as the pain, the worst I'd ever endured, ripped through all the drugs in my system, turning my numbness to ash. Writhing on the floor, all I could think about was the burning of my blood, and the flames I felt consuming me from the inside out. Lana's crying was barely discernible as were the words Kacey said while she hovered over me.

"I know, I know, Jac. I know it hurts. I promise I'm helping. We never told you—I'm a healer."

I nodded as I looked at her through my tears. I knew she was helping me; I trusted her.

Kacey suddenly let out a scream of her own as a Gaill guard ripped her off me.

Lana immediately pulled me up, and I was surprised to find that although a majority of my injuries were still there, the sharp pain in my ribs was much reduced, and most of the bleeding had stopped save a few cuts.

"Shit," Lana said in my ear, and it was then that I saw three more Gaill guards had joined the fight against Kacey.

"Go!" Axel shouted to us as he shifted in a blur of blue to help her. Literal ice shot from his eyes, striking the door in the back of the chamber and forging a hole right through it and the surrounding wall.

Lana and I stood stunned for several moments before she put her arm under me again and moved us forward. My limbs were still weak and my movements stiff, but we were faring a bit better than before.

By the time we reached the wall, it had been completely broken open to the outside, revealing a short embankment, ending in blue sky. We had just started to trudge up the hill when I felt someone grab hold of my outside arm. The person's nails dug into the exposed skin where my dress had been shredded as they pulled me back, away from Lana.

Stumbling, I attempted to fight them off to keep moving forward, but my movements were too weak. Even with Kacey's healing, I could do nothing while they dragged me back into the chamber.

"Not so fast, *Princess*." The voice from behind me was pure poison in my ear.

Romano.

So near I could sense him—smell the brandy on his breath, feel the movements of his chest.

I tried to run again. Tried to move. But my legs suddenly felt like granite beneath me. Crumbling granite. Old, broken, and so weary.

"Romano!" Dax's deep voice boomed across the chamber, causing both of us to freeze in place.

But only for a second.

Before I could blink, Romano had turned us both, unsheathing his sword from his back and holding me to his chest in the same movement. One of my arms was pinned behind me as the other instinctually came up to block him when he brought the blade to rest against my throat. Grasping his hand on the hilt, I ignored the shaking in my limbs as I attempted to keep him from digging the sword into my skin.

"You won't win this."

"Win what, Romano? You've already lost." Dax shifted to us, murder tattooed across his face as sure as the ink across his body. It was then that I noticed the mass of dead guards on the right side of the room. Dax had to have killed practically every guard in the chamber in a matter of minutes. Blood was dripping from his sword, steam curling above it into the chill of the prison cell. The other Devs were still fighting, but there weren't many guards left, and some were actively fleeing through the same door they'd entered.

We had won.

We won.

Adrenaline shot through me before I realized I was still being held by a madman. One who wanted my life and had nothing left to lose. Swallowing, feeling the steel of the blade on my throat with the movement, my eyes again found Dax.

"Release Jacqueline, and I might let you live."

It felt like an eternity passed as the two men held each other's gaze, but then the blade moved. Subtle at first, like Romano didn't want Dax to notice, but the pressure steadily increased as he began to press it into my throat.

He couldn't.

He wouldn't.

But he was.

I felt my power take hold then, like something buried deep, screaming to break free, it barreled through my bloodstream—an ultraviolet tsunami I couldn't have stopped even if I'd wanted.

Dax's blinding white gaze met mine. We didn't have to speak; we knew.

Bright violet sparked from my fingertips, and the smell of Romano's burning flesh assaulted my senses. He roared in pain, and I took my opportunity.

Using my last bit of strength, I pushed the blade away, falling forward as Dax shifted to us in a ray of white light. And I don't know if it was the slow return of my powers after Kacey's healing or something I dreamed up, but I saw Dax move. Saw him shift.

Majestic, animalistic, a savage type of beauty.

His face was flawless in its fury as he moved for Romano like the king of the jungle protecting his pride. Swirling his large Celtic sword above him as he moved, he drew electricity from what appeared to be every light in the palace before bringing the sword down and directing the path of light at Romano's chest.

Romano shifted, a blood red light engulfing him as he threw his own sword up, blocking the blow before Dax's energy reached him. Both men then unleashed the full extent of their powers on each other. Two of the greatest Gaill warriors fighting to what was sure to be the end of one of them.

Dax's sword, still glowing with the force of his energy, collided with Romano's. The two exchanged blows as Dax pushed Romano farther back toward the wall. Red light bled into Dax's, twisting its way from Romano before Dax broke their connection and lunged for a clear shot at Romano's heart. Time slowed to a crawl as Romano bent backward then shifted behind Dax, immediately taking aim at Dax's back.

My heart leaped into my throat as I watched Romano bring his sword down toward Dax.

Gripping the hilt in both hands, Dax whipped his sword behind him, blocking Romano's right before the sword sliced him in two. The sound of metal on metal echoed through the chamber as the blades slid against one another. Red light threatened to overtake white before Dax fully shifted to face the traitorous general. Dax's energy pulsed as he shoved Romano off, causing the general to stumble a few feet back before regaining his footing.

Both men breathed heavily as sweat shone on their brows. But neither was close to giving up.

Dax stalked toward Romano. "A behind-the-back blow, Romano? You continually prove yourself a coward." And with that Dax spun, bringing his sword down within slicing distance of Romano's neck. Time again stuttered as Romano shifted back slightly. He dodged Dax's blade by inches but couldn't escape Dax's energy as it swung out from the tip of his sword. Romano roared as Dax's energy hit him full force, sending him flying into the wall behind him.

Regaining his footing quickly, Romano shifted in a blur of red to Dax. Time froze, but Romano didn't. Instead, he swung his sword back before whipping it forward as he moved, carving through the air and cutting a line into Dax's abdomen.

I screamed as I watched Dax stagger back a few feet before Romano kicked him in the chest, sending Dax to the ground.

It was then that I felt hands wrap themselves around my waist as Axel held me in place—I hadn't realized I'd started to run toward Dax.

Romano moved again, bringing his sword down in what was sure to be a fatal blow before Dax shifted at the last moment, bringing his sword up to block Romano's. The two blades scraped against one another as the men fought for leverage. Dax spun then, rolling to standing as Romano's sword collided with the stone where Dax had just been lying.

Blood seeped through Dax's cut, but he didn't seem to notice as he strode for Romano. Romano turned just before Dax reached him, and their swords collided in a blur of clanking steel and light. The two fought, expertly spinning around one another in a deadly waltz as they exchanged blows and blocked each other's advances. Just before their movements became a total blur, Dax spun, catching Romano off guard, and put his full might into a swing that hit Romano's sword with such force that it flew to the ground.

Their gazes collided before Romano threw his hand to the side. Red light exploded from him and formed a circle with a black center. A cruel smile crossed Romano's face as he shifted into the swirling black energy. Within moments, the entire circle closed in on itself, and Romano disappeared from view.

A minute passed before I realized Romano was gone. A shocking silence hung in the chamber as everyone watched where he'd disappeared before Axel groaned in frustration behind me.

I watched Dax as his eyes remained on where Romano had been. His chest was rising and falling, jaw tense as his sword remained suspended above him, waiting to deal a deadly blow. Another minute passed before he slowly lowered his sword. His white gaze then broke away and moved to me.

A sob wrenched itself from my throat.

Dax dropped his sword and shifted to me in an instant. Cupping my jaw in his bloodied hands, his lips crashed into mine.

The metal tang of blood mixed with pine and ocean to overtake my senses as I fell completely into Dax's orbit. Our tongues and teeth clashed, a certain restraint snapping—the kiss as raw as the battle he'd just waged to save me. His grip on my jaw bordered on painful, but I welcomed the pain as a reminder that he was still here. And that our connection was as strong as ever.

"*Mo ghrá.*" Dax's voice was strangled as he broke our kiss to rest his forehead on mine. "*Mo ghrá*, it's over now. You're safe."

I looked up to find Dax's bright blue-green gaze swimming before me.

His thumb came up, deftly swiping away a stray tear I hadn't felt fall before he tipped his head down, gently kissing the spot where it'd been.

Scooping me up, he carried me through the chamber toward a table in the corner. I noticed the Devs throughout the room. Killian was hugging Lana who was crying but, thankfully, didn't appear injured as Mav, Kacey, and Axel rounded up what appeared to be a group of guards.

My eyes met Dax's again. They were still the brightest I'd seen them, whirlpools of swirling viridian.

"Dax, I'm so sorry." I choked out as he set me down on the table, my voice like sandpaper as the tears flooded over, reality hitting me full force. My thoughts became frantic, and I tried to assess the gravity of his injury only to realize the cut had almost healed itself due to his powers.

"No, Jacqueline. I'm sorry. I let my father convince me you were someone else when I already knew the truth." He paused, taking in my remaining injuries as sadness and anger welled in his eyes. Then a shadow of a smile crossed his face as he leaned between my legs, taking my face in his hands again. "Well, I didn't know you were the Calderonian Princess. But like I said, I knew you were no servant."

"I still should've told you."

"Jacqueline, it's okay. You were scared." He gently wiped away another tear that'd fallen. "And I'll spend the rest of my existence making sure you never feel that way again."

Reaching up, ignoring the aching in my muscles, I cupped his cheek, pulling him down to me. "*Tá grá agam duit*, Daxinius."

"*Tá grá agam duit*, Jacqueline."

And then he kissed me, before pulling me to him, hugging me like he'd never let me go again.

Dax had Kacey finish healing me—a task I both wanted and dreaded—while he, the boys, and his guard rounded up the rest of the Gaill guard and made sure the palace was secure. I wasn't sure if we were safe, where the king or Romano were, or what we were doing next. But for the time being, I told myself to focus on healing. I was no use to anyone in my current injured state.

I distracted myself from my thoughts, and the feelings of fire, by talking with Kacey and Lana during the healing process. They kept the conversation light as if none of us wanted to deal with the gravity of what had just occurred. It wasn't until Dax reentered the chamber sometime later that I remembered I never told him, or anyone, about my dream. And what I'd realized.

"How do you feel?" He leaned back as he stood between my legs to look at me, inspecting the now-healed cuts and bruises. He hadn't let me move from the table yet, like he was worried one movement would shatter me.

"Better. Still sore and weak, but better."

"Good."

Taking a deep breath and blowing it out slowly, I steeled myself for the last, and most important, confession I'd make. The one thing I was certain of after my last visit from the lady in black. "Dax?"

"Hmm?"

"I… I think I'm the One."

Dax's face broke into a knowing smile, and he gave me a relieved look like he was happy I'd finally solved the puzzle he'd finished ages ago.

"Wait, you knew?"

"I didn't *know*, but I strongly suspected. I doubted it when my father returned and spun his lies, but then I figured out the truth... and when I entered the chamber, I felt you. The same energy as always, amplified a hundredfold."

I sighed, shaking my head as I went to shove him, forgetting he already knew me too well. Grabbing my hand, he intertwined our fingers as he leaned into me, his other hand coming to rest on my low back, fingers splayed as he pulled me to him.

"*Mo ghrá*," he murmured as he nuzzled my hair, the familiar smell of pine and cold sea air flooding my senses.

"Get a room, you two."

I could feel Dax smile against me as Killian shouted at us across the chamber. Dax opened his mouth to reply when he suddenly turned away from me, looking to the hole in the outer wall Axel had made earlier. The rest of the Devs had become deathly still, and all had their eyes trained on Dax. I glanced at Lana, who looked equally perplexed—clearly the Devs were hearing something we humans could not.

Before panic could set in as to what this new threat might be, Dax turned back to me.

"A large air fleet is approaching. Likely the reinforcements I called in from Mikhail before we attacked." Dax brushed my dirt- and sweat-covered hair from my face before tilting my chin up and kissing my forehead. "We'll head to the Eur compound out west where it'll be safer. Now that we know for sure you're the One, you'll need more training. But I have no doubt that one day soon, together with the other Gaill, we'll be able to take down my father and the monarchy to save the innocents in Calderone."

I nodded, not needing any convincing to leave the Nor Gaill palace and its memories of the past twenty-four hours. "Where is your father?"

"Gone. As is Romano." Darkness crossed Dax's feature at the mention of them, and he dropped his hands, looking down before loosing a sigh. "That circle of black-and-red energy was a portal. Only those who can manipulate time are able to wield them. And that's Romano's area of expertise."

I swallowed audibly. That explained why time seemed to slow and start to Romano's advantage during their fight. "Will they be back?"

Dax pulled in his bottom lip as he met my gaze, nodding once. "They will. And with stronger forces no doubt. But next time, we'll be ready for them." He took my hand, placing a small kiss on my still-bloody, dirt-covered palm. "We'll take the servants and Deviants with us to the west."

"So this is really it? We'll head west, I'll train with the Coalition, and then the real war will begin? We'll take down your father and then save my people in Calderone with the Eur and other Gaill?"

"Yes, Jacqueline. That is my hope."

I couldn't stop the smile spreading across my face as the hum of an engine became discernible in the distance.

The bleak nothing that had hunted me the past twenty-four hours continued to beckon. We were still very much in danger. And things were still very much up in the air. But for the first time in a long time, it felt like everything might be okay after all. I knew, with a conviction I couldn't quite explain, that we would defeat Aidoneus and save my people someday soon. And that knowledge, that hope I had, was enough to keep the hollowness at bay for now.

Lifting me down from the table, Dax held my hand as I followed him, stiff-legged, toward Killian and Lana.

"You okay?" Dax asked Lana as we approached.

Her eyes grew wide as she looked at him and only nodded. "Thank you, Your Highness."

"Lana. I've told you before, call me Dax."

"Okay." A small smile crossed her face, and I could tell Killian was holding in his laughter from where he stood behind her.

I wasn't sure if I'd ever get over how the rest of the world saw the Gaill prince when he was so utterly *Dax* to me.

"You two go with Kacey to meet Mikhail. I know she mostly healed you, but you still need medical attention, Jacqueline. A few tonics will help with the weakness. Scarletti should be along soon."

Rolling my eyes, I sighed, too exhausted to protest something I knew to be true. Dax, knowing what I was thinking as always, leaned down, his signature smirk on his lips as he kissed me, then shifted away with Killian to help transport the Gaill guards we'd taken prisoner to the planes.

Lana once again put her arm under me as we made our way to Kacey and the Eur fleet, ready to take us to our new home. And a better tomorrow.

THE END

ACKNOWLEDGMENTS

So many people helped me in writing *The Gaill* that I don't even know where to begin. A million thank yous would never be enough!

To my rock, my best friend, my husband, Kevin—I simply would not be doing what I'm doing today without your support. I will never forget sitting in that tavern in Uptown back in 2017 and telling you that I had an idea for a novel. Never once did you express any doubts that I would write it; even though I'd just quit my insurance job to blog full time and was in way over my head. You always have been my biggest cheerleader and have sacrificed so much to allow me to pursue my dreams. I love you.

To my parents—two retired librarians who taught me that I'd never be bored so long as I had a good book to read. I think it's safe to say that all those nights spent reading *The Berenstain Bears*, *The History of US*, and *Harry Potter* really *really* rubbed off on me. You have always been my biggest fans. Thank you for helping me with every childhood poem, every college paper, and now *The Gaill*. And a special shoutout to my mother-in-law, Corinne; a retired school teacher who shares my love for YA. Thank you for cheering me on and allowing me to bounce cover ideas off you!

To my sister, brother-in-law, niece and nephews—your excitement for this book never wavered. Even when it took me three years to get it out to the world. Every time you asked about it, helped me formulate ideas, or simply allowed me to gush about the story meant the world to me.

To my friends and family—so many of you have asked for years about *The Gaill* and my plans. This story may never have gotten out there had so many of you not demanded I publish it so you could read it. Thank you for believing in me and pushing me to pursue a lifelong dream.

To Kari & Nia—my Lo Meyer team who happily held down the fort as I sometimes disappeared for days to write. My blogging business continues to be a success because of the two of you. I am immensely lucky to have you both in my life.

To the editing team (Anne, Abby, and Linda) at Victory Editing and the design team at Books and Moods—you have made this tricky self-publishing journey *much* easier. Thank you for always answering my (many) emails with grace and being such a resource for me during this time.

I would be remiss if I did not thank the educators who got me to where I am today. Principally, Janet Blimling, my high school AP English teacher. From guiding me through my first self-read of *King Lear*, to introducing me to the Brontës, to allowing me to be your TA, you had a profound impact on my love for reading and writing. And, if you hadn't pushed me to consider a career outside of education, I may not be here writing this today.

And lastly, but certainly not least, to you—my readers and followers. When I started The Lo Meyer Blog back in 2017, I never anticipated that this would be my life. You all have shown your support for me through every success, every heartbreak, and every major event. I simply would not be able to do what I do every day without your support.

ABOUT THE AUTHOR

Lo Meyer is a lifestyle blogger, social media content creator, and author of the new novel *The Gaill.* Growing up with librarians for parents, Lo developed her love for reading and writing early, earning a BA in English before starting her blog in 2017. Inspired by her love for all things fantasy, sci-fi, and romance, as well as her fascination with the way in which history repeats itself, she penned *The Gaill.*

Lo lives in Minnesota with her husband and three fur babies. When not reading or writing, she's spending time outdoors, buying more turtlenecks she doesn't need, and wrangling her zoo at home (husband included). Connect with Lo on Instagram, Youtube or TikTok (@_lomeyer_) or her blog thelomeyerblog.com.

Made in the USA
Monee, IL
19 February 2024

53246485R00229